04-1811

DARK

WILLIAM BERNHARDT

EYE

A NOVEL

RANDOM HOUSE
LARGE PRINT

Dark Eye is a work of fiction. Names, characters, places, and incidents are the products of the author's imagination or are used fictitiously. Any resemblance to actual events, locales, or persons, living or dead, is entirely coincidental.

The Library of Congress has established a Cataloging-in-Publication record for this title.

0-375-43459-3

www.randomlargeprint.com

FIRST LARGE PRINT EDITION

10 9 8 7 6 5 4 3 2 1

This Large Print edition published in accord with the standards of the N.A.V.H.

DARK EYE

FOR HARRY

I am so proud of you.

BOOK ONE

THE GROTESQUE

And all my days are trances;
And all my nightly dreams
Are where thy dark eye glances . . .

—"To One in Paradise"
EDGAR ALLAN POE

CHAPTER ONE

Three times I've fired my weapon. Three times. Twice because I had to. The third time was optional. But I never plugged anyone for making a pass at me, no matter how tempting it might be. It was a rule. Until that night in early October. When the whole damn mess began.

I really don't know how it happened. For starters, I looked like hell and I knew it, despite what the guy was saying. It was all bullshit.

"Has anyone ever mentioned that you have a gorgeous pair of eyes?"

"Only my ophthalmologist," I told the kid in the Polo.

"No, seriously, you do. My mom says I've always been an eye man." He leaned closer. I could smell the whiskey on his breath. "Are they different?"

"Different from . . . your mom's?"

"From each other. It's like . . . your right eye is darker than the left."

I nodded. "Cat scratch. When I was five."

"Well, it works for you. Gives you an exotic aura."

"If you like that, wait till you see my athlete's foot."

He smiled, which wasn't his best look. "You know what? You're funny."

"Not another reference to my appearance, I hope."

He scooted his chair closer to mine. "Look," he said, his voice suddenly low and tremulous. "I think it's obvious what's happening here. Why don't we cut through the baloney, go back to my place, and give each other what we both know we want?"

"At the moment, there's only two things I want."

"And they would be?"

"Another bourbon. Neat."

"I can arrange that. What else do you want?"

"You to leave."

The bar, Gordy's, was a hellhole I'd discovered when I was working on a case. Mind you, Vegas has some beautiful neighborhoods. This just wasn't one of them. Cops get called to some of the seediest parts of the city—actually, I think I've been to all of them. My specialty is the psychological profiling of deviant personalities. They call me a detective, but what I really do is provide detailed descriptions of creeps they haven't been able to catch, which can be plenty challenging. I love it. Anyway, I tracked some low-life child molester here. Hated him but loved his bar. I bonded with it; I don't know why. It wasn't at all a **Cheers** thing. Barely anyone there knew my name, and I liked it that way.

The décor was deadly. Tacky like the worst small-town plywood watering hole, except this was buried in Vegas's old downtown. Noise thundered relentlessly, assaulting your eardrums, not just music but an endless stream of chatter—sports, politics, and lame come-on lines. The place stank, maybe because drunks kept leaving the men's room door open, maybe because a wino on one of the bar stools kept vomiting on himself. Even the tables reeked, moldering wood soaked in way too much spilled hooch. There was a staleness to the air that made your head throb the second you stepped inside, that made cigarette smoke seem like a welcome alternative. And Gordy's teemed with men of the worst sort—not the bikers, pimps, prostitutes, mobsters, gamblers, and bookies that gave Vegas its colorful reputation, although they were there in force, but preppy types from UNLV in starched golf shirts who knew they could treat anything with breasts like dirt and still get laid because they were so damned hot and hunky.

Be it ever so humble.

I wasn't even thinking about work, so it came as a surprise when I saw Hikuru Mikimoto enter this two-bit saloon. He was a big-time drug dealer. And I hate drug dealers. I'd been consulting with some of the boys in Narc, trying to draft a profile that might help them find him. I really wanted to help, to prove that I could still do the job, but we'd been looking for more than three weeks without results. And then I just look up and there he is.

I wasn't entirely sure I was up to an arrest, but I couldn't let a godsend like this slip through my fingers. I pushed to my feet, bumping the table over, and fumbled for my badge.

"LVPD. Freeze, Mikimoto!"

He was a middle-aged Asian man, his paunch masked by a black T-shirt and what looked to be an Armani sport coat. As soon as I spoke, he took a decisive step backward. And two men behind him surged forward.

Personal goons. This was going to be more complicated than I had realized.

They came on strong and quick. My only

chance was to take them out before they could gang up on me. I pulled my gun and fired, but the shot went wide. It hit the mirror behind the bar and shattered it. The lounge lizards sitting at the bar scrambled. A second later, one of the goons knocked the gun out of my hand. I did a quick spin behind the table and a swing kick with my left leg, catching him full in the face. He dropped like a sandbag and didn't get up. The other one lunged from behind and grabbed me around the throat. I bit down on his arm, and when he released his grip, I gave him an elbow to the solar plexus. He doubled over. I grabbed him by the ears and propelled him into the hardwood bar.

Stupid fool didn't know when to quit. He pulled himself together and came at me again. I whirled around at the last moment and used a move they'd taught me at the academy, a little Judo 101, to flip him over my shoulder. He flew forward and crashed into that splintered mirror. Big chunks of glass sprayed the room. All the patrons ducked for cover.

Mikimoto tried to run away. Not likely. I dove for him, brought him down hard. By this time, the rest of the customers were racing for the doors, desperately trying to get out of my way. None of them offered to help.

I straddled Mikimoto, pinning him face-down against the filthy glass-strewn floor. He was raging, babbling incoherently in some language I didn't understand.

"You're under arrest," I said, wishing to God I had a pair of cuffs. "You have the right to remain silent. If you choose to waive that right—"

Mikimoto swung around with a speed that caught me by surprise. He had a small switchblade in his hand.

Now that pissed me off.

I twisted his arm at the socket, breaking it. The knife clattered to the floor. I wrenched his hand back, pinching it in the soft fleshy part between the thumb and forefinger. He screamed. With his slicked-back hair in my fist, I pounded his head against the floor.

"Goddamn drug dealer," I muttered. "Preying on kids. Pulling a knife on me." I shoved his face down again, hard, and then repeated it, again and again and again.

I felt someone pulling on my shoulders, trying to interfere. Another accomplice?

No. It was Harry, the old guy who worked behind the bar.

"Susan!" He'd been shouting, but for some reason it hadn't registered until now. "Stop it! Stop it!"

"Keep cool," I said as I let Mikimoto's limp head flop to the floor. "This creep's the worst scum in Vegas. Pushes hard drugs to schoolchildren."

"Who the hell are you trying to kid?"

I didn't understand him, didn't get it at all. But as I stared at Mikimoto's face, it seemed to, I don't know, sort of shimmer. Like a shape-shifter in a science fiction movie.

"This is police work, Harry," I growled, still staring at the face on the floor. "I'm doing my job."

"You're drunk off your ass is what you are. Did you bloody that kid up just 'cause he was trying to make time with you?"

I kept watching as the face changed, the whole body changed, and instead of a slick black T there was a pink Polo. How had the drug scum pulled this off? I wondered. Disguising himself as some preppy creep!

I pushed up to my feet. All at once, I realized how wobbly I was. The room began to spin, so I sat down again. The problem with that was, my eyes went back to the face, that kid's face, and I saw all the splattered blood and swollen flesh surrounding it. That finely chiseled face was like a pound of ground round.

Strong hands rummaged under my coat, taking my flask, and I didn't resist. "I told you to lay off the sauce an hour ago," Harry said. "Didn't know you had a private stash, damn you. How the hell am I going to explain this?"

The room was still spinning, even though I was sitting. I felt like I might rip my stomach out with a dull knife if I could. Then I noticed that I was bleeding, too, that I was sitting in a pool of glass, and that there was an especially large shard right in front of me, and I recall thinking someone should do something about that because it could hurt someone, and then I grabbed it and jabbed it into my left wrist. Blood spewed everywhere.

I fell over onto the floor, head first, and the rest of the world went away. After that, I don't remember anything. I assumed I was dead.

"Am I dead?" the young girl asked.

He stared down at her, stretched out on the table before him, a luminescent tableau so full of innocence and youthful curiosity. Her lengthy stay in the basement, so far from the bright lights of the city, had caused her skin to etiolate, but rather than detracting from her natural splendor, it seemed to enhance it. The primordial was strong with her, he sensed. He had chosen well.

"Of course you're not dead, my darling. You can see, can't you? Hear, smell, taste, and touch?"

"I can't move. Not at all. Nothing below my neck."

"I know."

"I think I've wet myself, but I'm not sure."

"You have."

"Even talking is hard."

He brushed a hand gently across her fore-head, straightening her bangs. "I'm so sorry."

"And I'm scared. Really scared. You're not going to hurt me, are you, mister?"

He was short of stature, but he liked to think he had a certain presence just the same. Did his accent thicken as he spoke to the offering? He suspected that it did. The genteel Southern gen-tleman rose to the surface.

He turned and gazed out the window, just above ground level. The sky was clear as glass; the air was pungently sweet. And oh, the stars—! The stars seemed to go on forever, traveling from his private retreat all the way to Dream-Land. Heaven was real here, far removed from the decay of the city, the fiberglass façades and organic stench. He did not look down but across, outward, into the desert, the vast un-touched expanse, the low-lying Spring Moun-tains, feeling the arid warmth as it bathed and reassured him.

"Mister?" Her voice was slow and stuporous.

"Yes?"

"Am I—am I—" Her hair was caught in her mouth. She tried to blow it away, but it was sticky and wet and wouldn't go and there was nothing she could do. She was like a rag doll, unable to help herself.

He reached down and brushed the hair out of her mouth. "Is that better, my dear?"

"Yes. Thank you."

"And your question?"

Her eyes were swollen and red from the anger phase. Screaming, shouting, threatening. Testing the waters, learning the abject futility of it all. Now she was more subdued, acquiescent. "Am I naked?"

"Yes, love. You're just as God made you."

"W-Why?"

"Because I wanted to see you as you truly are."

"Did you . . . do anything to me? While I was out?"

He pressed a hand against his black cotton vest. "What manner of monster do you take me for, madam?"

"Well . . . I didn't know."

"There has been no physical impropriety, I can assure you of that."

"Well . . . that's . . . good, I guess. So . . . could I have my clothes back?"

"I'm afraid not." He reached down and brushed another strand of hair out of her mouth. He held it for a moment, staring at the root. " 'The life upon her yellow hair but not within her eyes . . .' " He looked at her with opprobrium. "You're not a natural blonde."

"No."

"But your—your—" His face flushed.

"Dyed that, too."

"Oh, my. Oh, my." He assumed a stern expression. "My dear girl, this will never do. I mean, it simply isn't done."

"All the girls at my high school were doing it."

"Then I shall see that you never return to that pubescent whorehouse." He cleared his throat, fanning himself. "I couldn't help but notice when I undressed you. You were wearing"—he bore a pained expression, as if the very words hurt him—"thong underwear. Do your parents know about this?"

"No. A girlfriend bought them for me. Amber."

"I thought as much. Well, I destroyed the offending article." He leaned in close and whispered, "There's only one kind of girl who needs thong underwear, Helen. And you aren't that kind."

She spoke hesitantly, her words still slurring occasionally. "You can't know what kind of girl I am. You don't know me."

"You're wrong, my lovely. I've been watching you. When you slipped out."

"What?"

"I've even been to your Web site. I know you've been unhappy. I know your mother doesn't understand you. I know you were contemplating leaving home for good. You want something better than what you have been given, something richer. A Dream-Land."

The fear in her eyes was so intense he felt it in his heart as if it were his own. He had always been like that, sensitive to a fault, so in tune with the feelings of others that it sometimes became unbearable. He wished there were some way to turn it off, to flick the switch, to distance himself. But he had learned long ago that distance was not an option for him. He was a part of this world, and so he would remain. And if he could not escape the world, then his only recourse was to make it a better world.

Staring down into her fearful eyes, golden locks encircling her face, it was impossible not to think of another girl, another innocent, from that lost time so long ago. Following him through the forest, splashing him at the beach, she was the best of him, too pure to be tainted and forever young.

"Mister? Do you think if maybe I promised not to wear that underwear anymore, you could, um, let me go?"

"But my sweet, we have so much work yet to do." He returned to the basin and placed a washcloth in damp water. With great vigor, he began scrubbing her face.

"Mister? You're . . . you're hurting me."

"It's got to come off. All of it. A good girl doesn't need paint to make herself attractive."

"But—you're tearing—"

"A little elbow grease. That's what's wanted here." He made a small gasping noise. "Are those eyelashes false? Pity." He ripped them off.

"Oww! Mister, please—"

"And the same goes for these earrings, I'm afraid. Imagine piercing your flesh so you can adorn yourself with colored glass. They've got to go." He yanked them off through the lobe.

The girl shrieked. "Please! Oh, my God, stop, please!"

"Don't fret. I'll get something to stanch the bleeding."

The girl began to tremble helplessly.

"And that leaves us with the problem of the hair. What to do about the hair?"

"Maybe—I could just wear a wig?"

He considered. "I fear that would only intensify the artificiality. No, there's only one thing to be done." In the cabinet beneath the basin, he found a battery-operated electric shear.

"Please, don't. Please." She breathed heavily, twisting her head back and forth.

"I don't want to. But I have no choice." He switched the clippers on. "Please don't move."

He applied the shear to the crown of her head and moved over the crest in a long straight line, like a Marine barber buzz-cutting a new inductee. The girl let loose hopeless streams of tears that she couldn't wipe away.

In a matter of minutes, the cutting was done and the hair was gone. He took a brush and dustpan and cleaned up the girl and the table she rested upon. He retrieved his damp warm cloth from the basin and used it to gently, tenderly rinse her face and scalp.

He ran the palm of his hand across the top of her head. "Smooth as a baby's bottom. There now. That wasn't so bad, was it?"

"You—you cut off my hair," she said, her voice loose and broken.

"It was a necessary unpleasantness, but there's an end to it. Now we can relax and wait until the moment of—" He stopped short. His mouth twitched. "You've painted your fingernails."

Her eyes were wide, pleading. "Everyone does it!"

"No, not everyone."

"Please don't hurt me anymore. I'm begging you."

He smiled reassuringly. "Fear not. You'll barely feel it."

It was a simple procedure; they were artificial, press-on augmentations that left little dots of glue on the true nails after he tore them off. Then he pulled a chair to her side and rested.

This process was more difficult than he had anticipated. He gazed out the window into the crepuscular sky, contemplating the outlines of the pretend palaces of the Strip, the headlights rushing from one nowhere to the next, hustling people about like the miserable ants they were. He was so fortunate to be here—sanctified, removed, anointed. So lucky.

His eyes turned upward, tracing the rectilinear line where the horizon melted into the sky. This was his favorite kind of dusk, with no moon and just enough light to turn the sky a rich roseate blush. Gazing at this masterpiece painting, he thought: who could doubt that there was a plan for us?

"Look at the stars," he said after he wiped the tears and blood from her. "You can see the heavens so clearly. There must be a million of them. They're beckoning to us, leading us to the truth, telling us how we can live among them. But so few listen. So few can."

"Mister," she said. Her voice was dry and coarse, a staccato grating. "Are you going to kill me?"

"Why would you ask that?"

"Because you took me and you brought me here and I can't move and, and—" Her voice broke down. "And I think maybe you're going to kill me."

"Well, I'm not. Not precisely."

"Then why? Why have you kept me here so long? What are you going to do to me?"

He pressed his head close against hers, and his eyes shone with reflected starlight. "Something wonderful."

CHAPTER TWO

Am I dead? I wondered.

My last night in detox, I woke around five A.M. and saw David standing at the foot of my bed.

"Sugar bear?" I whispered, only marginally awake. My eyes were filmy and I knew I was mumbling, but I didn't think it would matter.

"I'm here, Susan," he answered. "How are you?"

"Not so good."

"Sorry to hear that." My God, but he was handsome. Made my whole body go warm and liquid. "I've been keeping an eye on you."

"Have you? I haven't felt it."

"Wasn't sure you'd really want to."

"Don't be dumb." I tried to move but my body wasn't responding. Just as well. I'd have been crawling all over him, probably violating several hospital regulations. "Did you see what happened?"

"Yeah. You screwed up big-time."

"Didn't mean to. I was . . . confused."

"It happens. So you're leaving today?"

"Thank God. I threatened to bust some doctors' heads if they didn't let me out."

He tucked his head, letting all that jet-black tousled hair cascade over his eyes. "I'm not sure that was the right thing to do."

"I had no choice. They're killing me."

"You need help."

"You've got some nerve, saying that to me."

He was so strong, even when he was silent. Muscled arms. Adorable chin dimple. "I miss you."

I reached out to him, but it was like touching a bubble: the instant you do, the filmy surface wraps around your hand and evaporates. I wanted to feel David so much. But my fingers fluttered like butterfly wings in the empty air.

Did I mention that I hated Dr. Coutant? Detested the man. I was only in that Popsicle joint six days, but it felt like a month in hell, thanks to Dr. Coutant.

"Let me state again that I oppose your early release. I think you need more time."

"Especially when you're billing by the hour, right, Doc?" I said it only because I knew it would infuriate him. The guy had been trying to get my goat all week—how could I resist the chance to give back a little of the same? I've been around doctors enough to know that they love to trash lawyers and other professional clock-watchers while ignoring the fact that their own bills are higher than anyone else's.

He had me at a card table in the main lobby of the detox ward, by the nurses' station, down the hall from the private rooms. The wing was all done up in calming shades of beige, with padded sofas and soft carpets. Like an airport lounge. "As long as the city's health insurance is footing the bill, what do you care how much I make?"

"I was just saying—"

"The fact is, Ms. Pulaski, you have a serious chemical addiction, and six days in detox isn't going to cure it. You need some time in a professional rehab facility."

"Do tell."

"I don't get the sense that you're taking this seriously."

"Not as seriously as you, certainly. . . ."

"Your addiction, I might add, was fueled by severe emotional problems, which you also are not dealing with." He was a stout, short man. When he went into his sapient counselor mode, he leaned back, his arms folded across a belly not even his white coat could disguise, and used an orotund, patronizing voice that affected me like teeth on tinfoil.

"Hey, I listened to your lectures. I took notes, even."

"That's not going to help when you get the urge to drink."

"Look, Doctor, I was never really addicted to it. I just let it get out of control. I'm not going to do that anymore."

He fingered the rim of his glasses. "That is, quite literally, what they all say."

"But in my case, it's true. I won't—"

"Ms. Pulaski, you do yourself no favors by minimizing your actions. You went on what apparently was a three-day bender that culminated in serious—"

"I made a mistake—"

"You had an alcoholic delirium, turned violent, and nearly killed a man!"

I clammed up. It was obvious he wouldn't let me go until he felt I had been sufficiently punished, so I just let it ride. He could inveigh against me till his beard turned gray.

"We need a plan," Coutant said, frowning. "I'm never comfortable releasing a patient unless he or she has a road map for overcoming the addiction. I want you to attend classes."

"Classes? As in school?"

"IOP. Intensive outpatient therapy. I'll put the information in with your release papers. Our group leaders are very gifted. You'll be surprised how much you'll benefit from it. And you should supplement that by attending a registered AA group."

"So, we're talking, amateur shrinks trying to get inside my head?"

He stared down at the table. I could tell he was choosing his words carefully, being oh so tolerant, which really drove me bananas. "You have a lot of anger, Ms. Pulaski. You may not be aware of it, but you do. That's what drives your self-destructive behavior."

I can't stand this business where some guy with a beard and a Ph.D. spends an hour with you and thinks he knows your whole life story. "Look—am I getting out or not?"

"I don't have the power to keep you against your will. I wish I did."

"Then give me my Get Out of Jail card and let me go."

"But we need a plan."

"Why? So you can magnify the paper jam in your file?"

"Because if we don't, you'll start drinking

again. Too often alcoholics have to hit rock bottom before they stop abusing alcohol and start putting their life back together."

"That's bullshit. If I say I won't drink, I won't drink." I got up and walked to the door—locked, of course—making it clear I was ready to leave. Hadn't I played his games long enough? Why was he so determined to prove that I had dark, insuperable problems that only he could solve? I had a job and a house and a niece who must be bouncing off the walls by now. Why should I let these people drain the insurance companies dry making referrals to one another? I had a life to live.

God bless Lisa. She was waiting for me when I finally got out of the treatment facility.

"Hail fellow well met," I said, wiggling my fingers in the air. "Thanks for the lift."

"My pleasure. Missed you, sweetie." She gave me a peck on the cheek.

"Ditto. Now get me the hell out of here."

Lisa is my oldest friend. We've known each other since kindergarten. I stole her cookie the first day and we've been girlfriends ever since, through school and college and her marriage to a bodybuilder with a leather fetish and her divorce and subsequent endless string of dates to guys remembered only for their kissing ability

or lack thereof. Not to mention all my little dif-
ficulties.

She put her convertible into first and
screeched out of the parking lot. She couldn't
begin to afford this car; it cost more per month
than her apartment. But she loved it. Lisa was
an inveterate speed freak, always had been. In
kindergarten, it was the swings. Now it was a
Porsche. I think she's in one of those Oprah categories: Women Who Love Their Cars Too
Much. And why not? We both pretended there
was nothing orgasmic about the smile on her
face when she shifted into high gear.

"Jesus Christ, I can't believe I spent six days
in there." It felt good, letting the wind rush
through my hair—like being in a cool shower,
that tingly sense of something cascading over
your entire body. She was taking me down the
Strip—what outside Vegas is called U.S. 9. Hotels and casinos. Volcanoes and pirate ships.
Fabulous multicolored neon view. Bright lights,
Sin City.

"They told me they wanted you to stay
longer," Lisa said.

"There's no money in miracle cures."

"That's a bit cynical, even by your standards."

"Did you ever wonder why it's always a
twelve-step program, Lisa? Three steps would
be insufficiently profitable."

She looked gorgeous in this car, with the wind whipping her hair back like a model in a shampoo commercial, which was probably another reason it was worth the money to her. She had long hair, perfectly blond, not a trace of dishwater. Or black roots. She worked out and never ate anything and looked great. She had those wonderful slender arms with firm muscles, the telltale identifier of a gym girl. I worked out, too, but on me it looked bulky and formidable, not sleek and sexy. If Lisa weren't my best friend, I'd hate her.

"Anything interesting happen in there?" she asked.

"Not much. It was evil."

"Evil?"

I nodded. "Doctors with lots of questions. Nurses taking your vital signs for no apparent reason. Some old gal who gave me a daily physical and enjoyed it way too much, if you know what I mean." Lisa giggled, which made me smile for the first time today. She was a tough audience. If I could make her laugh, I was doing something right. "Twice a day some guy would come in and lead a group session on the evils of substance abuse, and the whole time he's drinking coffee by the gallon." I gave her a grim look. "And they made us play games."

"You're kidding me."

"Scout's honor. Monopoly. Clue. Even Scrabble. It was compulsory."

"Now that's evil."

I hesitated a moment. "I saw David."

Her reaction was just a beat delayed, though she tried to act as if I had said nothing unusual at all. "You did?"

"Yeah. In my room."

"Were you having, um, dreams?"

A nice way of putting it. "I don't know. I guess. Didn't seem like it."

"But Susan, you know . . ."

"Yeah. I'm not that far gone yet."

"Well." Lisa focused her attention on her driving.

"He said he missed me. He said he was watching me."

"That's nice."

"Do you believe that?"

"Believe what?"

"That dead people watch us after they're gone. That they're up in the clouds, keeping tabs on the people they knew."

"Sure."

"I don't." I extended my arm out the passenger-side window, letting the wind ripple through my fingers. "I'm not even sure I believe in an afterlife. But if there is one, I can't imagine why anyone there would waste it watching the folks back on earth. I mean, if that was what you wanted to do, why leave in the first place?"

She didn't have an answer, so she concentrated on her driving, which was just as well.

He managed to get Helen into the back of his pickup, but just barely. Even though she was wrapped securely and he was using the flatbed dolly, it was hard work. But no matter, he consoled himself. At the end of days, one does not dwell on the mundane.

Afterward, he washed his hands, then dried them with a daisy-pattern dish towel, one of the few possessions of Nana's he had saved. She had taken such pride in those towels, he recalled, back when they were new. A small token of simple beauty in a life of utter squalor, he supposed. Where had she gotten them, anyway? Had the bank been giving them away? The gas station? A free gift in a box of detergent? He couldn't remember.

He walked back out the front door, whistling. Whistle while you work—that was what those dwarves said. He chuckled. And people called him short.

Ginny had loved that movie. Nana had the tape and they'd watched it together, over and over. He preferred livelier fare, truth be told, but his sweet Virginia loved it, and that was good enough for him.

It was a radiant night, almost a cerulean blue, and teeming with shadows. Perfect for his appointed task. Of course, he had planned it that way. Every detail in place, every jot and tittle. Just as it should be. As it was destined to be.

He had almost returned to his truck when he spotted the redheaded woman from the house next door. Divorcée, mid-thirties. Camille, she was called, like the victim in "Rue Morgue." Happily, she did not have her boyfriend with her today.

"Ernie?"

He stopped and waited as her crunched-gravel footsteps caught up to him.

"Hey, I'm sorry about last night."

He pulled himself upright. "My dear, there's nothing to be sorry about."

She grinned. "I love that accent. I wish Ty could do it. Gives me shivers."

He felt his face flushing, his stomach roiling.

"I tried to stop him, but he had to stir things up. You know how men are. Well, maybe you don't." She leaned in close. "They're all assholes. Except for you, Ernie."

He had been playing Mozart very loud last night. It was necessary to ensure that no one heard the screaming. In any case, it hardly merited her boyfriend's overreaction.

"He isn't a bad guy," Camille said, "not compared to some of the others I've had. But sometimes he can get . . . out of control."

Yes, he thought, especially when Ty was
bored and hungry for a fight. He wanted an
easy knock-down-drag-out he knew he could
win, and since he was a big, gym-muscled black
man, he felt no compunction against taking
on a somewhat smaller neighbor. People always
picked on short men, always had and always
would. It had taken all his comity and bon-
homie to get rid of the thug without an incident, but he'd managed.

Camille stood awkwardly for a moment, her
fingers fidgeting, her breasts all but spilling out
of the flimsy halter top. He felt her discomfort,
her longing to say something effervescent or
witty, some pointed observation that would
elicit his approbation. The woman liked him,
strange as that seemed. Apparently Mandingo
wasn't keeping her satisfied. She yearned for
something different, someone smart, someone
who could elevate her life from the drudgery
and banality that presently characterized it. She
was vulnerable. He had once considered her for
an offering, but she was too old, too large. She
could never fit the specifications.

"Say, what you got in the truck?"

He stepped forward, blocking her approach.
"Just some trash."

"Trash? I saw how you strained to scoot that load off the dolly. What are you throwing away, barbells?"

"Books. Nothing in the world heavier than books, you know."

"And you don't want them? Seems like I see you reading all the time."

"My interests have . . . evolved."

"Oh, yeah? What do you—"

"Camille . . . I must beg your pardon." He edged away. "I need to take care of this. Immediately." He slid into the cab of the truck and started the engine.

"You know, Ernie," she said through the open window, "you could come over sometime. Ty isn't around that much these days. We could have some fun, I think." She reached out and touched him on his cheek.

"Must dash, Camille. Please give my best to your beau." He rolled up the window and sped away. He drove quickly, but not too quickly, making sure she wasn't following him.

It should take no more than twenty minutes to get to the hotel, which was providential, because he had a limited window of opportunity during which he could get this bundle into his room without being spotted. From there, delivery to the ultimate destination would be a simple matter.

He tried to whistle again, but he seemed to have lost the tune. The encounter with Camille

had unnerved him. It had been a parlous moment, he realized, when she'd reached toward
the bundle in the back of the truck. Not that he
had done anything to betray himself, nothing
she was ever likely to comprehend, this woman
who couldn't master subject-verb agreement
and didn't have the sense to dispense with the
psycho stud who was servicing her. But he
didn't like the unexpected. He had planned
everything with meticulous care. Any deviation
from the designated path could only delay the
Golden Age.

I am the perfect passenger. Lisa has told me so
on numerous occasions. The absolute antithesis
of the bossy backseat driver. I figure if you're
behind the wheel, then you're calling the shots. I
don't mess with your radio, I don't tell you when
to change lanes, and I don't plot the course. So
I sat quietly as Lisa took me all the way down the
Strip, even though this was tourist season (every
season is tourist season in Vegas) and the traffic
was atrocious.

I love this town. Lived here all my life; never
had the desire to go anywhere else. There's so
much more to Vegas than what the tourists see.
But the truth is, I love what the tourists see, too.
From the austere Nevada mountaintops to the
concrete palaces to the sex clubs and the glut-

tonous buffets, I love it all. Even the Liberace museum. Honest.

My house was in a gorgeous neighborhood called Summerlin, near one of the area's many man-made lakes. Okay, ponds, depending on what you're used to. It was just down the road from the largest of Vegas's many pet cemeteries, where all three of my German shepherds are interred. I sat quietly while Lisa cruised through the south side. But when we were a good twenty minutes or so away from where we should be, I felt I had to speak.

"Are you taking me home?"

"Um, no."

I sensed immediately that this was a subject she had been deliberately avoiding. "I've been gone a long time, Lisa. I've got a million things to do."

"Yes, but . . . not there."

I laid my hand on her shoulder. "What gives? Tell me the truth."

"The truth is . . ." I could tell this was agonizing for her, which didn't make me any less insistent. "You don't have a house anymore."

"The goddamn bank."

"Yeah. 'Fraid so."

"I'm in the hospital for one lousy week and they take the house?"

"They told me you hadn't made a payment for four months."

"I've had a lot on my mind, as you well know."

"They said they've called and written and left messages but never heard anything from you."

"I don't recall any messages."

"And then when they found out you were in detox and no one knew when you might get out, that was it. They foreclosed."

"Can they do that? So fast?"

"Evidently."

"Greedy bastards. What do I have to do to get it back?"

The beautiful blond speed demon became a timid little girl. "I . . . I don't think you do, Susan. It's gone."

"Goddamn it." I slapped my hand down on the dash. "God**damn** it."

"I boxed up all your stuff and put it—"

"I don't care about that," I snapped. "Where's Rachel?"

Lisa's respiration accelerated. Her grip on the steering wheel tightened. All bad signs. "Oh, Susan, I'm so sorry."

"Where is she?"

Her forehead creased. "They've put her in a foster home, sweetie."

"Who did?"

"The state. NDHS. Human Services."

"I'm sick for one week and they confiscate my niece?"

"Susan, think. You never formally adopted her. She was just living with you, and that was okay for a while. But after . . . you know . . . what happened . . ."

"They had no right. None."

"They say you can visit. I mean, you can't take her away or anything, but—"

"I'm her family! I'm the only family she has!"

"I know. I told them. I offered to let her stay with me till you were released. I tried everything I could think of—"

"Apparently you didn't try hard enough."

"Hey, don't kill the messenger, okay?" For the first time, Lisa's voice rose. "You're not the only one who's had a shitty week, you know? I've been under continuous fire, trying to straighten out your—"

She stopped just short, for which I will always love her.

"They had no right to take my niece away."

Still driving, Lisa reached across and squeezed my hand. "Honey, you're an alcoholic—"

"I am not."

"—and there's no way the state is going to let a fifteen-year-old girl stay with a noncustodial nonparent alcoholic with proven violent tendencies."

"I've never hurt Rachel. I would never hurt her."

"I know, Susan. But you practically killed

that chump at the bar, and endangered everyone there, and that's all they're seeing."

"Goddamn it!" I pounded the dash over and
over again, which I'm sure Lisa did not appreciate, but she didn't say anything. "Goddamn
them all to hell."

Showing her usual perspicacity, she let me
stew for a while and didn't speak again until it
was necessary. "We're almost to my place,
Susan. Come in with me. I'll start a fire. You can
put on some woolly pajamas and I'll brew some
tea and you can just chill for a while, okay?"

"No. Take me to the office."

"Susan—"

"It's no good, Lisa. You know I can't tolerate
just sitting around, and I would hate being cod-
dled even worse. The best thing for me to do is
get back to my job and forget—"

She started to cry. This really bothered me
because, for starters, Lisa is my friend, and fur-
thermore, it seemed like if anyone should be
crying it should be me—and I wasn't, so what
right did she have?

And I wondered what she could possibly be
holding back that was worse than what she had
already divulged.

"Susan . . . you don't have a job anymore."

No.

"Don't blame Chief O'Bannon. It's not his
fault. IA was all over what happened, and that

boy's family is threatening to sue the department. O'Bannon had to do something."

"So—so—" I was having trouble forming the
words. "So—they suspended me?"

She shook her head. "No."

"What? **What?**"

She pulled up to a light, then turned to face
me. "They fired you, Susan."

"No way. I'll just talk to O'Bannon."

"He didn't want to do it. But he had no
choice."

"This can't be right. It can't be."

"But there are lots of things a trained psychologist can do, Susan. It might be good for
you to get away from police work, where there
are so many . . . reminders. This could be a
golden opportunity. Look on the bright side."

Sure. Other than that, how did you like the
parade, Mrs. Kennedy? "This isn't right. It can't
be. I'm the best profiler O'Bannon has, and he
knows it. I'm the one who solved the Wyndham
killings. I'm the one who—"

"That was before," Lisa said forcefully.

"Before this one stupid little incident?"

"Before you started drinking." The word hit
me like a brick. She continued to talk, but it
rolled off me like water on a slick surface. There
was a liquor store on the corner, and another on
the corner after that. Liquor was everywhere. It
was pervasive, and not just here in Sin City,

either. I spotted an ad for some tarted-up booze, Chivas Regal or some other stuff I couldn't afford. I remembered the smoky scent of a good scotch, the warm assurance as it glided down my throat.

"Lisa . . . could you stop the car?"

"You can't drink, Susan. Not at all. Not even once."

"I need . . . something. I can't . . . everything . . . it's all . . ."

"I'll stay with you tonight."

"You don't have to."

"I'm not asking—I'm telling. I'll stay with you."

"I'm not going to drink."

"Then you won't mind my being there."

"I don't need a babysitter."

"I've heard the first night is the hardest. For people in your situation."

So that's what I'd become. A situation.

I closed my eyes and tried to conjure up the memory of David just as I'd seen him that morning, but it wouldn't come. At best, I got a turbid glimmer, a toothy smile, a dimpled chin. Pieces of the whole.

It seemed I had nowhere to go and no one to see. Nothing to do. Nothing to live for.

The throbbing in my left wrist intensified. Beneath the bandage, it was sending me a message.

If ever there was a girl who deserved a drink, it was me.

He lifted his spade and began to dig. The soil was soft and loose, as he had known it would be. It was only about two feet deep, but that would be sufficient. It didn't really need to be buried. It was the suggestion that was important. The re-creation of the sacred image.

Despite the simplicity of the task, he found himself tiring and perspiring. But this entire area was deserted and he knew it would remain so until six in the morning, so it didn't matter how long he took. Just so the job was done right. According to plan.

He slowly lowered the long box off the dolly and into the freshly dug cavity. He lifted a spadeful of dirt and tossed it onto the box. The resultant clamor caught him by surprise.

Merciful Zeus. How could I be so forgetful? He leaned over the edge of the pit and lifted the half lid from the top section of the box.

Helen screamed.

He clamped his hand over her mouth. "My dear, I can't allow you to make a commotion."

She struggled to get free of his hand. She tried to bite him. She spit on him. Nothing worked.

"I'm going to release you in a moment. And

when I do, I don't want to hear any more screaming. You know, I could've deadened your entire body. And I still can, if need be. Do you comprehend what I'm saying?"

Slowly, he removed the hand from her mouth. She did not scream.

"Now that's more like it."

With the half lid open, she was visible from her bare shoulders up. "I couldn't breathe in there, mister. I thought I was going to die."

He made no comment.

"I could tell you were moving me, but I didn't know where we were going. And then I heard that thumping on the lid and I didn't know what was happening and I hate confined spaces and I panicked."

"Of course you did. Entirely understand-able."

She craned her neck, trying to see something other than the walls of the box surrounding her, gazing straight up at the cobwebs and skeletons and white sheet ghosts. "What is this place?"

"A gallery. A tableau, if you will. To honor the prophet."

"I don't know what that means," she said, choking. "I want to go home."

"And you will, in a sense," he said reassuringly. "To a far, far better home than any you have known before. Better than the one you kept sneaking away from."

"How do you know that? Did Amber tell you?"

"You must pardon me, but I really don't have time to continue this conversation."

Her eyes were red and watery. "You're going to kill me, aren't you?"

"Do you see a gun in my hand? Am I wielding a knife?"

"Answer me!"

"You have the potential to be reborn. To become something greater than you ever dreamed possible. To usher in a milestone in the evolution of mankind."

"Please don't kill me. I'm begging you! I'll do anything. You want sex? I can give you sex. You want to put it in my mouth? I can do that. Hey, I'd like to do it. I'd enjoy it. Just give me a chance, mister." She was babbling, rambling, desperate. "You've already hurt me so bad," she cried, her voice breaking. "Please don't kill me. Please let me go home."

"I can't," he said gently. "I know this is difficult for you, but it is for your own good. I'm helping you."

She stared at him, breathing in short, quick gasps. "Would you come closer, please? I'd like to whisper something to you. It's a secret."

He almost did it. But at the last moment, he stopped. "You were going to bite me."

"I—I don't know what you mean."

"And you thought if I came close enough you could bite my nose, maybe even my eyeball?" He made a tsking sound. "I suppose anything is possible for a girl who would wear thong underwear."

Her eyes closed. Her last hope was lost. There was nothing left now.

"This is a coffin, isn't it?"

" 'I could no longer doubt that I reposed in a coffin at last.' " He caressed her smooth bald head. "Don't focus on the here and now, my dear. The all-too-present present. Give your mind to the ineluctable truths of the cosmos. Cast your eyes to the stars!" He gestured heavenward, or ceilingward, like a master showman unveiling his main attraction. "There is so much more out there, so much more that we can become."

A tiny light blazed one last time. "I think you're a crazy man. I think you're an impotent little—"

With a single smooth gesture, he flung the lid of the wooden coffin closed and locked it. "I daresay that's enough of that," he murmured quietly. "I detest vulgarity."

He picked up the spade and continued shoveling dirt. It didn't take long. As he worked, he could hear her. She could move a little now, but alas, there was nowhere to go. She beat against the lid and scratched and clawed and screamed, but to no avail. In just under an hour the air would be exhausted, but the screaming and clawing would end well before that. She would be at peace.

And so would he. "'But out of Evil proceeded Good,'" he chanted softly to himself, "'for their very excess wrought in my spirit an inevitable revulsion.'" Cheerfully, he continued the spadework until the pit was full and smooth with only the merest tip of the coffin exposed to bring about its eventual discovery. And this time, the tune returned to him, and he whistled while he worked.

CHAPTER THREE

I awoke bathed in sweat. My cammies clung to me like glue, my whole body was cold, and there was an empty aching in my chest that felt as if someone had ripped my heart out while I slept. My wrist was throbbing, talking to me. I tried to stand but found I couldn't. Finally settled for rolling onto my back. I forced myself to inhale and exhale, hoping it would steady my nerves, which it never did.

I'd had some bad mornings before, but never anything like this. I felt as if I'd broken something, some part of my natural living apparatus. Am I dead? I wondered, and some part of me hoped I was.

After about two minutes that seemed like ten

hours, Lisa came into the room. She cradled my head in her lap and squeezed my hand tightly, stroking the side of my face.

"You can do it, sweetie," she said in soft, dulcet tones. I knew she was trying to be comforting, but I couldn't stop thinking that she sounded like a cross between a kindergarten teacher and a hooker. "I'm here for you. They told me you might have mornings like this."

"I—don't know what's happening," I said, breathing deeply. "I slept okay in the hospital."

"They were giving you drugs. Librium. It's a benzodiazepine. Eases the withdrawal symptoms. This is your first morning off."

"God." My lips were dry and cracked. "Lisa, I think I'm going to need a little something, just so I can function. It'll be the last—"

"No, Susan. No booze."

"I don't want the alcohol. I just need to kill this pain—"

"No booze."

"It's not like I want to get drunk. Once I get this anxiety under control, I won't touch another—"

"That's exactly what they told me you'd say, Susan. The answer is no. You've got to ride this out."

"Fine." I knew she was right, but at the same time I was cursing her under my breath, thinking what a stupid woman she was, how she didn't understand at all. I began plotting how I could get rid of her so I could live my own life. It wasn't as if one stupid drink was going to put me back on the skids and start me hallucinating. I could control it, and this time I would.

Took almost an hour to get to the point where I could walk. Showering made me feel a lot better. I cleaned up, put on some jeans and a clean shirt. Used some damn bubble-gum-flavored toothpaste I found in Lisa's medicine cabinet. Considered myself lucky I didn't have to use a Barbie toothbrush.

She'd already found me an apartment, not far from hers, and had my stuff moved into it. At the same time, she made it clear that I was welcome to stay with her as long as I wanted or needed. She hadn't lived with anyone for over a year, so she had a second bedroom that did nothing but collect dust. It was a generous offer. But I couldn't help noticing that she didn't suggest that I move into the spare bedroom on a permanent basis. We'd tried being roommates once, when we were both in college. It was a disaster. The fact that we are still friends is a testament to the healing power of forgiveness, or perhaps the evanescence of human memory.

"I want to see Rachel," I told Lisa as I finished dressing.

"I knew you would," she replied. "You've got an appointment at noon."

"So now I need an appointment to see my own niece?"

She didn't say anything.

I peered into Lisa's big lighted makeup mirror. At thirty-four years of age, I was still subject to pimples, and sure enough, there was a big one right at the top of the bridge of my nose. Makeup or straight pin? "Well, that'll be okay. We can get some lunch."

"You . . . aren't permitted to take her away from her foster home."

"What?"

"I'm sure they'll change that in time, but for now, your visit will be restricted to the Shepherds' home."

"Who the hell are they to tell me when and how I can see Rachel?"

"They're just trying—"

"I'm her only living relative."

"They know that, and—"

"They've got no business giving me orders."

I could sense that Lisa was getting irritated. "As far as NDHS is concerned, you're the sozzled psycho who attacked a kid in a bar and then—" She paused. "They're not going to let you take Rachel anywhere."

"Have they been spreading these slanderous remarks all over town? I will fight this—"

"Susan." I could tell she was checking herself, biting back words. "Give yourself a little time.

You're not going to put everything back together in a day. Your main focus should be on
getting healthy. And staying healthy."

"You're right, of course," I said, not meaning
it at all. I finished brushing my hair and adjusted
the lay of my bra. Nothing worse than poorly
aligned mammaries. "So what have you planned
to kill time till noon?"

"I thought we might go to the mall at the
Venetian. Do a little window-shopping for pur-
poseless trinkets we can never afford. Maybe
bump into Michael Jackson. Get a coffee. Ride
a gondola."

I shook my head. "Thanks, Lisa, but I'd go
nuts. Will you take me downtown?"

"You mean downtown as in police headquarters?"

I touched my nose. "Got it in one."

"I told you already. You're no longer employed there."

"Then I need to clean out my office, don't I?"

Lisa looked very dubious. "I suppose."

"So let's roll."

"And you won't cause any trouble?"

"**Moi?** Wouldn't dream of it." I tucked in my
shirt, wishing I still had a holster to strap on.
"I'm finished with that sort of thing. From now
on, I'm going to be amiable and even-tempered
at all times. Positively serene."

"What the hell did you think you were doing?"

Lieutenant Barry Granger stared at me with a placid expression that in no way disguised the contempt I knew he felt for me. It was quite a change. I still remembered a time when his stares signaled thinly disguised lust, or later, stares of envy, and, more recently, pity. I probably liked this one best.

"Clearing out the trash," he explained, his feet propped up on my desk. "Making myself at home."

"In my office?"

"Not anymore."

Incredible. In the space of one week O'Bannon had reassigned my office space. Actually, I could live with that, even understand it. But what I couldn't understand was giving it to this pig Granger.

"This is unacceptable," I said. My emotions were also pretty undisguised.

"O'Bannon needed a new detective."

"I was only gone a week. I've taken longer vacations."

"Not in the drunk tank."

I could feel my rage rising, and I really wanted to ream him in the worst way. But that would be playing into his hands. "Why would he promote you?"

"I was next in line."

"I was still around."

"You were drunk on your ass."

"And even drunk on my ass I would be a better detective than you."

To his credit, Granger remained calm. "I don't think Internal Affairs would agree."

"O'Bannon can't afford to replace a seasoned—"

"You don't get it, do you?" Granger was a handsome man, which made him all the more difficult to bear. He had sandy hair and a sun-baked complexion. He wore a light stubble, which even I had to admit made him look damn sexy. How did men maintain a light stubble, anyway? At some point, don't you have to shave or it turns into a beard? Do they make special razors with dullish blades for guys who look good with a little growth? "You're a behaviorist. I'm a homicide specialist. It's not that I'm replacing you. O'Bannon just needed someone he could depend on."

"Go to hell."

"And he can't count on you any more than—" He stopped himself, the bastard. Apparently this line was too low even for him. "Than anyone could."

"How the hell would you know?"

"I've seen what you've done to yourself. I've seen what you've turned into."

"There have been some extenuating circumstances, you son of a bitch. I lost my husband!"

"And I lost my partner!" He lashed out, letting loose something I knew he'd been holding back a long time. "Did you forget that?"

Granger had been David's last partner. Granger wasn't around when he died, but in a way, I think that made it worse. Sometimes cops carry this "my partner—my life" routine too far—the influence of excessive episodes of **T. J. Hooker.** But David and Granger had been close. Granger had genuinely loved David. And admired him. I knew that. But it didn't make me like him. How dare he fling the loss of my own husband in my face to score points, as if somehow he had more right to grieve than I did?

"I didn't forget," I said, pushing past him. "Where are my files?"

"You don't have any. They've all been reassigned."

I was reaching my limit. One more remark like that, and I knew I'd hit him. So much for my attempt to prove that I don't have any more violent tendencies. "I'm talking to O'Bannon."

"He's at the crime scene. Likely to be there all morning."

"What crime scene?"

Granger squinted slightly. "You **have** been out of touch, haven't you?"

"Don't play games with me, Granger. Tell me where he is!"

"No, that wouldn't be prudent."

I swore under my breath. Then I swore over my breath, several times. "You're still sulking because I wouldn't suck your dick that time at Gordy's, aren't you?"

"Jesus Christ, that was what? Ten years ago? Before you hooked up with David? I'd just met you."

"Yeah, but you haven't forgotten. Who was drunk **that** night?"

"I think you should go now, Susan."

"I think you're right. The smell in here is getting intense." I bolted for the door. "Have fun playing detective, Granger. If you need any help—go fuck yourself."

I slammed the door—**my** door—just for dramatic effect.

"How'd it go?" Lisa asked as I slid into the passenger seat.

"Fine. Swell."

"No problems?"

"Nah. They were all very kind. Glad to see me. Granger and I embraced."

"Granger?"

"Yeah. Who'da thought?" Well, if I couldn't live the fantasy, I could at least make Lisa think I did. While she drove to the house where Rachel was staying, I used her cell phone to call Eleanor, one of the young girls in Dispatch. She was nice, I thought she liked me, and I also thought she was gullible enough to believe anything.

"Eleanor? Susan Pulaski. I've got some lab reports for O'Bannon. Is he still at the crime scene?"

"Yeah," she answered. I heard a dozen other lines working in the background. "But I thought you—"

"He brought me back in. Said he needed my expertise on this one. So he's still out there?"

"Far as I know."

I noticed a light drizzle on the dashboard. "You think I should bring him a raincoat?"

"Nah. He'll be inside the hotel."

Getting warm. "And still working in that . . . that—what do they call it?"

"The Edgar Allan Poe Ballroom?"

"Right, right." That would have to be the Transylvania. One of the newer "family" resorts on the Strip. "Dumb of me. I never paid much attention in English class. I was thinking of that other guy. Hawthorne."

"No, it's Poe."

"Okay, thanks." For more than you know.

———

Annabel Spencer gazed nervously at the mirror-paneled walls, the smoky glass ceiling, the translucent corbels. Cameras behind every one of them, she thought. She had read that the camera positions were changed regularly to prevent anyone from knowing for certain what the security people could and could not see. Men on metal catwalks hidden behind the ceiling peered down 24/7. There was no telling how many people were watching her right now. Did they know she wasn't supposed to be here? How long would it take them to figure it out? And once they knew, what would they do to her?

As soon as she passed through the front doors of the casino, she knew her face was scanned by a computer running facial recognition software—developed at MIT, of course—which converted a fluid digital image of her face into mathematical data, translating facial landmarks into algorithms, then comparing the results to the millions of faces in a shared database. She didn't know if anyone had her cheekbones on file yet. In this day and age, it was impossible to be certain. The latest hot cyber-rumor held that Big Brother was constantly scooping up people's faces, taking them off Web sites and newspapers and airport security scanners. Today, almost anyone could be identified by an entity with the financial resources to pay for the data. Privacy was an illusion, or perhaps more accurately, a luxury that many big businesses could no longer afford. So the casino hard drives must be whirring away, she mused, trying to come up with a match, determining if she was a player or a patsy, a tourist or that most dreaded of all evils: a card counter.

Given the famous hatred of casinos for card counters, the minor detail that she was under-age might seem negligible—although it would certainly give them a no-questions-asked excuse to bar her from the premises. Not that they needed one. They could expel anyone, and would, if they thought the player was too successful at the blackjack table. It hardly seemed fair—they only allowed people to play the game if they weren't very good at it. Forget the signs saying the dealer rests on seventeen; the signs should read: SUCKERS ONLY.

Like many of her fellow students, Annabel considered herself a freedom fighter, not a card cheat. But she knew the casino would take a different view. Dark rumors circulated throughout the MIT campus about what happened to card counters in the back rooms of Vegas gambling emporiums. Since they were private property, they could ban anyone they wanted, and if you violated their ban, you could be charged with trespassing. But this was the town the mob built, after all, and casino bosses were known to employ means not sanctioned by law to convey the message that card counting was disfavored. She'd seen more than one MIT hotshot return to class on Monday morning looking as if he'd lost a fight with a tractor. And a few had disappeared altogether—never to return.

Trying to remain calm, Annabel strolled into the blackjack pit and scanned for an open seat. She was wearing her best DKNY **Sex and the City** black dress, and for an MIT math major, she looked pretty damn hot, if she did say so herself. Not that she wanted to attract attention— she just wanted to look as if she belonged there. Because everything depended on her having a successful night. Everything in the world.

She saw her mother's face on an overhead TV in the bar and froze. If her mother found out what she had done . . .

God. Annabel didn't even want to think about it.

A zombie dressed in tattered rags bumped into her backside. Clumsy, or copping a feel? Hard to be sure, but she was not inclined to give a guy in tatters and black eyeliner the benefit of the doubt.

"Sorry about that, ma'am."

Well, at least he was a polite zombie. "No problem."

"Can I get you something? Drink? Change?"

She suspected he really wanted to give her something altogether different. Damn those horny zombies. "I'm fine, thanks."

He moved on down the aisle, dragging his leprous skin and putrescent sores with him, brushing aside a cobweb and blending into the crowd of ghosts, witches, and assorted ghouls.

Welcome to Transylvania.

Not that she was an expert, but in her mind a casino should be sleek and elegant, like the ones in James Bond movies, where the men wore tuxes and the women wore beaded floor-length gowns with décolleté bodices. None of that here—this joint was pure Disneyland. Dolorous Victorian décor and bar stools that creaked when you sat on them. Your "ghost host" checked you in; the bell captain wore a long black hooded robe and carried a scythe. The gambling pit was decked out like a haunted house, with shutters blowing in the wind and tombstones with corny epitaphs. A Vegas casino with a Halloween party motif—it was enough to make you barf. And there were cops swarming everywhere, which also made her nervous. Apparently some horrible crime had taken place in one of the ballrooms; an entire wing of the hotel was roped off. But like it or not, this was the only house in town that still dealt a six-deck shoe all the way to the sixth deck. So here she was. Anyone want to suck her blood?

She found a stool at a hundred-dollar black-jack table and slid onto it. She liked sitting at the far left—Position Three, they called it at MIT. It gave her the most time to count cards before she had to play. Most amateurs thought the game of blackjack favored the dealer. It didn't. The dealer was stuck hitting sixteens and standing on seventeens whether it was smart or not. He didn't have the luxury of sitting pat on a twelve and waiting to see what happened. The only advantage the dealer had was that he played last. If you went bust, he collected your bet and kept it—even if he later went bust himself. A small point, but one that made a huge financial difference to the casinos. The only way to overcome that advantage was to count cards.

She ran the rules through her head. They weren't complex, but the cards moved so fast it was hard to keep up. Plus one for twos, threes, fours, fives, and sixes; minus one for tens and face cards. Take that running count and divide it by the number of decks in the shoe not yet dealt to come up with the true count. When the true count was plus eight or better, start increasing your bet. And most importantly, look casual, distracted, unconcerned, lusty, possibly intoxicated—but never give the slightest hint that you're counting.

She pulled out five hundreds and placed them on the table, waiting for chips. A moment later, a small man in a black vest slid onto the stool beside her. He had thinning hair and a little Hitler-style black mustache.

"Having any luck?" he asked.

"Just got here," Annabel answered succinctly. She didn't want to be unfriendly—but she didn't want to be friendly, either.

"I haven't caught a break all night," he said.

"Sorry to hear that."

"Guess the stars just aren't right."

"Maybe a zombie priestess put the hoodoo on you."

The corner of his lips turned up. "Anything's possible."

A waitress came by the table. She was dressed in a witch getup, but Vegas-style, with a plunging neckline, an obscenely short skirt, and fishnet hose. She did at least wear the traditional black pointed hat. Annabel ordered a mineral water. The man beside her asked for a Bloody Mary.

The first several decks were average. That was okay. She knew counting required patience. Favorable decks were the exception, not the rule. For the first hour and a half, Annabel remained almost exactly even. The count never rose above a plus five. She'd managed to rack up a few extra bucks by doubling down and splitting at strategic moments, but she'd had no justification for seriously increasing her wager. And the man sitting next to her talked almost continuously the whole time. He seemed uncommonly interested in her—where she was from, what she did for a living, whether she was here alone. Another hand or two and he'd probably be asking what kind of underwear she had on.

About two-thirds of the way through the next shoe, the count rose to plus twelve. With all those ten-spots in the deck, it favored the players, and coming this late in the shoe, the count was extremely reliable. It was time to increase her bet. Her hand trembled a bit as she pushed three hundred bucks' worth of chips into the circle. She was nervous, putting so much money on the line. But she had to do it. Everything depended on her game. Including Warren.

She felt a tapping on her bare shoulder. "Excuse me, miss."

She turned and saw a silver security badge. Damnation. Busted.

"Could I speak to you for a moment? In private."

Her first instinct was to run, but she got a grip on herself and followed the man to a private corner at the edge of the pit, just beneath a cartoonish polystyrene Satan. Had he caught her counting? Did he know she was underage? And what would he do about it? Her knees knocked. She was beginning to wish she'd had something stronger than mineral water.

"I've been watching you at the blackjack table, ma'am."

Great. So he knew she was counting. She should've realized that—

"The man sitting next to you has been watching, too."

Her brain jerked back front and center. "He has?"

The guard nodded. "I've had my eye on him for a while. I think he's a thief—pickpocket or purse snatcher or some such."

"How can you tell?"

"I've been at this job awhile, ma'am."

"Of course. I'm sorry—"

"I'd keep my distance from him. And definitely keep your eyes on your chips."

"Sure, I'll—"

"When you sat down at the table and pulled out your money, you flashed a huge wad. Looked to me like several hundred bucks, maybe more. And if I saw it, every crook in the joint saw it as well."

"I guess I should've been more discreet."

"We do our best to keep the casino safe, but the reality is, we have robberies every day. These creeps prey on nice people like you."

"I'll try to be more careful."

"That would be wise." He smiled. "Now go back there and get lucky, okay?"

"Sure. Thanks." She returned to the table. The dealer resumed the game. She won the hand. The count was still high, so she let it ride.

Not a minute passed before her neighbor spoke again. "Car parked next to a hydrant?"

Maybe if she was cooler to him, he'd go away. "No. Just a private matter."

"Trouble back home?"

"Nothing important."

More cards were dealt. Annabel got a natural blackjack, which paid off one and a half times the wager. She'd just made over two thousand dollars.

At this rate, she'd be married by sunrise.

The Shepherds' house was in one of the middle-range suburbs, not nearly as nice as the neighborhood where my house is—was—but decent. The vast preponderance of white picket fences and close-set houses told me the designers were striving for that old-time community feel. That these foster parents would live in such a neighborhood told me a lot about them from the get-go.

It was a brick two-story with green shutters and beige trim. A white trellis up the left side, with ivy snaking through the latticework. A long, curving walk led to the front door. The paint was fresh and the garden had been tended. It was all so **Leave It to Beaver** it momentarily engaged my gag reflex.

"They put Rachel in this Stepford house?"

Lisa ignored the commentary. "She was lucky to get a good placement as quickly as she did, Susan. I'm told the Shepherds are very nice people. She has her own room."

"She had her own room at my place."

"Which is now the bank's place." She popped open the car door. "Come on."

I didn't have to walk all the way up those steps. Rachel saw me coming. She burst out the front door and ran toward me, leaping into my arms.

I winced. I'd forgotten about my wrist, still wrapped and bandaged. The impact opened the wound and it began to bleed. I yelped.

"Oh, my God!" Rachel shrieked. "I'm sorry."

"It's nothing. It was already bleeding before I got here."

"Is that where you—you—"

"Cut myself. Accidentally." I took a step back and gave her the once-over. "Well, suburbia hasn't ruined you. Yet."

She laughed a little, but I could feel her edginess. "So . . . you're all right?"

"Of course. I was a little sick, but I'm better now."

"Can I go home with you, then?" She threw her arms around me again and squeezed tightly. God, but this girl loved me. I could feel the affection rushing through her fingertips. And I loved her back. I would do anything for her.

Behind her, standing in the doorway, I saw what must be the Shepherds. An elderly couple, trim and tidy, with smiles plastered on their faces that had nothing to do with happiness. They were watching every move I made.

"Rachel, honey, I guess the man says you have to stay here for a while. But I'm going to hire an attorney and fight. I'll get you back."

"Please hurry. I can't stand it here."

"Why?" I put a finger under her chin and raised her eyes to mine. "Have they hurt you?"

"No, nothing like that."

"Made you do a lot of chores?"

"They haven't made me do anything. They're just so . . . you know. Boring. I want to go home."

"About that." I figured the best approach was to come right out with it. "I lost the house."

"What?" Almost instantly, water welled up in her eyes.

"Yeah. Bank took it."

"But—all my stuff—"

"Lisa saved it. And I've got a new place."

She wiped her eyes. "Where's the new house?"

"It's . . . an apartment. But it's nice-sized and there's a room for you. So all your stuff will be waiting for you once I bust you out of Stalag 13."

Rachel was a lovely girl—she took after my brother, not me. She had auburn hair, getting redder by the day. Clear-skinned and pretty. I knew for a fact she was popular with the boys at school. So far she'd shown good sense about that, for which I was grateful. "Can I see it?"

"Well . . . let me talk to Ozzie and Harriet."

Their expressions changed when they realized I was coming for them. They made no approach but braced themselves, as if I were some malevolent force they couldn't escape. I knew it would be awkward—a meeting between the guardian who'd lost custody and the guardians who'd been given custody. But I wanted to minimize the discomfort. What was the point in hassling them? Better to try to charm them, at least until such time as a court put custody back where it belonged.

"Hello," I said, hand extended. "I'm Lieutenant Susan Pulaski. I want to thank you for taking care of my niece while I was in the hospital."

The man took my hand and shook it feebly. The woman just stared.

"Looks as if you have a fine home."

"We like it," he said. "Been here twenty-seven years."

"That's wonderful. I've just moved into a new place. Rachel is anxious to see it." I laughed and acted very casual. "Probably what she really wants to see is her stuff. Pick up her Discman and some eyeliner. Mind if I show her the new spread?"

The Shepherds exchanged a silent look.

"What do you say? I'll have her back in an hour."

The man took forever, like he had to crank up his motor before he could speak. "We were told not to let you remove her from the premises."

"Oh, I wouldn't leave town. I just—"

"We were told not to let you take her anywhere."

Stay calm, I told myself. A portrait in tranquility. This old man can't get to you.

"We only want what's best for the child," the woman interjected.

"Well, ma'am, I've kept Rachel for the last three years, so I feel as if I can be trusted to—"

"We were told that Rachel has had a most unstable home environment," the man said. "That you worked odd hours, were gone for extended periods of time. That she was habitually late for school and missed extracurricular activities, the few she was involved in. That her grades have dropped dramatically."

"We've both had a difficult year. I'm sure you

know why. But Rachel is tough. All us Pulaski girls are."

"Nonetheless—"

"She'll bounce back. As long as her spirit isn't smothered under your two-car-garage, sex-every-Thursday mentality." Damn. Shouldn't have said that . . .

"I don't appreciate that kind of talk."

I couldn't stop myself. "And what is it you've got to give her that you think is so hot? A riding lawn mower and a color TV? Now I remember where I've seen you before. In the dictionary, under **mundane**."

"You can stop that abusive talk right now." He was nervous, twitchy. My God, what had they told him about me? "You aren't going to take her anywhere."

"Is that right."

"That's right."

"And what makes you think you could stop me?"

He leaned close to me and sniffed the air. "Have you been drinking?"

"Are you out of—"

"I know all about your substance abuse. The NDHS people told me. And Rachel told me."

"Look—I don't do that now."

His silence clearly communicated how little weight that statement carried with him.

"I'm serious. I'm not drinking anymore."

"Good."

"I mean it."

"Good." He paused. "But you're still a drinker. And drinkers are liars."

It took all my restraint—never my best quality—to keep from decking him. "Look, Mr. High and Mighty, I don't need any crap about—"

"This interview is over." He raised his voice. "Rachel. Come in now." She reluctantly obeyed.

"Wait just a goddamn minute. I'm not—"

"If you don't leave my property immediately, I'll call the authorities."

"I didn't do anything. I just—"

"Goodbye." He tucked Rachel behind the door, but she rushed forward and hugged me, hard. He eventually pried her away. Then he shut the door and left me standing like a goon on his well-swept porch. Alone.

Annabel raked in the dough, all the while giggling and acting as if she barely knew what she was doing, as if her big wagers were made out of boredom rather than expertise. She'd ask the dealer for advice—they do that now, ever since Vegas decided to become friendly. Not that they could tell her anything she didn't already know. It was all for show.

Back around 1994, a team of six MIT students began flying to Vegas to prove what many had speculated for years—that a keen understanding of advanced mathematics could pay off at the blackjack table. Half the team—the Spotters—would spread through the casino and sit at various blackjack tables making normal bets, never varying the amount—but counting cards. Some of these guys were absolute geniuses. They could bring off a slick trick called shuffle tracking, which took advantage of probability-distribution mathematics and the fact that most dealers do a light shuffle so as to resume the game as quickly as possible. Shuffle tracking allowed the Spotters to follow a pocket of favorable cards from one shoe to the next, calculating the amount of low-card infiltration caused by the shuffle. Some Spotters would even intentionally blow hands to control the flow of cards—that is, to make specific cards they were tracking come up when and where they wanted them.

When the deck favored the players, the Spotters would signal one of the Gorillas, who wandered the floor, usually pretending to be drunk or inexperienced or both. When they got the signal, they sat at the Spotter's table and made the big bets, cleaning up until the Spotter signaled them to leave because the deck was no longer favorable. The Gorillas couldn't be accused of counting cards; they barely looked at the cards. And it was nearly impossible to nail the Spotters, since they never made any money and often lost. At the end of the day, all members of the team shared the loot. In this manner, the MIT invasion managed to make big bucks and not be detected.

For a few years. Then the casinos caught on and came down on the students—hard. Not only were they all banned, but some were beaten, apartments were robbed and raided, and everyone was terrorized. House rules were changed to make counting less reliable. But new students kept coming. They became the scourge of Vegas; rumor had it the big security firms were willing to take drastic steps to stop the students. Annabel thought it seemed like a crazy risk and had never expected to do it herself.

Until she found out she was pregnant.

Warren had saved her life. When she first came to MIT, she was all alone, had no friends. She was awkward and isolated and tended to stutter in class. Even with a famous mother, she was a standout nerd—and at MIT, that took some doing. She knew some of the boys made fun of her behind her back. But not Warren. He adopted her, took care of her, showed her the ropes, invited her to parties. They'd been going out for more than a month before he even tried to have sex with her. And by then, she was so in love that she melted like an ice cube.

She loved Warren, but he was in no position to marry her, not now, when they were both in school and had no money. He told her it would be a mistake and she knew that he was right. Once again, he was looking out for her. But she couldn't bear the thought of having an abortion. And even less could she bear asking her mother for help. The mother who could spend hours with the network suits she belittled but couldn't find time to see her daughter win the Academic Bowl state finals. She had never given Annabel any direction or advice or help other than financial. Her mother had chosen to make her job Priority One, to never be seriously involved in Annabel's life. Well, fine. She wasn't about to go running to the woman now.

Which meant she needed to come up with some cash, fast. So she'd flown west, slapped on this blond wig, and come to the Transylvania. And on the eighth hand, the last dealt from the favorable shoe, she split two tens—not normally a smart move, but the deck favored her, and the dealer had a six showing, his worst possible card. It paid off. She doubled a two-thousand-dollar bet twice, took all her winnings, and quit. Now she had the stake she needed. She could marry Warren, give this baby a name, and continue their education without involving her mother.

She pushed away from the table. "That's

enough for me. It can't get any better than that."

The little man sitting beside her grabbed her hand. "You're not leaving, are you?"

She yanked her hand away. Something about the man's touch made her skin crawl. "I'm afraid I am. B-B-Best of luck to you."

She cashed out, then quickly made her way to the elevators that descended to the parking garage. She didn't want to risk being stopped by pit bosses or mashers or thieves. All she wanted was to get back to Warren and start their life together. This development wouldn't advance her plan to be the youngest woman ever to win the Fields Medal, but she didn't mind. She liked the idea of settling down, being a married woman. And she loved the thought of being a mother. Annabel would take a different approach than her own mother had done. Better. She would turn her heartache into empowerment.

The elevator doors dinged and she stepped out into the cold, barren garage. It was quiet and dark, shadowy. This was one area where the haunted house motif did not need to extend, she thought.

Her pace quickened; she heard each step echo in her wake. Chill bumps rose on her arms and legs. She moved even faster.

That was when she heard the footsteps.

No one had come off that elevator since she

arrived, she was certain of that. Nonetheless, someone else was here. She fumbled in her purse for her keys. She was practically running now, her heart thumping in her chest. She was alone, dressed provocatively, carrying a big wad of cash—an obvious target, an easy one. Please, God, just get me back to the rental. . . .

She rounded a lane of cars and sprinted. Just a few more steps and she'd be safe. Just a few more steps . . .

He jumped right in front of her. She screamed.

It was the man from the blackjack table. The little man with the mustache.

"Where you going in such a hurry?" he said, his vulpine eyes dancing.

"Leave me alone." She held her purse up, brandishing it like a club.

He was quick, smooth, as if he'd had martial arts training. He knocked the purse out of her hand, then grabbed her by the hair. The wig came off in his hands.

"Not a natural blonde? That's disappointing." He tossed the wig away and grabbed her brunette locks, jerking her head back. He pressed his face close to hers. "If you take that pretty dress off yourself, I won't have to rip it."

"Please leave me alone. Please."

"After, bitch."

"You don't want me. I—I'm pregnant."

"Sure you are," he said, flinging her back against the hood of the car. He grabbed the front of her dress with both hands, one over each breast. "Don't forget that I gave you a chance to do this the easy way."

"Freeze!"

Her assailant's head jerked around.

It was the security guard from the casino. He stood about ten feet away and had his gun pointed right at them. "Good thing I kept my eye on you. I thought you were a thief, not a rapist." He stepped closer, keeping his weapon level. "Now let go of the little lady."

Instead the assailant thrust Annabel forward, locking his arm around her neck. "She's my shield, man."

The guard continued his steady approach. "Do you think I can't hit you without hitting her? Think again." He adjusted the aim of the gun, obviously training it on the man's head. "She won't even get dirty."

"All right, all right!" The man released Annabel and pressed himself face-first against the car. "I give up."

"Very wise." Lowering his gun, he grabbed the assailant's right arm and swung it behind his back.

In a sudden flurry of movement, the man whipped around and knocked the gun out of the guard's hand. He pushed the guard backward and tore off running.

"Stop!"

He bolted down the parking garage, back toward the stairs.

The guard scrambled under a car to retrieve his gun, then gave chase. Before he was halfway across the expanse, the man had disappeared through a stairwell door.

"Damnation!" The guard pulled out his radio and called for help. Then he returned to Annabel's side. "Are you okay, ma'am?"

"I'll live," she said, steadying herself with one hand on the car roof. "You think they'll catch him?"

"The way he was running? He'll be at the Luxor before the men upstairs are on their feet. I'm sorry."

"Hey, I'm just glad you showed up when you did. You're my hero."

His eyes twinkled. "Told you that man was dangerous, didn't I?"

"Yeah, you did."

"You'll need to fill out a report."

"Ohhh . . ."

"You can do it tomorrow if you'd rather."

"I would, thanks." She smiled. He was kind of cute, really.

"Got your purse?"

"Sure." She bent down and picked it up. "Well, thanks again."

"Of course." He started to go, then stopped. "One other thing."

"Yes?"

"That dress you're wearing? I don't like it."

"Excuse me?"

"Look at yourself in the mirror. Your breasts are on display, as if you were a southern plantation slave girl."

"I—I didn't realize—"

"Your teats are for nursing children, my dear. Not for attracting men." His voice seemed to slow, to acquire a more pronounced drawl. "Not for producing unholy thoughts. Luring men to their doom. Throwing your sex at them like some kind of harlot."

She turned toward her car. "I—I think I should go."

"Too late for that, petunia." One hand on the back of her head, he jabbed a syringe into her neck. Her legs wobbled.

He scooped her up into his arms and carried her to his pickup. "I am sorry about the pain, my dear. But you won't feel it for long."

Annabel was dazed, limp. "What . . . what are you going to do . . . ?"

"I'm going to help you. Help you be something better than you are. Something wonderful."

CHAPTER FOUR

Chin up, Susan, chest out, I told myself as I made a beeline toward the yellow crime scene tape. Walk like you know exactly what you're doing and you're in a hurry to get there. That's how I've managed to bluster my way past guards, thugs, reluctant witnesses, and on one occasion, Secret Service agents.

I nodded at the patrolman posted by the entrance to the ballroom—and kept on walking. I could read his confusion, his uncertainty. No doubt he'd heard that I'd been relieved of duty and didn't know what I was doing here. But he didn't stop me. There was also a hotel security guard standing by the door, a little guy with a tangled mess of black hair and a big bad gun.

He was watching me carefully, too. But I kept on walking.

This ballroom was something else. I had been out to this hotel before, not for work but for pleasure. I liked the joint. It appealed to my sense of the macabre. Of all the themed casinos that had sprung up over the last couple of decades, this was my favorite. It was built back in the early Nineties, when Steve Wynn and some of the other high rollers were doing their Vegas Is for Families initiative. Disneyland of the Desert, that's what they wanted. That's when the new improved Strip got Treasure Island (pirates) and the Excalibur (Camelot) and the Luxor (fantasy Egypt). Then we got the geographical reconstructions—the New York, complete with a fake Statue of Liberty, and the Paris, complete with a fake Eiffel Tower (like the original, only better-lit). By the end of the decade, the pendulum had swung back again and Vegas was refocusing on its old reliable: vice. This has always been a city of addictions—booze, drugs, sex, money, risk—and now they were back in fashion. Most of the new resorts focused on providing premier shopping or replicating high-dollar vacation spots. Truth was, most of the chumps who came to Vegas had never been to Europe and would be bored stiff at the real Bellagio. But they loved the chance to pretend to be cosmopolitan sophisticates—with girlie shows and free drinks, of course.

The Transylvania had come in about the same time as Treasure Island and the Excalibur. With a choice spot just up the Strip from Circus Circus (now there was an interesting concept— Gambling for the Whole Family!), it had done a brisk business, specializing in those with a taste for the outré. Most of the joint was more tongue-in-cheek than terrifying. Scary more in the sense of, say, Disneyland's Haunted Mansion than, say, a Jason movie. That showed in the galleries, too. That was another hot Vegas trend—everyone wanted a exhibition. The Bellagio had originally sported Steve Wynn's art collection. The Venetian had a Guggenheim museum. Mandalay Bay had art treasures collected from around the world. And the Transylvania had a series of ballroom galleries exhibiting re-creations of various fright classics such as **Frankenstein, Dracula,** and **Dr. Jekyll and Mr. Hyde.**

This gallery was dedicated to Edgar Allan Poe. I didn't know enough about his work to identify most of the references. But there was a spooky Victorian house, crumbling and decayed, with a façade that looked like a human face—windows for eyes, et cetera. There were cobwebs and skeletons and, of course, the requisite graveyard, which was where I found Chief O'Bannon, crouched on the floor examining something in a tiny evidence baggie. He was surrounded by a swirl of activity, at least a dozen forensic technicians carefully combing the site with dusters and infrared lights. Chemical swabs. Tweezers. I wondered if they knew about me. For a brief moment, I thought about turning tail and running before I was spotted. But that's not my style. That would be too sensible.

One of the techs approached O'Bannon. Tony Crenshaw. His specialty was dactylograms—that's **fingerprints** to the rest of the world—but he was so good O'Bannon let him mess around in hair and fiber and pretty much anything else he wanted to do. I decided to keep my mouth shut for a moment—a novel idea, for me—and just listen.

"We've gone over the box pretty carefully, sir. Lots of good trace evidence."

"From the victim?" O'Bannon asked in his usual gruff manner. "Or the killer?"

"Certainly from the victim," Crenshaw said, wincing slightly. "But we're hoping we'll get something from the perp."

"What have you found on the girl?"

"Hair. A few latent prints. Blood."

"How much?"

"Not a lot. She does not appear to have been wounded in any significant way."

"Anything else?"

Crenshaw hesitated a moment. "Sir . . . have you looked inside the box?"

"Briefly."

"The inner side of the lid?"

"No. Why would I?"

"Claw marks."

O'Bannon squinted. "Like a wild animal?"

"Like she was desperate to get out. The marks match the victim's fingers, which you may have noticed were raw and bloody."

His eyes narrowed. "You mean—she was still alive when—"

Crenshaw nodded grimly. They both looked as if they were about to be sick. I crept forward to get a look at the box they were talking about.

Just below O'Bannon, sticking out of the mock graveyard adjoining the haunted house, was an open coffin. With a very scratched inner lid.

"Christ," O'Bannon said, wiping his brow. "What have we got now?"

Crenshaw shook his head and went back to work. O'Bannon did the same, but I could tell he was shaken.

A moment later, O'Bannon spotted me out of the corner of his eye. "What the hell are you doing here?"

I moved closer, hoping to avoid a scene. "Looking for you."

"You should've been stopped on the other side of the tape."

"C'mon. You know no one can stop me."

He grunted unhappily.

"I wanted a few words with you, Chief. About my job."

"Here's your few words: you don't have a job anymore."

"Chief, I know I kind of screwed up."

"That's like saying Rush Limbaugh is kind of conservative."

"Let me make it up to you. Reinstate me."

"No can do."

"Please."

He started to speak, then stopped, glancing at all the people surrounding us. He grabbed my elbow and dragged me off to where we would be less conspicuous, then looked me straight in the eyes, glowering. "Do you have any idea what I've had to deal with this past week, while you were off taking your rest cure?"

"It was hardly—"

"I've been dealing with a family—a very rich and influential family—that doesn't understand why one of Las Vegas's finest beat their oldest son to a pulp. It's amazing how unreasonable people can be about things like that."

"The kid was a jerk."

"Oh, well, in that case, you should've just killed him."

"Chief—"

"They've been threatening to sue the department, something that would decimate our already strained budget, not to mention create some incredibly bad press."

"If there's anything I can do—"

"But there isn't. You created a big shitpile and left me to clean it up."

I had to take a step back. O'Bannon was way angrier than I had anticipated. I'd never seen him like this, and I'd known him even longer than I'd been on the force. His left eye was twitching, for God's sake, and the little purple veins on the bulb of his nose were throbbing.

"Of course, I've had to deal with the IA boys, who were all over us, calling for an investigation, policy changes. The usual bull. I tried to point out that you were not exactly acting ex cathedra when the incident occurred—although apparently in your drunken stupor you thought you were—but that didn't placate them. They're demanding prompt action, which is just IA code for 'throw us a scapegoat.' "

"And I'm the scapegoat."

"What'd you want me to do, pin it on the kid you creamed?"

"So you just fired me. While I was seeking medical attention."

"Technically, I didn't fire you. Internal Affairs did."

"Bastards."

"IA wanted to go the whole dishonorable-discharge route—put a permanent stain on your record that would guarantee you couldn't get hired as a security guard at Piggly Wiggly. But I told them you were dealing with personal problems and had a chemical dependency and a lot of other crap, so they just fired you and left it at that."

"Thanks so much."

"Don't thank me. I didn't do it for you. I did it for your dad. **He** earned my loyalty."

I can't pretend that one didn't kick me in the teeth pretty hard. My father was a cop. He and O'Bannon had been peers. I think they were even partners for a while.

"Chief—please. Listen to me."

He pushed my hands away. "Pulaski, we've got nothing to say."

"I need to work right now."

"They're hiring at McDonald's."

I gestured toward the coffin. "Looks like you've got a weirdie on your hands. Some kind of psycho?"

"God, I hope so. Maybe if we have a real case to work, IA will ease up on my former behaviorist's drunken brawls."

"You're going to need someone with expertise."

"I've promoted Granger to homicide detective."

"Granger couldn't detect his ass with both hands."

O'Bannon leaned right into my face. "But you know what? When I get back to the office tonight, he'll be sober."

They found Helen. Just as he'd planned.

He was experiencing so many emotions at once, it took a moment to sort through them, to catalog them in his brain. There was a calm, yes, definitely a peace that came from knowing it had begun. His actions had begun to concatenate. He had taken the prophet's nebulous meliorisms and converted them into a concrete plan of action. There was no chance of turning back, losing faith, rethinking the agenda. It was done, and because it was done, nothing would ever be the same.

But he couldn't deny that he also felt a certain disappointment. Did anyone appreciate what he had conceived? Of course not. Who could appreciate how dramatically their lives would soon be changed, irrevocably? What had begun with Helen would soon affect every soul on this earthly plane. **Helen, thy beauty is to me / Like those Nicean banks of yore . . .**

He continued observing the busy proceedings in the ballroom; his security uniform gave him an entrance pass to anywhere he wanted to go. So much energy, but so little of any importance being accomplished. They would not be among those who understood, these poor functionaries charged with an impossible task. Not a one of them.

Except perhaps . . .

He watched the woman, the tall one, the one most of the others studiously avoided. What had she done to make herself such a pariah? he wondered. He sensed that he himself might be more welcome than she was at the moment. And yet there was something special about her, something he sensed, something he felt in his heart.

He watched as she approached the remains of dear Helen. The others had obsessed over her shaved head—still did, in fact. He could well imagine what they were thinking. Obsessive-compulsive, perhaps. Organized nonsocial, the shrinks would proclaim. Woman-hater, the chief was probably grumping. Fools. Children.

But not the tall one. Her eyes had already moved to the torn earlobes. Then the damaged fingernails. She knew instinctively what was important. What was telling.

She was strikingly attractive—tall, slender,

athletic. Her face seemed drawn, strained, but her features were sound. And she had hair the color of his totem.

But there was more than that. Her eyes.

They were not the same. One was darker than the other. The left was a smoky gray, but the right was pure ebon.

He closed his eyes. **Now all my hours are trances; / And all my nightly dreams / Are where thy dark eye glances . . .**

Her presence here was no accident. She had been sent to him.

She was part of the plan.

Could it be she who would share his dream? That he might work in solitude no longer?

No, Ginny, I am not being unfaithful. But it's hard to be alone always. So hard . . .

He opened his eyes and peered all the more intently at the woman. She was older than his usual; she could not be an offering. But why not a colleague? Poe had taken a young girl for his bride, but he had chosen an older woman for his companion, his true soul mate. Maria Clemm had been with him longer than his child wife, and in the end, she had been far more important to him.

He gazed longingly at her eyes again, wondering at their importance. And this time, he saw more than just their color. There was pain in those eyes. She had been hurt, this one. Scarred. She was still reeling. Trying to find her place in a world that had turned against her.

She needed him.

His shift was over. One quick stop at the dentist's office, and then he could return his attentions to the new offering. Darling Annabel. But all the while he walked and later drove, he thought about the woman he had seen in the gallery, the one with the hair of the raven. How could he reach out to her? How could he make contact? A blessing such as this could not be ignored.

I tried to give the IOP classes a chance. I really did. I played Dr. Coutant's game. But it didn't take long to realize that this wasn't going to be helpful.

As I predicted, it was mostly a big group therapy session run by two former users, neither of whom was remotely qualified to lead a big group therapy session. They'd probe with their little questions, trying to get people to talk. I was willfully noncooperative. I couldn't relate to anything anyone was saying, most of which was incredibly stupid. As a trained psychologist, I resented seeing these nudniks turn therapy into Ted Mack's **Original Amateur Hour.**

Okay, so I was the only one in the group with

a college degree. I wasn't going to be snotty about it. I've never had any trouble mixing with people from all walks of life. And I remembered Dr. Coutant saying that intellectuals rarely did well in these programs. Does that mean they're only successful with dunderheads? People who buy into anything anyone tells them? At any rate, I had a hard time relating to the travails of guys working on the loading dock making eight bucks an hour who got hooked on street drugs mostly out of boredom because it wasn't football season and there was nothing on television. And I detested hearing people whine about their personal problems, most of which didn't amount to a hill of beans.

Of course, they had the AA twelve steps up on the wall. We all recited them in unison, then the group leader talked about each of them, even though the first eight or so all seemed to me to say pretty much the same thing over and over again. What is all this "admit that I am powerless" crap, anyway? Wouldn't it be a better technique to admit that I am powerful, that I have the strength to overcome my troubles? I had a real problem with this sniveling approach to better health. I couldn't help wondering if that was why AA and other similar programs didn't have a better recovery rate.

We also had this guy, Herb, a little salt-and-pepper-haired man who fancied himself a motivational speaker. He had lots of standard routines, gimmicks, anecdotes, acronyms. I thought it was just a matter of time before he tried to sell us his three-hundred-dollar award-winning series of inspirational cassette tapes. He asked us how we were, starting with me.

"I'm fine," I said succinctly.

"That's not an answer."

"I'm fine," I repeated, a little louder.

"That's not an answer. That's a blow-off." He pointed to a poster on the wall next to the twelve steps. It was basically a long list of adjectives. "Pick three that describe how you are."

Okay. His class, we'll play it his way. I chose three at random. "Optimistic. Determined. Reverent."

Herb arched an eyebrow.

For the following hour, we were treated to this blustering rodomontade about Herb's successful battle against demon rum. We were supposed to be inspired, but I couldn't help thinking that if the guy had ever had one day like most of mine, he'd be back in the gutter with a dollar bottle of muscatel.

Then, for his next act, Herb wrote PEOPLE PLACES EVENTS on the chalkboard. "You abuse substances," he announced, "because of one of these three things. Something a person in your past did. A place that hurt you. An event that traumatized you." He used examples from his own life, so we got to hear about how his mother threw plates at him when he was six and how his drunken daddy left when he was nine and how he got busted up in 'Nam. And oh yeah—his daughter is a sex addict, so he won't speak to her anymore. Thanks for sharing.

Mental note: next time I develop an addiction, sex addiction sounds a lot more fashionable, not to mention pleasurable, than substance abuse. All the major movie stars are sex addicts, right? But no one treats them like they would a wino. Alcoholism gives a girl ruddy skin and liver damage. Sex addiction adds luster.

Anyway, this guy's sermon opened the floodgates on what all the women in the group wanted to do anyway—blame it on their spouses. This was not remotely helpful to me, but I have to admit listening to it had a certain addictive quality, like tuning into a poorly written soap opera—just one damn thing after another. I listened to hours of the running battles between Jill and Buddy, every last mean thing he ever supposedly said. Oddly enough, she never did anything to provoke his invective. At least as she told it. Jacqueline was slightly more honest. She admitted that she argued back when her husband came after her for no reason. But she was blameless. Those bad men made those nice girls drink.

Yeah, right.

So at the end of this interminable three-hour session, one of the leaders, a heavyset gal named Margie, decided to pick on me. I hadn't said much, so I guess she felt obliged to try to get me into the whining bee.

"Why do you think you drink, Susan?"

"Drank. I don't do that anymore."

The smile only flashed for a second, but I didn't miss it. "Why do you think you drank?"

"I liked it."

She batted her long false eyelashes. "That's all?"

"Yup. Tastes good. Makes me feel good. What more do you want?"

"You don't think it . . . could have anything to do with your work?"

"Of course not. I love my work." I left out the detail that I didn't actually have work at the moment.

"You don't think it could relate to . . . what happened with your husband?"

"No," I said, giving her a stony glare. "I don't."

"You took a piece of glass—"

"I don't want to talk about that."

"You seem to have a lot of anger. Why is that?"

"Maybe I don't like having people prying into my private life."

"We're only trying to help you."

"You're talking about things you know nothing about."

"Then tell us. We want to learn."

"There's nothing to learn."

"No problems?"

"No. Everything is fine. Perfectly pleasant." I even forced myself to smile.

Margie leaned forward. "Susan . . . what's your secret?"

"Excuse me?"

"What's your secret?"

"I don't have one."

She paused a moment. "I remember a patient I had about three years ago. He said everything was fine, too. Then one day I asked him, 'What's your secret?' And he looked at me for a long time. Then he finally told me he was sexually abused when he was six years old. And he started crying. All that fear and anger tumbled out of him. He's been well ever since."

So that was what she wanted. Some big fake Hollywoodesque **Prince of Tides**–like single-event explanation for every problem I've ever had. Talk about trite. I considered making one up: **I was stolen by Gypsies and forced to work on a coffee plantation in Kenya.** But I knew I would be the only one laughing.

"There's no secret. Your whole approach is

psychologically wrongheaded. You can't boil all of a person's problems, all of their life, down to one person or incident."

She remained implacable and insistent. "Susan . . . what's your secret?"

What was this—some kind of hypnagogic brainwashing technique? "How many times do I have to say this? There is no secret."

I could see the other patients in the room shaking their heads sadly. Margie sighed. "I hope that's true, Susan. For your sake. You have a lovely smile, and I'm glad to see you using it occasionally. Beautiful eyes, too." She paused, staring at me. "But when I look into those eyes—I see pain."

At the next break, I left, never to return.

He heard Annabel even before he opened the door. That was unfortunate. He had not expected her to regain consciousness so quickly.

"Who is it?" she shouted as he came through the door. She twisted her head around; it was all she could move. "Who's there?"

"Just me again, my lovely. Back from the trenches."

She was lying flat on the table, as pure and unsullied as the day she was born. Her wide limpid eyes stared up at him. No restraints were necessary. She would not be able to move her limbs for some time.

"Why am I here?" she asked. "Where are my clothes?"

"You're in my laboratory," he said, maintaining calm, genteel composure. "And it was necessary to remove your garments."

"I don't—don't know what you—what you—" She was trying to fight the drug, to gather her strength. It was hopeless, but he couldn't help but admire her for trying. "I don't know what kind of sick bastard you are—"

"I assure you my parents were married at the time of my birth, dear."

"My boyfriend knows where I went! And when I don't return, Warren will do whatever it takes to find me."

A feisty one, this offering. A pleasant contrast to her predecessor. Exhilarating. "Dear me. Do you suppose he might call the law enforcement authorities? My heart's atwitter."

"Worse than that, you asshole. He'll call my mom."

"Do tell."

"That's right. She may be shit as a mother, but she's got power and money and she won't let you get away with this."

"You should not speak ill of your parents, Annabel. It's most unbecoming."

"They'll show you unbecoming, you sicko."

"Annabel, I don't care for your tone."

"You won't care for anything when my mother gets her hands on you. Now let me out of here!"

He looked down at her with genuine sadness. "That, I am afraid, I cannot do. My plans for you are not complete. But when they are, you will be released."

"And I'll be free to go?"

He hesitated only a moment. "You'll be free."

"What are these plans?"

"You'll see."

"What are you going to do to me?"

"Nothing improper, I assure you."

"Then why did you take my clothes off?"

"Did you think I had no legitimate purpose? That I did all this for my personal delectation?" He touched her sternum experimentally with his finger, then drew a long, slow line down her breast bone. He used his most mellifluous voice, hoping to calm her. "You can't appreciate what I'm doing, but it is for your own benefit, to help you fulfill your destiny, to complete your spiritual efflorescence. It was necessary."

"Necessary for what? For you to get your rocks off?"

He twitched. "You know, my dear, my plan does not require me to advance to the next step until tomorrow. But under the circumstances, I think mayhap it's best that we proceed immediately."

"What do you mean? What are you talking about?"

He set down the brown bag he had brought in with him. "Allow me to prepare my tools. Then all will be made clear."

"What's that? What is it?" Panic set in. Her voice quavered. She was no longer shouting, no longer demanding. She was scared.

He opened the bag wide and held it before her so she could see the scalpel, clamp, wedge, prong, and drill. "These are my dentistry tools."

"W-W-What are you going to do with those?"

"I'm afraid you are due for an oral examination, darling."

Her eyes grew wide and watery. "Are you— are you going to hurt me very much?"

"Yes, I'm afraid I am. I can't deaden this pain—not without making you unconscious. And you need to be awake as long as possible. So you can appreciate what is happening to you."

Her face caved, as the horror of her situation became clear. "P-P-Please don't do this. I'm going to be married. I'm going to have a baby."

"I don't think so." He leaned forward, the metal clamp and wedge reflecting light into her eyes. "Open wide."

CHAPTER FIVE

The lawyer sat on the other side of his desk, wearing a three-piece suit with a watch chain dangling from his vest pocket. His expression was so earnest it made me want to barf.

"You must understand, Susan. There are many competing factors involved here."

"What's so complicated? I'm her only living relative."

"Granted. But there are complications."

"I've been raising Rachel for three years without any problems."

His head swayed. "Well . . ."

"Certainly nothing major. And then I get sick for a week and they steal her away and stick her in a foster home."

He took a deep breath, then slowly released it. "I don't want to make you angry, Susan. But if we're going to get anywhere, we have to be realistic. You did not get sick. You were committed to a detox clinic. Because you are an alcoholic."

"That's bullshit."

"That's the position of the state, at any rate. And NDHS is not going to allow an alcoholic to retain sole custody or guardianship of a minor without a fight."

"NDHS needs to mind its own business."

"This **is** its business."

Jerk. Of course, like any good cop, I'd been trained to despise lawyers, so having to go to one for help was excruciating. I'd used this guy, Quentin Delacourt, a few times after David died, for wills and estates stuff that I never really understood. But he didn't know me. And I didn't much care for having him make these blanket proclamations about who and what I was.

"I'm not going to sit here defending myself to my own attorney," I said. "Will you take the case or not?"

"That depends on what you mean."

"I mean getting my niece back."

"Are you sure that's what you want?" He leaned back in his burgundy leather chair, adopting what he undoubtedly thought was a deep, contemplative pose. "There's no rush. Maybe you should give yourself some time."

"I gave myself a week. Look what happened."

"Give yourself a month. Just to relax. No stress, no work. And no alcohol, of course. Give your body a chance to recover. I don't think you've taken any time to get your head together since—"

"I'm not wealthy, Mr. Delacourt. I don't have the luxury of indulging myself in some spiritual walkabout. I want my niece back—now. I want you to file a motion or whatever it takes to get her yanked out of that hideous foster home."

He opened a file on his desk and thumbed through it. "From what I can see, the Shepherds' home is far from hideous. Apparently they have taken in many minors from—um—difficult situations."

"Rachel was perfectly happy with me. And she hates it where she is."

"That's to be expected, at least at first."

"So will you bring the motion or not? I want a hearing."

He gave me the contemplative look again, this time even steepling his fingers for added effect. "If you're sure that's what you want, then I'm honor-bound to get it for you. But I can't say that I'm optimistic about your chances. NDHS wouldn't have intervened unless they thought they had due cause. They've really papered this file."

He was starting to piss me off, big time. "How much mileage can they get out of one stupid mistake?"

"It goes way beyond that." He continued thumbing through the file, not making eye contact with me. "You're currently unemployed."

"I'm going to fix that."

"I won't lie to you, Susan. As long as you're unemployed, there's no way you're going to get custody."

"I told you, I'm going to fix that."

"Rachel's grades have been falling for the past year."

"It's hard losing a father figure. For the second time. Hasn't been a real picnic for me, either."

"Her school counselor says she's been depressed."

"I think that's somewhat understandable, given the circumstances."

"NDHS says you often leave her alone at night, while you're ostensibly working."

"Ostensibly? What is that supposed to mean?"

He closed the file. "One has to wonder, given the frequency . . ."

I stood up. "What are you implying?"

"Have you been drinking around Rachel?"

"I never drink at home."

"I ask again, have you been drinking around Rachel?"

"Absolutely not. Look, I screwed up once. I wasn't drinking that often."

"If you make that claim at the hearing, NDHS will bring out your blood work and prove you a liar."

"What the hell do they know about it?" I screamed. And immediately felt embarrassed. I was proving myself just as unstable as NDHS said I was. Playing into their hands. "Let those sons of bitches lose a husband! Let's see how well they handle it."

"We all know you've had some difficult trials. But the focus at the hearing will be on what's best for Rachel."

"I'm best for Rachel. She needs me!"

"Or is it more that you need her?"

I felt as if the top of my head was going to blow off. Literally. I gripped the edge of the man's desk, consumed with fury. "Are you going to get me the damn hearing or not?"

"I'll get the hearing," he said quietly. "But I can guarantee the attorney for NDHS will be much rougher on you than I have been. And if you behave in court the way you're behaving now, you haven't got a snowball's chance."

It took him more than three hours to remove all of Annabel's teeth. He used no anesthetic and nothing to stanch the bleeding. She bled profusely, down her chin, onto her bare neck and shoulders, mixing with saliva and coagulating to create a nasty bubbling paste. He had no means of measuring the quantity of blood lost, but it seemed enormous, an endless flow from those torn and ravaged gums. He had no idea if, as in the story, she would bleed to death, but it certainly seemed possible. And if she did not do so as a natural consequence, he knew how to see that she did.

After the first tooth was removed, she began to scream. He turned the Mozart up high. Fortunately, Camille's boyfriend was not nearby; it would have been an inopportune time for a visit. After the third tooth, the screaming ceased, as did the threats about her mother's revenge, the name-calling, the inappropriate remarks about his parentage. By the tenth tooth, she was entirely broken, shattered, incoherent. She began to hallucinate. She lost all sense of who and where she was. She called him Warren, made sexual advances. She alternated between pleading for mercy and babbling about her schoolwork. He was moved by her pain, truly. It took great force of will to remind himself that there was a higher purpose behind all this. The path to godhood was strewn with sacrifice.

"Am I dead?" she asked at one point just before unconsciousness descended, her pulpy gums mashing together. "I feel dead."

"The sleep will come, my sweet Berenice."

"Thasss good," she said, and her last thought was expressed as a single word. "Why?"

" 'And still the phantasma of the teeth maintained its terrible ascendancy,' " he murmured, and with gentle fingers closed her eyelids for the last time. "Make a place for me in the firmament, my darling. Tell my love I will soon be reunited with her. That we will all be together once again."

He walked upstairs and gazed out his window at the striking sunset. It was a glorious evening, bright and clear, a vivid orange and blue curtain draped across the skyline. He could almost feel the warmth of the light emanating from the Luxor pyramid, a forty-billion-candle-power beacon said to be the most powerful spotlight in the world. It shone for ten miles into space, carving a swath through the heavens. Was it the light that illumined sweet Virginia's face? Was it a trail of bread crumbs Annabel might follow? There was no basis for these beliefs in the prophecies. But it seemed so in his dreams, and the prophet did teach that dreams were a portal into the land of the ideal. If he could dream there, he could be there. And so he would. And so would they all.

After dark, I told Lisa I was going to the grocery store for some Vanilla Heath Bar Crunch. Hated to lie, but it seemed simpler than having an argument about whether I should do what I already knew I was going to do. I had to see O'Bannon. And I'd decided to confront him in an environment in which he couldn't so easily blow me off.

Short drive with the top lowered down the streets of neon did me a world of good. Saw the transparent dome of the Fremont Street Exposition, my new favorite tourist joint. Basically, they tarted up the old Strip so it could compete with the new, and did a darn good job of it, in my opinion. Hey, beats seeing David Cassidy lip-sync or the ten billionth magic show, right?

Once I arrived at his house, I pounded on his front door, literally pounded. Guess my rage was still boiling. When I thought about what he'd done to me, after all I'd done for him, the cases I'd solved, only to have him shaft me the first time I'm vulnerable—it just infuriated me. I pounded and pounded, and when he didn't come to the door immediately, I started shouting.

Some kid opened the door.

Okay, **kid** might be pushing it, but he seemed like a kid to me. He was probably in his early-twenties. He had peach fuzz on his upper lip and cheeks, and long brown hair that wasn't very well groomed. He was dressed in a green T-shirt and was tall and lanky. Actually, my first thought was of Shaggy from those Scooby-Doo cartoons.

"Do I know you?" he asked.

I blinked. "I . . . don't think so."

We stared at each other.

"Is this the O'Bannon residence?"

"Uh-huh."

More staring.

Finally he spoke: "Did they give you ice cream?"

"Umm . . . excuse me?"

"I wondered if maybe they gave you ice cream. They gave me ice cream. I like ice cream, don't you?"

"I never had much of a sweet tooth. Who is they?"

"The hospital."

"The . . . hospital?"

"I had to be in the hospital once and I didn't like it. But they gave me ice cream and I liked that."

I checked my reflection in the glass in the door. Did I look sick? Was I still wearing the ID bracelet? I had on a short-sleeved blouse, but I had replaced the gauze bandage on my wrist with a plain wide Band-Aid. "How do you know I've been in the hospital?"

He gave me a sheepish look. "Did you have to wear one of those gowns with your butt hanging out?"

"Um, I don't—"

"Do you mind if I say **butt**? I think **butt** is a funny word, but my dad says I shouldn't say it."

"How did you know—"

"This." He grabbed my arm—a little too roughly, but of course he didn't know I'd recently punctured myself. At least, I don't think he knew. "See?" He turned my left arm around so the crook of the elbow faced up. There was a red pinprick where they had drawn blood and now that I noticed it, a couple of faint bruises above and below. "I bet you have small veins. I have small veins, and it took them three times to get the needle into me."

"Could I possibly see your father?" I assumed O'Bannon was the previously mentioned dad and I was speaking to his twenty-something boomerang boy.

"Do you have a dog?" he asked.

"Not currently. Why?"

"I don't like dogs. Do you like dogs?" With each new remark, I became increasingly aware of the oddness of his voice. He talked too loudly, for starters, given that we were only about a foot apart. And the inflections were all wrong. It was almost like one of those computer-generated voices that are assembled by syllables, so the intonation goes up and down with no relation to what is being said.

"Well . . . some dogs. I used to have German shepherds—"

"If you have a dog, I can't let you in the house."

"That's cool. No dog."

"Did you know that dogs were first domesticated around fourteen thousand years ago near Israel?"

"No . . ."

"I think it was a mistake."

I stared at him, but not as intently as he was staring at me. He never actually made eye contact. Every time my eyes came near his, he averted them. I tried to get a fix on who I was talking to, without success. There was something odd about his expression, a certain vacancy behind the eyes. Almost as if he wasn't really there. Like his body was on the front patio with me but he wasn't. Like he was gazing out through an invisible acrylic barrier—he could see through it, but he couldn't make contact. It disturbed me.

One of my chief assets has always been my hyper-empathy. I've had it since I was a child. I don't know why. And I can't really explain what it is. But I've had this ability to tune into what other people are feeling. It isn't a mind-reading trick. But it's real. Of course, it's always been a great asset to me in my work as a behaviorist. One of the reasons I've been able to create useful profiles is that I've had this talent for understanding what motivates people, what impels them to take action. But it wasn't doing me any good with this guy. When I put out my feelers toward him, I got nothing.

"So . . . is your dad home?"

"He's in his study." No movement.

"Can I talk to him?"

And the kid disappeared. Didn't say yes, no, or go to hell—just turned around and dived back into the house.

So what was I supposed to do? I decided that I'd been invited in, so I stepped into the foyer and closed the door behind me.

And nothing happened. After a minute or so of waiting, I escorted myself down the front hallway in the direction I'd seen the boy go.

I found O'Bannon's study. It was a gorgeous room, with walls of dark wood paneling and hundreds if not thousands of books. Two of the walls were completely covered with bookshelves stuffed to capacity. Beautiful books, leather-bound editions with gilt-embossed lettering on the spines. Some of them were police-related—criminology texts and such. But most were fiction, literature I was supposed to read in college but never did: **Wuthering Heights, In Search of Lost Time, Ivanhoe, Bleak House, One Hundred Years of Solitude.**

Chief O'Bannon sat in a plush recliner, obviously designed to be a reading chair. The spine of his book faced me. He was perusing **Jane Eyre.** Yes, you heard me correctly. My tough-guy supercop boss was reading **Jane Eyre.**

And he was drinking. There was a crystal snifter on the table beside him, and an open decanter of brandy beside that.

I could smell it, even across the room. It smelled good.

The kid who had opened the door was sprawled across the carpet. He was reading something, too.

I guess this room was far enough back that O'Bannon was insulated from the noise at the front of the house. Neither of them appeared to have heard me approach. Neither realized that I was standing in the doorway staring at them.

"Chief?" I said quietly.

He jumped, actually jumped, out of his chair, slamming his book shut. His elbow knocked over the brandy snifter. It spilled onto the table and soaked some papers. One of them caught my eye. It was a photocopy of a page torn from a spiral-bound notebook, filled with block lettering and symbols.

"Damn it." O'Bannon tried to wipe the mess up with his sleeve. Fortunately, there had not been much left in the snifter. Once he had the mess contained, he focused his attention on me. "What are you doing here?"

I pointed. "Your son let me in."

He looked down at the kid, frowned, nodded. "Well, what do you want?"

"You know what I want."

"It isn't going to happen."

"Just listen to me for a moment."

"No."

"Come on. We can help each other."

"I don't think so."

"I need work."

"And that's why you came here?"

"I want to help."

"I don't need help. I need peace and quiet."

"Chief, listen to me!"

"Go home."

"A-A-Are you guys fighting?"

It was the kid, still lying on the floor, but now twisted around and watching us like a spectator at a tennis match.

"No," O'Bannon snapped. "We are not fighting."

"'Cause it sounds like you're fighting. Do you need to go to time out?"

"Darcy . . ."

The boy looked at me. "Do you know that if

you make him mad, you will have to go to time out? Or maybe military school."

"Darcy!" O'Bannon barked. "We are not fighting!"

The kid's eyes widened. He ran the tips of his fingers through his hair, as if he were washing it with invisible shampoo. He made a strange, excited noise, over and over again, something between a snort and hysterical giggling.

"Hey, it's okay." I don't know why, but I walked over to him and tried to lower his hands. "Your dad and I work together. We always talk like this. It doesn't mean anything."

His arms were stiff and resistant. "S-S-S-Sometimes my dad talks like that, and it means he's mad."

"Well, it doesn't now. Your daddy adores me and I know it. Even when he tries to hide it."

Apparently O'Bannon'd had enough of this fun. "Susan, you're wasting your breath. The only reason I'm tolerating this intrusion is out of respect for your father. But that respect can only go so far."

"Look," I said, "I know you've got a weird homicide on your hands. I know the victim was buried alive. Obviously, you've got a seriously twisted killer. My specialty. You need me."

"Like hell. I assigned the case to Granger."

"Right, Granger—hawkshaw extraordinaire.

Give me a break, Chief. Granger doesn't know squat about aberrant psychology. Except maybe what he picks up when he looks in the mirror."

"We'll catch the killer, Susan. Without your invaluable assistance."

I pointed to the photocopy on the table, the one with all the gibberish. "Is that part of the case?"

He shrugged. "We found that inside the girl's coffin. But we can't make heads or tails of—" He stopped short. "You are not getting involved, Susan. Give it up. Go home."

Why was everything so difficult? Everyone kept babbling about how they wanted to help me, but every time I needed help, no one could deliver. "Chief, I need my job back. If I don't get work, I'm going to lose Rachel."

"That ship has already sailed."

I was so frustrated, so furious, my hands tightened into fists.

"Are you going to spank my dad?" the kid—Darcy, I guess—asked.

If I thought it would help . . . "No. I told you, we talk like this—"

"Because whenever Unca Donald gets mad like that, he gets a switch and chases after his nephews and spanks them."

There was something so strange about this young man, something so childlike and yet not,

something unnerving because it was so ineffable. But I kept my attention focused on his
father.

"Is this because of that jerk's rich family?" I
said. "Because if you're doing this because you're
afraid of a lawsuit—"

"There isn't going to be a lawsuit."

This about-face caught me off guard. "Excuse me? This afternoon, you said—"

"No lawsuit."

"Someone pulled some strings?"

"For you? Hell, no. You just got lucky."

"What happened?"

"At the hospital today, some helpful RN
knocked over a table where the frat boy had laid
the pants he was wearing when you worked him
over. And guess what fell out of his pocket? A
little baggie filled with crystal meth."

"You're kidding me."

"Like I said, you got lucky. Of course, there's
no evidence that he was using on the night in
question. But it would certainly explain his aggressive and violent behavior."

"Did he have aggressive and violent behavior?"

"Sure. That's how the fight started, right? You
had to defend yourself."

"To tell the truth, I'm a little fuzzy on the details. . . ."

"At any rate, that's going to be our story, and it persuaded the guy's family to entertain second thoughts. Even if they managed to overcome this brilliant defense at trial, the whole world would know their son was a drug user. Possible dealer. They didn't think it was worth it."

"That's fabulous."

"That's dumb luck, which does not in any way excuse or justify what you did. I can't use a cop I can't trust, Susan. I can't use a cop who might lose it at any moment. I can't use a cop who might be sneaking drinks on the side."

"Chief, that's all behind me."

"So you're all cured now, huh?"

"Well . . . yeah, I'm over it."

"Fit as a fiddle. One hundred percent. Ready to carry a gun again. Ready to be some other cop's partner. Ready to have someone count on you, depend on you. Ready to have someone put their life in your hands."

I didn't bother answering.

"I care about you, Susan. I **do.** And that's why I'm saying this. I will not reinstate you. You need to get help—professional help. This may be your last chance to save yourself before you've lost everything."

"I've already lost everything."

"No, you haven't. But you will if you start drinking again. Now get out of here."

I wanted to scream. "Fine! Have it your way. You won't see me back here begging. Not for a blue moon. Not if—"

"And try not to be so angry all the time. Relax. Read a book. Get healthy."

I couldn't leave without giving it one more try. I dropped a scrap of paper on his table. "I'm leaving you my new address and phone, just in case you change your mind."

"I won't. Go."

Darcy walked me to the door. He still talked in that too loud voice with the odd inflections, but he seemed to have lost the stutter. "Will you be coming again in two and a half years?"

"Why—?"

"That's what you said."

"I said I'm never coming back here."

"Uh-huh." He gave me that sheepish grin again. "What you said was: 'You won't see me back here begging. Not for a blue moon.'" The amazing thing was, he not only repeated what I had said verbatim, he mimicked my inflection. Then he shifted into a colder, almost singsong tone, as if he were reciting in front of a school-room. "'A blue moon is the second full moon in a given calendar month, which in North Amer-ica occurs approximately once every forty-one months, or approximately every two and a half years.'"

I gave him a long look. "I'm not coming back."

"Oh. Is the reason that you will not come back because of me?"

"Of course not."

" 'Cause if it is, it's okay. I know sometimes people don't like me. My dad says it's not my fault, but he still yells at me sometimes. Everyone yells at me sometimes."

"It wasn't you. Really."

"Then—" His hands began to flap up and down. "Do you think that maybe you could come again sometime? My dad gets real lonely. I think he misses having a girl around."

"I think your father made it clear. . . . Never mind." I wiggled my fingers, smiled faintly, and left. I probably should've said something more, but I couldn't manage it. I was so depressed, so frustrated, so . . . empty. I didn't have anything to spare for anyone else.

At first I thought the tall girl had a dog and I was worried because I don't like dogs and dogs are scary mean and smelly, but it wasn't a dog. The tall girl was sweaty and the hospital smells were still there a little and maybe one of those perfumes that she put on way too much of. I liked the girl and I think Dad likes her even though he was mean to her and she said he wasn't mean to her but he was and I know that look like the coach at the YMCA when I was in the eighth grade. He smelled too and Cleanliness is next to Godliness and get your hands out of your hair and what is that smell and I liked her she was nice to me. I don't know why she was nice to me but she was she touched me and I don't like it when people touch me but sometimes I wish they would more. **My love for Heathcliff resembles the eternal rocks beneath—a source of little visible delight, but necessary.** I was right when I said I hoped she would come back because Dad is lonely but sometimes I'm lonely too and I like the tall girl with the eyes that don't match and the bump on her nose and the yellow Post-it stuck to the sole of her shoe. The girls at the day care act nervous around me but this girl didn't I think she liked me at least some maybe a little but when Dad talks to me I can't talk any more and he gives me that look like he's so disappointed in me. He spent hours on that simple puzzle and he never asked me never once did he ask me even though I like puzzles and he doesn't. The girl was keeping secrets and not just that she's been in the hospital but I like the girl and I hope she comes back.

I wonder if she has babies because my dad said you need a girl to have babies and I like babies. Babies are nice to me. They don't mind when I'm around.

He rolled her remains into an old carpet, which made it easier to transport her to the pickup. He was learning, wasn't he? He was an innovator, never content with the status quo, always searching for ways to improve himself.

He drove the short distance to his chosen disposal place. This would be much easier than the last. Almost no chance of being spotted here, not this time of night. It was perfect—thematically appropriate (though the police were unlikely to get the joke), risk-free, and certain to be discovered.

Only an occasional plane passing overhead reminded him where he was. The glittering silver created a reflected brightness, but if he stayed on the far end of the lot, he would be safe. He opened a curved and unlocked silver door and laid her body to rest.

He hesitated. A ceremony before he departed seemed appropriate. Perhaps—some sort of prayer.

He lowered his head and spoke in susurrous tones.

" 'And so, all the night-tide, I lie down by the side of my darling—my darling—my life and my bride.' "

He took a handful of dirt and, just to give this a semblance of burial, sprinkled it over the body. " 'In her tomb by the sounding sea.' "

"You've got a date? A true-to-life, honest-to-God date?"

Lisa batted her eyelashes. "Control your envy."

"And this isn't with . . . what was his name?"

"The Human Plunger? Not him." Lisa had an endearing habit of identifying all her boyfriends by reference to their kissing technique.

"No, I mean the advertising guy."

"The Tongueless Titan. Ditched him."

"Dare I ask why?"

"Kissed hard with his mouth open, but never any tongue."

"Was that bad?"

"It was weird. Like he was administering CPR. And I asked myself, if he's so reserved with his tongue now, is he ever going to—"

"Lisa!"

"Well, a girl has to wonder."

I leaned through the open car window. "Have a good time. I'll expect a full report."

Lisa took my hand and squeezed. "Are you sure you'll be okay, honey?"

"Of course I will." Lisa was so sweet. She would do anything for me, I knew that. It frustrated her, not knowing what to do, what she could do.

"I don't feel right, leaving you by yourself."

I patted her reassuringly on the shoulder. "Don't be silly. You can't babysit me forever."

"But it's only—"

"We'd drive each other crazy and we both know it. You're my best friend, Lisa, but even you can only tolerate me in limited doses." We both laughed. "You've gotten me a great place to stay. I need some time to get it in order."

"I could help."

"Hey, you did all the packing. It's only fair that I unpack."

"There's no rush."

"I want the place looking nice before Rachel comes back."

Lisa fell silent.

"You run along," I said quickly, papering over the gap. "I'll call you later."

She smiled a little. "Okay. But if you need something, call me on my cell."

"I will."

"I won't be far. I could be at your place in a heartbeat."

"You shouldn't say that. I might call. Interrupt some CPR."

Her smile faded a bit. "I wish you would. But I know you won't."

Lisa hugged me again, then drove off in a

sports car cloud of smoke and I made my way to the new apartment.

She'd done a terrific job, especially considering how little time she'd had to work on it. Wasn't too expensive, either. The monthly rent was considerably less than my mortgage had been, when I paid it, so I might end up with a little extra spending money—a pleasant thought.

What little furniture I had was in storage, so I was stuck with the rudimentary apartment-provided stuff. The mattress was lumpy and hard, but I had a hunch I'd be sleeping soundly anyway.

I started by doing what little had to be done to make the joint habitable—sheets on the bed, Mr. Coffee in the kitchen. Most everything else could wait. I really needed to relax. What an ordeal this day had been. I was exhausted.

I should've just watched television, but I couldn't resist going through the packing boxes, making sure everything was safe and still in one piece. Lisa had taken great care with my belongings. But she couldn't know everything. She couldn't know that the scruffy, torn T-shirt that looked as if it must be a dust rag was actually my favorite pajama top. She couldn't know that I folded my sweaters along the vertical bias, not the horizontal. And she couldn't know that I had left a full bottle of bourbon in my gym bag.

But I knew.

CHAPTER SIX

He had just unfolded the morning paper when Harv Bradford entered the canteen.

"Can you believe those cops are still running around outside, Ernie? Took me twenty minutes just to get into the hotel."

He shrugged. "They have a job to do. They must keep the crime scene secure."

"Yeah, right." Harv poured himself a cup of coffee, took a sip, then winced. "Are we reusing yesterday's grounds?" He tossed the drink into the sink. "You had any contact with the cops?"

"No."

"Neither had any of the boys on the night shift. Kind of a snub, if you ask me."

"They're LVPD. Why would they consult with us?"

"We're the hotel security force. We work every damn day right here where they found the body. Seems like we might be able to tell them a thing or two."

"Such as what?"

"Well . . . I don't know exactly. But something. At any rate, they could ask. To treat us like we don't exist . . ." Harv shook his head. "Just seems disrespectful."

"City cops never have any respect for private security," he replied. "They call us rent-a-cops."

"I think that sucks." Harv was a little over six feet, but he carried a spare tire that made the gray uniform bulge in all the wrong places. He looked ridiculous, out of shape, stupid. And he wondered why the police didn't want to consult with him. "I could tell them a thing or two."

He lowered his paper. "You know something about the body they found?"

"Well, no. Not exactly. But it's possible I might've seen something without knowing I saw it, you know what I mean?"

I know you're a fool, he thought.

"Hey! Is there something in the news about it?"

Harv snatched the paper out of his hands without even asking. It was because of his

height, of course. Because Harv towered above
him, that gave him free rein to disregard common courtesy.

"What do you know?" Harv said, slapping
the paper. "The Transylvania made the front
page. Did you read it?"

"I **was** reading it," he answered sharply.

"This is pretty cool. Look at the size of the
headline. I bet this is getting national play."

"We can but hope."

"Kinda exciting, ain't it? Being a part of a big
story like this."

"I don't believe that either of our names is
mentioned."

"Maybe not. But it happened right where we
work. And I know the guy who found the
body."

"You're a celebrity, Harv."

"If you ask me, this is what the money boys
get for choosing such a creepy theme for this
place."

"The children like it."

"Yeah, and since when did Vegas care about
children? This new crowd—they got more
bucks than brains. I liked the town better when
the mob ran it."

"Those were the good old days."

"You really don't think those cops would
want to talk to me?"

"I really don't, Harv."

The paper crumpled in his hands. "Know what? I always wanted to be a cop. A real one, I mean. When I was a kid. But I couldn't afford the school and I couldn't pass the test. So I went into private security."

"And isn't that satisfying? You wear a uniform. You have the occasional opportunity to hustle prostitutes. Strong-arm card cheats."

"It ain't the same. People look up to cops."

"Do they?"

"Cops are like heroes. They make TV shows about cops. When was there ever a series about a private security guard?"

And that of course proves, a posteriori, that security guards are without merit. "I suppose you have a point."

"I mean, here I am, right on the premises, with a badge and a gun and everything, but those guys outside would never dream of asking for my help. Wouldn't even cross their minds." He released a slow sigh. "Here." He tossed the paper back. "All that little print makes my head hurt."

There were smudges on the main story, big black remnants of Harv's Frankensteinian thumbs. He hated that. He didn't want to read a paper that had been pawed over by illiterates. And this one was important; he needed this story for his History. He would have to pick up another copy on his drive home.

His eyes returned to the main story under the banner headline:

MURDER VICTIM "BURIED" IN CASINO GRAVEYARD

BY JONATHAN WOOLEY

An unidentified nude female corpse completely shaved of body hair was discovered early Tuesday morning in a mock graveyard located at the multimillion-dollar Transylvania resort hotel, authorities revealed yesterday afternoon. The body was placed in a wooden coffin and buried under a thin layer of dirt. The graveyard is part of the hotel's Edgar Allan Poe gallery, one of several horror-themed tableaus on the ballroom floor.

"We're just glad the body was discovered before the doors were opened," said Transylvania owner Katherine Wentworth. "We wouldn't want any of our guests to be disturbed."

Police officials remained tight-lipped about the investigation, but LVPD Chief of Police Robert O'Bannon indicated that they were pursuing several leads.

"Obviously, the irony of depositing a body in a fake graveyard was more than someone could resist. We've taken evidence, which should allow us to identify the victim in time. The large number of tourists coming in and out of Vegas makes a quick ID difficult. Nonetheless, we have all our top officers working on it and have every reason to believe we will identify the victim—and her assailant—in short order."

At a press conference later in the day, a representative of the LVPD Homicide Department, Lieutenant Barry Granger, stated that preliminary tests indicated that the victim had died of suffocation. Several unanswered questions still remained about . . .

In other words, they knew nothing. He allowed himself a tiny smile. They didn't know who Helen was, they didn't know who he was, and they had no glimmer of the magnitude of what they had stumbled across. At least not most of them . . .

His eyes scanned the page and then the continuation on page three, searching for the information he wanted. Yes, yes, he knew O'Bannon, that blowhard was on television all the time. There were repeated references to Lieutenant Granger, who during his initial crime scene appearance seemed almost deliberately slow-witted. But what of the raven-haired beauty? Who was she? What was she doing there? Given the way she was treated by most of the other police officers, it was tempting to conclude that she was an unauthorized visitor, that she had no connection to them. But he knew that was wrong. He had seen the way she moved, the way she carried herself. She was on familiar ground. She had done this before. Had she been brought in from another jurisdiction? He had to find out.

"So I'm thinking maybe I'll just march right up and introduce myself to 'em. What'd'ya think about that?"

"What?" He looked up. Had Harv been babbling the entire time he was reading? "Who?"

"The cops, Ernie. I'm thinking maybe I'll tell them I'm available. Who knows? They might like the chance to work with someone who knows the lay of the land."

"They won't give you the time of day," he replied. "If you had something to tell them, then maybe—"

He stopped short. That was it. If he had something to tell, something they really wanted, he could command anyone's attention. Even hers.

"I'll be out this afternoon," he said, tossing down the paper. "Cover for me in the casino."

"Sure, but—"

"Keep your eyes open and your lips sealed," he added as he slid into his coat. "And most importantly, Harv—don't hassle the police and don't go near the Poe room. You never know what might happen there."

CHAPTER SEVEN

The phone must've rung twenty times before it finally registered in my brain. Exerting all my available strength, I managed to pull my head out from under the pillow. It throbbed. More than throbbed—it felt as if someone were running an electric mixer inside my cranial case, scrambling my brains.

I grabbed the receiver, knocking over the end table in the process. The bottle fell to the floor with a bang but thank God didn't quite break.

" 'Lo," I managed. My tongue felt like Velcro.

"Pulaski? Is that you?"

I stiffened. It was Chief O'Bannon. "Yes, sir."

"Are you all right?"

" 'M fine."

"Took you forever to answer the phone."

"Sorry. I was in the shower."

He was silent for a moment. "Are you able to come out to a crime scene? As soon as possible."

Truth was, I felt like shit. But I wasn't going to tell him that. "You want me at a crime scene? After last night—"

"I've changed my mind. Decided to give you a second chance."

"Out of the goodness of your heart?"

"Out of respect for your father. And David."

"Bullshit." I shifted the phone from one ear to the other and pushed my aching self up to a sitting position. "There's been another murder, hasn't there?"

"Yes, but—"

"Buried alive?"

Again the silence. "No. This one's worse."

"You've got a psycho on your hands."

"Looks that way."

"And that's the real reason for this call. Not any charity toward me. You need my expertise."

"Look, I don't have time for this. Are you coming or not?"

Get a grip, I told myself. Take the job before he changes his mind. "All right, I'm in. I'll stop by headquarters and get my badge and—"

"No badge. No gun."

"But you said—"

"I'm willing to hire you on a part-time

consulting basis with respect to this one case. That's it."

"No way."

"Those are my terms. Take it or leave it."

"You—" I pounded my fist into the pillow, biting back what I really wanted to say. "Why are you doing this to me?"

"You're not ready to be reinstated."

"How the hell would you—"

"You have a problem, Susan. A major problem. And until you've overcome it, you're not going to play on my team. But I still need a behaviorist, at least until the Feds move in."

"Feds?" I whistled.

"So I'm asking one last time. Will you take the consulting position or not?"

"I'll take it." Even though I found the whole situation offensive, I needed work if I wanted to get Rachel back.

He told me where to meet him. "I'll be there in about an hour."

"Twenty minutes," he answered. "Or you're off the case."

"But I just got up—"

"I thought you just got out of the shower."

I pressed my hand against my forehead. Dumb, dumb, dumb.

"See you in twenty." He made a grunting noise, then disconnected.

My entire body ached. The head was the

worst, but it was just part of the overall miserable package. I felt broken, shattered, both in body and in spirit. I looked down at the bottle rolling around on the floor—empty—and it made me sick in so many ways I couldn't count them all.

My first night alone since the big breakdown, and I'd found a hell of a way to celebrate. I couldn't be trusted for one night. I'd done exactly what everyone said I would do, and I was lying about it afterward, just as everyone knew I would.

Hell. I had work to do. That would be my cure—bury myself in a case. Get too busy to indulge in bad habits. I'd made one mistake, but I was determined not to let it happen again.

The hollow anxious aching in my chest reasserted itself. My wrist tingled.

I found the crime scene on the back forty of McCarran International. Out here in the desert, you could barely tell you were anywhere near a major city. The airport terminal was to the north; other than that, it was big-sky country. Hard to imagine what could've inspired those Mormons to settle down here all those years ago. John Fremont, now mostly remembered for the tourist trap street that bears his name, first wrote about the area he discovered in 1844 while he was out harassing Indians. But Mormon cattle ranchers set up the first settlement in these fertile plains, around 1855. By 1905, we had a train station—and casinos—and they held the first Las Vegas land auction, the event that put this city on the map.

Bugsy Siegel always gets the credit for founding Vegas—especially after they made that movie with the far-too-handsome Warren Beatty—but he was only one of several people who established Vegas as a fantasy pleasure destination. He was a gangster, for God's sake, not a visionary. There were already a couple of hotels out here when he made the scene. If he'd been that insightful, he'd have bought all the land in the area, not just one lot, right? Meyer Lansky and a host of investors—one of whom probably had Siegel offed—were also major players. But everyone remembers Bugsy. There's even a memorial garden shrine to him, out at the modern-day Flamingo. Lisa and I went there once, just for laughs. It was a hoot. Of course, I was snockered at the time.

After I parked my car, I stumbled down a sharp paved declivity to the recessed tarmac where the body had been found. The crime scene was in the midst of dozens of disabled aircraft. Apparently this was where the big birds came to die. One of the patrolmen on duty filled me in. The body had been stashed inside one of the retired jets. Judging from appearances, this young naked woman had already been dead before she was brought here. Why would the killer stash the corpse in an abandoned airplane? How was this connected to the woman who had been buried alive?

I wasn't surprised to see Granger lurking about. Wasn't surprised, but wasn't happy, either. His face expressed his feelings about me pretty clearly, too.

"Took you long enough," he grunted.

"You're in a jocund mood this morning. Someone put castor oil in your coffee?"

"Just for the record," he said, "your involvement in this case—or any other case, for that matter—is against my strong objection."

"I assumed any smart idea wouldn't come from you," I replied, walking past him without stopping.

I found O'Bannon inside the plane, running down a checklist with Crenshaw. When he saw me, he glanced at his watch. "Twenty-nine minutes," he said. "And you look like hell."

"Top of the morning to you, too," I answered, smiling.

He walked up to me and widened my eyes with his fingers, like I was a damn cow he was thinking of buying. "Your eyes are bloodshot."

"I had trouble sleeping. You know how it is. First night in a new place."

He frowned, then sniffed.

"Anything on my breath?"

"About half a tin of Altoids, unless I'm mistaken." He gave me a long look, and believe me, I didn't need hyper-empathy to know what he was thinking.

"Who's the victim?" I asked, hoping to redirect his scrutiny from me to, well, anything. I stepped closer to the body, which the coroner's assistants were in the process of transporting. She was young, probably sixteen or seventeen. Something odd about the way her face was set, but she had been a pretty thing, that was obvious, and she still had her hair, unlike the last one. Fingernails, too. Her skin was an icy white, so drained of color her lips were almost invisible. There were no apparent wounds or injuries.

"Don't know. She was found with no identification. We'll run her picture in the paper and with luck someone will recognize her."

"What makes you think this is the same killer?" I asked, although I was certain it was. "Seems like an entirely different MO."

"He left another note."

O'Bannon handed me the evidence, already encased in a transparent sheath. It was similar to the one I'd spotted last night—letters and symbols and general nonsense on a sheet of lined notebook paper. "Any idea what this is?"

"No. I've got some of our biggest eggheads working on the first one, trying to see if it's some kind of code. So far, no luck. It may just be psychotic rambling."

"Can I get a copy? I know someone who might be able to help." I surveyed the crime scene. "Who was the first responder?"

"Harrelson. Lucky choice, really. He did a solid, clean job."

The first responder has the job of securing the crime scene. This is critical, not only to obtaining pure and useful information, but to being able to use that information later at trial. He or she must protect the evidence, then initiate safety procedures—in this case, make sure the killer wasn't still around—and then contact the proper criminalists and finalize the relevant documentation, which with a homicide, was enormous. Once the crime scene experts and homicide investigators arrived, supervisory authority passed to them.

Contrary to what everyone thinks from watching **C.S.I.,** the Vegas Metropolitan Police Department has no department called a C.S.I. Level III. Or for that matter, a Level II or Level I or Level 427.5. Those TV creations are a blanket fiction that allows characters to do the work of a wide range of criminalists: forensic lab techs, photo techs, latent print examiners, firearms experts, medical examiners, document experts, hair and fiber teams, and evidence custodians, just to name a few. The only thing the

TV show doesn't exaggerate is the importance of this work. Most cases are solved—and proven in court—thanks to the work of these technicians.

"How was she killed?" I asked O'Bannon.

"Naturally, Dr. Patterson won't offer an opinion this soon. But judging from her skin tone, she bled to death."

I was puzzled. "You mean, she had internal bleeding?"

"No."

I glanced again at the body. "I don't see any injuries."

"Right. That's the mystery."

I stared down at the corpse, hoping to get some kind of fix on who she was or what she had been doing. What happened to you? I wondered. Who did this? And why?

I scrutinized the whole picture, the neck, the chest, the legs. Not only were there no signs of a wound, there were no signs of any kind of struggle. No signs of restraint, except perhaps some faint redness across her upper arms. Were you too scared to fight? I wondered. She looked healthy enough. Why didn't she claw his eyes out?

I put the coroner techs on hold and, against their heated protest, took a closer look at the body. I found signs of a body piercing on her navel. But the stud was gone. Ripped out.

A pattern was forming in my mind. Far from

a complete picture—a hint at best. But something. Taking two tongue depressors from one of the coroner's boys, I pried open her mouth. And gasped.

Now I knew why there was something odd about the set of her jaw. Her teeth had been removed. Every single one. The tearing of her mouth, her gums, was enormous; the extraction had not been executed by a trained professional. This was how she had bled to death. Not from any bodily wound. From the mouth.

Thank God I'd had no time for breakfast. Throwing up would not only be unprofessional, it would convince O'Bannon I'd been drinking. I'd seen some seriously twisted, weird, ugly stuff in my time, and it took a great deal to get a gasp out of me, even on a day like this when I was well off my game. But I was sickened by the thought of the pain she must have endured, both mental and physical. This was not the work of any ordinary killer. Not even an ordinary psychopath. This was something—someone—altogether different.

"I'll want to see the coroner's preliminary report," I said, letting her mouth relax. "As soon as it comes in."

"Natch."

"I'll want the files on the first victim, too. Everything you've got."

"I've already had them sent to your office."

O'Bannon coughed. "Your temporary office. Downtown."

"Criminalists got anything useful yet?"

O'Bannon shrugged. "Not that I've heard."

"What about blood splatters?"

"Do you see any?"

"No."

"Neither do we. Even after we went over the area with leucocrystal violet."

Which confirmed my feeling that the young lady was killed somewhere else. And cleaned up afterward. "Firearms?"

"No indication."

"Forensic entomology? Botany? Zoology?"

"Possible they'll turn up something. But so far, no."

"Hair and fiber evidence?"

"Nope."

"How could the guy bring a corpse all the way out here without leaving something behind?"

"By being very careful."

And that in itself was telling.

I searched for, spotted, then approached Crenshaw. He was crouched on the ground, going over the metal floor of the plane with a small brush. Beside him was his fingerprint examiner's field kit, a five-level tool chest filled with everything he might possibly need—powders, lifting tape, ink, flashlights, petri dishes, baggies, tweezers, distilled water, and a lot of other stuff I couldn't identify. "How's it hanging, Tony? Seen any exciting friction ridges lately?"

He smiled a little. "Are you working this case?"

"Strange but true. Got any identifiable prints?"

"Not yet, but I'm still working. I'll have to take some of this stuff back to the lab before I can be sure."

"I would've thought the killer would get his paws all over the place, dragging a heavy corpse into the plane."

"I would, too, but he didn't. We found nothing inside the plane—except for one little smudge. On the body." He pointed down at the corpse with which I was now altogether too familiar. "Probably touched her before he transported her. Possibly even before he killed her. Maybe when he undressed her."

"Could the print belong to someone other than the killer?"

"Anything's possible, but I got it off her back, so it isn't her own. If she's been captive for a while, it almost has to be the killer's."

"What is it? Index finger?"

"Unfortunately, it doesn't appear to be a finger at all. I can get a print off any section of volar skin—fingers, soles, lips, ears. This is a palm. It could be worse—some courts won't admit non-hand or -foot prints. But it could be better, too. Although palms are just as unique in pattern as fingerprints, no one is databasing them."

"So even if your print pays out, we won't be able to run it through VICAP."

"Right. We might use it to verify a suspect—once you have one. But that's it."

I nodded. "Keep looking."

"Will do."

I wandered around a bit longer till I found the impression examiner, a woman about my age named Amelia Escavez. She'd joined the force maybe six months before.

"Whattaya got?" I asked, crouching at her side. God, this felt good. Back in the swing of things. Doing what I did well.

"Tire print." She tended to be succinct when she spoke to me. Perhaps if I'd ever asked her out to dinner, made a friend of her, she'd be more forthcoming. But of course I hadn't.

"The killer?"

"Possible. He must've used some kind of vehicle to get the body to that plane. Since he couldn't get through the locked gate, he presumably needed something sturdy enough to make it down that steep off-road slope. And the airport officials tell us none of their personnel has had any reason to be out here recently. So . . ."

She reached into her field kit, took out a fixative, and began stabilizing the impression. She'd use dental-stone casting or some similar material to transfer the print. I noted that her kit was even bigger than Fielder's. She seemed ready for anything we might throw at her— evidence vacuum, envelopes, bottles, boxes, cutting implements, disposable filters, glass slides, measuring tools, bindle paper, lifters, acetate covers, lifting tape, even an infrared spectrophotometer. Left the electron microscope in the car, I supposed. Looked cool, though, I had to admit. Maybe I should get a kit. What would I put in mine? Rorschach ink blots, multiphasic personality tests, a copy of **The Silence of the Lambs . . .**

"It's a small print," she explained. "There was a spot of oil, still somewhat damp, on the pavement. That's what caught it."

"Just the one?"

"'Fraid so. I looked for a matching opposite-side impression but didn't get one. This concrete isn't a very good surface for that sort of thing, absent the oil."

"Can you identify the tread?"

"I don't have enough to do it by sight, but once I get it into my computer, I may be able to give you a brand or even make. The FBI has a huge tire tread database."

"I need anything you can give me now. Can you at least put me in the neighborhood?"

She hesitated. I could see she was reluctant to make an unverified guess that might come back to haunt her if it turned out to be wrong, especially since she didn't have any reason to trust me. But she did it anyway. Good woman. "Looks like a pickup to me."

I nodded. Yes, that seemed right. Would make it easier to transport the body, and you could get it down that sharp slope.

"Any footprints?"

"I wish. Sorry, no."

"You'll get me a copy of that print?"

"Sure."

"Lifting material?"

"Thought I'd use overlapping tape affixed to white card stock. Soon as it dries a little more."

"Sounds like a winner. Thanks."

I stayed another hour or so, chatting up the techs, the ones who would talk to me, and trying to learn whatever I could. For the most part, I just absorbed. The place, the victim, the whole scenario. Tried to get inside the killer's head. What was he playing at? What made him do the things he did? I don't like to admit it, but I was more than a little creeped out. Maybe it was just the effect of being hung over on a body that was already in poor condition, but I couldn't shake this ominous feeling. I mean, I've worked some horrible crimes in my time, but that business with the teeth—who would be capable of that?

At the edge of the crime scene, I saw O'Bannon motioning to me.

"I'm on my way back to HQ," he explained. "Will I see you there when you finish up here?"

"Sure."

"I'd like it if you could drop by my house tonight. Maybe around nine-thirty."

My eyes narrowed a bit. "May I ask why?"

"Well, I'm not coming on to you, if that's what you're thinking. Bring a chaperone, if you like."

"What's the occasion?"

"I want to review the case. Get your preliminary thoughts. You know the press is going to be all over this case. I want to be ready to tell them something."

"And it couldn't wait until tomorrow morning?" I looked him straight in the eyes. "You don't want to hear my thoughts on the case. You want to make sure I'm not drunk."

"I'm trying to help you, Susan."

"You think if I'm alone tonight, I'll drink. Do you know how offensive, how utterly—"

He cut me off with a harsh glare. "Don't be stupid, Susan. When people offer you help, take it."

"I don't need help!"

"See you at nine-thirty," he said curtly. He waved to Granger, and together the two of them left the scene.

When I got back to headquarters, I was in for a few surprises. The temporary office set up for me was a desk, an old crappy one, wedged into an alcove just a few feet from the men's room. This not only guaranteed that I would be constantly bombarded with manly odors, but also ensured that every guy in the building would trip over me at least twice a day.

Fine. Let O'Bannon play his little games. I was going to solve his case.

First thing I did was call that pettifogger of mine and tell him I was gainfully employed.

"So how much are you going to make as an LVPD consultant?" Delacourt asked.

"I'm a little fuzzy on that."

"Not as much as your previous salary."

"Probably not."

"Well, it's better than nothing." Man was damn hard to please. "Look, I got you a hearing. Two weeks from yesterday."

"Two weeks? Why so long?"

"In case you haven't heard, Susan, the Las Vegas family courts are swamped, and there was no emergency."

"I think there's an emergency!"

"The child is not in danger."

"I think she is. The longer Rachel is forced to stay with Darby and Joan, the more they're going to warp her mind."

"Susan, I had to pull a lot of strings to get two weeks. Would you just ride with it?"

I closed my trap. "Anything I can do?"

"Yes, since you ask. You could become a model parent. Keep regular hours. Stay sober. I got a report from NDHS that says you're not going to the IOP classes."

Goddamn spies. "I can't very well earn a living and support my niece if I go to classes all day long."

"A sound point, but not one they're likely to be sympathetic to. I'll let you know if anything else turns up. In the meantime—keep your nose clean. For your sake, and Rachel's."

After that entertaining badinage, I got to work. My desk was already buried in paper. The reports on Murder Victim Two were just trickling in, but O'Bannon had sent over the voluminous reportage on Murder Victim One. I started at the top and tried to become familiar with the case, all the while pretending that I didn't feel as if I'd been buried alive myself, as if my head weren't throbbing, as if I didn't desperately want a drink. Not to get drunk—that had been a stupid mistake and I wouldn't do it again. I just needed a little pick-me-up, something to take away the pain so I could focus on my business. I'd stop after one.

I started with the autopsy protocols for the first murder and what little preliminary information they had provided regarding the second. I'd done this often enough to know I could safely skip the pages of minutiae on the body organs and glands, which would probably not be helpful and which I wouldn't understand even if it were. In both cases, the coroner reported an increase in serotonin and histamine levels. In the first murder that was to be expected. She had a long, painful time to be terrified before she finally suffocated. But it was present in the second victim, too. What's more, the second victim's gum wounds showed much higher histamine than serotonin. So she lived a good while after the teeth were removed. O'Bannon was right—she'd bled to death, aspirating blood making it increasingly difficult to breathe. A slow, painful passing.

With considerable reluctance, I opened the envelope marked PHOTOS. Death had caught Victim One's face in a hideous rictus, eyes and mouth wide, terrified, like that Edvard Munch painting. She died screaming, with no one to hear her.

The forensic analysis reports on Murder One were not helpful. The criminalists had vacuumed and grid-searched thoroughly. Even taken the trap from the vents and examined them. Found a few soil deposits, but nothing useful. Organic stains were unavailing. The preliminary victimology reports were even more of a joke. We didn't know who either victim was, making it almost impossible to speculate as to motives or why the victims were chosen.

Now here was an interesting tidbit—Victim Two was pregnant, just barely. Did the killer know? Was that why she had been chosen? Or why she had been killed?

I read the handwriting, ink, and paper analysis that had been performed on the two messages left with the corpses. Although the notes were handwritten—probably a necessity given that many of the characters used don't appear on a standard keyboard—the writer was probably not using his usual hand. A rightie using his left, or vice versa. It was the most common way of concealing handwriting. It would account for the shakiness of the lines, the inconsistency in character size. But that made it impossible for the expert to draw any conclusions regarding the personality being masked.

The handwriting expert did provide one interesting bit of information: the writer was using a fountain pen, gold-tipped broad nib. In this day and age. When you could find a fifty-

cent Bic in any drugstore. He was using a fountain pen and a blotter.

I spent the rest of the workday messing about
in the database for psychological profiling of serial killers maintained by the FBI's Behavioral
Science experts. I am a huge admirer of the
work John Douglas did, interviewing serial
killers and cataloging the patterns and similarities in their backgrounds, as well as their modus
operandi. But I didn't find much that pertained
to the case at hand. With each new piece of information, however small, I got a growing sense
that we were dealing with something entirely
out of the ordinary, something I had never seen
before.

Maybe something no one had seen before.

Las Vegas Metropolitan Police Department—
Central Division—was more hectic than M&M
World on a Saturday night. Chaos reigned
supreme. You'd think they had slots in there, the
way people wandered in and out, back and
forth. Twenty conversations going at once, not
to mention a few scuffles and one flat-out
fistfight between a plainclothes vice cop and a
young lady of the evening he had in custody.
The room was humid and noisome, reeking of
sweat and stale coffee and fetid breath.

How did people work under these conditions? he wondered. What utter banalities these officers were, with their rolled-up sleeves and underarm stains. All they needed were Irish accents and a box of crullers to complete the picture. It seemed unlikely that this crowd could apprehend a purse snatcher. And these were his adversaries?

He was astonished. And in all honesty, a bit disappointed.

Where was she, the raven woman? The one who tried to understand.

He'd chosen his disguise with exquisite care. It had to be subtle; she would detect any major attempt at subterfuge. And he did not want to bury himself so deeply that she could not perceive his true self. Just enough that any formal description she might give at a later time would be useless. He wore a false mustache, a simple bit of misdirection, but one that seemed to alter the entire character of his face. He'd forgone his contact lenses and was wearing the wire-rimmed glasses of his early youth. And in his boldest stroke, he'd darkened his hair. He had considered going blond—he'd always fancied the effete, sensitive poet look—but he sensed that she would be more comfortable with dark hair. Black, like her own. Black like the raven.

He would be forced to prevaricate, for his own safety, and he wasn't happy about that. A southern gentlemen does not tell tarradiddles. Except, he felt it fair to add, in self-preservation. His appearance itself was a lie, come to that, so what additional damage to his integrity could a few words do?

He waited for what seemed an interminable time but saw no traces of her. In fact, he saw no female at all, discounting the ones wearing handcuffs. How was he to learn anything about her when he didn't even know her name?

He approached the front desk clerk. "Beg pardon, sir. I need to speak to someone."

The clerk looked up. "Wanna give me a hint?"

"It's about the young woman found at the Transylvania."

"Okay," he said wearily. "What about her?"

"If you don't mind, I need to talk to someone working on the case."

"Granger isn't here."

"Actually, I need to speak to the woman. . . ."

The clerk seemed lost. "The dead woman?"

"No, the one working the homicide."

"Granger hasn't brought in any female detectives."

Patience, he told himself. Patience. "I wonder if perhaps you might be mistaken. I'm quite certain I saw her yesterday at the crime scene."

No reaction from the clerk.

"I don't recall her name, but she was quite

tall. Slender." He paused. "And hair the color of the raven."

"You talkin' about Pulaski?"

"Perhaps I am."

"She isn't on the case. Not officially, anyway. She isn't even on the force anymore. She's just been brought in to give advice or something. Weirdos are her specialty."

"Do tell."

"Yeah." He lowered his voice. "Big mistake, if you ask me."

"You don't care for . . . Miss Pulaski?"

"Not that I'm one to talk out of school." He lowered his voice to a whisper. "Bitch and a half."

"I'm sorry to hear that."

"She was never exactly Shirley Temple. But since her old man died . . ." He whistled.

"Is she . . . coping with her loss?"

"Oh, yeah. She's coping." He made a drinking motion with his hand. "In the worst possible way. Look, if you want to talk to her, she's coming up the stairs right now." His voice dropped again. "But if I were you, I'd stick with Granger."

He pivoted and cast his eyes down the staircase that bisected the room. There she was. Hair as black as the night. And those eyes—that magnificent dark eye!

It was the Eye that transfixed, that vexed me . . .

"Are you Lieutenant Pulaski?"

The woman peered at him, a quizzical expression on her face. "Sort of."

"My name is Ethan Jenkins. I need to talk to you."

She gave him a quick once-over. "I'm sorry, but I'm very busy right now." She started to pass.

"I know. I heard about the second victim on the news. That's why I'm here."

She stopped. "You know something about the murders?"

"I think so, yes. I saw the most recent casualty, just two days ago. At the Tropicana. She was gambling."

Pulaski's eyes narrowed. "You're sure about this?"

"I am. I saw her picture. It's the same woman. And someone was following her." He looked around, frowning at the distracting clamor all around them.

She pointed her head toward the front door. "Walk with me."

"So he escaped?"

"I'm afraid so," he explained. "I just happened to be in the parking lot at the time and was able to intervene on her behalf. I'm no fighter—I'm an accountant, actually. I think he had some martial arts training."

"We haven't received any reports from the Tropicana."

"I don't think they know it happened. As far as I could tell, no one at the hotel was aware of the incident."

"With all those cameras they have? I'm surprised anyone could escape notice."

"I believe the cameras are in the casinos. Not the parking garage."

"But muggers love to lurk in parking garages!"

"Lieutenant, I've been in Vegas long enough to understand that casinos install those cameras to protect the casinos, not the patrons."

"Right, right." She pulled a notepad out of her back pocket. "Do you know if she filed a report?"

"I told her she should, and I assumed she would."

"But she didn't. The creep must've gotten her before she had a chance."

"It would appear that way. If only I'd realized. I thought he was gone for good. I never imagined he might come back and try for her again. He must've really wanted the woman's purse."

Susan shook her head slowly. "I don't know what this guy is, but he's not a purse snatcher."

Indeed? He remained silent.

"I don't think he was after her money. And I don't think it was a random selection. It was . . . considered. I think he'd been watching her, investigating her, and she met . . . some kind of criteria." She paused. "I think he **chose** her."

It was all he could do to keep from kissing her. She was brilliant. Instinctively brilliant. "But how can you know?"

"I can't **know.** Not exactly. I just . . . get stuff. About people." She frowned. "It's hard to explain. It's more a feeling than anything else. A sense of what fits and what doesn't."

His first impression, even as he had observed her from afar, had been correct. She was a very special woman, this Lieutenant Pulaski. Her intuitive powers were great, possibly even equal to his own. She would be a worthy opponent.

Or better yet, a partner.

"And you're sure this was the same girl we found at the airport?"

"Positive. I talked with her for some time."

"But she didn't give you her name?"

"No."

"Did she tell you where she was staying?"

"I'm sorry, no."

"Well, we'll check the records at the Tropicana. Mention any friends, family?"

Should he tell her about Warren? Of perhaps even the girl's mother? That would be a bold move, wouldn't it? But too fraught with risk. Lieutenant Pulaski might not have much data to work with at the moment, but she was not stupid. Far from it. He couldn't know too much.

"I'm afraid we never talked about anything other than the incident."

"Sure. I was just hoping." She scrutinized the notes she had scribbled onto her pad in a hand far too tiny and slovenly for him to read. "Can you give me a description of the assailant?"

"I can try. He was a big man—strong, obviously."

"Height?"

"Almost six feet."

"Hair?"

"Blond. With lots of curls. And he had a beard."

Her head tilted to one side. She was considering, he realized, running the description through her mental database. And it didn't fit. Because it wasn't true. But she couldn't know that for a fact. Not yet.

"I wish we could be sure the man you saw was the killer. But . . ." Her voice drifted.

They had rounded a complete city block and returned to the street on which they had started. "I suppose it's possible this guy had nothing to do with her murder," Susan said, closing her notebook. "But it's still worth checking out." She extended her hand. "Thank you for coming forward, Ethan." She paused, not in front of headquarters, but across the street from a place called The Golden Bear. A bar and grill. "Now, if you'll excuse me—"

"Lieutenant?" He took her hand.

"Yes?"

He glanced across the street. "That is not what you need."

"Excuse me?"

"A little early, don't you think?" He smiled. "If you start drinking now, you'll be useless for the rest of the day. Then you'll become angry at yourself for drinking and being useless. Wouldn't it be smarter not to start?"

"You're pretty damned impertinent, Ethan." He thought she would be mad, but the steam never rose. The corner of her lips turned up. "But you're right. I guess I needed to hear someone say it." She checked her watch. "Anyway, I've got an appointment with an old friend. Thanks again."

He hesitated. "I . . . wouldn't mind seeing you again sometime, Lieutenant."

She grinned. "Call me Susan."

He watched as she made her way up the steps and away from him. He would see her again. He knew it. But there was much work to be done in the meantime. Another offering to be secured—according to the prophet, a trinity was necessary to bring about the holy objective.

And he had to find an axe.

His plan would move forward. And Susan Pulaski would be a part of it. Onward unto glory, now and forever.

I was still thinking about that distinctly decent-looking witness when I arrived—perhaps I should say descended—into Colin's office.

He peered across his cluttered desk at me, one hand still on the computer keyboard. Was he umbilically attached to the thing?

"You want to consult with me? On a murder case?"

"If you're willing."

"Well, sure, yeah. I mean, I guess." He rubbed his hand through tousled hair that looked as if it hadn't been combed for days. "But why me?"

"Because of all David's friends, you were the . . ." Nerdiest? "The best at solving puzzles."

"And you think that's what these are?" He took the photocopies of the two messages left at each of the crime scenes. "Anyone else working on this?"

"Chief O'Bannon has assigned his best and brightest, but I don't think they have any real expertise in this field. He also faxed copies to the professional code breakers at the FBI and even cryptanalysts at the CIA—but so far, they got nothing. He's talking about running the messages in the newspaper, a prospect I really dread."

"Why?"

"Because the press will eat this up with a spoon. They've already gone big with the photos of the victims. These coded messages will take the story right into comic book land. The press will glamorize them and hype them and make it all the more difficult to conduct a serious investigation."

"It may just be delusional psychotic ranting."

"I'm hoping not."

"Why?"

"If it's gibberish, as my superior suspects, it's not going to be any help to me. But if it's a message, something the killer so desperately wanted to say that he left behind a potentially incriminating note . . . well, that could tell me a great deal."

Colin laid the copies flat on his desk and stared at them. He was wearing a T-shirt and sweatpants, mismatched, but he worked at home and I suppose if you know you're not going anywhere you don't have to dress for it. His posture recalled a vulture, his neck craned over the desk, his glasses so thick he could probably perform microsurgery without additional instrumentation. David had met Colin in college and they'd stayed in touch after, right up until David's death. They weren't best friends—their tastes were worlds apart, Colin being more cerebral—but they were close enough that I knew him, and I knew what he did for a living, too.

He created puzzles. Crosswords, mostly, but also acrostics and word searches and this godawful impossible wordplay-infused variant of traditional crosswords called cryptics, clearly the products of demented brains. Best of all, I knew he considered himself an expert on cryptograms. An entire shelf on the wall behind him was dedicated to codes and ciphers.

"Well, if it is a code, it isn't a simple substitution code, I can promise you that," he said about a minute later.

"Simple substitution code?"

"Yeah. One letter representing another. Like the cryptograms in the newspaper. Easily solved by reference to letter frequency and patterns of orthography."

"Orthography?"

He grinned. "That's what the nonpuzzling world calls **spelling.**"

"And how do you know it isn't one of those . . . simple substitution codes?"

"Because if it was, I would've solved it already." He continued staring at the pages. "There are more than twenty-six characters in use here, which also rules out a simple substitution. Some of these symbols aren't letters at all. Decoding is also complicated by the fact that there do not appear to be any breaks for sentences or words. The symbols are grouped in large blocks, and I rather suspect that the blocks may not be in the proper order. Looks like it may contain some decoy characters, too."

"Decoy characters?"

"Right. Blanks. I see that **Q** appears in here twelve times, far more than any other letter, which would suggest that it represents **E.** But it doesn't."

"How do you know?"

"Because if it did, I would've solved it already. No, it's more than just a cipher."

I wondered if I should subpoena the subscription list to his puzzle magazine. There had to be something wrong with people who spent their spare time busting their brains over stuff like this. "If it isn't a substitution code, what is it?"

"Well, I'd say there's a remote possibility it's a translated anagram."

"Huh?"

"Letter scrambles. Like those Jumbles in the paper. He takes the message, then rearranges the letters at random. In a message this long, it would come out looking like gibberish."

"How would I ever solve it?"

"You wouldn't. Or me, for that matter. A

computer might, once it figures out what to do with the nonalphabetic entries. Might at least be able to generate a menu of workable solutions."

"Any other possibilities?"

"Oh, there are lots. Codes are literally as old as language, and over time people have devised a lot of devious ones. It's possible that breaking the code requires reference to some external text. Like you have to know what page of the King James Bible to use as a reference key. Those were popular during World War I. Or it's possible the solution requires a code-breaking machine, like Enigma in World War II."

"I doubt if that's the case."

"Why?"

"Because if this code requires either of those two external devices, we have no realistic chance of solving it. And I have to think at least some small part of this guy wants us to solve it. Otherwise, why would he leave it? He wants it to be hard. He wants us to appreciate his brilliance. But eventually, he wants us to read the message."

He nodded. "You know, there is precedent for this sort of thing."

"Codes?"

"Left behind by psychopathic killers, yeah. You heard of Zodiac?"

"Of course. Studied him in school." I snapped my fingers. "He left messages, too, didn't he?"

"Yup. Coded. His crypts have appeared in some of the puzzle magazines. They were insidious. Stumped all the experts, including the government. Three of the four were never solved. Only one was. As I recall, it was a schoolteacher who finally cracked it, some regular Joe who saw the codes in the paper and worked on them in his spare time. Took months."

"I don't have months, Colin. This guy's on a killing spree."

"Understood. I'll do my best." He shrugged. "Maybe I just think this because I want to think it, because it would be more fun, but I don't think this is gibberish. I don't think it's the work of an amateur, either. I suspect your killer knows something about codes. A little, anyway. My hunch is there's a message hidden in there, but it's incredibly complex. Different. And it's going to take a different kind of brain to figure it out."

"Then I've come to the right place."

He sat up, stretching. "I'll give this top priority. I'll even put off doing today's **New York Times.**"

"I'm surprised those puzzles are any challenge for you."

"I do them without the grid."

I blinked. "You mean, without the little white and black boxes?"

"Right. I work out the grid on my own, from the clues and their numbering."

"If you keep talking like this, Colin, I'm going to move you to the head of my suspect list."

He grinned. "Hey, you holding up okay? I heard you were having some problems."

My chin rose. "None to speak of."

"If you need anything—"

"I don't need any help." I paused. "But thanks."

"Okay." He reached down and pulled up his socks, which didn't match. God, but this man needed a wife. "You know, when David died like that—it hit us all pretty hard. But I have to think it hurt you most of all."

"Nothing I can't handle." I pushed myself out of his chair, bringing this line of conversation to a dead stop. "If you get anything on those codes, let me know, okay? The sooner, the better. No telling how many young women's lives may be at stake until we catch this whack job." I left as I came in, all business, no crack in the exterior.

I couldn't afford a crack, and I damn well resented his trying to pry one open. We live in such a Jerry Springer world—everyone wants to go public with all their problems. Whatever happened to the virtue of circumspectness? When did we become such a nation of whiners?

Besides, I had work to do.

CHAPTER EIGHT

I was pissed as hell about being forced to report to O'Bannon's house just so he could make sure I'd been behaving myself. At the same time, I knew if I didn't appear, he'd jerk my tenuous little consulting position like the handle on a one-armed bandit. For now, I had to play it his way.

I left the top down and stoked myself on the night air. Did I mention that I love this city? People talk about New York and its nightlife, but for my money, Vegas has it beat. People crawled down Fremont till the wee hours of the morning, and for the most part, they enjoyed themselves, acting like kids, blowing money they don't need, being royally entertained. Granted, our shows may not have the sophistication of

Broadway, but people came to Vegas to have fun, not to get clubbed over the head with Pulitzer Prize–winning angst. And for the most part, the tourists were nice folks. Writers always portray them as seekers of sin, but what I see is mostly plain, decent folks who want to get away, play, gamble a little, gorge themselves at a buffet, and sleep sweet dreams.

While I drove, I called Lisa on my cell. To my surprise, she was home.

"How's it hanging?"

"Oh, fine. I'm washing my nylons." Which was code for no date. "I checked by your place but you were in absentia."

"On my way to O'Bannon's. He's got me working a new case."

She gasped a little. "Not those girls who—"

"That's the one."

"Oh, geez, Susan. Do you think you're ready for this?"

I tried not to take offense. Anything she said arose from her concern about me. "Best thing. Keep me off the streets. How was your big date last night?"

"Ohh." I didn't have to see her to see her face falling. "Disappointing."

"Not a tiger?"

"More like a lap dog."

That was a new one. "I'm not sure I—"

"Visible tongue. Before my mouth was even

open. I think I'm going to become a nun. Stop
by on your way back?"

"I . . . it'll probably be too late. Definite date
for tomorrow?"

"All right. You're sure you're all right?"

"Couldn't be better. Couldn't be better."

By the time I got to O'Bannon's, it was almost ten, but I hoped he'd cut me some slack
since I'd been working like a busy beaver. I was
surprised to find that kid of his on the front
porch—sort of. He stood just off the edge of the
concrete, about three feet from the door. His
entire body was stiff, shoulders hunched, like
he'd just been injected with a paralytic drug.

"Hey, Darcy," I said, flashing my best smile.

"Do I know you?" he said, but his expression
almost immediately brightened. He remained
stiff. "I like your voice. You're Dad's friend from
work."

"Yup. He inside?"

"Yes . . ."

"Shall we go see him?"

It was difficult for him to speak, but when he
finally started, the words burbled out in that
strange voice of his, too loud, the inflection all
askew. "Would you be afraid of spiders? Because
some girls are afraid of spiders. Did you know
some, a lot, a lot of girls are afraid of spiders?"

"I've heard that."

"So, if, then, are you afraid of spiders?"

"Nah. I'm not afraid of anything."

"Do you think that would be poisonous?"

He pointed downward. I didn't see anything. "Can you be more specific?" I moved in closer and eventually realized there was a small gray spider on the front porch, barely noticeable. "I don't think it can hurt us, Darcy."

"Did you know there are four kinds of poisonous spiders indigenous to North America?" He was lecturing me, but he never made eye contact. "The widow spiders, the recluse spiders, the hobo spiders, and the yellow sac spider."

"I'm fairly certain this little fella is none of the above."

"You can never be sure. Sometimes they can trick you. Did you know that sometimes spiders can try to trick you?"

"I didn't know that."

"I think that maybe we should go around to the back door."

"Not necessary. I'll take care of it." I raised my foot, hovering over the offending obstacle.

"No!" Darcy fairly screamed. He raised his hands, flapping them in the air. "Don't kill it!"

"I thought you were afraid . . ."

"I don't like to hurt things. I don't think anyone should hurt anyone, do you?"

"But . . . it's a spider."

"It's still alive. Isn't it still alive?"

"But eventually we need to get inside. Don't we?"

"Maybe you could just . . . just . . ."

"Capture and release?"

"That would be good."

I picked up a fallen leaf, slid one edge under the spider, and tossed it into the hedges.

"Will he be all right there?" Darcy asked.

"That's its natural environment," I assured him. "It'll be like a kid in a candy store." Judging from Darcy's nonresponsive expression, I needed to modify my cliché. Abstract language was lost on him. "It'll be like—what's your favorite room in the house, Darcy?"

"The library."

"It'll be like you with a good book in the library."

"Oh." His head twitched a couple of times. "Good."

"Can we go in now?" I looked back at the front door and found O'Bannon standing there, watching. "Chief."

He pushed open the screen door. "Come on in. Darcy, why don't you go finish your book?"

"Oh." He seemed reluctant to leave. "Okay."

Once we were alone, O'Bannon showed me into his den.

"Sweet boy you've got."

"That's one word for it."

"Wouldn't even hurt a spider. That's pretty

endearing, in this day and age. Most guys his age spend the evening pretending to blow people to smithereens in video games."

"He's always been like that. Entirely nonaggressive. Doesn't want to hurt anyone. Kids at school used to rough him up pretty bad. But he never struck back. Never did anything to anyone. Practically a saint." He stopped by his desk and gave me a searching look.

"You going to sniff my breath?"

"Don't have to."

"Because you trust me?"

"Because I've been on the police force thirty-four years, which unfortunately gives a man a lot of experience with alcoholism. I can spot a drunk at ten paces."

"Ooh. Scary." I jerked my thumb toward the other room. "So, that boy of yours. Autistic?"

He raised an eyebrow. "Not bad, Pulaski. Most people think he's retarded. Or just weird."

"Well, I am a trained professional. I've worked with autistic children."

"I guess that gives you an advantage." I could tell this wasn't something he talked about often. At the same time, I got the impression that while he was accustomed to keeping it private, it might be a comfort to talk about it with someone who had some understanding of the condition. "Most people, all they know about autism is what they got from that Dustin Hoffman movie, where he acted all weird and twitchy—but not particularly autistic. People looking for a hyperactive toothpick counter aren't going to peg Darcy."

"He must be very high-functioning. He's obviously smart, and he speaks clearly enough. He interacts. He's in our world, at least to some extent."

O'Bannon nodded, dropping onto the large sofa. "It wasn't always that way. At the age of three he was profoundly autistic. Didn't answer questions, showed no emotions, was totally withdrawn. Took years of aggressive behavioral intervention programs to get him where he is today. Worked with a guy named Dr. Lovaas out in L.A. for years. Made a huge difference."

"That's controversial therapy, isn't it?"

"It shouldn't be. Got too many damned romantics trying to pretend that there's something special or magical about an autistic kid's private world. He's in his own little paradise, they say. Why do we have to force him to conform, to live in our world? What bullshit. Anybody who's ever spent time with a seriously autistic kid knows better. They're confused, frustrated, unhappy, isolated. Bringing them into our world, trying to make it possible for them to interact, to be productive, is a gift."

"I'm sure you're right. He seems very knowledgeable."

"Well, he remembers everything he ever read. Wish I could say the same for myself. Autistics are known for their prodigious memories. When Darcy's focused, he's incredible. The trouble is getting him to focus, getting him interested, giving him the proper incentive. He's flooded with stimuli. His head is like a radio receiver getting messages from fifty different places at once. It takes a lot of concentration to sift through that, to focus on one particular line of thought."

"Aren't there drugs that could help him?"

"No. Everything his docs ever tried just made him listless. Dreary. I'd rather have an autistic boy than a zombie." He drew in his breath. "I've had to face facts. He'll never be normal, no matter what I do."

"Well," I said, depositing myself on the sofa, "normal is overrated."

O'Bannon's gaze turned inward. "You can't imagine how hard it was on Connie and me. Our first child. By the time he was two, he was reading. Honest to God. Knew the alphabet, could count as high as you want, remembered everything you told him. Sang, even played the piano a little. Had perfect pitch. We thought we had a little genius on our hands. Then somewhere around his third birthday, it all started to go south. He didn't come when called. He disappeared, hid. All his incredible speech disappeared."

"That's frequently the way neurological disorders work. At first they manifest as prodigious intellectual abilities. Then the other shoe drops."

"Yeah." O'Bannon kept his face stoic; everything I got, I got from the eyes. He did a good job of keeping it in. But I suppose he'd had a lot of practice. "He does have some special abilities. Memory. Math. Reads fast. Plays the piano—and he never had lessons. Does the whole puzzle page in the **Courier** in less than five minutes."

"Okay, now I'm starting to hate him."

O'Bannon grinned. "He really tries to get along in the world, to understand what's going on around him, hard as it is for him. He's done a hell of a lot with the hand he's been dealt."

"But I notice he's still at home. What is he, twenty-one, twenty-two?"

"Twenty-six. It's the angelic countenance that throws you off. Autistics are renowned for their sweet good looks. As for moving out, I don't know if he'll ever be able to live independently. He sure isn't now. Most autistics end up in some kind of home, but . . . I don't know. I couldn't bear it. He's my only family."

"I get that."

"I had hoped that one day, with enough therapy, he might be able to do some kind of work. But that's probably not realistic. He helps out at a day care center. He loves to work with small children. I think he's comfortable around them in a way he'll never be with adults. But . . ." His eyes wandered. He was feeling uncomfortable. I could tell he wanted to change the subject. "So what've you got on this case? Solved it yet?"

"Give me another ten minutes."

"Have you at least got a working theory?"

"Guy's hard to get a grip on. A lot of the information I've received is contradictory. And it doesn't fit the standard profile of a psychopathic sexually motivated serial killer."

"Are you sure that's what this perp is?"

"I can't imagine anyone burying a woman alive, or tearing out all her teeth, for any logical reason. Can you?"

"But does he have to be sexually motivated? Neither of the girls was molested."

"He's probably impotent. That's not uncommon. They can't get off the normal way. They get gratification from killing and torturing the helpless. Any progress on identifying the victims?"

He shook his head. "Nothing so far. Eventually someone will miss them. But it might take a while."

"If we knew how the killer was selecting his victims—or why—we'd be better able to protect the populace. This has already gotten a lot of press—"

"And it's going to get a lot more."

"Right. So we need to be able to tell them something about the man."

"Are we sure it's a man?"

"Serial killers almost always are. Comes with the testosterone."

"But you said this killer doesn't fit the standard patterns."

"True enough." Leaning back, I noticed that Darcy was crouched in the entryway. How long had he been there? "Need something, Darcy?"

"W-W-Would it be okay if I sat with you guys? I think that would be fun. Wouldn't that be fun?" He walked over to the sofa and sat between us, brushing shoulders.

His father grunted. "Darcy, we're talking about a case. You should go to your room."

Darcy was crestfallen.

"I don't see any reason he can't stay," I cut in. "Maybe he'll inspire us." I don't know why I did it, except that I could see that he really wanted to be there with us. And I've always had a soft spot for Shaggy.

O'Bannon spoke as if he weren't there. "He isn't usually this social. Especially with strangers."

"But we are not strangers," Darcy said, looking at me. "Are we strangers? Don't I know you?"

"Yes, of course you do."

"That's what I thought. Then we are not strangers. What are we talking about?"

I suppressed a smile, then leaned forward so I could see the chief. "I don't suppose any of your experts have had any luck on the coded messages."

"No," O'Bannon grunted, reaching back for one of the two photocopies. "They don't think they are messages. Which of course is the obvious response when you aren't able to decode them."

"I took them to a geek friend of mine. I'm hoping he'll figure something out. I'd really like to know what they say, but—"

Darcy jumped in. "W-W-Would it be okay if, do you think, could it be okay if I took a look at them?"

"Darcy," his father said, "this is police business. It might be better if you watched one of your videos."

"Please," he said. "I want to read them."

Read them, I noticed he said. Not solve them. Read them. "Why don't we give him a shot?" I took the copies and handed them to Darcy.

O'Bannon's face was pained. "Susan . . ."

"You said he was good at puzzles. Maybe he'll see something the experts missed. Maybe he'll spot some clue that will make it possible for the experts to—"

Darcy cut me off. " 'Deep, deep, and for ever, into some ordinary and nameless grave.' "

O'Bannon and I both looked at him. "What?"

He repeated it.

"What?" his father said, irritated. And then his voice softened: "Is that a poem or something?"

Darcy looked up nervously. "I—I—I—I think that's, what you were, you were, can't you read it?"

I took the photocopy he was holding, the one that had been stuffed inside the coffin with the girl who was buried alive. "You're saying that's the translation of this message?"

"That's what it says."

"You decoded it?"

He gazed at me with that deceptively vacant expression. "That's what it says."

"Darcy . . ." His father sighed. "We could all make up something that could be the message. Sometimes it's fun to pretend—"

"I—I—I—" I noticed his stuttering became much more pronounced when he was speaking to his father. "I read it."

"That's impossible. You looked at it for, what? Twenty seconds?"

"Does Darcy normally make things up?" I asked.

"Well . . . no."

"Does he tell lies?"

"I don't think he knows how."

"Is he given to flights of fancy?"

"He wouldn't understand what a flight of fancy was."

"Probably never engaged in imaginative play as a child, right? No make-believe. No cowboys and Indians. That would be typical for kids with his . . . situation." I turned back to Darcy. "Say it again. Read it."

He glanced down at the paper. " 'Deep, deep, and for ever, into some ordinary and nameless grave.' "

"Sounds like something that belongs in a coffin, doesn't it? Darcy, is it a substitution code?"

"What?"

"Does one letter—or symbol—stand for another?"

"I guess—I mean, no, not really. Well, sort of."

I resisted the urge to pound my head against the wall. "Darcy, can you explain to me how you can read this?"

"Can you, do you—I mean—I just read it."

No cheese down that tunnel. "I wonder what it means. Maybe if I went on the Internet—"

"It's from a book."

I gaped. I mean, it was incredible enough that this kid might solve the puzzle the experts couldn't. But now he was going to identify the quotation?

He jumped off the sofa and raced to the wall

behind the desk, one that was covered with books. It was as if someone had flipped the ON switch; suddenly, he was alive, more than alive. His eyes darted back and forth, his hands flapped frenetically. His fingers brushed against the spines of the books as if they were his friends.

It didn't take him long. He pulled down a large black volume, crouched on the floor, and began rifling through the pages. O'Bannon stood to the side, watching.

"Here it is," Darcy said, barely a minute later.

I knelt down beside him and read the passage he indicated. There it was. Verbatim.

"Darcy . . . how did you find it so quickly?"

"I—I read it once."

"Recently?"

"No. But I remembered."

I flipped the book around and looked at the spine. **Tales of the Grotesque and Arabesque,** it said. The subtitle was: **The Poems and Stories of Edgar Allan Poe.** The quote he had found was from one of the stories: "The Premature Burial."

Of course.

But what was the connection to the second story? That awful business with the teeth . . .

"Darcy, I want you to look at the second message."

"I already did." He held it in his hands. " 'In

the multiplied objects of the external world I had no thoughts but for the teeth.'"

"Do you recognize that quote? Is it from—"

He was already turning the pages. Less than thirty seconds later he found it. In a short story I'd never heard of, titled "Berenice." I flipped to the end. **. . . there rolled out some instruments of dental surgery, intermingled with thirty-two small, white, and ivory-looking substances that were scattered to and fro about the floor.**

The story was about some maniac pulling out a woman's teeth. And letting her bleed to death.

"I told you he had a prodigious memory," O'Bannon said. "Eidetic. Not only can he recite back word for word something he read years ago, he can tell you what page it was on."

I'd heard of such things in school, but never actually encountered it. "And he reads a lot?"

"Constantly."

"That's . . . an amazing gift."

"Yeah. With virtually no practical application. Or so I thought." O'Bannon frowned.

I held the book up. "I read a little Poe in college. Kind of liked it, as I recall. But I didn't see the pattern."

"And now you do?"

"I'm beginning to. Thanks to your son." I patted Darcy on the shoulder. He immediately reacted to the touch of my hand. It was sort of like he was wriggling away and sort of like he was snuggling against it. "I hope you're not one of those collector types who won't lend reading materials."

O'Bannon shook his head. "It's just a book."

I hope he agreed that this interview was over. Because I had some real work to do now and I wanted to get to it. The book was more than a thousand pages long, for God's sake. It would take me hours to get through it, to see what other clues might be in there. I needed to re-examine everything in light of this new lead. And then . . .

And then I got an idea. "Is the first crime scene still restricted?"

"Sure. We've got men posted."

"Good. I want to go back out there tomorrow morning."

"Okay."

"Would it be all right if I bring Darcy?"

Darcy's eyes lit.

O'Bannon's didn't. "Are you out of your mind? What for?"

"He might be useful. He sure as hell was tonight. There might be more Poe clues lying about. Stuff only he would spot."

"Susan." He sidled closer to me and lowered his voice. "Darcy may look like a man, but in-

side, he's a little boy. You saw him with that spider. What's he going to do at a crime scene?"

"The body has been removed."

"But still—"

I hated this business of talking about Darcy as
if he weren't present, when he was standing
barely two feet away. But I had a strong feeling
that I was right about this. I couldn't even explain why, not coherently. But when you're Em-
pathy Girl, you learn to trust your instincts.
"You said you wished he could learn to do something productive. Hold a real job. So humor me
here. Maybe you've got a budding detective on
your hands."

"Susan . . ."

"As I recall, Sherlock Holmes was pretty odd
himself."

"Susan!" I was not prepared for his anger.
"You've known Darcy for what? Ten minutes?
I've been living with him for twenty-six years."
His voice dropped. "There's no way in hell he
could cut it as a cop."

"I'm not asking you to give him a badge. Just
let him tag along. Humor me."

Darcy jumped in. "C-C-C-Can I go, Dad? I
would like, would you, I could, I could be
good. Can I go with that one?"

He gave me a long look. "Don't make me regret bringing you in on this case, Pulaski."

"I won't. Darcy—pick you up at nine in the morning." I winked. "Don't be late."

See I knew I could help I knew I could help if only he would let me but he wouldn't but the girl did and the girl's name is Susan I heard that was her name and she was nice to me just like she was before. There was a girl at the clinic who was nice to me like that and she was pretty too but not as pretty as Susan and she told me to read one of her music books so whenever she forgot the words I could tell her and she was nice but I think maybe Susan is nicer and smells better. She has something funny about the way she smells but it's not so bad I remember people's smells and everyone has a smell if you smell hard enough. I'm glad I could remember those stories like I did and my dad didn't he read the stories too but he forgot and I remembered. **You shouldn't be reading those horrible stories. You should be reading a nice book like** The Hardy Boys **or** Two Years Before the Mast. Susan says I could go see where they found this lady's body and I don't like killing I think it's mean to hurt things but if I go with her it would almost be like I'm a policeman and I know that would make my dad happy even though he pretends like he doesn't care whether I'm a policeman but he does. I hope it's not too

gross. I don't like gross. I would never hurt anyone, no matter what.

Mostly I want to go because I'll go with
Susan. I like Susan. Susan is pretty even though
she has a cigarette burn on the back of her right
pant leg and she bites her fingernails so much
two of them have been bleeding. Susan is babies
and sugary and I like the way she flips her hair
back when she's being funny even though I
don't understand the joke I can tell she's being
funny and she smiles at me and lets me sit next
to her and I think she must like me and that's
good because I know I like her.

CHAPTER NINE

He felt such intense revulsion that it became difficult for him to breathe. He was physically ill. He knew his face was ashen, and he feared he might soon relinquish custody over his lunch. It was so disturbing, so depraved.

Certainly he had expected to be offended. But he had no idea how bad it could be. Sexual relations were a gift given us for the perpetuation of the species, not, he thought, a commodity to be bought and sold. But here, in this Haunted Palace of a sort Poe never imagined in his most fevered dream, it was all garishly on display, everywhere he turned. He had never seen so much unclothed flesh in his entire life—and it sickened him. Everything here sickened him.

From the start he had understood that his visit to Nighthawks was one of duty, not pleasure. Vegas sex clubs were notorious, and this one had a reputation worse than most. Its dark ambience, the decorative whips and chains, bespoke a debased sensibility with a strong sadomasochistic bent, inimical to all standards of decency. Not a place for the avatar of the prophet. To begin with, there was the music—which was not at all musical. How could this electronic rap dissonance be music, which by definition is a melody played in rhythm and in counterpoint to a harmony? Where was the melody in this hip-hop mishmash? It was just sound, mindless decibels, played blaringly, unbearably loudly. And the light was blinding—silver shards glittering all about him, reflecting off the mirrored walls and the discothèque balls on the ceiling. It was a grotesque de Sade bacchanalia, all justified by suggestions that indulgence and degenerate fantasy fulfillment were salubrious for the psyche. Well, he did gainsay it, as would any decent soul with an eye on Dream-Land.

"Good evening," said the woman at the door, who was wearing a skintight black leather bodice exposing extraordinary mammarial engineering. "I am the mistress of pain."

"Good evening to you, madam," he replied in his most elegant southern accent.

She rammed a riding crop under his chin. "Your heart's desire can be yours. All you need do is ask."

"Most obliging." He removed the crop and stepped inside. The décor reminded him of those hideous films of the 1960s purportedly based upon the prophet's stories. Victorian furnishings, faux marble pillars, red curtains, padded sofas and love seats. A throne at each table, such as it was. Waiters dressed in silk Italianate tunics. He almost expected to see Vincent Price emerge from behind the drapes. But in fact, the most noteworthy figures inside were women, naked or all but. He didn't object to nudity in and of itself. But it was never meant to be distorted and turned into a weapon, much less an industry. He was surrounded by unclad women, more than a hundred of them in bikinis, G-strings, negligees, all manner of exiguous attire. Some wearing nothing more than a few carefully cantilevered scarves. None of them much older than their teens. Undulating and thrusting and rubbing and pressing. Trying to excite the worst of passions. Parading their sex for the entertainment of the unworthy.

He staggered through the narrow corridors, his mouth dry, searching for a spot with an open seat and a modicum of oxygen. The music, the smoke, the cachinnation, and the Caligulan revelry all assaulted and oppressed him. Most of the rooms had stages upon which young women re-moved their clothes in time to the rhythm of that relentless music. He saw one stage—he couldn't help but look—with an uncommonly limber woman spread across the floor, twisting and writhing like a snake, hands flat, breasts pressed against the stage, her thighs locked around the head of a middle-aged man in a blue leisure suit. In some of the smaller, more private alcoves, women performed one-on-one, straddling the men's laps, rubbing themselves against their pa-tron's personal areas for his despoiled gratifi-cation.

He was tempted to run outside, retrieve the axe from his truck, and bring them all to ac-count for their crimes against decency.

But that was not the plan. He pressed his hand against his forehead, forcing himself to maintain focus. He had a destiny to fulfill, and he would not shirk it.

He found an empty chair wedged between two young men in matching shirts, both in the throes of lap dances. He tried to make himself comfortable, but the girls on either side con-stantly poked him with their stiletto heels or other protuberances. They giggled, smiled, then returned to their business. Their **business.**

A woman wearing a red lace teddy appeared before him. She had no concept of personal space—or perhaps she did—and stood so close to him that the tips of her fairly enormous and probably artificial breasts touched his face.

"You look as if you could use a friend."

He tried not to stammer as he spoke. "We could all use a friend."

"I'd like to be yours." She had vivid red hair—not natural, he felt certain—parted in the center, and a mole strategically positioned just below her lower lip. He rather suspected that wasn't natural, either. She appeared to be about twenty, which in this place made her a senior citizen. "Can we do business?"

"I'm looking for a girl."

"That's why I'm here."

"No, you don't understand. I'm looking for a particular girl."

Her smile faded a few notches. "Don't be put off by the laugh lines, Skippy. I'll rock your boat like it's never been rocked before."

"I'm sure, my dear, but—"

"Just give me a chance." She pressed a knee into his lap and leaned closer. "I know what you want."

"I don't believe you do."

"Trust me." She squeezed.

"Stop that!" His voice came out much louder than he intended as he slapped her hand away. Fortunately, the music was so thumpingly loud that even his immediate neighbors did not notice. He took several deep, cleansing breaths, trying to regain his genteel demeanor. "Listen to me. I am looking for a specific girl who works here. Her name is Lenore."

The redhead arched an eyebrow. "You like them young, don't you?" She pulled away. "What else is new? Give me a minute, slick."

He waited. While he did, the young man to his left apparently reached climax, shouting and bellowing and putting a very satisfied expression on the face of the purposeful titian-haired teenager who climbed off his lap. Money changed hands, a lot of it.

And then he saw Lenore. She was an Asian girl, as he'd known, but her hair was dyed blond. Or perhaps it was a wig? She was much smaller than her predecessor, and younger. Almost a child. Poe would've loved her. He thought he perhaps loved her himself, in his way.

"April said you wanted me?" she said with a ruby-red pout.

"She was correct."

"Okay, so a table dance is two hundred, all right? You want anything more, we negotiate."

He gazed at her, the impossibly rouged cheeks, excessive bee-sting lipstick, breasts like pomegranates. She was wearing a tight red bustier with dragons embroidered on each side. She was a lovely thing, delicate as a rose blossom.

He had been right. She was the offering. And the third would fulfill the prophecy.

"This may seem odd to you, dear," he said, oozing gentility, "but all I want to do is talk."

"You like to watch. That's okay, I get it."

"No, ma'am. Listen to me carefully. I want to talk. With you."

"Believe it or not, mister, that's about the only thing we're not allowed to do here. They don't want us wasting time with conversation. And they don't want patrons getting hung up on a particular girl and starting some kind of trouble."

"I can pay you. Well."

She pursed her oh-so-red lips together. "I don't know."

"Please. I'll make it worth your time."

She considered a few more moments. "I wouldn't do this if it hadn't been such a shit of a night." Her eyes scanned the room, checking for supervisors, then scrutinizing the numbered lights on a neon sign by the door that told her where vacancies existed. "Okay, look. I can get us a couch in a semiprivate room. But it'll be three hundred to me. And you'll have to tip the bouncer."

"And we can talk?"

"You can do anything you want. I'll be working. Come on."

She led him through the madding crowd to an alcove farther down the main hallway. After he took care of the bouncer, Lenore gave him a gentle push onto a black upholstered couch. A moment later, a woman wearing a black dominatrix outfit appeared bearing a tray with two glasses of champagne.

"I'm sorry, ma'am," he said, charming her with his smile, "but I do not partake of strong spirits."

The waitress stared at him. "It's just champagne."

He wagged a finger. "Nonetheless. Spirits destroyed the prophet, you know."

The waitress and Lenore exchanged a look, then a shrug. The waitress disappeared.

Lenore reached behind herself and snapped open the bustier.

"Just a moment," he said, holding out a hand. "You don't need to do that. I want to talk."

"No doubt." She pushed his hand away and crawled onto his lap. Her bare breasts tickled his nose.

"I mean it!" he said, holding her back. "This is not—"

"Do you want me to lose my job?"

He relaxed. Even in a semiprivate room, the night must have a thousand eyes. "At least give a man a chance to breathe, would you?"

Lenore giggled. "Whatever." Her hips began to sway.

"That's not necessary, either."

"Got to please the client."

"Rest assured you will receive my highest encomiums."

"Just relax," she said, stroking the back of his neck. "We have to look as if we're doing proper business. Even if we're not. Believe me, girls who don't follow the rules don't last long here. And I've got a living to make."

"Some living. A girl your age. Performing lap dances for strangers."

"I don't do lap dances," she replied. She squeezed her thighs together, tightening her grip on his groin. "I do friction dances. It's my specialty."

He felt his internal temperature rising.

"Now what is it you wanted to talk about, you stud?" she growled in his ear, her hips grinding. She was eager and energetic but not that practiced. "Don't I interest you even a little?"

"This isn't—isn't—"

"I know what to do." Her hand found the zippered fly of his trousers.

He knocked her hand away. "Stop!" This was becoming too intense, too potentially awkward. "I want to go somewhere private."

"We are somewhere private."

"Someplace else. Away from here. Someplace we can do . . . more than this. You know what I mean."

"I don't know if I think that's a good idea. . . ."

"Please. Vouchsafe me this one cherished boon."

She peered at him with a harsh eye. "If we leave the club, I'll be out for the entire evening."

"Yes."

"You'd have to compensate me for the loss. Me and the management."

"I understand."

"Do you? We're talking, like, three thousand dollars here."

"I can do that."

She gave him a long look. "I can't pretend it wouldn't be good for me. Bring my average up. You're sure?" She hesitated only the merest of moments. "Okay, I'll do it."

"Most munificent of you."

"Let me clock out and get my coat." She stopped just before she left the room. "You're sure? You're serious about this?"

He nodded, smiling pleasantly. "Dead serious."

I was pumped. For the first time since I got out of the hospital I was actually feeling somewhat good. I might not have the case solved, but I'd had some breakthroughs—the eyewitness, and now the decoded messages. My first steps in the psychologically right direction.

I decided to treat myself. Dinner at Elmer's. Not a million-course buffet, not fancy French cuisine. No elaborate décor. No décor at all, really. Just good old American down-home comfort food, ribs and chicken-fried steak served straight, at a very affordable price. Once upon a time, Vegas was famous for places like this, for their ninety-nine-cent all-you-can-eat shrimp and buck-ninety-nine filet mignon. Nowadays, the big resorts hired Michelin-quality chefs to entice people to pay for the prestige of a ridiculously overpriced meal in a room with minor French impressionist paintings. Wolfgang Puck had four restaurants here, for Pete's sake.

Elmer's was much more to my liking. It had a lot of sentimental value. David and I used to come here on our anniversary. I hadn't been back since he died, and hadn't wanted to. But I had a sense now that I was ready.

I felt like Dolly Levi after a long absence. I smiled at the maître d', a freckle-faced kid engaged in a losing battle with acne. "Party of one, please. I'd like a table—"

"By the window. With a view of the skyline." He grinned. "Good to see you again, Miss Pulaski."

I was floored. "What a memory you must have."

"Not at all. You're one of our most regular customers."

"I—you mean, before—"

"On the seventh, every month. It's your anniversary date, right?"

"Well, yes, it was, but—"

"And you never miss a month. Very admirable."

My neck stiffened. "But—I haven't been here for more than a year."

He blinked, still smiling. "You were just in last month."

"I—was?"

"And the month before that. And the month before that."

"But—I don't . . ."

"Shall I have the bartender bring you your favorite?" He winked. "Or maybe we should save time and have him bring you a pitcher."

My stomach felt like lead.

"When you're finished, let me know. I'll call you a cab." He winked again. "I think that's best, don't you?"

The elation I'd felt before deflated like a collapsed artery. The gnawing in my gut, the panicky, breathless, acidic sensation reasserted itself. "All of a sudden, I—I'm not feeling well. Maybe I'll skip dinner."

I stumbled out of the restaurant, knowing damn well that I was not skipping dinner. Only mutating its form.

"Where are we going?" she asked as they made their way to his truck. She had pulled a white embroidered wrap—a kimono, perhaps?—around herself to cover her virtual nudity.

They arrived at the pickup. He opened the passenger side door for her. "Huh. I didn't figure you for a pickup man."

"What did you have in mind?"

"I don't know. Thought you were more the Lexus type."

He closed her door securely, then walked around to the other side. "I find my truck very practical. And reliable."

"Yeah, I guess that's right. Mind if I turn on the radio?"

He winced, ever so slightly. "Would it be more music such as what they play in your workplace?"

"Guess you're pretty tired of that, huh?"

He smiled. "I don't mean to be bilious with you. But one must have standards." He looked over his shoulder, making sure the path behind him was clear. "That noise does not even qualify to be called music. It is an assault on the eardrums."

"It wouldn't be so bad if they didn't play it so loud. But it helps with the dancing. And it creates a party atmosphere. Most of the girls are so stoned they don't hear it anyway." She glanced down at the seat. "What's this?"

She had found the axe which he had left lying on the floor beneath the glove compartment.

"That's . . . just what it appears to be. I have some stumps on my property that require removal."

"Oh." She handed it to him. "Creepy." She slid into the seat. "Do you have one of those new places out in Grover Mills? I've heard those are—" She stopped again. "Now what's this?"

Edgar turned. His eyeballs bulged as he realized what she had found. "Don't—"

"There's something rattling around in there." She picked up a shoe box he had left under the seat. "I think it may be broken."

She opened the box.

And screamed.

The box fell out of her hands and all of sweet Annabel's teeth, all thirty-two of them, caked with blood, flew across the cab of the pickup.

"Oh, my God," Lenore said, pressing her hands against her mouth.

"I can explain," he said rapidly. "I'm a dentist and—"

"I heard about that girl—" She pushed open

the passenger side door. "I'm getting out of here."

He grabbed her arm. "Please don't."

"Look, keep your money. I'm leaving."

"But I can explain."

"Let me go!" She brought her fist down on his arm, as hard as she could. It was all he could do to hang on.

"Give me one more chance."

"I'm not giving you anything, you pervert." She sank her teeth into his wrist.

"Oww!" She'd hurt him, broken skin.

She scooted toward the door, but he managed to grab her shoulders and yank her back. The kimono slipped, exposing her. "Stop this immediately!"

"You stop, asshole." She rolled back, bringing her legs around and kicking him in the face. He slammed back against the driver's-side door.

She was already upright and moving toward the open door. With a sudden lunge, he sprang forward and grabbed her by the neck, then flung her head against the dash.

She was slowed, but not unconscious. "I'll scream . . . ," she mumbled.

"No, you won't." He snatched a loaded syringe out of the glove compartment and jabbed it into her neck. "Sweet dreams, Lenore."

It took more than a moment for him to regain his composure. Perhaps the insufferable music was a blessing after all, he noted, since it ensured that no one inside could possibly hear anything that happened out here.

He had to remember not to blame the girl. What could she know? She only acted out of fear, ignorance. He bent over and lightly brushed his lips across her forehead. **Thus I pacified Psyche and kissed her, / And tempted her out of her gloom . . .**

He threw a tarp over her, hid the axe behind the seat, and pulled out onto the street.

That was sloppy, he scolded himself, driving away. He'd been clumsy, foolhardy, as if he wanted to be caught. And it had almost cost him everything.

He could take no more risks. His work was too important. She was the third, the final component in the sacred trinity. First Helen, then Annabel, and now Lenore. The chosen offerings. After this, there would be only rejoicing. He was the Instrument who would usher in the Golden Age. As it was meant to be. As it was foretold.

CHAPTER TEN

It was a miracle I woke at all, much less before nine o'clock. I didn't know which was dragging me down more—the reading all night or the drinking all night. I'm not sure when I finally gave it up. I was in the middle of "A Tale of the Ragged Mountains"—a jolly Poe yarn about someone being killed via a poisonous leech—when my eyelids finally gave in.

A quick glance at the watch told me I had less than thirty minutes until I was supposed to pick up Darcy, who was about ten minutes away. My first instinct was to just grab my keys and go—what would he care if I was groomed or not? But O'Bannon might be lurking about, and he'd know something was up if I came in looking disheveled, distraught, or drunk. He'd fire my sweet ass in a heartbeat, and then I'd have no chance of reclaiming Rachel. So I showered quickly, steaming the smell out of my skin, and I brushed my teeth relentlessly.

I stared at the smoky brown liquid resting at the bottom of the bottle on my nightstand. If I polished that off, I could ditch the bottle. That would be smart. Get rid of the evidence, just in case Lisa or O'Bannon dropped by.

But if you start drinking first thing in the morning, I reminded myself . . .

Don't be idiotic. It was barely a swallow. I raised the bottle to my lips and downed it. It burned going down, but it burned good.

And then I brushed my teeth some more.

I may have violated a few traffic regs making my way to O'Bannon's, but they were minor ones, I'm sure. After I'd been in the car a few minutes, my cell beeped out the theme from **Dragnet.**

"Pulaski."

"Susan, it's Colin. I've got something for you."

"Talk to me, Einstein."

"Those messages you left behind—they really are messages. Coded messages. I can confirm it."

Since he couldn't see my face, I figured it was safe to smile.

"It's a code, but an insanely complex one. A normal substitution cipher has twenty-six characters, for obvious reasons. This one has three hundred and forty."

I raised an eyebrow.

"And given the relative brevity of the messages, that leaves a lot of characters to decode on not much information. Over half of the symbols appear only one or two times. See, he starts by substituting each letter for another symbol, then transposes these symbols, creating a hybrid substitution-transposition cipher. The cipher alphabet changes after every seven letters. So each letter of the plaintext is represented by several different symbols in the cipher-text. It's called polyalphabetic cryptology."

"So," I ventured, "have you cracked it?"

"No way. It's a major accomplishment just to have figured out what it is. I suspect a full decoding will require one of those mainframe code-breaking computers at the CIA. All I have is a few words. That first cipher says something about a grave. A deep one, I think."

"'Deep, deep, and for ever, into some ordinary and nameless grave.'"

There was a pause. "Could be. Where'd you get that?"

"And the other one reads, 'In the multiplied

objects of the external world I had no thoughts but for the teeth.' "

"Teeth?" He fairly squealed into the receiver. "No wonder I didn't— What kind of message is that?"

A damn good question. "You ever read Edgar Allan Poe?"

" 'The Gold Bug.' "

" 'The Gold Bug'?" I hadn't gotten that far yet. "What's that?"

"Short story. Big hunt for pirate treasure. Which they find by solving a substitution cipher."

"Poe wrote about ciphers?"

"He was the first writer to ever use one in a story, if I'm not mistaken. He's probably the granddaddy of American codes and code break-ing. He was really into it. The story gives a mini-lecture on how to solve cryptograms. As I recall, he ran ciphers in whatever magazine he was editing at the time and challenged people to send him one he couldn't crack. I don't think he was ever stumped."

Codes were important to Poe. And so of course they were important to anyone to whom Poe was important.

"You know, Susan, if your killer's really into Poe, he may be up to some seriously bizarro business."

I let Colin sign off, with that sobering thought ringing in my head.

After a brief stop, I pulled into the O'Bannon driveway at a quarter after nine. Darcy was waiting for me on the front porch.

"You came!" he said, plainly delighted. Was he worried that I wouldn't? I approached bearing tall ones from the corner Starbucks clone. I needed a cobweb clearer, and I thought he might, too.

"How 'bout a cup of jamoke? Your choice— regular, or the more exotic white chocolate mocha."

He stared at them, not taking either. "On Wednesdays I have two eggs and bacon and the eggs sunny-side up and not touching the bacon and a half glass of orange juice at eight o'clock. Then I take Bus 17 to the day care center so I can be there by nine, except today I called and told them I wasn't coming so it's okay that I'm not there yet."

And they say autistics are inflexible. "So you want coffee or not?"

He was still staring at the cups. "Did you know that most coffee comes from the west coast of Africa?"

"I thought South America . . ."

"Less than ten percent comes from South America. Most comes from Africa, where acid rain is constant and bathes the coffee beans all year round."

That explains the rich aroma. "Come on, Darcy. Choose your poison."

"Caffeine has been used as a highly effective poison in many agricultural arenas."

"Well, I'm not a plant. Take one."

He hesitated, looking at the cups the same way he had looked at the spider. "Did you know that caffeine is more addictive than cocaine?"

My arms were getting tired. "No . . ."

"It's also a diuretic. It dries you up and creates an addiction. Causes headaches and diarrhea and other physiological ailments."

I sighed. "You don't want any coffee, do you?"

"Scientists say that it's best to avoid addictive substances. Do you think that it's best to avoid addictive substances?"

The cups were starting to burn my fingers. I poured the mocha into the grass. "Absolutely. Horrible things, those addictive substances. Avoid at all costs."

The Poe Gallery. Of course. The significance of this burial site was increasingly apparent, thanks to Darcy.

There were only a few cops left at the Transylvania. A couple of techs and one uniform standing guard. Another day or two and the room would likely be released back to the hotel. What they would do with it, I had no idea. I suspected the memory of a real corpse turning up in this Disney-Meets-Death joint might spoil the fun for some of the patrons.

Tony Crenshaw was on the scene. I decided to walk over and give him a good chin-wag. "Anything new?"

"No. Not here, anyway. There's a rumor the coroner might release something later today."

"Be still my heart."

I noticed that Darcy was hanging back. Probably shy around people he didn't know. I thought about introducing him around, then decided it was probably best to let him absorb the crime scene in his own way at his own speed.

"You see my e-mail on the Poe connection?" I asked.

"Jesus Christ, yes. The whole office was buzzing about it this morning."

"What's the general opinion at the water-cooler?"

"Either the killer is crazy or you are. Possibly both."

I smiled a little. "What do you think?"

"I think you should've kept your theories to yourself. Something that warped is bound to leak out."

"What if it does?"

"This is nutty stuff, Susan. The press is already leading with this story. If they get wind of this development . . ." He made a slashing gesture across his throat.

"I just wanted to get my theory on the table so I could get input from the other geniuses in the department."

"Other?"

And of course I wanted to show everyone that I wasn't too inebriated to do my job. That O'Bannon hadn't committed a spectacular error in judgment by involving me. I wanted to make sure I got credit. Even if my brilliant breakthrough was mostly attributable to a twenty-six-year-old autistic guy. "You read much Poe, Tony?"

He shrugged. "I'm more of an Anne Tyler man myself."

"Just as well. Better for you." I saw that Darcy was hovering over the grave site. The body was gone, of course, but the coffin was still where it had been found, the half lid open. I walked over to him. "Kind of spooky, isn't it?"

His hands were flapping in tiny circles. "I think it's strange that that one died. Do you think it's strange that that one died?"

I didn't quite grasp his line of reasoning. "I . . . think the whole scenario is strange."

"In 'The Premature Burial,' the man gets away."

I thought back to my reading the night before. It was all a bit hazy, but I could recall a few details. "Yeah, that's right."

"In 'The Fall of the House of Usher,' Madeline is buried alive."

"Oh, yeah?"

"She gets out, too."

"Huh." Hadn't gotten to that one yet.

"In 'Ligeia,' a woman is buried alive."

Jeez Louise. Poe was really hung up on this plot device, wasn't he? "Does she get out?"

"Sorta." He glanced down at the coffin. "But that one did not get out, did she?"

"No, Darcy. She didn't." Which raised an interesting point, at least in my head. If my killer was trying to re-create scenes from Poe, and the characters in the stories don't die, why had he let this victim die? What purpose did he think the deaths would serve? "She must've been awake, though. Look how she clawed at the lid, trying to get out."

"At the top. Not at the bottom."

"I suppose it's everyone's first instinct to use your fists to try to pound your way out of something."

Darcy's head tilted to one side, as if that computerized brain of his was momentarily processing information. "Are your arms stronger than your legs?"

I thought for a moment. "I suppose not."

He pointed to the coffin. "Were that one's?"

"I don't know for sure, but—"

"Did you know that men usually have more upper-body strength than women?"

"Well, I've won a few arm-wrestling matches in my time."

"But girls sometimes have strong legs, don't they? Especially young ones. How old was this one?"

"We're not sure. Sixteen or so."

His head tilted again. "Why do you think she did not use her legs?"

"I . . . guess she didn't think of it." Which sounded lame even as I said it. "Or she couldn't."

"Were her legs tied up?"

"No."

"Then—"

"He's using a drug." Damn. It was obvious— once the kid fed it to you. "Some kind of paralytic agent. That's how he controls his victims." I pondered a moment. "But nothing showed up on the preliminary tox screen."

Darcy jumped up and down eagerly. His voice sounded as if he were reciting at high speed. "Some paralytic drugs, like poisons, will not be detected by general screening procedures. Progressive laboratory screening from the general to the more specific is required. For example, an anion gap on the electrolyte panel combined with metabolic acidosis on arterial blood gases would prompt an inquiry into ASA, methanol, or ethylene glycol as potential etiologic agents."

I stared at him, doing my best not to gape at this astounding feat of mimesis. Even if he didn't understand everything he was saying, his memory was preternatural. "Did you go to medical school while your father wasn't looking? How on earth do you know this?"

"My dad has books about criminology. Lots of them. When books at his office were replaced by newer editions, he always brought the old ones home."

"For you to read. And memorize." I began to get the picture. "Darcy, you're a one-man forensic lab. I'm going to call the coroner. Patterson hates interference from detectives, but if I gently pass the word that a singular screen for paralytic agents before he files his report might be a good idea, he can do it and act as if it were his idea."

I punched my cell and delivered the message. When I finished, I found Darcy staring at the double doors that led to the main hallway outside.

"That's how the killer got in," I explained. "Looks like he fired up an acetylene torch to weaken the chain, then used his spade to break it."

Darcy didn't respond. He continued staring at the door, the jamb, the place where the chain had been.

"We think he came in around two or three in the morning," I continued. "The coroner should be able to nail the time for us. There's a service driveway on the other side of the hallway. No one would've been out there early in the morning. He'd have the time and opportunity to drive up from wherever, break in, and do whatever he needed to do."

Darcy was still staring at the door, doing that weird head-tilting thing.

"We've photographed the door, of course, and the chain is back in Evidence. I can take you to see it, if you like. I can show you the enlargements of the doorway—"

"That's an ugly black spot."

He was pointing to a longish horizontal mark, slightly triangular, that scarred the green paint at about the level of the doorknob. It was widest on our side, then narrowed toward the hallway.

"Yes, very unattractive. Hotel employees can be such slobs. Probably some workman carting in furniture in a big hurry."

Darcy scraped the black place with the tip of his fingernail. It flaked off a bit. "It's burnt."

"Burnt?"

He nodded. "My dad works with a torch, in the garage. For his pottery."

Okay, this time I had to do a triple take. "Your dad makes pottery?"

"Yeah. I like pottery. Do you like pottery? He's good at it. He has a kiln for the big stuff, but he uses a torch on the ashtrays."

"Let me make sure I'm getting this. Your dad makes ashtrays?"

"And bud vases."

"Chief of Police Robert O'Bannon makes bud vases?"

"I think he is very good at it. He whistles while he does it, so I guess it makes him happy."

I had no reason to doubt the guy. But I had a hard time conjuring a mental image of this big gruff cop straddling a potter's wheel, much less baking dainty knickknacks.

Darcy redirected my attention to the black scar. "This is from the torch." He tucked his chin, made that irresistibly silly face. "One time my dad made a mark like that on his work-bench. He said some very bad words. I could tell you about them but he told me I was not to repeat them."

"That's quite all—"

"The only other time I heard my father talk like that was when I dropped his first-edition copy of **Brideshead Revisited** in the bathtub and—"

"Is there some significance to this, Darcy?"

He had no answer. I could tell something was bothering him. But the cranial computer hadn't quite lined up all the data yet.

"Don't sweat it, Darcy. You've been brilliant enough for one day. I can't believe you know so much about toxicology."

"Do you think that I know a lot of things? My dad says I know more stuff than an encyclopedia, but it doesn't matter because I don't have the sense to know what to do with it."

"That's okay, my friend," I said, linking my arm around his. "Because I do. Let's go to the next crime scene."

Did I make her happy I think maybe I made her happy and she looked happy but I remember sometimes Mommy looked happy and it turned out she wasn't. She made me go to those places I didn't like and Susan brought me to this place I didn't like but it's okay if it makes Susan happy. I found out that Susan is not married anymore and if she's not married then she could marry me and we could have babies. She doesn't have any babies but she could I know she could and that would be even better than the day care center. **An unhappy alternative is before you, Elizabeth. From this day you must be a stranger to one of your parents.** I don't know why it made her so happy all I told her was what was obvious but her voice was faster and higher and she touched my arm so I think that means she was happy so I'm happy too. I wonder if my dad will be happy. I wonder if he will let me go out more. Maybe he would even let me be a policeman. He thinks I don't want to be a policeman, but I do. I want to make him happy. I just don't understand why people do all these things they do. People always think I act crazy but I think the things other people do are crazier and I don't understand them.

Maybe Susan can explain it to me. I would like that.

Even as I drove him out to the second crime scene at McCarran, I knew I had no right whatsoever to expect Darcy to come up with more breakthroughs, or to spark new ideas in me, or whatever it was he was doing. But I couldn't help hoping, just the same. I wonder if that's why God stopped with the miracles after the New Testament days. People are never satisfied. They always want more.

I asked one of the patrolmen to give Darcy access to the crime scene, then let the boy do as he pleased. Far be it for me to direct him. He spent almost an hour just wandering in and around the plane. He crouched down where the body had lain, looking at it from all angles, his head tilted with that uncanny android expression on his face. He paced the perimeter of the entire pavilion where the retired planes were stored. But he always came back to the place where the body had been found. He crouched down on all fours and pressed his face to the floor, his butt sticking up in the air. He looked like a bird dog sniffing for a scent. I could see one of the techs watching him out of the corner of his eye, laughing. I gave him the finger and told him to get to work. Asshole.

"The criminalists have been all over this site," I told Darcy, just to hear myself talk. "They didn't find much. No useful stains or residue. No blood. A few bits of carpet lint on the body."

Darcy's head rose, as if he had detected a new scent. "Carpet? Or rug?"

"Whatever. Something from her home or his that—"

"I think maybe it was a rug. Do you think maybe it was a rug?"

I paused. "I don't know. I'm not sure I see the—"

"Did you know that murderers sometimes wrap bodies in rugs to make them easier to carry? During the 1934 torso murders in Cleveland, the killer—"

"But if the killer brought the corpse in a rug, where is it?"

"I think maybe he must've taken it home with him."

I considered. "No. The body couldn't have been wrapped, and he must've dragged it part of the way. There was dirt on the body."

Darcy crouched down low again. "There's a lot of dirt on the floor of the plane. Why would there be dirt on the floor of the plane?"

"I . . . guess the door blew open and—" Right. We were in a sea of concrete. "He brought the body from somewhere else. Probably got tired at some point and dragged it. It got dirty."

"I didn't see the body," Darcy said. "Was it all scraped up?"

"Well, no. Actually, it seemed well cared for, even washed. Almost like he really cared about her."

Darcy brushed his hands off and stood. "I think that maybe he brought this one here in a rug."

And damn it all, I knew he was right. "But where did the dirt come from?"

"I think that maybe he brought that, too."

"But why? For what reason?" I asked, but I

realized that brilliant as he was, Darcy could never deduce the answers to these teleological questions. Because that required someone who understood the wild and wooly ways of people. Perhaps someone blessed with hyper-empathy. Yours truly. I thought a moment. . . .

Because this was a burial, that's why. At least in his deranged mind, this was a burial, so he'd brought dirt. Why hadn't I seen it before?

I knew the answer to that question, too.

Because I hadn't had Darcy before.

I put my arm around his neck and gave him a squeeze. He pulled away but not too hard. "Darcy, my friend, I think this could be the beginning of a beautiful friendship."

He smiled cautiously, eyes up but chin tucked. "Did I—did I do something good?"

"You hit the ball out of the park, slugger." Bizarre as it sounds, being with Darcy, working with him—if you can call it that—made me feel . . . better. Stronger. Like maybe I really could still do this.

"Does this mean that we could go for custard later? I like to eat frozen custard. Custard is my favorite thing because I know whenever I have custard it's going to be a Very Excellent Day. On Wednesdays, my favorite is vanilla toffee, but my dad likes the bubble gum flavor—"

"Your dad likes bubble gum custard? Get out of here."

"Sometimes he gets Oreo Cookie Mash. If we went now I think my dad wouldn't mind and it would be okay and I don't think it would spoil our dinner, do you?" He grinned that goofy grin again. Irresistible.

From a landing bay outside the Arrivals deck, he watched the crime technicians work through high-powered binoculars. His hand still hurt from the bite, but he had cleaned and dressed it and all his fingers were functional, if a bit weak. He was wearing his uniform, which was not the same as those of airport security but was more than enough to keep people from interfering with him. When a man in a uniform went to the airport, no one messed with him, especially these days.

Watching the crime techs at work was fascinating—and rather discouraging, too. It was of considerable interest to him to see where they focused their attention. The careful steps they took to ensure that no tracks or footsteps were obliterated—not that he had left any. All right—one tire track. He was human. What could they possibly do with that? He would change the tires on the truck tonight, just to be safe.

These people spent hours coating the area with a fine white dust, hoping to find a fingerprint. Absurd. To leave behind clues of that caliber, one would have to be a fool. No, he wanted to scream at them, I didn't leave behind any hair—I wore a net the entire time. Did they think they were dealing with a beer-sozzled redneck? A tripped-out tourist? Had he not made it abundantly clear that he was a serious man doing serious work?

Thank heaven Susan finally arrived. His sweet, beautiful Cassandra. Yes, his totem had been right, had been prophetic. It was still early days, but he felt certain that she would be the one to appreciate what he had done. She'd barely been on the scene a minute yesterday before she had Annabel's mouth open, something none of her predecessors, not even the representatives from the coroner's office, had the sense to do. **Her understanding encompasseth mountains. . . .**

But Susan's return to the scene today was fraught with disappointment. For starters, she did not come alone. Who was this new companion? He hadn't been at the police station. He was dressed casually and didn't appear to have any official status. And yet, Susan talked to him constantly. It was as if she was feeding him information, soliciting his opinion about every aspect of the case. Was he her friend, her partner? Or something more? He seemed younger than she, surely too young to be . . .

And yet there was something between them, something real, important. He tightened the focus on his binoculars, zooming in for a closer look. He stared at the young man's eyes, watching the way he moved, the way he talked, for a considerable period of time. And yet, he couldn't get a reading on him. The young man's eyes were like reflecting mirrors. There was something . . . elusive about him. Something inscrutable. As if there was an emotional lacuna where a soul should be. As if . . . as if he wasn't entirely a part of this world.

Dream-Land? No. He might not be able to discern what drove Susan's young cohort, but he was certain it was not enlightenment. There was more confusion about him than determination.

And yet he couldn't help but wonder. . . .

Did he pose a threat? The others, with their by-the-book approach and mundane sensibilities had little hope of ever discovering the truth. But this new interloper . . .

He would have to keep a close eye on this young man.

On his way out of the airport, he bought a newspaper from a self-serve kiosk. He would want the day's story for his History. The article about the discovery of Annabel's body was rather disappointingly small, even though there were no other stories of great import. Was this town so jaded that murder no longer captured its imagination? What was this distorted mentality that bestowed more attention on Siegfried and Roy than a messiah?

SECOND BODY FOUND IN ABANDONED AIRCRAFT

BY JONATHAN WOOLEY

Another naked corpse was discovered late Friday afternoon by FAA investigators in one of the many abandoned aircrafts housed on the rear field at McCarran International, authorities confirmed at a noon press conference. Although officials did not offer an opinion as to whether this death was linked to the body found two days before at the Transylvania Resort Hotel, they did acknowledge that both bodies were entirely naked, and that both were found with a mysterious written message.

"We're doing everything we can to solve this case," said Chief of Police Robert O'Bannon. "Even calling in federal experts. But it would be a mistake to prematurely conclude that the killings are linked without more information." When pressed, Chief O'Bannon acknowledged that there was a strong possibility that both crimes were committed by the same assailant or assailants. He offered no opinion as to who that might be or what motive might lie behind the crimes. He did note that the two deaths were very different in nature. The woman found at the Transylvania died of asphyxiation, while preliminary indications were that this latest victim had died from exsanguination.

Even if the crimes are linked, O'Bannon noted, it is important not to create a panic. "Las Vegas is a large city, and there is no reason to believe that anyone, especially tourists, are in danger." Lieutenant Barry Granger, the homicide detective assigned to the case, also urged that . . .

He closed the paper, disgusted. Why did they always interpellate O'Bannon and Granger? They didn't know anything. O'Bannon was a supervisor and Granger was a fool. Why didn't they talk to Susan? Susan understood that this was not just another murder case; he was sure of it. She could give them a story worthy of publication. He would be interested to hear what she had to say. What she thought of this case, these crimes.

What she thought about him.

He had always considered himself a paragon of decorum and chivalrous behavior. He had modeled himself after the prophet in word and deed, sensibilities, even adopting the euphuism of his era. But there were so many unanswered questions. He would follow Susan constantly now, as much as he was able. To keep an eye on her. To ensure that her interest didn't flag. And as to this new man—perhaps he would have to arrange a meeting. If there was danger afoot, he had to know. So he could take the appropriate action to eliminate it.

CHAPTER ELEVEN

There were some advantages, I was beginning to learn, to having an office adjoining the men's room. True, it meant I was on display like a museum exhibit, or perhaps more accurately, like a zoo animal, caged all day long. But it also meant that no one could avoid me, certainly no one male, no matter how much they might like to do so. Even Granger did not possess a cast-iron bladder. Earlier, he had tried to slip past by pointedly looking the other way, so I complimented him on something, I think on the way the coffee stain on his tie matched his underarm stains. For his afternoon visit, he decided to take the offensive. And he was pretty darned offensive about his offensive, too.

"Pulaski," he growled, even before he got to my desk. "What the hell were you doing with O'Bannon's kid?"

"I was investigating, sir. It's what investigators do. Perhaps you were absent the day they covered that at the academy. Darcy was quite useful."

"I know the kid's story, Pulaski. And I saw how he acted at the crime scene. There's no way—"

"You don't know anything about it."

"I know he's been nothing but a burden to his father. I know O'Bannon never mentions him. Never."

I wondered if that was true. "There's no reason for anyone to be embarrassed about a neurological disorder. It's no one's fault. It just happens. We don't know why."

"None of which explains why you were dragging this poor boy all over two grisly crime scenes. Are you trying to suck up to O'Bannon?"

"Don't be imbecilic."

"You really think if you play out this charade with O'Bannon's son you'll get your old job back?"

"The thought never entered my mind," I said quite honestly.

"Well, leave the kid alone. Let him work in that day care or whatever. No telling what a crime scene might do to a mental case like that. Might give him ideas, even."

God grant me the serenity to accept the things I cannot change and not kill Granger in the process. "I'm just trying to catch the murderer. Just like you."

"Which reminds me. You were not hired to sniff around the forensic evidence or to repeat the work of others more qualified to do it. You were hired to prepare a psychological profile. Have you done that?"

"I'm working on it. It's difficult when we don't know who the victims were."

"I can help you with that." He slapped a folder down on my desk. "If I were you, I'd get something down on paper. The FBI profiler will arrive tomorrow."

My head jerked up. "What?"

"I'm told he's one of the best. Most of the boys think O'Bannon hired you so he could tell the press he was doing everything possible to catch the killer. But after the Feebie arrives, I can't imagine what the point of paying for an outside consultant would be." And on that note, he galumphed toward the men's room.

"Thanks for stopping by, Granger," I couldn't resist saying. "You honor David's memory."

He stopped short, his shoulders rising. "Better than you do," he muttered under his breath. Then left.

I didn't allow myself to focus on what the son of a bitch had said or what he meant by it. I had work to do. If Granger remained in charge of this investigation, the killer could work his way through Poe's collected works three times over without getting caught.

A federal profiler? Why? Had O'Bannon requested it? Because he had no faith in me anymore?

I put it out of my mind. If the man was coming, I would have something ready to show him.

The file Granger dumped on me was more helpful than I could've imagined. The two victims had been identified, thanks to the pictures run in the daily paper. The first was named Helen Collier, and she lived here in the Vegas 'burbs with her mother. Mom had been visiting friends and didn't know her daughter was missing—till she saw her pic in the paper at the airport on her way home. Hell of a shock that must've been. Helen had been a petite girl and cute, judging from her school photo. Too cute to end up suffocating, clawing for air in a buried coffin.

The second girl was named Annabel Spencer.

She was originally from New York but was going to school at MIT. No one had any idea what she was doing in Vegas. The only person who even knew she was gone was her boyfriend, and so far he wasn't providing any details. But here's the kicker: Annabel Spencer was the only daughter of Dr. Fara Spencer, acclaimed TV shrink. Her afternoon TV show was huge; Lisa swore by it. Sort of a cross between Dr. Phil and Judge Judy, Fara alternated between administering homespun wisdom to the worthy and tongue-lashing the unworthy. Her hour was the hottest thing in syndication.

And her daughter was the second victim. As if this case could get any weirder. Or more complicated.

I jotted down the address of the Collier residence. That had to be my next stop.

I was almost out the door when an intern brought me a message.

"Lieutenant?"

She was a Hispanic woman who I knew worked in toxicology. She'd been here more than two years, but if she hadn't been wearing a badge I wouldn't have known her name was Jennifer. "Yes?"

"I have a report for you."

"I'm kind of in a hurry, Jen. Can you give me the highlights?"

She spoke quietly, almost timidly. "Despite Patterson's protestations, we ran the tests you requested, the progressive tox screen."

"And?"

"A lot of time had passed on both corpses, but we found distinct traces of tetraodontoxin."

"And that is?"

"A neurotoxin, basically. It causes paralysis, speech difficulty, shallow breathing, and slowed pulse till it gradually wears off, usually permitting brain functions and speech before it allows movement of the rest of the body."

"Is it dangerous?"

"Given in large doses, it can be fatal." She paused, fidgeting with her fingers. "Do you like sushi?"

"I'm more a cheeseburger and fries girl. Why?"

"Heard of fugu?"

"The blowfish that's a Japanese delicacy, but if it's not prepared right it can kill you?"

"That's the one. The toxin is found in the ovaries of the blowfish, and it isn't destroyed by cooking. Prepared properly, just enough remains to give diners a pleasantly flushed and tingly feeling. Prepared improperly, it's fatal."

"I think I'll stick with Quarter Pounders. Any idea where the killer might've gotten this stuff? I assume it's restricted."

"Theft from a lab or clinic or drugstore or hospital is always a possibility. Or he might've gone to Haiti."

"Haiti?"

She nodded. "I understand you can buy it on the street there. It's used in voodoo religious rituals. That's how they zombify plantation workers."

"And that's how our man keeps his victims under control. Wow. Thanks." I grabbed my coat.

"Lieutenant?" Jennifer hadn't budged. "We never would've found that if you hadn't asked for the additional tests. How did you know?"

I smiled. "Years of experience. And training. Proper training is so important." I grabbed the report and headed out the door. Darcy, you little genius. I'm keeping you in this investigation. Whether Granger likes it or not.

I've lived in this city all my life, so there was no excuse for it. If you live by only one rule in Vegas, it should be this: avoid the Spaghetti Bowl at all costs. But it would be the quickest way to get to the Colliers' place if traffic was down . . .

But traffic was never down, not in the loop formed by I-35 and U.S. 93-95 around downtown Vegas, joining just to the north and west of the Old Strip. The long strands of highway gave it its culinary name, and all the locals knew traffic there could be more congested than L.A. Fortunately, I had Darcy in the car, and he entertained me by reciting the crime statistics for every violent homicide in Vegas for the last fifty years.

I left Darcy outside while I went in to meet the first victim's mother. Mrs. Collier was remarkably informative, all things considered. It had to be unbearable, losing a daughter. I still stung from being separated from Rachel; imagine how it must feel to know your little girl was gone forever, and worse, that the psychopathic killer who snatched her did it while you were off on a holiday. The guilt would be enormous.

"She was the sweetest girl," Mrs. Collier kept saying. She had not wanted to talk to me. She had already been quizzed extensively by Granger's investigators. "Sweet, sweet, sweet. All my friends told me that girls were the worst. That once they were teenagers they became monsters. But not my Helen. She was always so sweet."

"I'm sure she was," I said, wishing the woman would come up with a more useful adjective.

"She never went in for those naughty activities some of the other girls did. She didn't chase after boys. She didn't stay out late. She didn't like to party. She preferred to tap-dance."

"Did you say tap-dance?"

"That was her grand passion. Her idol was Shirley Temple, ever since she was a baby. She could've been great, given her chance."

"Was she taking lessons?"

"Yes. She and her best friend, Amber, went to Miss Claire's School of Dance on South Fremont. Almost every Friday, they went to the dance recitals held in the basement at Trinity Episcopal."

"Any nights other than Friday?" I asked, remembering that she was last seen on a Thursday.

"No."

"Never?"

"Absolutely not. I had a strict policy on bedtime by ten o'clock on all the other nights of the week, but on Fridays I let her stay up till midnight. I checked to make sure she was in bed, safe, every night. And I locked the doors."

"Could I see her room?"

After a moment of hesitation, she escorted me upstairs.

If I hadn't known the girl was sixteen, I certainly wouldn't have gotten it from her living quarters. It was all decked out in pink frillies and lace and flowery dust ruffles and stuff I don't even know the names for. My parents never went in for this junk. Even at an early age it was clear I wasn't a Barbie girl. But evidently Helen was.

Or someone thought she was.

"Had this furniture some time?" I asked the mother, who was hovering awkwardly by the door. I figured she'd probably bought it when the girl was five and couldn't afford to replace it later.

I was wrong. "Actually, we picked this set up last year. They were having a sale at Conway Brothers."

Hmmm. "You know, I'm probably going to be a while. I like to soak up the atmosphere, get a feel for who your daughter was. You don't have to wait for me. I'm sure you have many other things to do."

Couldn't be any less subtle than that. "Very well." She was still reluctant, but she retreated. "I'll be in the kitchen. If you need anything."

Thank heaven. Behaviorists don't work well with an audience. I couldn't get inside Helen's head with her mother monitoring and censoring me the whole time. Helen's desk, her closet, and for that matter her entire room, were uncommonly clean. I realize I was not the prototypical teenager, but my room had never looked like this. Had her mother cleaned up before the cops arrived? Or did Mom always keep the joint like this? Was she one of those hausfraus who scurried around telling people to take off their shoes and not touch anything, making it more like a museum than a living environment? How would young Helen react to being raised by a single parent who had that obsessive-compulsive approach to life?

I combed through Helen's closet, finding nothing of interest. She had a lot of clothes and tons of shoes, but I supposed that wasn't unusual for girly-girls of her age. All her outfits appeared to be of the sort her mother would approve. Tasteful knee-length tea dresses that kept the body well covered. Pep club uniform. One-piece swimsuits. No Britney Spearsish midriff-revealing outfits. No hip-hugging blue jeans. No cleavage-boosting brassieres or clinging sweaters. No Victoria's Secret lingerie.

Maybe her idol really was Shirley Temple.

Nah.

I checked the bathroom, too, but I felt certain that if there had ever been anything of interest, Mom would've removed it. I not only found nothing useful, I found nothing that suggested this girl had ever hit puberty, unless you counted the box of tampons shoved to the back of the cabinet beneath the sink. No pills, no diaphragm. Not even Clearasil.

I was hoping for a diary, but no such luck. In the bottom desk drawer, however, I found a stack of collage books. Helen was a scrapbooker.

But this was not your garden-variety scrapbook. There were no pictures of actors or pop stars, no Eminem or Brad Pitt. Most of the pictures came out of magazines, and all were of people in authority, people in helping professions. Police officers, doctors in white coats, firemen. Wholesome role models.

Was this girl really the Pollyanna her mom thought she was?

Possible. But I still didn't think so.

On the back page of one of the scrapbooks, I found a Web URL. I jotted it down in my notepad. I was putting them away when something spilled out of one of them, something that had been wedged between the pages.

A torn bus ticket. Now that was interesting. She wouldn't need to ride the bus to get to Trinity Episcopal.

I didn't expect to find anything useful under the bed. Wasn't that the first place parents always looked? That was where I'd kept my pot when I was her age. And God knows I'd gotten caught often enough.

But under Helen's bed, hidden in a small box wedged between the bottom of the mattress and the wooden slats, I found an outfit of clothes. It was all black. A sheer, tight lacy bodice. An equally tight, short leather skirt. Matching bra and shoes. Fishnet hose. A pair of black Ray-Bans with purple lenses. Something that looked like a white shoe polish brush but which I knew (thanks to Rachel) was actually used to put a temporary streak of color in your hair that washed right out once you were home from your revels. All told, a very exotic, erotic, interesting little outfit.

Granger's investigators would've seen this, too, of course, but they wouldn't grasp the significance. They'd laugh embarrassedly, or maybe make some off-color joke about the little girl getting some action. Then they'd close the box and put it away and proceed to look for bloodstains or something else they could understand. But to me, this box spoke volumes.

Helen was a closet Goth girl.

Downstairs, I found that one of Helen's friends had arrived. I knew from a picture wedged into the side of the mirror above Helen's dresser that this was Amber. She was more distraught than the mother, her cheeks still red, her eyes watery. When I asked if I could have a few words with her, I thought she might faint. But she agreed. That only left the more difficult chore of getting rid of Mom.

"I don't see what you could possibly have to ask that I couldn't hear. This is about my daughter, after all."

"That's just it," I tried to explain. "Your presence could . . . inhibit the discussion."

"This is still my home, and if you're going to talk to my daughter's best friend, whom I've known since she was six, you're going to have—"

"If you won't cooperate with me, ma'am, I'll be forced to call some uniforms and take her downtown. Is that what you want?"

She stared at me stonily, lips tightly pursed.

"They'll come with the siren blazing. They'll put cuffs on her. She'll ride in the back of the cop car and be processed and printed and strip-searched before being interrogated." All of which was total bullshit, but I figured this lady wouldn't know.

She relented. "Very well. But Amber, dear, listen to me." She took the girl's hand, and I got the immediate impression the girl wished she wouldn't. "You don't have to say anything. You don't have to tell this woman anything. If at any time you want the questioning to stop, you just call for me. Understand?"

"Yes, Mrs. Collier."

The woman disappeared herself, leaving us alone. Amber was taller and beefier than Helen had been, with lighter hair and a way of talking that seemed both lazy and smart.

"Kind of controlling, isn't she?" I said, hoping to break the ice.

Amber shrugged. "I'm used to it."

"I guess you must be, if you've known her since you were six. Were you over here a lot?"

"Most times we hung at my house. It's closer to school, and my dad keeps the pantry well stocked. Over here I was always worried that I might drop a cookie crumb on the carpet and give Mrs. Collier a heart attack."

I grinned. Mordant Humor R Us. "But you and Helen were tight?"

"Yeah. Best buds."

"And when the two of you took off on Friday nights, you weren't going to a church and you weren't going to any Shirley Temple show either, right?"

Now she became wary. Which I could understand. Why should she trust me? "What makes you think that?"

"My psychic powers. Am I right?"

She didn't answer.

"I found one of Helen's bus tickets."

Still nothing.

"Found Helen's party suit, too, and I feel certain she wasn't wearing that getup to any church."

Amber smiled a little.

"Where's the Goth scene these days, Amber? Was there a bar you two liked? Maybe something on campus?"

"Nothing like that," she said quietly.

"Did you go down to the Strip? Pretend to be hookers just to amuse yourselves?"

I was getting warm, but I hadn't arrived. "We did go to the Strip sometimes."

"To do what?"

"Whatever. Just hang. Went to shows sometimes."

"And not tap dancing."

"Helen was more into heavy metal."

"But there wasn't always a concert."

"Sometimes we'd just walk. Go to the mall at Caesar's or the Aladdin. See what was happening at the hotels."

Of course. "The Transylvania. She liked the Transylvania, didn't she? Where else would a Goth girl go?"

Amber nodded. "She got off on all that creepy stuff. Haunted houses. Horror movies."

Sure she did. Anything that was the antithesis of her mother. That was her quiet rebellion. "Anyplace else?"

"There was this club near the Transylvania. An Army grunt hangout. Helen was kinda sweet on military types."

"Do you know where she went the night she disappeared?"

"No. I had to go to Los Angeles with my parents. So I guess she went out without me."

"Maybe with another friend?"

"Maybe. But I don't know who it would be."
Her eyes lowered. "I bet she went alone."

I bet she did, too, damn it. That's why she'd
been so easy to snatch. "Do you have any idea
what happened to her?" I asked, but I knew
Amber didn't and I was right.

I left the house excited. I still had a long way
to go, but I was definitely making progress. And
the bizarre thing was, I wasn't anxious to get
back to HQ and wow O'Bannon. I wasn't
aching to spill the beans to Lisa.

I couldn't wait to tell Darcy.

I found him more or less where I'd left him,
out in front of the house. He was crouched
down in the rather bosky garden that lined the
north side of the house.

"Do you think Helen wore a size six?" he
asked as soon as he saw me. "Because I think
maybe she was a size six."

"No," I replied. "She was too busty."

He looked at me, puzzled. I made an ex-
planatory gesture. He blushed, then averted his
eyes and ran his fingers through his hair.

"Did you know that I was asking about her
shoe size?" he muttered, staring at the ground.
"I was asking about her shoe size."

"Oh, geez, sorry." Pretty adorable really,
watching him flush up like a radish over nothing. "Size six, huh?" I remembered the shoes I'd

seen in the girl's closet. "That sounds about right."

"I think she was a size six," Darcy repeated, still flapping his hands nervously. "At first I thought maybe her mother was a size six. But I saw her feet when she came to the door and they were like boats."

I giggled. I thought I was allowed, since my feet were also of the boatish variety. "Why were you wondering about Helen's shoe size?"

He pulled me into the garden, behind a row of hedges, then crouched down and pointed. Behind the hedge, close to the house itself, there was a faint but discernible impression in the soil. A footprint. The tread looked like some kind of spiked-heel number.

I looked up. We were directly beneath Helen's bedroom window. There was a drain-pipe attached to the wooden siding that could provide some support. Not that much was really required. Her window wasn't that high off the ground.

Thanks to Darcy, I had a pretty good idea how Helen could walk on the wild side on nights other than Friday. Even if her mother did make sure she was in bed at ten and locked the doors.

"You've got a good eye, Darcy. That looks like it could be a size six. Maybe seven."

"Six."

"Well, to be sure, we should—"

"It's six and five-twelfths inches long. That's a size six."

I'd been around this wunderkind long enough to know not to argue. "Let's get some plaster out of my car and make a cast."

"And after that?"

I grinned. Something about this guy brightened my spirits, just being around him. "I think you've earned a custard. Don't you?"

He grinned excitedly. "Very Excellent Day! Very Excellent Day! Are you going to try the Strawberry Mash?"

"Maybe. What about you? Vanilla Toffee again?"

"I usually have Vanilla Toffee on Wednesdays and Strawberry Mash on Thursdays, unless there's a new flavor, and then I substitute the new flavor for whichever flavor on my list has the most letters in its name. If there's a tie, I cross out whichever one comes last in the alphabet, unless the Thursday falls on the last day of the month, 'cause then I reverse the alphabetical order and . . ."

He was so close. She was the third and final offering, and once he was done with her his work would be complete. He had crossed the Rubicon. The Golden Age would soon be upon them.

"You hurt me," he said as soon as Lenore opened her eyes.

It was a long while before she could reply. Her eyelids fluttered as she slowly shook off the soporific. She parted her lips, then worked them slowly, soundlessly, as if taking them for a test drive. She tried moving other parts of her body and soon found that she could not.

He watched it all, reading her emotions as they raced through her head. Her first instinct was panic, but she stifled it. Even in this dazed state, she was smart enough to realize a cool head would be required if she was going to save herself. Her next emotion was anger, but that too she managed to sublimate. She thought that he was probably some kind of sexual deviant—how could she know?—and that she was more likely to survive by acting submissive and helpless. And waiting for her opportunity.

It was more than a minute before she actually spoke. "I—I'm sorry. I can see your hand is sore."

"I don't mean there," he said. He placed his injured hand over his heart. "I mean here."

"I—I—I'm sorry," she said. She must be tired, lethargic from the drug. But he still sensed that she was playing him, exuding vulnerability until she had enough strength to make a break for it. Poor little offering.

"There was no justification for that sort of behavior," he said firmly. "You forced me to retaliate in kind. I was not pleased." He lowered his head. "I abhor violence."

"I—I guess I just panicked."

"So you did."

"Why can't I move my arms or legs?"

"I've given you a little something."

"Is it . . . permanent?"

"It will wear off altogether soon, if I don't give you another dose."

"I—I'd rather you didn't." She was laying it on a bit thick now, he thought, with the stuttering and plangent baby-girl vocalization.

"Then I won't."

"Really?"

"I give you my word. No more injections." He paused. "It won't be necessary."

"That's good. I'm glad you feel that way. Um . . ." She batted the lashes over those lovely Asian eyes. "Sir? Am I naked?"

"You are. Cap-a-pie. And let me just say— never have I had an easier time removing someone's clothing."

"So you've . . . you've done this before?"

"Once or twice." She was testing, exploring. To his surprise he saw that she was already able

to move the fingers of her right hand, just a bit.
A strong girl, this one was.

"Are you a dentist?"

He cleared his throat. "I don't have a degree.
But I am not without skill."

"Are—are you going to remove my teeth?"

"No, dear."

"Are you going to remove . . . anything?"

He sighed. "Yes, I'm afraid I am. I do regret
it. But it's essential."

"What . . . are you going to take?"

"Your head." He revealed the axe she had discovered in the truck. "I should never have left
this lying about. That was inexcusable."

"Please don't," she said. Her voice was tiny,
almost invisible.

"I have no choice, my darling."

"I'll do anything. Anything you want."

"That's most generous of you. But I can't accept your offer." He closed his eyes. " 'Vainly
had I sought to borrow, from my books surcease
of sorrow—sorrow for the lost Lenore.' "

"Don't, sir. Please don't hurt me."

" 'For the rare and radiant maiden whom the
angels name Lenore.' "

"Please. **Please!**"

He smiled at her. " 'Nameless here forever-
more.' " And then he raised the axe over his head.

CHAPTER TWELVE

Got to work without incident, thank God. Took a little more than I should've before I brushed my teeth, but it was right there in the open bottle, and I had to be sure I could work without distraction today, without that stifling, panicked feeling, without my temper getting out of control. I mean, it was one thing to be drinking last night. You needed something to get you through all those bizarre Poe stories. But in the morning? I probably shouldn't have. . . .

Damn them all. I can handle it. I can handle it. It'll wear off in an hour or so, and I am not going to make a habit of it. It was just this one last time. . . .

I slid behind my desk, bound and determined to avoid the obvious stereotype. Sure, I know the cliché. The FBI comes to town and the local cops get bent out of joint. They're coarse and resentful. The Feebs are all cool, steely-eyed authority. There's a lot of chatter about jurisdiction—wait, no—"turf." That's the way it's supposed to happen, in TV shows and movies. And, unfortunately, in real life.

But I wasn't getting sucked into that trap. I didn't need any more problems and I certainly didn't need anyone filing negative reports on me. I had to keep my job and to stay on my best behavior, at least until that custody hearing. So I was prepared to suck it in and be deferential. Why not? We were both trained professionals. Psychology was a fluid science. Two professionals could hold differing opinions and neither necessarily be wrong. There was nothing threatening about it, no harm in having a partner.

Just so I was the one who caught the killer.

Maybe half an hour later, Granger strode superciliously to my desk, avoiding eye contact, white shirt in tow. I braced myself for the inevitable fatuous remark.

"And this is the former Lieutenant Pulaski whom you've heard so much about," he said. "She has been working on a temporary basis as a consulting profiler. Up until now, anyway."

Subtle, Granger. Very subtle. I stood and held out my hand.

Then my eyebrows rose, of their own accord. I was prepared for the Fed to be cool and authoritative. I was not prepared for him to be hunky.

"Patrick Chaffee, Behavioral Science Unit. Good to meet you, Lieutenant." His grip was firm but not oppressive. He was a couple of inches taller than me, which is saying something. He had a kind face, a friendly one. He seemed relaxed, at ease. Not like he was planning some macho squeeze play.

"Call me Susan. And just for the record, I've been working as a behaviorist for—"

"Oh, I know, I know," he said, still shaking my hand. "I'm familiar with your work on the Wyndham case. I read your report in the American Academy Journal."

"You did?" I said, totally nonplussed.

"Absolutely. It made the rounds at Quantico. First-rate work. Thorough and innovative."

Did I say he looked like a nice guy? Obviously, he was the spawn of Satan. "We got lucky on that one."

He blew air through his lips. "There's no such thing."

"Look," I said, "I've got all the files you'll want to see. I'll clear out and let you dig in."

"I'd rather you walked me through it."

Yet another surprise. "You would?"

"Absolutely."

My eyes narrowed. "So . . . when you say

you're from the FBI, would that be the one in D.C.? In the J. Edgar Hoover Building? Or is this perhaps some kinder, gentler FBI?"

He laughed. "Let me clarify, okay? This is still a Vegas PD case. Two killings, weird as they are, aren't enough to put it on our threshold. I was just asked to help. Although with you on retainer, I'm not sure why they bothered." He flashed his smile, the sort of smile that turned George Clooney into a twenty-million-a-flick property. "Think we can work together?"

My chin rose slightly. "Possible."

Granger looked disgusted. "I'll leave you two psychos alone," he said, chuckling quietly at his own nonjoke. Nebbish.

Patrick clapped his hands together. Did I mention that his eyes were blue? Oh, man, his eyes were blue. Vivid, liquid blue. "Shall we get started?"

As it turned out, he wasn't reading anything until he had a shot of java in him. A man after my own heart. Literally, I hoped. I took him down to the kitchen. Despite his initial generosity to me and my favorable first impression, I thought it was important to set a few ground rules.

"Let's just get this straight up front," I said, passing him a Styrofoam cup filled with the brackish stuff that passed for coffee around here. "You may be the big-shot FBI behavioral specialist. That's okay, I can respect that."

He took it straight—no cream, no sugar. Brilliant. "I sense a **but** coming."

"But I know my stuff, too, even if I didn't train at Quantico. I've been working this beat for nine years and I've earned my propers."

"Understood."

"So let's skip the usual business of lording it over me because you're fed and I'm not. I've studied John Douglas's work on sexual killers, all the interviews, all the compare-and-contrast. Hell, I've read every word the man wrote."

"I was trained by John Douglas."

"And I'm not inexperienced. My work has led to the capture of twenty-seven sexual or habitual offenders."

"Excellent. I've caught forty-two, myself."

"And I am up-to-date on the new research in my field. I read the Behavioral Science Unit's annual report from cover to cover. I read last year's twice."

He smiled. "I wrote it."

I leaned back in my chair. "You're doing this to me on purpose, aren't you?"

"And loving every minute of it." The twinkle in his eye was irresistible, even though every instinct in my body told me I should resist.

"They gave you the scoop on me, didn't they?"

"I've seen your resumé, yes."

"That's not what I mean." I watched his eyes carefully.

"What do you mean?"

"I think you know."

"That your father was a cop—till he was murdered? And the case remains unsolved."

"That was a long time ago. What I'm concerned about . . ."

"The drinking?"

I nodded.

"I'm okay with that."

"Not a problem?"

"Long as you're sober when we're working, I don't figure it's any of my business."

"You aren't afraid I'll relapse and destroy the case or something? Everyone else is treating me like the Creature from the Black Lagoon."

He shrugged. "I might have a little more perspective on this than they do. I used to be hooked on heroin."

"Heroin? You?"

He spread his hands. "See? Least booze is legal."

"Heroin?"

He nodded. "But I kicked it. You will, too." He crumpled his empty cup in his fist. "Tell you what. Let's hold off on the files. Show me the crime scenes. Take me to the house where the first victim lived. We can read papers later. Make it a late night. Maybe an all-nighter."

"Sounds great." I headed toward the door.

"So," he said, stopping me. "You think we can work together?"

What could I say? I gave him my best squinty-eyed, tell-me-no-lies look. "Did you really have a heroin habit?"

He grinned a little as he led the way out. "You'll never know."

After two burials, a hanging was almost exhilarating. He had allowed himself to have fun with this one—why not? If the eyes of the world were going to be focused on his work, as it now seemed evident they were, he should make the most of it. He should see that the word was given to those with the perspicacity to understand it. And for the rest—well, at the very least, he could entertain them.

He'd almost fallen asleep waiting for the owners to shut off the power. It had been a sea of lights, a blazing neon panorama, garish and lovely all at once. And so much to choose from! What sort of message should he seek? The profound? The prophetic? The risible? Most of the older casinos had deposited signs here, as well as restaurants, hotels. Even theme parks. There were so many possibilities. . . .

In the end, the choice was obvious. Puns might be the bailiwick of the insipid humorist, but this was irresistible. A huge, towering, crane-held sign. The front proclaimed FIRE SALE. While the back read HALF OFF.

That was where he left Lenore, the biggest part of her, anyway. Hanging beneath the HALF OFF.

Such a beau geste! How would dear Susan react? he wondered. It was amazing how completely the woman had come to dominate his thoughts in so short a time. It was impossible to resist thinking about her. Somehow, knowing that there was someone out there with the potential to appreciate his work made what he did so much more thrilling. The thought of carrying on without her was intolerable. But what if she was replaced? He had read in the paper that the FBI was sending the LVPD a federal expert in the same field. What if O'Bannon decided Susan's services were no longer needed?

He couldn't let that happen. He would have to do something to prevent it.

CHAPTER THIRTEEN

Oddly enough, Granger had not arranged high-speed Internet access for me, possibly because he hadn't arranged a computer terminal for me, so I had to sneak into O'Bannon's office while he convoked his top detectives in the conference room. Once I was in, I checked out Helen Collier's Web site. She had obviously done it all herself. The signs of amateur webmastering were everywhere. The layout was functional but unadorned. A lot of hyperlinks led to nothing. But what was there was interesting.

Helen had scanned some of her own artwork, the same kind of drawings and collages I'd found stuffed in the bottom drawers of her desk. I wasn't surprised. One look at the meticulous living room was sufficient to tell me that Mrs. Collier was never going to put her daughter's art on display in the house. Not even on the refrigerator. So Helen had found another way to exhibit it. She'd kept a blog, too—a Web diary. It hadn't been updated for two months, but what she had written was fascinating. Darcy was right—she'd been creeping out at night through the bedroom window for at least a year and a half.

All the photos of Helen were distorted, maybe for security reasons, maybe just because she thought it was cool. But using my imagination, I could get a pretty good idea what she had looked like when she hit the street in that outfit. False eyelashes, black fingernails, big hoop earrings. She would definitely attract attention. Even more clearly, she had a taste for the dark side. I could see this dodgy girl talking to a stranger, particularly if he gave her some reason to trust him. I could even see her getting into his car. Making the biggest mistake of her too short life.

I should've stopped reading the blog right then and there, but of course I didn't. I kept moving backward in time until I got to an entry describing a family trip to Carlsbad Caverns. As soon as she was down in the cave, she'd freaked. Totally lost her head. Turns out that prissy mother of hers used to exact punishment by locking her in a small, dark closet and she'd been claustrophobic ever since.

So just imagine what happened when Helen found herself locked up in that coffin. No light, no air. Barely able to move. No one to hear her screams.

Small wonder her fingers were shredded, the lid of the coffin was so scarred.

I had to catch this killer. Soon.

"Seen this?"

Patrick tossed the morning paper on my desk. The double-sized headline was easy to read: KILLER INSPIRED BY POE!

I scanned the story by Jonathan Wooley, the reporter who had been covering the case. He knew about the quotes and he knew the murder methods re-created scenes from Poe's fiction. "I thought we were keeping this to ourselves."

"So did O'Bannon," Patrick informed me. "He's furious. Who do you think leaked it?"

"I have no idea. For his sake, I hope O'Bannon doesn't find out."

Patrick propped his feet up on the edge of my desk, leaning his chair back against the men's room door. It was generous of him to stay out here with me. I knew perfectly well Granger had given him a nice private office.

"I read your preliminary profile. Good, solid work."

"Thank you. I appreciate your—"

"So you won't mind, I hope, if I say we should tear it into pieces and start from scratch."

Slow burn. "You think I'm on the wrong track."

"Not at all. I just prefer to build from the ground up. I've had previous cases where I came in late and tried to operate within the parameters of preexisting profiles. It doesn't work. Even when I have full and free license to edit."

"Okay." I was not going to throw a fit. I was not going to act defensive. There would be no turf war, damn it. "Why don't you work up your own profile, then we'll compare—"

"No, no," he said, looking at me with those baby-blue eyes that could probably persuade a chimney to give up smoking. "I want us to do it together."

"Look, you don't have to humor me—"

"Not at all. You've got the experience with this case, not me. And you've got a solid background in behavioral sciences. I might be able to contribute some of the latest thoughts and theories. We'll work together."

Like I said before, almost too perfect. "Okay, where do we start? What do we know?"

"Statistically speaking," Patrick began, "our killer is most likely a white male between the ages of twenty and forty-five. Over ninety percent of all American serial killers are."

"The cops already know that. What else can we give them?"

"Let's start with preliminary classifications."

"Organized and disorganized?"

"Essentially. But that terminology has fallen out of favor. Roy Hazelwood has modified Douglas's work somewhat in this regard. He prefers to start by distinguishing between the impulsive offender and the ritualistic offender."

"I'd say our guy is ritualistic."

"Definitely. A thinking killer. Someone who has spent an enormous amount of time working out his fantasy and bringing it to life. He's not taking the easy way, or the approach that would be most likely to avoid detection. He's planning everything in accordance with some loony scheme."

"The Poe fetish."

"So it seems. Bringing those weird stories to life has become an idée fixe for our man. But what does he hope to accomplish?"

"Good question. Wish I had an equally good answer."

He sat up to let one of the sergeants pass into the bathroom. "Hazelwood has delineated the five components of the ritualistic killer: rela-

tional, paraphilic, situational, victim demographics, and self-perceptional."

"You're going to have to explain."

"Relational has to do with the relationship
between the victim and the offender—or more
accurately, what he fantasizes the relationship to
be. Girlfriend? Wife? Slave?"

"And the answer is?"

"We don't know. We need more information.
Your coroner says the victims haven't been sexually molested, at least not in the sense of pene-
tration. Our man may be a kidnapper, but he's
no lothario."

"Probably impotent."

"A distinct possibility, but we both know
there are still ways for a crazed man to inflict
sexual damage and humiliation on a helpless
woman. If we knew more about what he does
with them before he kills them, that might yield
some answers. Or if we knew how he selects
them. How he lures them in."

"Next component?"

"**Paraphilia** is the currently vogue term
for sexual deviation. Voyeurism, pedophilia,
necrophilia, transvestitism—you name it."

"You think this guy can't get it off the normal
way, so he's grabbing little girls off the street."

"I'm not saying that. This could be a twisted
form of sexual sadism. A way of asserting his
power over them. He renders them powerless

with the drug, then subjects them to some Poe-inspired horror. A form of slavery, I suppose."

"But there's no indication that he's trying to break their will. Play with their minds. Turn them into true slaves."

"Not yet, maybe. But this guy is just getting started." A grim expression crossed his face. "Let's hope we catch him before it gets to that."

"Situational?"

"That's key to understanding what our boy is up to. What's the situation he's trying to create? What setting is he trying to realize?"

"I'm not sure I follow."

"For instance, when I'm giving lectures back at Quantico, the setting I'm trying to create is a classroom. The relationship is teacher-student."

"I got you."

"Or here, for instance, with us, the setting is master-servant." His eyes sparkled. "The young protégé learns at the feet of the seasoned master."

"Is that what this is? I thought it was more like the hopeful acolyte worships at the temple of the earth goddess." Okay, maybe that was a little obvious, but he'd started it.

He cast his eyes about. "Not much of a temple."

"I'm a rose-colored-glasses girl."

He dragged the conversation back on track, darn it. "So I'm thinking the setting this guy wants to create must be a sort of torture chamber."

"Like Robert Leroy Anderson?"

He arched an eyebrow. "Very good. You are up on the literature."

"I do my best."

"So he's using Poe for inspiration but is basically serving his own sadomasochistic need to inflict pain on helpless victims."

My face scrunched. "I don't know."

"You have a different theory?"

"No. I don't know. Maybe you're right. I just sense there's something more going on here. He's had so many opportunities for cruelty, but actually there's been little evidence of it. Kidnapping and murder, yes, but—I don't know. Sadomasochistic lust just doesn't explain everything."

"Which leads us to our fourth component. Victim demographics."

"Well, they were both young girls. Teens."

"Both girls look young for their age."

"That's true. A baby-doll fetish?" I shrugged. "They came from very different backgrounds. One was solidly lower-middle-class. The other came from a super-wealthy background, daughter of a celebrity. Both appear to have been raised by their mothers."

"But did the killer know that?"

"Seems unlikely."

"So he was just going by appearance?"

I have to admit, I hadn't thought I'd like working with a partner, but I did. Bouncing ideas off someone who had the same grasp of the field was exciting, almost electric. I felt a tingling run through my body that wasn't all about serial killers, either. Good thing Patrick wasn't in any position to make advances. I would've melted like a custard. "I don't think so."

"Why not? It's the logical conclusion."

"Despite the age and gender similarity, both girls looked quite different."

"He can only choose from what's available."

"This is Vegas, Patrick. You can find any- thing you want, and plenty of it. Take a short walk down the Strip and you'll find a dozen girls who fit any possible physical description. No, he chose these victims because they fit some specific parameter—we just haven't figured out what it is yet."

"And as to the killer's self-perception?"

I pondered a moment. "That's more diffi- cult."

"He obviously likes being in control. Exert- ing power over others."

"Ye-es . . ."

"He enjoys inflicting pain on his victims."

My neck twisted. It would be easier just to agree than to try to explain my reluctance. But as always, I had to go with my feelings. "We don't know that."

"Susan, think about what he did to these two girls."

"I know. But that doesn't mean he enjoyed it."

"What other possible reason could he have for burying a woman alive? For making someone bleed to death?"

I shrugged. "This may be a rather heterodox theory, but I don't believe this guy perceives himself as an evildoer. Or even a punisher. He's communicated with us twice, but there've been no jeremiads about whores and harlots. No suggestion of guilt on the part of the victims. I get the sense that he somehow thinks what he's doing is . . . honorable. That he's acting purposefully to accomplish . . . something."

"Like what?"

"I can't imagine. You think our guy has a personality disorder?"

"Duh."

"Psychopath?"

"Actually, we don't use that term anymore."

"Oh, spare me."

"The currently preferred mental health term is antisocial personality disorder. APD for short."

"Whatever. You think that's our guy?"

"Not if you're right that he thinks he's doing

a good thing. That would be more like . . . I don't know. Schizoid personality disorder."

"Or a narcissist."

Patrick batted a finger against his lips. "That's not bad. Delusions of grandeur. Belief that he's special and his actions can't be comprehended by ordinary people. Feeling of divine entitlement."

"If I'm right, what does it tell us?"

"That he needs constant admiration. That he won't hesitate to take advantage of others in order to achieve his plan, whatever it is. That he will be indifferent to or unaware of the needs or feelings of others. Basically, the world is his stage, and the rest of us are just props at his disposal."

"How does that help us catch him?"

"Well, he'll be seeking attention. Praise, even."

"He's going to try to contact us, isn't he?"

"Almost certainly. He already has, with those coded notes that were bound to lead us to the Poe connection. But he'll do more. He'll talk to us."

"Good. That would help me understand him, what he wants. Empathize."

"With a serial killer? Is that a good idea?"

I stood up and stretched, wondering whom I'd have to sleep with to get a fresh cup of coffee. " 'Is that a good idea?' hasn't really been the touchstone question of my life."

We were well on our way to a solid and surprisingly useful profile when we were interrupted by O'Bannon's secretary, Madeline. She looked put out, probably because she'd had to walk across the station to deliver the message herself—Granger hadn't given me a phone.

"O'Bannon wants to see you. Right now."

As if she thought I might keep the man waiting for an hour or so. Maybe stroll down to the pub and have a few drinks first. Whatever—I didn't have to look at the woman to see that she had it in for me. So I obediently pushed myself off the Naugahyde and headed for O'Bannon's office. I was almost there when I was accosted by an attractive middle-aged woman with large red spectacles and a neatly tailored suit. I didn't have to look at the label to know it hadn't come off the rack. And I didn't need an introduction to know who she was.

"Are you Susan Pulaski?" she asked.

Moments like this, one has to wonder about the wisdom of the saying "Honesty is the best policy." "I am."

"I'm Fara Spencer. The mother of Annabel Spencer. She was—"

"I know who she was," I said, sparing her the explanation. "I'm sorry for your loss."

"Thanks, but that really isn't good enough. I want to catch the bastard who did this."

"We all do, ma'am."

"That's what I keep hearing, but as far as I can tell, no one is doing anything."

"I can assure you—"

"I have some serious complaints about the way this investigation is being handled."

I tried to edge past her, but she wasn't budging. "Any complaints should be directed to Lieutenant Granger. It's his case."

"My understanding is that he's essentially a supervisor. All my sources tell me that in a case such as this, a proper psychological analysis is critical to catching the killer. And that's your department, right?"

"I'm also working with—"

"So let me be blunt, Ms. Pulaski. Do you think you're up to this?"

Every joint in my body stiffened. "I've been working as a behaviorist for over—"

"I'm aware of that. I'm also aware that you were recently fired and have not been reinstated. I know about your personal problems. As well as the . . . addiction that led to your hospitalization."

"You're terribly well informed, aren't you?"

"In my business, it's essential."

"Well, in my business, it's essential to know what the hell you're talking about. We're running a first-rate investi—"

"I've had recovering alcoholics on my show, Ms. Pulaski, as well as experts in the field of substance abuse. And I know you can't just square your shoulders and be cured a week after you go into rehab."

"It was detox, not—"

"Frankly, I'm appalled to think that a critical role in the apprehension of my daughter's killer has been relegated to someone who only weeks before was suffering paranoid alcohol-infused delusions and behaving in a violent and psychopathic manner."

"We don't say **psychopathic** anymore," I told her through clenched teeth. "I'm surprised all those experts on your show haven't told you that."

"My point, Lieutenant Pulaski, if indeed it is still appropriate to refer to you as a lieutenant, is that you have no business working on this case. I want you to resign so that someone better qualified can take your place."

All right then, the gloves were off. "Ms. Spencer, this isn't some daytime TV show dispensing feel-good bullshit to bored housewives. This is reality. And the reality is, I'm good at what I do. You're not going to find a replacement who does any better."

"I find that very difficult to believe. Your judgment is clouded."

"Ma'am, don't talk to me about clouded judgment. With all due respect, I'm not the one who just lost her only daughter. In every case of this nature we have grieving parents, and they are almost always obstacles, not assistants. We put up with it because we are service-oriented professionals and we realize that dealing with the death of a loved one is difficult."

"Certainly you're a testament to that," she said dryly.

I sucked it in, showing a degree of restraint that surprised even me. "My point is, we're doing everything we can to catch the killer and we will continue to do so. If you're not going to help, get the hell out of the way!" I pushed her aside and marched on toward O'Bannon's office.

"You haven't heard the last of this," she shouted after me, confirming what I already knew all too well. "I'm not that easily brushed off."

I entered O'Bannon's office and slammed the door behind me. He was sitting at his desk, pretending to rifle through some papers, but really just marking time till I arrived.

And to my surprise, Darcy was there, too, sitting in a chair just behind him.

"Hey, Darce," I said, wiggling my fingers. "How's my main man?"

He blinked. "Did you know that coffee is the second largest trade commodity in the world market? Americans consume more coffee than the inhabitants of any other nation on earth."

"It's my fault. I skew the average." I turned my attention to the boss. "What's up, Chief?"

"How are you getting along with the Feeb?"

"Swimmingly."

"No complaints? On either side?"

"Not that I'm aware of." I looked at him. "You seem somewhat incredulous."

"I'm glad to hear you've finally learned to play well with other children."

"So what's Darcy doing here?"

O'Bannon squirmed slightly. Not physically; he was too savvy for that. But I saw it, just the same. "He . . . asked to come. He wanted to see you."

I smiled. "No new developments today, Darce. No more crime scenes."

"Nonetheless, he . . . wanted to be involved."

"Okay by me. But Granger apparently has a problem—"

"I'll speak to Granger. He's pissed at me already because of the press conference."

"We're doing a press conference? I thought you hated—"

"We don't have any choice. Do you realize how much attention this case has been getting?"

"I've seen the local papers."

"It's not just local. It's everywhere. Only thing worse than a serial killer is a serial killer during a slow news week. I guess it's to be expected—this case gets weirder and weirder every day. The press has a million questions about the Poe connection. And now we've got a beloved television celebrity involved. We're the lead story on CNN Headline News, for God's sake."

"So if the press is all over it already, why hold a conference?"

"We've got to do something. Tourism is down dramatically. People are canceling their vacations. I guess no one wants to gamble badly enough to risk being buried alive. Or bled to death."

"But unless they're young women—"

"Which is one thing we need to explain. But the main chore will be to convince everyone that we're working hard and we have substantial leads."

"We do?"

He ignored me. "I've got the Chamber of Commerce breathing down my neck, Susan. The mayor. The hotel commission. We need to put on a dog-and-pony show."

"Okay. So Granger is traumatized because he has to go before the press?"

O'Bannon's eyes drifted down to his desk. "Granger isn't doing it. You are."

"Me? But he's—"

"You know as well as I do that once those re-porters get going with Granger he'll come off looking like a doofus. He's a good cop, but quick wit isn't his specialty. Besides, what does he have to tell them? The only person who's come up with anything useful is you."

"And Darcy. But what if the press hassles me about my recent demotion to consultant status?"

"Tell them it's none of their damn business. Stick to the case."

"But—"

"Don't bother arguing. You're doing it. Un-less you'd like me to terminate that consulting agreement."

I fell silent.

"Good. The press will assemble at five. So go change your clothes and do something with your hair and get ready. If you want to bring your FBI guy, that's fine, but I want you to do the talking. We have to impress upon them the fact that the LVPD is in charge and has the in-vestigation under control."

"Great. Just great." I checked my watch. "I'd better—"

He held up a finger. "One more thing." He turned. "Darcy, can you get me some more cof-fee?" O'Bannon held out his mug. "I'd really ap-preciate it."

Darcy tilted his head. "D-D-Did you know

that Americans drink over forty million cups of coffee a year?"

"Fascinating. So refill my mug, will ya?"

Darcy left the office. And O'Bannon gave me the harshest look I'd had since I got out of detox. "Don't hurt him."

I was totally flummoxed. "What?"

"You heard me. I don't want my boy hurt."

"I wouldn't dream of hurting him. He's adorable. And I think he loves working on this case."

"What he loves is—" He stopped, shook his head.

"I'd think you'd be pleased. You know, in his own weird little way, he has a real aptitude for detective work."

"There is no way in hell Darcy could cut it as a detective. He can't even carry on a coherent conversation."

"He might need help in certain areas, but who doesn't? Lots of people can't carry on conversations. I don't know anyone who can do what Darcy does."

"How could he interview a suspect? How could he organize his thoughts and come up with a theory? Write a report? It's ridiculous."

"I think you're being too hard on him."

"I didn't just stroll into his life last week. I think I know a little something about what he can and cannot do." He muttered something under his breath. "Look, you can take him around to the crime scenes. Let him talk to the techies. Fine. But I don't want him hurt. Are we clear?"

I stood quietly at attention. "Yes, sir."

The door opened again and Darcy entered. "Here's your coffee, Dad."

O'Bannon took a deep drag, then winced. "What the hell is this? This isn't—"

"I got you decaf. Because caffeine is not good for you."

"Decaf?"

"In controlled studies conducted at Stanford University, caffeine and caffeine withdrawal were linked to headaches, nosebleeds, stomach disorders, irritability, impotence . . ."

O'Bannon pressed a hand against his forehead. "One more thing to remember about this press conference, Susan. Your psycho killer may be watching."

"Almost a certainty," I said. "So I'll be careful not to make him feel challenged, offended, maligned. No telling what he might do if that happened."

He was disturbed.

He had done everything according to plan. He had sacrificed the offerings. He had followed the directions in the prophet's work. But the Golden Age had not come. Ginny had not been returned to him.

Was it possible he was wrong?

It must simply be delayed. A transformation of this magnitude cannot come about overnight. This would give him more time to get the word out. The media coverage had exceeded his most fevered imaginings. It seemed he was everywhere, or his work was—on newspapers and magazines, on the television, on street corners and newsstands and even the giant electronic billboard on the MGM Grand. A condign response to actions of this boldness, of this import. His great commission had been to spread the good news, to tell those who would hear of the coming of Dream-Land. He'd become a sensation.

Such success could only presage greatness. Such acceptance could only validate the rightness of his path. With this degree of exposure, he could be assured that any receptive ears would hear the message. Not everyone would understand it, of course. Some would write it off as just another news story. Another pathetic wretch trying to get his fifteen minutes. But the enlightened would see more. The prophet had known his message would not be heard by everyone: **To the few who love me and whom I love—To those who feel rather than to those who think—To the dreamers and those**

**who put their faith in dreams as the only re-
alities—I offer this Book of Truths. . . .**

On the television, a popular talk show host was interviewing an English professor about how Poe's dark and nihilistic visions might inspire an unbalanced personality. The professor appeared delighted to be consulted. Not surprising, in this age in which colleges push professors to become media consultants as much as they push them to publish. An expert in American literature probably receives few calls from the six o'clock news.

"Tell me the truth," the host said, leaning forward in her swiveling chair. "This Poe stuff is mostly for kids, isn't it?"

"Not at all," the man replied, straightening the cuff on his tweed jacket. "Poe was an important figure in American literature—indeed, in world literature. He invented, or at least defined, the modern short story as a literary form. He invented detective fiction, wrote the first true science fiction story. He invented symbolist poetry and the New Criticism, which would be fully realized only half a century later, during the Modernist era. He may not be America's greatest writer, but I would be hard pressed to identify one whose contributions were more widespread. Poe had a huge impact on many great writers. Oscar Wilde. Jules Verne. Thomas Pynchon. Nabokov. Poe has fallen out of favor with my academic colleagues at this time, who tend to favor Faulkner as the chief figure in American literature. But Poe's influence has been vastly greater."

"But Dr. Watson . . . Poe may have been a good writer, but wasn't he kind of a freak?"

"Much of the Poe persona as we know it today was the creation of his literary executor, Rufus Griswold, who was jealous of Poe's work and sought to destroy his reputation. He began this stereotype of Poe as a dark, cruel, nasty, abusive alcoholic. In fact, most accounts from contemporaries who knew Poe describe him as charming, witty, intelligent, generous, courteous, even chivalric. Women adored him; toward the end of his life he was seeing several wealthy socialites at once. He had lived in the North, the South, and even England, but always considered himself a southern gentlemen and behaved accordingly. Except when he was drinking, of course."

"But those stories he wrote—that's really twisted stuff. Burying people alive—"

"Premature burial was a widespread and much discussed phobia in the nineteenth century. Not just with Poe. There had purportedly been a true incident that got great play in the papers. People began buying coffins with escape hatches that could be activated from the interior

or that had a bell the interred could ring if consciousness returned."

"Okay, and how about that teeth-pulling
business?"

The professor held up his hands. "Make no
mistake about it—Poe wrote some strange tales.
His imagination was given to the macabre and
sensationalistic. But he was trailblazing—writing a kind of story that had never been attempted before. And to some extent, all of his
work is united by his strange belief system. Poe
believed that there was another world, a better
one, that we saw glimpses of when we dreamed.
Poe even believed it was possible . . ."

He switched channels to the press conference, which was late in starting. No doubt they
had woodshedded Susan, drilling her on what
could and could not be revealed. With so many
eyes watching, they must be concerned about
her somewhat mercurial temperament. Either
that or they were pouring coffee down her gul-
let, sobering her up, poor thing.

How interesting that she should share the
prophet's infirmity. Remarkable—or a sign of
shared destiny?

At last, Susan approached the podium, looking elegant in a sleek blue jacket and white
slacks. In the background, he spotted Lieutenant Granger and that new companion, the

one who looked as if he barely knew where he was. Susan adjusted the microphone and began.

"My name is Susan Pulaski. I'm a behavioral expert and consultant to Lieutenant Barry Granger and the Vegas PD. I have a prepared statement, and then I'll be able to answer some questions.

"Let me make one point up front. Our investigation into these murders is ongoing. All available resources have been assigned to this case, and we are also working in consultation with federal authorities and various experts in the fields of serial crime and sexual deviancy."

He raised an eyebrow. Sexual deviancy? He had never touched any of these girls in that way. Surely she must know that.

"All our available manpower and then some is working around the clock to bring this killer to justice. While we are not prepared to make an arrest at this time, we have several very promising leads. We are working closely with a top FBI profiler and we hope to be in a position to make an arrest soon."

A bit of bravado? he wondered. Probably fed to her by O'Bannon, necessary to keep the press at bay. But unwise. He had no intention of being apprehended.

"This is what we know for certain. The first victim, as I believe most of you already are aware, has been identified as Helen Collier. She died of asphyxiation after being buried in a mock coffin at the Transylvania hotel. The second victim was Annabel Spencer, a mathematics student from MIT, apparently a weekend visitor who had been gambling at some of the local casinos. She died from acute blood loss. Her body was hidden in an abandoned aircraft stowed on a back lot at McCarran International. We have one possible eyewitness and a host of physical evidence."

Hands shot up, but Susan ignored them, continuing with her statement.

"It is true, as has been speculated in the press, that the killer obtains inspiration from the works of nineteenth-century American writer Edgar Allan Poe. Both bodies were left with cryptic messages drawn from the works of Poe. The murders appear to be reenactments of scenes from Poe. While this is colorful and good for headlines, it is not particularly helpful in tracking the killer, nor is it unprecedented. Past serial offenders have been known to derive inspiration from the zodiac, old movies, **The Catcher in the Rye,** even Beatles songs. What is important is that we focus not on the superficial trappings but on the personality that lies beneath it. Understanding that personality, we believe, is the key to preventing future crimes."

She folded her notes and looked out into the crowd. "I can take a few questions now."

Again, the hands flew upward. Susan scanned the gallery. She's looking for something, he realized, but what? A familiar face? A friend somewhere in the valley of the vultures?

She pointed.

"Lieutenant Pulaski, do you have a description of the killer?"

"I'm not prepared to provide that information at this time."

"Does that mean you don't? Because if you do—"

"I'm not prepared to provide that information at this time."

He supposed she was hesitant to reveal the description he gave her when he was disguised as Ethan. Very smart, Susan. He hadn't given her enough detail to make it possible for anyone to find the killer (even were it accurate). Revealing it now only risked potential embarrassment if (when) it turned out to be wrong.

"Do you have a psychological profile of the killer?"

"We are developing and refining our profile every hour of every day. I am not authorized to provide details of the current profile to you."

An anorexic reporter in the front row cut in. "You know, Lieutenant Pulaski, that will lead some to speculate that you have no valid profile."

Such thinly disguised calumny. Susan was

doing a good job of masking her reaction, but he felt it, all the same. "I can assure you, ma'am, that my colleagues and I are more than able to perform our jobs, and as I mentioned, we have been working in consultation with federal specialists. But we do not feel it would be advantageous to reveal everything we know about the killer at this time." She apparently couldn't resist adding, "Use your brain. It isn't hard to figure out why."

"What's his motive?" someone else asked.

"We can only speculate. Certainly we do not believe there is any rational motive, such as greed or jealousy. Given the vagaries and inconstancies of the psychotic mind, determining what delusion motivates him can be extremely difficult."

He felt a flash of anger—**psychotic?**—then checked it. No, he told himself, don't blame her. She doesn't understand, not yet. She couldn't possibly know.

A handsome middle-aged man with a salt-and-pepper goatee spoke up. "Jonathan Wooley, **Vegas Courier.**"

He inched forward. Wooley had written all the best pieces he had pasted into his History.

"Ms. Pulaski, I respect that you don't want to reveal everything you know—you don't want to force the killer to change his MO, and you probably need some undisclosed details to distinguish crank informants from people with actual knowledge. But surely you can understand our position. Basically we're asking: are we safe?"

"The LVPD is taking all possible steps to ensure—"

"Pardon me, but you weren't able to stop the previous killings and you've given us no reason to believe you can prevent any future ones. Are the citizens of Las Vegas safe?"

He noticed that Susan's fingers tightened, almost imperceptibly, on the lectern. He knew what she was thinking. She wanted a drink.

"The LVPD is advising citizens to take extreme caution until the assailant is apprehended, particularly young women who are—or look— ages fourteen to twenty."

"Should we close the casinos? Are the discos safe? How can people protect themselves?"

The hesitation in her voice—first time yet— told him this was something that had been discussed before the conference. He suspected that she favored telling people to lock themselves in their homes and shutting down the whole city. But of course the powers that be would never permit that.

"We have to keep our heads on straight and not let fear get the best of us. For the most part, people should proceed with their normal lives. But they should exercise extreme caution, particularly those in the target gender and age group. Don't travel alone. Have someone walk you to your car. Don't speak to strangers. And most especially, don't get in a car—or truck—with someone you don't know."

"But how can we know what situations create jeopardy, when we know so little about the killer?" This Wooley was relentless. He supposed that was why the man was a successful reporter, but it was beginning to wear a bit thin. "Are his victims chosen at random?"

"I've said all I have to say on the matter," Susan replied firmly. "Now if there's nothing more, I—"

"Perhaps you wouldn't mind answering this question, Lieutenant Pulaski. That is, **former** Lieutenant Pulaski." A camera pivot revealed a woman barreling her way through the heart of the assembled press corps. "Are you qualified to work on this investigation?"

He edged toward the television. It was that woman, the TV host. Annabel's mother.

Susan cleared her throat. "Mrs. Spencer, as I think you know, Lieutenant Granger is in charge of the investigation. I'm only consulting on—"

"You're the behavioral expert. The only one on the force."

"Actually, I'm working with a representative from the FBI who—"

"But so far, you haven't come up with any-thing. My daughter's killer is still at large. And I am outraged."

The reporters drank up this unexpected bit of conflict. Pens scribbled madly. The minicams shifted their gaze from the podium to the ag-grieved mother.

"Mrs. Spencer, everyone at the LVPD is sorry for your loss—"

"But not sorry enough to do anything about it, apparently. Why hasn't this man been caught? Why aren't you doing more?"

Solipsistic firebrand. Quarrelsome quidnunc. She had no right to embarrass Susan in public. She was just trying to steal the limelight, the glory hound. Everything Annabel had said about her was true. She was unworthy, as was this behavior. She'd be better served to consider how her daughter could be with child and in Las Vegas without her knowing about it.

"Again, let me make it clear that everyone is doing their best—"

"But that's not good enough, is it?" The mother stepped up on the raised platform. "I am publicly calling here and now for a clean sweep of the LVPD team and full federal as-sumption of this investigation."

"That isn't even constitutional and it wouldn't—"

"Talk is meaningless. We're looking for a deranged killer, a psychopath. We're not going to catch him with these Deputy Fife officers."

Susan's cheeks burned. "I can assure you, ma'am—"

"In the meantime, I'm demanding the immediate removal of several LVPD personnel who have done nothing but obstruct reasoned efforts to bring this fiend into custody. Beginning with Robert O'Bannon."

"That's uncalled for. Chief O'Bannon has years of—"

"His conduct has been grossly negligent."

"He knows more about police work than you could learn in—"

"He hired a drunk to work on my daughter's case!"

The harsh words sliced through the press conference like a laser. Susan took a step back, almost staggered.

"I guess you didn't cover that in your opening statement, did you, Ms. Pulaski? Perhaps you'd like to explain why you are no longer a member of the LVPD. Why your employment was terminated. Perhaps you'd like to explain where you were residing only ten days ago or why you have a bandage on your wrist."

Susan's teeth were tightly clenched. "This conference is over."

"I'm calling a press conference of my own!" the mother all but shouted. "I want some action! And I'm willing to put up my own money to see that it happens."

"I don't need this," Susan said, folding up her materials.

The mother grabbed her arm. "I want my daughter's killer found!"

Susan pushed her away. "We all do, ma'am." She left the stage, and the live feed gave way to background commentators rattling about the "surprising and dramatic turn of events" at the press conference. Although they didn't come right out and say they agreed with the mother, they were quick to note that she was not the only one who had criticized the way this investigation was being handled. They couldn't resist adding that there were many unanswered questions about Susan Pulaski's involvement, suggesting that they had known all along about her alcohol addiction and time in detox which, of course, none of the lazy mouthpieces had.

He shut off the television in disgust. His anger at that hideous woman and the ignorant press was intense, but not so intense as the sorrow he felt for his poor damaged Susan. She must be devastated. She would try to act tough, as if it didn't bother her. But it would. It would eat away at her like an earwig burrowing through her brain. And before the day was done, she would drink.

The department would be all over her, pressuring her, just as they would now be pressured to terminate her. His resolve was redoubled: he had to give her something. Something to make her indispensable to the investigation.

That contemptible Spencer woman—how he loathed her. She was projecting, of course. Annabel had said she was a wretched, inattentive mother. No doubt she was trying to sublimate her guilt by lashing out at others. She had slandered him and, more importantly, his Susan. If it happened again, he would be forced to take action. For Susan's sake. And that of the world to come.

I don't like that one with the frozen hair and the painted face and the big glasses and the guitar calluses on her left-hand fingers. I didn't like it when that one was mean to Susan there was no reason she should not be mean and that's what they taught me in Sunday school didn't she ever go to Sunday school that one was mean I'm sorry she lost her little girl but maybe if she'd been watching she wouldn't have lost her and it isn't Susan's fault. She was mean to Susan and said lots of loud things I didn't understand and she smelled bad too like something out of one of those bottles at J. C. Penney's where the lady is always asking if you want a sample and I don't I don't I hate those smells get those smells away from me and I screamed and knocked over her tray and my dad was so mad at me and she smelled just like that. I didn't think my dad would let me come to his office today but he did and he said I could come again if I wanted to if I didn't get in Susan's way because Susan has problems and he doesn't want me to make them worse like I would. **The world is full of obvious things which nobody by any chance ever observes.** I got to see Susan and I know she likes coffee even though it's bad for you so I read up everything about coffee so I could tell her and I think maybe it made her happy but I saw her talk to those camera people and saw the glasses lady be so mean and for no reason. Bad lady! I bet she likes spiders and I bet she has a dog.

She shouldn't have been mean to Susan. No one should ever be mean to Susan. I want her to be happy. I want to have her babies.

I turned on the water, stepped into the shower fully clothed, and screamed. Screamed like a banshee, an elemental force of nature. Everything that had been pent up inside me I tried to release in one piercing blast. All my anger at the lawyers, at the people who took Rachel from me. At Dr. Coutant. At O'Bannon. And most of all at that obscene television gorgon Fara Spencer.

And David. David, David, David. I shouted and shouted until my throat hurt.

It wasn't enough. It was still with me. It would always be with me.

What had that hideous bitch thought she was doing? As if nothing mattered but her own self-centered quest for vengeance? Normally, I was scrupulously considerate of the feelings of the bereaved, however their actions might complicate my work. But this woman had crossed the boundaries. She was using her celebrity status to interfere with the detective work. Worse, she was threatening my job. I knew that O'Bannon would be under all kinds of pressure to cut me loose. It would be the easiest thing to do, especially now that he had a federal behaviorist working on the case. And if I lost this job, my chances of getting Rachel back were less than zero.

I stumbled out of the shower, dripping water all over the floor. I didn't know what I should do. I didn't know what I could do. I dreaded going back to work tomorrow, knowing what everyone would be saying, or at least whispering. Knowing it was just a matter of time before the word was given. Before I was pink-slipped into oblivion.

I tore through the sacks in the kitchen, all the shopping I had done on my way home from the office. I thought about calling Patrick—after the conference, he had more than hinted that he would be available if I wanted to get together tonight. But I couldn't, not now, not on these terms. Not when I was so goddamned vulnerable. There was only one thing I could do under these circumstances.

I had swallowed half the bottle before I came up for air. After that, I don't remember much of anything.

CHAPTER FOURTEEN

I skulked into the office feeling like death on a plate, wondering if they could tell. If they would suspect. Everyone always suspects the worst, don't they? At least about me they do.

I had not gone by the O'Bannons' to pick up Darcy this morning—for a reason—so I was surprised to see him sitting beside my desk.

"Morning, Darce," I said.

He scrunched his face up. "You smell funny."

"I do?" I had showered, groomed, perfumed, brushed my teeth about six times, and consumed Altoids as if they were a breakfast food. "Must be my perfume."

"Chanel No. 5?"

I stared at him. "That's right. How did you—"

"One of the ladies at my day care wears Chanel No. 5. Till she stopped 'cause they use animals to test stuff."

"I see," I said, amazed. We were a good five feet apart. "You like it?"

He shook his head. "Stinky."

I laughed.

"I like the normal way you smell better."

"Okay. I'll lay off the Chanel."

He didn't say anything.

"Because that explains why you thought I smelled bad."

He fidgeted with a lock of hair curled behind his ear. "Did you know that a bottle of vodka contains more sugar than a Giant-Size Snickers?"

I slid behind my desk.

"That's fascinating, Darcy. Did you get that from one of your almanacs?"

He shook his head. **"Hollywood Squares."**

I was relieved to see a kid from the mail room loping up to my desk with a small package. "We found this on the front counter. It's addressed to you. Someone must've dropped it off when no one was looking."

I took one of the end flaps and started to tear it open.

"I don't think that's wise." Patrick appeared

at the top of the stairs. "It could be dangerous. I'll call for a fluoroscope."

"What, like it might be a bomb? Nah."

"You can't be sure."

"Well, I've read two-thirds of the way through the complete stories and poems of Edgar Allan Poe, and I've yet to encounter anyone being blown to smithereens."

"Susan, you know the proper procedure as well as I do. Let's call the bomb squad and—"

"He doesn't want to kill me. He wants to impress me." Once I had the wrapping off, I closed my eyes and opened the box.

Nothing happened.

I peeked into the box. My lips parted.

I guess my shock registered, because Patrick immediately said, "You know, we can't be sure this came from the killer. A case that garners as much publicity as this one is bound to generate copycats. This could be from some crank or would-be martyr or—"

I pursed my lips. "No. This is from the guy."

"How can you be sure?"

I tilted the box toward him. And thirty-two blood-caked teeth slid into view.

It took us a few minutes to notice, but there was a note in the box, too, taped inside the lid.

I put on some plastic gloves and carefully un-folded it.

The same old code, or another one like it. But it appeared to be longer than the previous messages. "Darcy?"

I showed him the note. It was fascinating to watch him go into action, his head tilting, his eyes slightly contracting. "Is it the same cipher?"

"No," he said quietly. He continued staring at the paper. "This is a toughie."

I suppose the killer realized, since we'd made the Poe connection, that we had broken his code. So he provided a new and even more in-sidious one. "Look, Darcy, it isn't fair to put you on the spot like this. I'll call my friend Colin—"

"No." He seemed bothered. I don't know if he was offended or just determined. As always, he was hard to read. But I let him work.

It was a full five minutes before he spoke again. " 'Misery is manifold. The wretchedness of earth is multiform.' "

"I remember that," I said. "It's from one of the stories."

Darcy nodded. " 'Berenice,' " he said, pro-nouncing the c as if it were English, not like the Italian ch sound. How would he know? "The first line."

The first line. Something we would be sure to identify. He was making it easy for us. "That's the story where the psycho yanks the girl's teeth. We already knew about that. I was hoping for something—"

Darcy interrupted. "There's more."

Patrick and I huddled around him, as if we might be the slightest help.

"It's hard," Darcy said quietly. "This one has five different symbols for each letter, but some of the letters don't appear five times in the entire message." As far as I was concerned, that made the whole thing impossible, but not a minute later Darcy read us the remainder: " 'I hope you like my present, Susan.' "

"Susan?" I said, eyes wide. "It says that? He calls me by name?"

He nodded, then continued: " 'There will be more messages. But only for you.' " He looked up. "And I guess the rest of it is numbers."

"Numbers?"

"Seven of them."

"A phone number. Can you read it? Did he give us a number where we could contact him?"

Darcy's head twitched. "Do you think the bad man lives with you?"

"What? What are you talking about?"

Darcy looked at me with sad eyes. "It's your phone number."

Thank God I'd hidden the booze before I left the apartment that morning, because when I returned, it was with an entourage of twelve cops of various types, not to mention Darcy. While the trace team set up some extensions and all their recording equipment, I scurried around picking my underwear up off the floor and other such essential housecleaning chores.

Patrick had come, too, and I have to admit it gave me a bit of a charge, having him there, in the very place where I sleep and all. I made a resolution—as soon as all these interlopers cleared out of my apartment, I was going to insist that he go out with me. Shameless, I know, but let's face it—I'm a squeaky wheel.

And I didn't want to spend another night alone. Not if I could help it.

"We've added two extensions," Tony Crenshaw explained, "so we can listen in and make a recording. We've also added an open line to Bell's electronic switching center—ESS—and to humor Agent Chaffee, a hotline to the FBI's communications room."

"Sounds good," I said. "How long does it take to make a trace these days?"

"Not as long as you might think. Depends on how the call arrives, but if it comes on all-electronic switches—and if it's a local call from a residence, it will—we should have it in a minute."

"So I have to keep him rambling for sixty seconds."

"Not even. We've got a tone generator connected to your line. As soon as he calls, we'll pick up and start tracing—but the tone generator will make a false ringing noise and fake him into believing you haven't answered. We'll cut it after four rings—otherwise he might hang up."

"So that leaves me with, what? Fifty seconds of talk?"

"We could have someone else answer. Try to put him on hold."

I shook my head. "He won't buy it. He may be crazy, but he's also smart."

"Fine. After the fourth ring, click the interrupt button quickly to simulate the sound of the phone picking up. Then start talking."

"Don't seem too eager to chat," Patrick said. "He'll get suspicious."

I agreed. "I think I can keep him talking. He's concocted this brilliant scheme—in his eyes—but has no one to appreciate it. He wants me to be his audience. Who better to appreciate what you've done than the police officer who's trying to catch you? He wants my admiration." I gave Patrick a sly smile. "But I'll make him work for it."

Darcy sidled up beside me. "I think sometimes people's voices on the phone sound scary. Do you think sometimes people's voices on the phone sound scary?"

I patted his shoulder reassuringly. "I can handle it."

His father cut in. "Darcy, why don't you catch the bus home? Susan is very busy right now."

Darcy frowned, then started stuttering again. "I—I—I would rather stay with Susan, I think. If—if—if—" He swallowed. "If you get scared, Susan, I'll talk to him for you."

My eyes got strangely itchy. "Thanks, Darce. Appreciate it." Which I did, especially given how scared he was of the voice on the other end of the line.

After that, we sat around and stared at the phone. We had no idea when he might call. I wished I'd bought the latest **Cosmo** or something. My new apartment was distinctly short on reading materials, other than that Collected Poe. All my books were still packed up in boxes. It occurred to me that Darcy could probably recite any number of books to me from memory, but I declined to ask.

"Remember this," Patrick said, "next time you're asked to talk about the glamorous and exciting world of law enforcement."

I laughed. "When I finally lose the rest of these chumps," I said, "wanna go out and get—" I checked myself. "A sandwich?"

He beamed back a smile filled with potential. "I'd like that."

"It's a date," I said, just in case there was any doubt about the direction I was heading. Before I could elaborate, the phone rang.

We all stared at each other. This was it. This was really it.

The machine picked up the line and the tone generator kicked in. I patiently waited for four rings. Crenshaw gave me the signal. Then I clicked the interrupt, took a deep breath, and spoke.

"Hello. Susan speaking."

"Hey, Suze. Whatcha been up to?"

Breath poured out of me like a deflated balloon. It was Lisa.

"Haven't seen you today."

"Well . . . I've been busy. O'Bannon is working me like a plantation owner."

"Want me to come over?"

"I do, but the problem is—" I glanced at O'Bannon. He gave me the okay. "I'm currently surrounded by about a dozen police officers."

"What? What's going on?"

"I can't go into it now. How about I meet you for breakfast tomorrow? Krispy Kremes sound good?"

"I could live with that. Eight too early?"

"See you then." I hung up the phone and stared out into a sea of irritated faces. "Well, forgive me for having friends."

And then we all sat down to wait some more.

———

After another hour or so, Patrick excused himself so he could review the security detail. I felt like I was probably safe at the moment, since I was surrounded by half the Vegas police force, but whatever. Maybe he just wanted to stretch his legs.

I killed time by showing Darcy the two card tricks I had learned in Brownies about twenty-five years ago. The problem was, he could always see how it was done. In fact, after watching it once, he could duplicate the trick himself.

"Hey, Chief," I said, "did you know you have a potential cardsharp on your hands? I could see him running a three-card monte operation on the Strip."

O'Bannon grunted.

We were all having a perfectly merry time—when the phone rang. Tone generator, four rings, and then I was on.

"Hello. Susan speaking."

"Did you enjoy my gift?"

I closed my eyes and tried to focus. Friendly, but not too eager. Don't challenge him. "It got my attention. I think the forensic lab will probably have more fun with it than I did."

"They won't learn anything."

"You never know."

"What are you doing, Susan? You're not falling back into bad habits, are you?"

What the hell was that supposed to mean? "Just spending a quiet evening at home."

He chuckled. Actually chuckled. "I rather doubt that."

"So what are you up to, anyway? Why are you doing this?"

"I can't tell you. You're not ready."

"Aw, please. Fill me in. So I can appreciate what you're doing."

"You're very clever, Susan. If you open your mind, you will find the truth. I only have time to tell you this: you would look beautiful in neon." And then the phone went dead.

I checked my watch. Thirty seconds, tops.

I looked at Crenshaw. He was on one of the extensions, talking to the switching center. "Did we get a fix?"

After a few moments, he put down the phone. "No."

Granger pounded a fist into his palm. "Nothing at all?"

"It's local. We're sure of that. But we don't know where he is." He looked at me sadly. "I think we should leave the recorder on and the equipment in place. In case he calls again."

"Sure," I said. "But he won't. He's already accomplished what he wanted."

"We'll get that tape recording to the sound lab. See what they can tell us."

"And then?" Patrick asked.

"Then," I said, "we have to figure out what he meant by that gibberish about the truth. And that crack about me looking good in neon."

"It was just bullshit," Granger said. "He was flirting with you."

"Maybe, but I don't think so."

"Then what?" O'Bannon asked.

Good question. I fell back against my sofa and thought a good long while before answering. "It was a clue. To whatever he wants us to find next."

This was a new experience for me. Being at a bar—The White Feather—but not ordering a drink. It was almost as seedy as Gordy's, but it was near my apartment, and they served sandwiches as well as libations.

The three of us found a table—Darcy tagged along—and I ordered a club soda. Patrick relaxed as soon as I placed my nonalcoholic drink order. Maybe Darcy did, too. I felt proud of myself. I'd passed the test.

And periodically, as needed, I excused myself to powder my nose. And safe within the confines of a stall with the door closed, I took a deep swig from the flask tucked inside my jacket. Crunched a few Altoids and I was back in action.

As I passed by the bar on my way back to our table, this guy leaned backward from his bar stool and blocked my path. He was big and black and had a shaved head. He couldn't have exuded more testosterone if he'd poured a bottle of it over his head.

"What you doin' in a dive like this, Susan?"

I gave him a look. I knew him from somewhere . . . the courtroom, that was it. He was a bail bondsman. He'd made a few passes at me through the years; I'd never given him the time of day. I thought his name was Jake, but I wasn't sure enough to give it a try. "Just drinking in the atmosphere."

"I think you came lookin' for me."

"Do you now?"

"Yeah. Me, or somebody like me." He had a laconic, deliberate way of speaking that set my teeth on edge.

"Well, you're wrong. I'm with someone. Two someones, actually."

"You sure about that?"

"Yeah, positive."

He gave me a look I didn't like at all. "You change your mind, you come back and see me, okay? I'll give you what you want. I'll make you feel alive."

Jesus Christ, some guys. I pushed past him and returned to my seat.

"You've changed your perfume," Darcy said upon my return.

Was he talking about Chanel No. 5 again? Or did he know what I'd been doing in the ladies' room? The kid was a damn bloodhound. "Yeah. I prefer something smokier when I'm out at night."

"What do you think he meant?" Patrick asked. He was nursing black coffee, but oddly enough Darcy hadn't given him the lecture on the evils of caffeine. "That crack about neon."

I waved my hand, smiling, my eyebrows arched provocatively, leaning forward. I didn't want to be obvious, but I was feeling pretty bold. Maybe it was the Jack Daniel's coursing through my system. "I don't want to talk about business tonight."

"Neon is an inert gas," Darcy informed us. "It's odorless, colorless, tasteless, nontoxic, and monatomic. In a vacuum tube, neon glows reddish orange. Its chemical symbol is Ne. Its atomic number is ten."

"Fascinating," I said, fluttering my eyelashes, still gazing at Patrick. "But like I said, I don't want to talk about work."

Darcy grew quieter. "I was trying to be

useful. It's the most important thing in life. To be useful."

"That's a lovely sentiment."

"John Adams, the second president of the United States, said that in 1814 to his—"

"Darcy . . ." I sighed. "It's late. I appreciate you seeing me here, but this might be a good time for you to head home."

"Are you also going home? I'm sure the police officers have left."

I ignored him. "I'll be along. But you should go now. I'll pick you up early tomorrow morning. We'll see what we can get out of that phone call. Till then—get some rest."

"I never sleep more than four hours a night. Some nights my dad turns out all the lights and I just stare at the clock for hours."

"Darcy—" I tried to smile. "There's a bus stop at the corner. Just turn left outside the door. You can ride it all the way home without changing."

He stood, looking uneasy, fidgeting with his hands. "Do you think that you will be all right?"

Adorable. I was amazed at how much affection I felt for him, after knowing him only a short while. But I wasn't going to get laid with him around. "I can take care of myself, Darcy. Good night."

" 'Night." He stumbled out of the bar, glancing back at me over his shoulder.

"Cute kid, huh?" Patrick said, sipping his coffee. "And what a memory."

"Yeah. Incredible." I leaned forward. Had I remembered to unbutton the top button of my shirt? "I don't want to talk about him, either."

"Indeed. What do you want to talk about?"

I leaned in even closer. "Come to think of it, I don't really want to talk at all."

"I'm astonished." My God, but he was sexy up close. Or far away. Or with a paper bag over his head. "I was told you were very aggressive."

"Me? I'm a pushover. Try me." Just another inch, and my lips were planted firmly on his. They tasted sweet. I'd almost forgotten. He put his hand at the base of my neck and sent tingles radiating up and down my spine. This was going to be good. I knew this was going to be good.

"What do you want?" he whispered to me.

"I want to feel . . . something different," I said, peering into his beautiful blues. "I want to feel like I'm really alive. Not just going through the motions." Enough with the damn talking. I pressed my lips against his and we didn't come up for air for a good long while. I didn't care who saw or what they thought. I needed this. I needed this.

"Come home with me," I said finally. "Or I'll go with you. Whatever's closer. What'd'ya say?"

He looked at me a long moment. His expression alone was sufficient to convey everything I needed to know. Everything I didn't want to hear. "No, I can't."

"But—I thought you felt like—"

"I do."

"Then come on." I snaked my hand between his legs and gave him a squeeze in a strategically chosen area. "I'll make it worth your while. It'll be great. Promise."

"I know it would," he said, pushing my hand away. "But you'd hate me in the morning."

"Don't be dumb. I—"

"You would. You'd be embarrassed and ashamed and regretful. We wouldn't be able to work together anymore."

"Are you saying—we can't ever—"

"No. I'm just saying it's too soon." He stood. "I think it's best if I go."

"Please—"

He took my hand. "You'll be glad. Later."

"I doubt it."

"You will." He let my hand fall and left.

Way to go, Susan, I told myself bitterly. Chased him right out of the bar. Came on too damn strong, just like always, and bulldozed him right out of the ballpark.

I needed a drink, and I wasn't talking about club-fucking-soda, either. I made my way to the little girls' room again and raised the flask. It burned good, going down. After a swallow of that, I felt much better about myself. What the hell—I knew I was going to drink it all eventually. I pressed the bottle to my lips—almost as tasty as Patrick was—and emptied the flask.

I left the restroom feeling stronger, complimenting myself on handling it and not losing the knack and walking and talking as if I really were only drinking club soda. I had about decided to give up on the place and go home when I saw a man's leg blocking my path.

"Can I buy you a drink now, Susan?"

It was that same guy, Jake or whatever, the shaved head. "I don't drink anymore."

"Fine. You figure out what you want yet?"

"I . . ." I looked at him through blurred eyes. "I want to feel something different. Alive."

"I can handle that."

He threw some bills on the bar, took me by the hand.

"We can't go to my place," I said. "Is your place near?"

"Not near enough." He led me down an alleyway behind the bar. It was dark, but not so dark I couldn't see it was filthy. Nothing but dirt and slime and upended trash cans. "This'll do."

He whipped me around and grabbed my

hands. "You ready to feel somethin' different?" He didn't wait for me to answer. He ripped my jacket open, sending the empty flask smashing onto the pavement. With unrestrained brutality, he pulled down my pants and panties, then sat me down on one of the trash cans.

"I'm thinkin' a little back door action might do the trick," he said while he unzipped. "That work for you?"

I didn't say anything.

With one powerful move, he pushed me to my knees, then swung me around until I was spread stomach down across the trash can. No talk, no warning, no foreplay.

"Ahhh—!"

It was my first time and the pain was searing. I wondered if he had done this before, used the same lines, gotten what he wanted the same way. I wondered where he came from, what he really liked, what he saw when he looked into my eyes. I didn't think he was heartless or even particularly selfish. He just had needs, like we all did. When it was over and he woke up the next day, he might feel a little guilty about it.

But I wouldn't, and I wouldn't care if he did. I needed to feel something. Pain. Humiliation. Rage. It was all the same. I just wanted to feel alive again.

CHAPTER FIFTEEN

The next morning, I hurt like hell. My head throbbed, sure, always, but that wasn't the worst of it. I could barely walk. Somehow I managed to stumble out of bed and make it to the front door before the bell had rung more than, oh, fifty times or so.

"Susan. My God, what happened to you? We were supposed to have breakfast, remember?"

Lisa. "I, uh, slept in. I had kind of a rough night."

She rushed in, putting her arms around me. "You look like someone beat the hell out of you."

"No, no, just trouble sleeping."

She stiffened slightly. "Susan, I'm sorry. I

know I'm not your mother, but the counselors told me that the best way to be your friend was to try to help you keep your promises. Have you been drinking?"

"What? Are you kidding? No."

"Really?"

" 'Course. You called last night." Thank God I could remember that much. "I was home, remember?"

"But—"

"Wanna smell my breath?" What a bluffer I am.

"Frankly, no." She guided us both to the sofa in the living room. It was green and faded and showed traces of all the cop butts that had been on it the night before. "I got enough of that last night."

"The new guy?"

"Oh, yeah."

"Memorable?"

"Human Dental Pik. Tongued every incisor in my mouth. Thought he was attempting a root canal. Do you still want to see Rachel?"

"Right. Damn." I brushed my straggly, stinky hair out of my eyes. "I forgot."

"How long has it been since you've seen her?"

"Well, uh . . ."

"When I talked to her last night, she said you hadn't been in for several days."

"Well, she should know."

"Susan, this is exactly the kind of behavior that caused you to lose her in the first place."

"Look, Lisa, I had a horrible night. That killer, the Poe guy, he called me. Here."

Her eyes ballooned. "He called **you**? Why?"

"Hard to say. I think he was threatening me. Or trying to help me. Or none of the above."

"Oh, my God." She cradled my stinky head in her hands. "No wonder you're a wreck."

So here I was, using a serial killer to excuse my erratic behavior. I felt pathetic.

"That explains why you were so weird when I called. What did he say?"

"Well, I think he may have given us some clues."

"My God, Susan. Should you be working on this case? He knows who you are."

"True."

"I don't think this is good for you at all. Especially not now. You need out."

"I need work."

"I'm talking to your doctor."

"Don't you dare."

"Susan, it's for your own good. I'm just trying to help."

My blood burned. "I don't need help!"

"You do." Despite my nastiness, she hugged me all the tighter. "I love you, Susan. I'm not going to let you kill yourself. I'm not."

"May I come in?"

We had left the front door ajar, and Darcy was standing just outside, peeking through. Lisa still had her arms around me, and I could see he was confused. "Is that one your girlfriend?" Darcy asked.

I cleared my throat. "Well, yes . . ."

"Did you know that four percent of all women prefer other women to do sex with?"

"Darcy . . ."

"I don't think there's anything wrong with that, do you? But my dad says it's bad."

"Darcy . . ."

"But the weird thing is he loves his videos where women are with other women and—"

"Darcy!" He fell silent. I had to remind myself—he doesn't see faces; he can't read facial expressions. He's not going to get any nonverbal cues. You want him to be quiet, you gotta say so. "What are you doing here?"

He looked nervously at Lisa, fidgeted with his hands, then started again. "I think maybe Mr. Granger figured out what that 'neon' remark meant. He called my dad. The killer wanted us to go to this place where they store old neon signs."

"Why would he want us to go there?" But I was certain of the answer before I had finished asking the question. "Let's go."

The usual rant against Vegas is that it isn't really a city, just an oversized vacation destination. After all, there's no urban blight, like cooler-than-cool New York. There are no high-rises, other than the hotels. How can that be a city? What some of these geniuses don't get—Hunter S. Thompson, for one—is that this is a **Western** city. It's out in the fertile desert plains. It's meant to be flat. The houses were designed to go out, not up, in the traditional hacienda style. It was built for the automobile, not the pedestrian. No one wants to walk in Vegas. It's too hot. You don't walk home from work. You don't walk to the store for a loaf of bread. That doesn't make it any less of a city.

I got to see a lot of that flat landscape on my way to the Vegas Neon Graveyard. We parked and walked down a lovely pine-bordered alameda till we arrived at the main lot. A lot of memories were stored there, especially for someone like me who'd lived in Vegas all my life. Remember Sassy Sally's, on Fremont? That huge neon marquee was here, in all its glory. Or the gigantic guy in the leisure suit who used to shoot pool on the marquee for Binion's? Also here. Some of this stuff went back to the very earliest days of postwar Vegas. Remember the crown that used to sit atop the Royal Nevada? Well, neither did I. I'm not that old, for God's sake. But one of the lab techs pointed it out to me.

Apparently the guy who owned this place was a collector who just couldn't bear to see these Vegas icons destroyed. So whenever one of the casinos or hotels replaced their signage, he bought it, usually dirt cheap. He'd had to move his collection three times, on each occasion to a larger tract of land. He was outside the city now—probably too far from the Strip to attract much tourism, not that the average Vegas visitor was all that interested in historical memorabilia. He sold new signs, too, but I got the impression that was mostly a front to finance the acquisition and upkeep of this gaudy but sentimental collection.

It must've seemed like a unique and harmless specialty field. Until the headless corpse turned up.

The other half, the head, was hanging separately.

"Half off," I muttered, wishing to God I had something to drink. "I guess that's a joke."

Darcy looked at me, puzzled. "Is it funny?"

"No, but—" How was I going to explain this? His father had warned me that most humor passed Darcy by, and given all the language oddities associated with autism, he was less likely to get wordplay than anything. "Never mind."

Darcy turned away, staring at what looked like the old frontispiece from the Horseshoe. Poor kid. I remembered what a gentle spirit he had—how he wouldn't even hurt a spider. And here I was dragging him around to see decapitated corpses. Well, technically, he'd dragged me, but still. Maybe Granger was right.

Speaking of whom: "Glad you could make it, Lieutenant Pulaski. Hope you don't mind us taking your clue and running with it."

Just had to rub it in, didn't he? "Not at all. Give my congratulations to your team. How'd you figure out what it meant?"

Granger gave me the sort of smile that makes you desperate to erase it with the flat of your hand. "That's why we're called detectives."

"Of course."

"What were you doing last night after we left your place?"

Was there something about my face? Clothes? Smell? Had that brute from the bar gone to the press? "I was a little shaken up, actually. After that phone call."

I brushed him off and scouted around for Darcy. He'd been here a good two minutes. More than enough time for the Boy Wonder to start making his bizarre and brilliant deductions.

"So what Poe story are we in now?" I asked. Darcy was staring at the ground. "I've read several that involved decapitations."

" 'The Black Cat,' " he said flatly.

"I kind of remember that one. Similar to 'The Tell-tale Heart,' right? Guy tries to kill a cat, and when this woman rushes in to save it, he kills the woman instead. What makes you think that's the one?"

I could tell this poor gentle soul didn't want to talk about it. But he did. For me. "He used an axe."

Eww. "Did you get that from the coroner?"

He shook his head.

"Then how?"

"I looked."

Double eww. 'Course, I looked, too, but apparently I lacked Darcy's eye for detail. Or maybe it was that I hadn't read Carston's twelve-volume **History of Criminology** cover to cover and memorized each page. "Did you have a chance to look at the note?"

He nodded, then recited it for me—without looking. " 'From the one Particle, as a center, let us suppose to be irradiated spherically—in all directions—to immeasurable but still definite distances in the previously vacant space—a certain inexpressibly great yet limited number of unimaginably yet not infinitely minute atoms.'"

"That's kind of different. Is that Poe? I don't recognize it." Not that my brain came equipped with photographic memory. "Do you?"

Darcy shook his head. It bothered him. I could see that.

"Maybe our killer has begun composing original works? In the style of the master?"

Again he didn't answer and I didn't blame him. Even as I suggested it, it didn't sound right. The psycho was still using Poe for his blueprint. There was no indication that he had broken free of that particular part of his psychosis. So where did this bizarre and cryptic message come from? Evidently I needed to know more about Poe than was contained in his complete works. I resolved to stop by the city library on my way home from work and see what I could learn about the man himself.

I saw Tony Crenshaw near the spot where the torso still dangled. His body was stiff, almost rigid. Only his mouth moved. He reminded me of one of those talking statues at Caesar's Palace.

"Got anything for me, Tony? More of those rug fibers?"

"Not a one."

"Anything at all?"

"Not much. No prints, that's for damn sure.

Nothing we can get DNA from. A few almost microscopic traces of clothing."

"Can you tell what it is?"

He shrugged uncomfortably. "I'd like to get it under a microscope before I make any definite pronouncements. But it looks as if it might be lace. Red lace."

"Lace." I turned to Darcy. "You remember any references to lace in the Poe stories?" He didn't. "Well, he couldn't have carried her here in anything made of lace. Wonder why he didn't use the rug?"

"He may have destroyed it after the last time," Tony suggested.

"That one is small," Darcy said, edging forward. It took me a moment to realize he was talking about the victim.

"Yeah, it's a shame."

Lines crossed his forehead. Obviously, I hadn't taken his meaning. "She's light. Especially in . . . two pieces."

"Are you saying . . . he didn't need the rug?" And as soon as I said it, I realized Darcy was right. That Asian girl couldn't've weighed a hundred pounds—even before she was subdivided.

"We found a robe covered with blood," Tony explained. "We figure he used it like butcher paper—put it under her when he killed her to soak up the blood. But it's possible . . ."

I followed his meaning. Wrapped her in her own robe and tossed her into the back of the truck. The robe was already wrapped in plastic for protection, but I gave it a good once-over. It was silken, if not actually silk, and rather exotic. Long, sinuous Chinese dragons were stitched all over it. Victim was very involved with her Asian heritage? No, that wasn't it. . . .

"Hey, I've got something."

It was Jodie Nida, a tech from the coroner's office. Given Patterson's normal reticence to say anything in advance of the official report, this was nothing short of amazing. I hurried to her side. Darcy followed close behind.

Wouldn't you know it—she was examining the disembodied head. I felt my gorge rising, and this time it wasn't due to Granger's belligerence or drinking my dinner last night.

"Let me guess—she died of lack of oxygen to the brain."

Nida didn't smile. "Technically, that's correct. It appears to have taken two blows to sever her head. Not the easiest task, even with a sharp blade. And there are other body wounds, probably slipups. One is about two centimeters long between the fifth and fourth intercostal spaces at the medial border of the right breast. Another wound at the anteromedial right deltoid."

"Administered before he cut off her head? Or after?"

"I can't be sure. But that isn't why I called you over here. You see it?"

I had no idea what she was talking about.

"The teeth," she said helpfully.

I leaned in closer, even though it was the last thing on earth I wanted to do. She used a dentist's tool to pull back the edge of the mouth.

"See?" There was a small but discernible red dot on one of the victim's incisors.

"Blood?"

"Looks that way. We'll confirm it in the lab."

"Could this mean . . . she tried to defend herself?" I hoped for a yes. It would be nice to think she hurt this bastard before he chopped her in two.

"Either that or he treated her to a T-bone steak, rare. But I'm seeing no signs of a recent meal, and I've found skin flakes on the lining of her mouth. I think she got him."

"Good for her." I wondered what had allowed her to get in even that tiny blow of resistance that none of the others had managed. "Looks like she was in good shape."

"Agreed," Nida said. "Excellent muscle tone, even after rigor. I'm guessing she was an athlete."

"Dancer," Darcy said quietly, looking away, hands flipping.

We both turned and stared at him.

"How can you possibly—"

"Did you see the calluses on her feet?" he asked.

"Darcy, anything could've caused that. She might have a job that required her to stand on her feet for long periods. Waitressing, or—"

"Dancer," Darcy gently insisted. "Did you know that dancers get special calluses in special places? Look at the calluses on her feet."

I did. I saw how they formed a semicircular arc at the base of her heel. A firm ridge down the sides and across the center.

Nida and I stared at each other, utterly wordless.

"Maria Tallchief had the same calluses, according to this biography my dad brought home from the library once. Did you know that she was the first truly great prima ballerina in America? She was born in Fairfax, Oklahoma, and—"

"No, I didn't," I said, not informing him that I didn't even know who Maria Tallchief was. My mind had already wandered to another place. Red lace. Exotic wraps. Dancing. I punched my cell phone. "Madeline? Check the missing-persons reports for the last few days. See if anyone is missing an exotic dancer. Showgirl. Anything like that." If I could figure out where the victim came from—sooner, this time around—I might finally figure out this creep's pattern and anticipate the next one. "I wish I understood how he chooses his victims," I said, not really realizing I was speaking aloud. "Or how he chooses where to leave his victims."

"They are all graveyards," Darcy said.

"Huh?" I snapped out of my reverie.

"Did you notice that they are all graveyards? The make-believe graveyard at the Transylvania Hotel. The old airplane graveyard at McCarran. The neon sign graveyard."

I slapped myself for being such a stooge. It was obvious—after Darcy explained it to you. "What could be more natural for a Poe freak? Fake graveyards. He wouldn't use a real one. That would be too ordinary. Too nonpsychotic. So he put a twist on it. His idea of a joke."

"Is this funny?" Darcy asked, and this time, I thought it was a valid question. It could be humorous, in a twisted sort of way. Dragging the police all over town, from one faux grave site to the next. What fun it would be for him to—

I froze up. He wouldn't want to miss all the action. He must be watching. Just so he could savor the fun a little longer.

I looked all around. We were on the very outskirts of town, surrounded by high, dusty hills. Lots of potential vantage points.

I waved for Granger. I wanted him to send his boys into the hills to see what they could find. But even as I told him, I knew they wouldn't catch our killer. He was much too careful for that. He was already leaving.

Because he'd been watching me all along. I was certain of it.

A cold shudder coursed down my spine. He was way ahead of us. He had been way ahead of us all along. We were just playthings to him.

I grabbed Darcy and tugged him back toward my car. I didn't want to be here any longer. I didn't want to be anywhere near here.

How could I possibly catch this man when he was so much smarter than I was?

I don't like going to these dead places. I don't like seeing dead people or touching them or thinking about them. I don't like killing things. No one should ever kill someone. I would never kill someone.

Susan was still stinky today. She smells like that yucky bottle with the brown stuff that looks like apple juice but isn't that my dad opens at night when he's reading or writing or thinking about Mom. It makes him stinky, too, but he never drinks enough of it to last long. I know Susan has brushed her teeth and crunched on mints and she has a pretty smile doesn't she but she's still stinky I can smell it even when she thinks it isn't there anymore. I wish Susan wasn't stinky because I like Susan but I don't like stinky. People should not be stinky.

Coffee is also stinky, but not as much stinky. I hope I never find the axe I hope no one does because I don't want to see it like when Margaret Hayes bumped Alice Tucker at school and she cut her lip on the water fountain and the blood streamed everywhere and I thought it was funny and everyone told me it wasn't funny but I couldn't help but laugh because she looked so silly with her lip swollen and that red stuff all over her face. I got in trouble but I don't know why because I didn't push her and she wasn't really hurt but I wish the bad man would not cut up his people I don't like it when he cuts up people. I don't like him at all but I like Susan and if Susan wants to take me to these places I guess I'll go.

Why doesn't she see it? It is so obvious. I would tell her but I'm afraid then I'd get in trouble like I did with the water fountain because I don't understand something like they always tell me I just don't understand and I don't want to get in trouble anymore ever again. Especially not with Susan.

I wasn't particularly upset when I returned to headquarters and found Patrick sitting at my

desk. I'm not that easy to set off. But I was surprised—and enraged—to find daytime TV's favorite non-doctorate-possessing doctor sitting
on the opposite side.

"May I ask what you're doing here?"

Dr. Spencer barely even looked up. "I'm trying to catch the man who killed my daughter.
Not to mention another—make that two other
girls."

"Don't you have some important housewives'
crisis you could be working on? The heartbreak
of psoriasis or something."

That got her. "I've begun my own investigation. I'm setting up shop at the Transylvania,
where this case began. I came here to inform the
local authorities. Even though we are conduct-
ing separate inquiries, I hope we can still share
information."

"I'll bet you do. Since we have some and you
don't."

Patrick evidently thought this would be a
good time to intervene, with the hope of possibly avoiding bloodshed. "Under instructions
from Washington, I've given Dr. Spencer se-
lected portions of our draft profile, Susan."

"What?"

"Particularly those parts dealing with what
we know about the killer's preferred victims."

"Are you crazy? That could compromise the
whole investigation! What if she reveals every-

thing we've got to her television audience? She could force the killer to change his MO."

"That is a possibility, but—"

"This stinks to high heaven, Patrick. Did she threaten the department?"

Spencer rolled her eyes. "Don't be so melodramatic, Lieutenant. I simply informed your superiors that I will be giving a prominent prime-time interview tonight. They thought it best to arm me with information so that I could protect potential victims. Frankly, I don't understand why you haven't already done this yourself. I can only assume that it is another reflection of your . . . currently unstable condition."

The problem was, she said it so convincingly I almost believed it myself. "You're just ticked off because you couldn't get me fired."

"That was never my goal."

"Like hell. You gave it your best shot at that press conference. Turned out you didn't have as much clout as you thought."

She rose out of the chair and looked me square in the face. "The only thing that saved you, Lieutenant Pulaski, is that timely care package that you say came from the killer. Since he has chosen to communicate with you directly, your superiors thought it would be unwise to dismiss you at this time. But that won't last forever."

She grabbed her coat and purse but couldn't resist a final addendum. "Not if I have anything to say about it. And believe me, I do."

They didn't want to let her see me, damn it. And I had made a point of stopping at a gas station, checking my looks. My breath. Putting on makeup. Hell, I even tweezed! And Ozzie and Harriet still didn't want to let me see her.

"I called NDHS. They say I'm allowed."

"At designated times," Ozzie said. He was standing tall, but his nervousness showed. We both knew I could knock him down like a bowling pin. But that probably wouldn't be in my long-term best interests. "You've missed the last two."

"I've been very busy at work. Big murder case. Maybe you've read about it."

"We saw you on the TV," Harriet said. She was barely visible under the crook of her husband's arm. "I thought that Spencer woman was very rude."

"And honest," her spouse groused.

"Look, could I just see my niece? I'm not planning to take her away. I don't understand why this is such a big deal."

I stared at the man. We were practically nose to nose. "You're trying to sniff my breath."

He gave me a "Who, me?" look.

"Here, let me make it easier for you." I leaned forward and breathed on his nose. He winced. "Okay?"

"You come back at your designated visitation time. You've got one on Monday after school."

I wanted to scream. "Why are you being like this?"

"If we are to establish any order in young Rachel's life, we have to maintain a schedule that she can depend upon and—"

"Susan!" Without warning, Rachel surged past him. He reached for her, but she was too fast for him. She threw her arms around me and hugged tightly. I buried myself in her lovely auburn hair. "Susan! God, I've missed you!"

"I've missed you, too, honey." I stared at her, long and hard. "You look great. Is that a new dress?"

"Yeah." She whispered in my ear. "I think they're trying to buy my good graces. Of course, it isn't working."

That was my Rachel.

"Where have you been?"

"I've been chasing this killer, sweetie. Have you read about it?"

"Are you kidding? They don't talk about anything else on television. Have you seen the guy?"

"No. But I've talked to him."

"Really!"

"Yup. Called me on the phone last night."

"Get out of here!" She was so pretty, so pure. God, but I loved this girl. "All my friends are jealous that I know the famous Susan Pulaski."

"Famous?"

"Don't you know? Everyone watched that press conference."

"Swell. All of it?"

"Yes. Even when that cow attacked you. My friends are boycotting her show now."

"Well . . . don't be too hard on her. She's lost her only daughter."

She gave me another squeeze. "Susan, how long till I can come home with you?"

Above us, I saw Ozzie's frown intensify. "My lawyer is working on it. We're supposed to have a hearing in a few days." I pulled her away a bit and addressed her captors. "Mind if I take her to my car? I'd like to talk to her privately for a moment."

Ozzie was succinct. "No."

"We're not going anywhere."

"You step off the front porch, I call the police."

I sighed heavily. He was probably bluffing. But given the current delicate circumstances, I couldn't take the risk. "Rache, I'm sorry I haven't been by. But it's important that I work on this case."

"I know. He's so sick."

"It's more than that, honey. I have to be able

to tell the court that . . . that I'm working. That I have a steady income. That I'm gainfully employed. I need good references." I could see she didn't really understand. But that was okay. Just so she knew I hadn't forgotten about her. "But as soon as I get you back home, we're going to spend some major time together."

She looked at me carefully. "Just the two of us?"

I didn't know what she meant. Well, I couldn't be sure. "Just the two of us."

"You'll come by again soon?"

"Sure. How about tomorrow night?" Which of course was not my next scheduled visitation.

I heard the tiniest hesitation in her voice. "Oh—geez. I have church tomorrow night."

"Church?" I gave Ozzie and Harriet the long look. "Trying to bring her to Jesus?"

"They've got a big youth group," Rachel explained. "It's kind of cool, actually."

"It is?"

"Yeah. I mean, it's real queer banana," she added hastily. "Corny like you wouldn't believe. But I'm tolerating it."

Uh-huh. I gave her foster parents another once-over. They were more dangerous than I realized.

"You won't let that crazy man hurt you, will you, Susan?"

I stood and smiled. "Are you kidding? I'm

going to put him behind bars where he can't hurt anyone. Just a matter of time."

It was well past dark, but he continued reading, reading and rereading, poring over the prose-poem that for him held all the keys to under-standing. The answers were there, buried beneath its cryptic passages. They had to be.

Had he erred? Had he somehow misinter-preted the prophecies? Why had the Golden Age not begun?

All along, he had been buoyed by an innate confidence, an ineffable sense of rightness. He had always been an edacious reader, but for years now he had perused nothing but the texts, reading them over and over, subjecting them to the most intense lucubration. He had discov-ered the truth and he would use it to work mir-acles. But the offerings had been made, the triumvirate had been sacrificed. Each of them—Helen, Annabel, and the lost Lenore—in turn had been translated in a manner prescribed by the texts. But there had been no passage to Dream-Land. No Golden Age.

No Virginia.

Why had it not happened as prophesied? **The final globe of globes will instantaneously disappear, and God will remain in all.**

There must be something he was missing,

something he had yet to do. But what was it? What could it be?

He staggered away from his reading table, his hand pressed against his brow, his heart filled with sorrow. Why did it have to be so hard? Was this despair that the prophet had felt? Was this why he had ultimately failed? Why he had drunk himself to a crapulous demise on the streets of Baltimore?

He threw his arms up toward the heavens. Why must the road to redemption be strewn with thorns? Would he never find peace?

Don't go near the ocean, Ernie. Nana told you not to go near the ocean.

He closed the door to his bedroom and entered the living area, then turned on the television and began scanning channels. It was a little early for the news broadcasts, but perhaps there would be something to transport his mind for a brief time. . . .

In only a few moments, he had found a program of interest. That woman. The mother. And another man, prematurely gray hair, bulge around the center.

They were talking about him. His work.

That part didn't interest him much. The media attention had ballooned to such an extent that he had almost tired of hearing about himself. Idle speculation, repetition, sidebars on other cases not remotely similar to his own. It was all the same uninformed claptrap, over and over again, signifying nothing.

But this woman had something very different to say.

"Dr. Spencer," the host said, "you've been caught in the eye of the hurricane. After building a career based upon helping others, including those bereaved by violent crime, you find yourself crime's victim. To the rest of the country, perhaps even the world, this is a fascinating, gruesome murder mystery. But to you—it's personal. How are you dealing with the loss of your daughter?"

She was wearing a red dress, he noticed, red like the blood of the offering, with a neckline more suitable for a prostitute than a mother. No doubt she had used that costume to get on the air, to excite impure thoughts in unsuspecting men. She cared nothing for sweet Annabel. She craved attention for herself.

"It's a struggle, Chet. I won't lie to you. Pulling myself out of bed. Facing a new day. Confronting the horror of . . . of what happened to Annabel. A loss like this—it's just devastating."

"I can only imagine," he said, his eyes watery. "And yet you've managed to keep going."

"It's been hard. But I—I have an obligation to Annabel. And her child—my unborn granddaughter. Annabel was a fighter, right to the very end." As if she would know. "So I have to be, too. I have to be strong for her."

"I think you're doing an impressive job of that, wouldn't you agree?" The live audience unleashed a supportive round of applause.

Spencer smiled slightly. "I've always thanked the Lord for my blessings—especially Annabel. No matter how busy things were in the world of television, I never forgot that Annabel was my top priority."

He choked. *Not what she told me, you two-faced harridan. You were an absentee mother who didn't even call on the weekends. She told me you couldn't identify her boyfriend, didn't even know she had one. Why don't you explain to the man why you didn't know your own daughter was pregnant? Why she flew to Vegas rather than to you for help?*

"Now Dr. Spencer, you've been quite active in the investigation into your daughter's murder."

"Chet, I have no choice. She was the dearest thing in my life."

"And you haven't been afraid to criticize the law enforcement officers investigating the case, either. You've been quite vocal about your objections."

She paused thoughtfully. "I never thought of myself as a tub-thumper. But how can I remain silent? This killer tortured and murdered my daughter! Most crimes are solved shortly after the crime is discovered or they aren't solved at all. I first talked to the LVPD officers twenty-four hours after my daughter's remains were discovered, and they knew nothing. That hasn't changed—even now, when a third victim has been discovered. All my suggestions, all my offers to help fell on deaf ears. And they've made the most inexplicable, unforgivable personnel assignments."

"You're talking about the behavioral expert, aren't you? Susan Pulaski."

"Among others. God knows I hate to single out the only woman working on the case. But she's an alcoholic. Barely out of rehab. It's inexcusable."

She was doing it again. Making her ad hominem attacks on Susan for her own petty reasons. Spreading Susan's secrets to every moron with a television. Had she no sense of decency? Of propriety? How would she like it if her secrets were bared on the open airwaves?

"Now, to be fair, Dr. Spencer, my sources tell me that Lieutenant Pulaski does have some solid experience with aberrant criminal psychology. And she's not exactly in charge of the case, is she?"

The woman squinted slightly, but there was no wrinkle. Plastic surgery, he surmised. Probably lots of it. And she was barely middle-aged.

How telling. "Any contact is too much, Chet. I want my daughter's case to have the best. I insist upon it. That's why I've taken steps."

He reached for his teacup, but his hand was shaking. Steps? What . . . steps?

"Please tell the audience what you've done, Dr. Spencer."

"I can't tell you everything. But I've hired private detectives, several of the best. They're looking into this case, and they've already made several interesting discoveries. Things the police totally overlooked."

"Can you give us an example?"

"Sorry, Chet, no. You never know who might be listening."

"I understand."

"I would like to say this, though." She turned slightly, adjusting her seat so that she was looking not at her host but directly into the camera. "My first instinct was to make an appeal to the killer. But everything I've learned about this case, everything my detectives have discovered, suggests that it would be useless. This man is sick. A sexual deviant. Someone who likes to torture little girls. My experts tell me he probably started when he was young, maiming animals, deriving pleasure from it. Setting fires. They tell me he enjoys torturing his victims before killing them, that it makes him feel powerful, sexually gratified, taking off their clothes, doing—" Her voice choked. "Doing hideous things to them."

His lips parted as he stared wordlessly at the television screen. No. **No!**

"The experts tell me it's even likely that . . . that . . ." She turned away, wiping her eyes. "That he probably . . . did things to Annabel and the others . . . after they were gone. That he would seek sexual gratification from the dead."

He stumbled backward, knocking over the chair. Calumny!

"We are dealing with the worst scum who ever walked the face of the earth. A human worm. So I won't bother appealing to his better nature. But I will say this to all the other people out there, the good people, the ones who want to catch this man as badly as I do. He has struck three times. Common sense tells me someone must know something. Someone must work with him. Someone must live next door to him. Someone must've sold him a cup of coffee. Someone must've seen or heard something that made them suspicious."

She leaned into the camera. "Please come forward. Call me at the command center I've set up at Las Vegas's Transylvania Hotel. I will personally reward anyone who brings us useful information with a no-questions-asked award of a hundred thousand dollars. All you have to do is call."

"Talk about putting your money where your mouth is." The host gazed at her with adulatory eyes. "But Dr. Spencer, shouldn't any potential witnesses call the police?"

She drew in her breath. "Of course, I can't suggest that any informant should not contact the police. All I can ask is that you call me, too. Give me a fighting chance to find this monster."

"Given that kind of incentive, Doctor, I think anyone out there with information will be calling you first."

"That filthy murderer had better hope they don't." Her eyes lowered, then darkened. "Because if I get to you first, mister, it won't be so I can read you your rights."

He clutched the remote, punching the power button, then flinging it at the set.

He was breathing rapidly, perspiring. His entire body was shaking.

She was coming after him. That woman was coming after him. That damnable whited sepulcher—pretending to be so noble, when in fact she was as base and vile as the serpent. Destroying his reputation, tainting his good work with her relentless animadversions.

She was threatening him, threatening him with her money and her detectives and her sick sick words. She had called him a sexual deviant. A torturer of young women. She had sat there in front of thousands of people, perhaps millions, and told them he was a demented necrophiliac!

And she had sent them hunting for him, enticing them with her petty little cumshaw.

He paced around the living room, trying to calm himself, to get a grip on his thoughts. This could not be permitted. He was working at a sacred cause. He sought the truth and the light, the Golden Age. And he wasn't just doing it for himself; he was doing it for all of them. Even Annabel. Even that hideous woman, so determined to repugn him at every step!

He had tried to maintain some degree of gentility throughout this process, but if more direct means were required, then he had no choice but to provide them. Even if it wasn't in the plan, even if she could never be an offering. She must be stopped. And so she would be. And so would be all those who stood against him at the dawn of the Golden Age.

CHAPTER SIXTEEN

H er name was Lenore Johnson," Granger said, not bothering with any niceties such as "Good morning" or "Hello" or even "How's tricks?"

"Lenore? The lost love in 'The Raven' is named Lenore."

"Must be a different chick," Granger brilliantly opined. "This one worked at an S&M club a few blocks off U.S. 69."

I stared at the photo he slid onto my desk. It was her, all right. I'd recognize that head anywhere. "Lenore Johnson, huh? Not very Asian-sounding."

"Mixed-race. The Asian is all on her mother's side."

"Positive ID not twelve hours after we found

the decapitated body. Nice work. How'd you manage it?"

"That's why—"

"—they call you detectives. Right, I remember. Know what, Granger? You're full of it."

"Least I still have a job."

Why, why, why? Why did he have to be such an asshole? "It wasn't my fault O'Bannon yanked my badge. He was being pressured—"

"Don't make excuses. By all rights, you should be out on your—"

"Can't you see that I'm trying!" I screamed at him, so loud that I attracted attention all across the office. "Can't you see I'm trying to do better? I need this job!" My eyes began to water up. I hate that. It's so . . . girlish. I felt humiliated. "Why do you have to hate me so much?"

"You know the answer to that question," Granger said quietly.

"Do you think you're the only one who loved him?" I cried. "You goddamn, self-righteous—"

"Hey, whoa, **qué pasa,** man?" It was Patrick, riding in on his white horse. "What's going down? Big case discussion?"

I threw myself into my not very comfortable desk chair and wiped the water from my face. "Granger was telling me about his big breakthrough in the case. He's identified the last victim."

"That's his big breakthrough?" Patrick turned toward Granger. "I thought one of your detectives recognized her from the head shot. If you'll pardon the expression."

I raised an eyebrow.

Granger stammered. "W-Well . . . we were assisted by a certain degree of facial recognition pattern in—"

I gave him a look that would turn flesh to stone. "You mean your great moment of deduction came because one of your detectives is into S&M?"

He cleared his throat. "It's important that detectives stay hip to the mean streets of the city. You never know when—"

"Oh, give me a break." I did my best imitation of his whiny voice. " 'That's why they call us detectives.' Jesus. More like 'That's why they call us porn addicts.' "

"Hey," Granger said, "I didn't see you finding the corpse. Figuring out what that 'neon' reference meant."

Patrick spoke again. "Didn't O'Bannon tell me that the owner of that sign graveyard found the corpse? And called you."

I couldn't believe it. "And this was how you obtained your other big insight?" I stood up and did my best impression of a macho stud walk— even groped myself. "We be studs. We be detectives."

"You're disgusting," Granger said, walking away.

"Sticks and stones," I muttered, watching with pleasure as he departed. Probably stupid to piss him off so badly. But if he'd had the clout to get me fired, it would've happened a long time ago.

Darcy made his way up the stairs. I grabbed his hand. His face lit up like a lightbulb. "Darcy, guess what the third victim's name is."

He thought for, like, a nanosecond. "Lenore."

"What? Someone already told you."

"I do not think anyone told me. I just got off the bus. But I thought that maybe all of the girl's names were from Poe poems. And Lenore is the most popular—"

"Why didn't you tell me?"

"I do not think you asked me."

"You don't have to be asked, Darcy. If you know something, you should just . . . volunteer it."

"My dad does not like it when I do that. He says I tell people a lot of boring things they don't want to hear, and sometimes I say things that get me into trouble because I don't understand. He says I should be quiet unless—"

"Listen to me, Darcy. New rules. If you know something—anything—you tell me. Immediately."

Patrick stepped in. "So the victims' names are all found in these poems?"

"Right. I was suspicious when we had an Annabel—'Annabel Lee' is one of Poe's most famous verses. But having a Lenore clinches it. That's the name of the girl in 'The Raven,' and he used the name in other poems as well. Always to represent some lost love. Actually, all of these names represent some unrequited or lost love." I tossed Darcy my library copy of **Poe: His Life and Legacy** by Jeffrey Meyers. "Would you mind reading this tonight?"

"Okay," he said with alacrity. "Why?"

"Because you'll remember it."

A line crossed Patrick's forehead. "You really think this biographical material will be important?"

"It may be critical," I answered. "It may hold the key to the whole puzzle. Even that last message."

"So in your view, our killer thinks he's Poe?"

I squirmed. "I don't know that he literally thinks he's Poe. It's more that . . . that . . . he takes inspiration from him, his work. Not just when he's selecting his murder methods, but—everything."

"Edgar Allan Poe is his role model?"

"Kind of, yeah. Which explains a lot. According to this book, the public image of Poe as this ghoulish creepazoid is inaccurate. His work was creepy, but he wasn't." Except when he was on a drinking binge, of course. "He thought of himself as a proper southern gentleman. He was offended by vulgarity, impropriety."

"And what does that tell us about the killer?"

"Well, for starters, it might explain why he removed the painted nails. Piercings."

Patrick nodded slowly. "Shaved Helen's hair."

"Because it was dyed an unnatural color."

"This is beginning to make sense. I mean, a twisted, narcissistic, antisocial, delusional kind of sense." He thought for another moment. "But if the women in these poems represented some sort of Poe ideal—"

"They all died," I said, thinking off the top of my head. "That's the key. Helen was a woman he admired when he was an adolescent. Annabel Lee and Lenore were versions of his wife, Virginia, who died of tuberculosis."

Darcy spoke. "'And so, all the night-tide, I lay down by the side / Of my darling—my darling—my life and my bride . . .'"

"Exactly. Annabel Lee, Lenore, and a dozen other characters in Poe's poems and stories. They're all his dead wife."

"But," Patrick said, "what's the point of it all?"

"I don't know. But that quote—the last one. I think that's the key. We have to figure out what it is. What it means."

"And," Patrick added, "we need to make a list of all the female names used by Poe in his stories and poems."

"It's going to be a long list," I said, "but I agree. It might be useful. Maybe we can put out some kind of warning. Darcy, are you up for it?"

"Did you know that Poe wrote fifty-three poems and seventy-three short stories?"

"No, but you do, which is why you're the best man for this job."

"So the guy has been choosing women with these Poe names," Patrick said, his mind still racing. "But why so young? Are they easier to control? Is the killer a repressed pedophile?"

I shook my head. "Don't you know?"

"What?"

Even when the agent was a decent guy, knowing something the FBI didn't was not an altogether unpleasant sensation. "That bride of Poe's? Virginia Clemm? He married her when she was thirteen."

Overnight, the Van Helsing Ballroom had been converted into the nerve center for Dr. Fara Spencer's Wanted Dead or Alive operation. The room was a beehive of noise and activity, a bombinating assault on the senses. And yet, he observed, it was not chaotic. There was an almost serene order as all concerned careered from one area to the next going about their designated tasks. A dozen operatives milled through the room in straight ties, white shirts, and rolled sleeves, some of them private detectives, some retired police officers, some specialists hired to lend expertise or to screen potential informants. Security officers were posted on all doors. Interviews were conducted in private alcoves. Two rows of phone banks, with over two dozen phones, filled the length of the ballroom, and they were constantly ringing, ringing, ringing . . . **to the tintinnabulation that so musically wells, / From the bells, bells, bells, bells, bells—**

He soaked up the view, smiling. The hive was running smoothly. But where was the queen bee?

Dr. Spencer did not so much walk as march into the ballroom, two men on either side of her, several behind, all talking constantly. At least one of the hangers-on was a reporter; he was not sure about the others. He knew she had a fleet of so-called behavioral experts advising her on the case, suggesting potential avenues to explore. Earlier, while posted at the front door, he had managed to overhear most of an absurd exchange between the queen and two of her minions.

"Fundamentally," a pedant in horn-rimmed glasses had explained, "serial killers can be divided into two categories. Social and nonsocial. Organized and disorganized."

He had to bite his lip. Even given the vagaries of modern psychiatry, it was absurd. The whole world divided into four lame labels. And these people called themselves experts.

"So which is this pervert?" Spencer had asked.

"Keep in mind that we're working with precious little information," the partner said, an obese man in an unseemly green tie. He was making excuses for himself in advance, as they always did. "But all indications are that he is very organized. Three crimes so far—that we know of—and he still hasn't left behind any determinative trace evidence."

"And we can safely assume that he has some social skills," Horn-rims intoned. "Since he appears to have been able to capture his victims without the use of force. So far as we know."

"All right," Spencer said, holding up her hands. "So he's an organized social. What does this get us?"

Despite his profound dislike of this contemptible woman, she did have a knack for cutting through the balderdash.

"Well," Horn-rims said, "once we've made our diagnosis, we can get a fix on who the killer is."

"I don't care who he is," Spencer shot back.

"I don't want to know his inner child. I just want the bastard to fry."

"Right, right. So we must create a profile—"

"Forgive me for saying so, but this is starting to sound like the same bullshit I got from the police department's so-called expert. I'm not laying out all this money to get more of the same."

"Of course not. I'm probably not explaining myself clearly." He licked his lips and tried again. "Once we know who the killer is—what kind of person he is—we can begin to anticipate his moves. Perhaps even trace him to his lair."

His **lair.** He stifled his laughter. It was like something out of a comic book.

"Now we're talking." Spencer's interest level markedly increased. "So how do we do that?"

"Well, Doctor, one salient fact we have observed is that all the victims have been women."

Bravo, Auguste Dupin. How much was she paying these fools?

"According to the group consensus, our killer is driven by a psychosexual hatred of all women."

Still pretending not to listen, he stifled a yawn. Wrong.

"He is physically unattractive, or at the least not handsome. Because he is unable to attract women, he came to hate them."

Wrong, wrong, wrong. Every bit of it.

The partner cut in. "Perhaps it would be more accurate to say that he focuses the sublimated anger he bore toward his mother figure on randomly chosen women."

Randomly chosen? Now that was truly offensive.

"This speculation is all well and good, I suppose," Spencer said, "but where does it get me? How do I catch him?"

"By keeping a close watch on all the places it would be easiest for an organized social to find women alone," the partner answered. "The streets, obviously, especially downtown. Strip clubs, casinos. We've prepared a list."

Spencer took the proffered paper. "I don't see this hotel listed."

Horn-rims nodded. "Our feeling is that he's unlikely to strike at a place already associated with him. Plus, since organized socials tend to follow the media coverage of their crimes obsessively, he must be aware that you've set up shop here. He won't come anywhere near this hotel."

It was all he could do to keep from laughing.

Until the woman stood beside him.

"So . . . your name is Ernie?" Spencer said, reading his badge.

He stiffened. "Yes, ma'am."

"Keeping an eye on things?"

He was on loan-lease from the hotel to Dr.

Spencer and was currently assigned to watch one of the side doors. "Doing my best. Lot going on here."

"Yes, there is. Try not to be distracted by it all." She leaned in closer. "I'm probably safe here, but, still my experts say there is . . . some reason to believe the killer might lash out against me."

"Surely not, ma'am."

"I know, it seems incredible. But I'm being extra careful, just in case. There's more than one way to skin a rabbit."

She was so close to him. Mere inches away. In his coat pocket, he had a hypodermic, loaded and ready. In the wink of an eye he could have it in her throat.

But then there would be the difficult matter of her escorts, getting her to his truck on the other side of the casino, removing her from a ballroom teeming with people. . . .

"I'll make sure nothing happens here, ma'am."

"I'd appreciate that."

"And if I may say so . . ." His southern accent came trippingly off his tongue. "Speaking on behalf of all the security officers here at the Transylvania, we very much appreciate and admire what you're doing. We're behind you one hundred and ten percent."

Her eyes went slightly out of focus, glistening. "Thank you, Ernie. That . . . that means a great deal to me. I hope we can talk again sometime."

"I feel certain we will, ma'am," he said, smiling sweetly.

"Seriously, Darcy, I think it would be better if you stayed in the car."

"But I do not want to stay in the car. I cannot help you if I stay in the car."

"You can. I'll tell you all about it."

"I want to go in with you."

We were parked outside Nighthawks, still in my car. Truth was, I would rather he came in, too—you never knew what he might notice. But I had a feeling it might not be a good idea. "You see, Darcy . . . this place . . . this is a grown-up place."

"All those places where girls died were grown-up places."

"Yeah, but this is . . . this is . . ." I took a deep breath. "Darcy, has your dad ever . . . had that talk with you?"

"My dad talks to me all the time. Sometimes I wish he wouldn't talk to me so much."

"Yeah, but has he ever talked to you about . . . the birds and the bees?"

His eyes widened. "I've read lots and lots of books about birds and bees. Did you know that the hummingbird is the fastest—"

"That's not what I mean, Darcy." I took a big breath. "See, Darcy . . . this is a sex club."

He looked at me, then at the building, then back at me. "Do you mean—they do sex in there?"

"Yes. I mean, probably not. Certainly not all the—"

"I have never seen anyone do sex. Can I go in with you and see it?"

I pressed the palm of my hand against my forehead. "Are you sure you'll be okay with this, Darcy?"

"Of course. This is not like gong to all those places where people got killed. Killing is bad. But I think doing sex is a good thing. Do you think doing sex is a good thing?"

I popped open the car door. "C'mon, Casanova."

"Good afternoon," the woman in black said as I stepped through the door. "I am the mistress of pain."

"Stow it," I replied, flashing my ID. "I'm the mistress of pain in the ass."

She blocked my path, pressing up against me. "You prefer to be dominant?"

"I prefer to get what I need without any hassles."

Her fingers toyed with my collar. "You should open yourself to new experiences. I could—"

I slapped her hand away. "Let's get one thing straight from the start. If you think you're going to intimidate me with your lesbian chic bullshit, forget it."

Darcy was behind me, staring with a total absence of subtlety. But of course subtlety was a personality quality he didn't have. The mistress was wearing brown riding pants, very tight, and a black leather bustier top. Not hard to guess where Darcy was staring.

"Do you have trouble breathing?" he asked. "Because it looks like you might have trouble breathing."

The mistress pointed her riding crop at him and winked. "Breathing is overrated."

"Do they make you wear that?" he continued. "Are you being punished because you misbehaved?"

"No, dear."

"I've never seen a shirt that had to be tied up in the front like that. Do you like to be all tied up like that?"

She turned her withering expression my way. "One of your crack detectives?"

"As a matter of fact, yes. I have a few questions for you."

"I've already spoken to several—"

"You haven't spoken to me. I have some additional queries."

"Well, I have a business to run."

"I can change that."

She jammed that crop under my chin, forcing it up. "You like to play rough. Is that what you're into?"

"You don't have any idea what I'm into."

"I've been at this a long time. I can tell what a client wants in about thirty seconds."

We were practically nose to nose. "I'm not a client, and if you don't cooperate, I'll send Vice over to shut you down for good."

"Bitch."

"Lady, you don't know what bitch is till I get started. So are you going to talk to me, or what?"

"Well . . ." She glanced beyond the red curtain, down a corridor. "These are business hours."

"And what business would that be? Nothing illegal, I hope."

"Of course not."

"I would certainly hate to find out there was"—I made a little gasp—"prostitution on the premises, because that's still not legal in Vegas."

"Contact dancing is permitted. At least for now."

She was right. Despite Vegas's rep as Sin City, prostitution had never been legal here. Customers had to leave town and go to joints like the famed Chicken Ranch for that. For it to be legal, anyway. In reality, prostitution was not uncommon. A lot of it passed under the guise of "outcalls" or "room dancing." Escort services with girls who met you at your hotel room fronted a lot of it, too. After a 2002 law change, lap dancing became technically legal in Clark County, but dancers were not permitted to touch or sit on the customer's genital area, which some would have said was the definition of a lap dance. What many people didn't realize was that the Las Vegas Strip—and most of the clubs on it, including this one—were outside the city limits. Municipal officials had no jurisdiction.

"Is that what you give your customers?"

"In part. We're about fantasy fulfillment."

Darcy probably only understood a tenth of what was being said, but he was still red in the face, and I knew it was only going to get worse. "Darce, why don't you take a stroll around the premises while we talk? See if you can spot anything the detectives missed."

I could tell he didn't want to leave me, but he did as I asked. If only my previous partners had been so compliant.

This chick was way over the top, but by Vegas

standards, she was a perfectly average, ordinary working girl. After all, Vegas was the one city where a girl with no training, no education, and not incredibly bright could still make a good living, own a house, raise kids. Thanks to the Culinary Union, even nongaming cocktail waitresses got nine bucks an hour, plus tips, which was where the real action was. Gaming waitresses got fourteen. Where else could a cocktail waitress afford a mortgage and car payments? Where else could a high school dropout park cars and make enough to send his kids to college? Call girls—even run-of-the-mill ones—took home anywhere from five hundred to three thousand bucks a night, depending upon what exactly they were willing to do. Anywhere else in the world, this woman would be sleeping under a bridge in a cardboard box. In Vegas, she was the mistress of pain.

Hey, it wasn't called Sin City because of Wayne Newton.

"What can you tell me about Lenore Johnson?"

"Nice girl," she answered. "Did whatever she was asked. I like that in an employee."

"How long had she been here?"

"About three months."

"Know anything about her background?"

"She came from Kansas, poor girl. Father was

a police officer. She didn't do drugs—something of a rarity in this field. She was well mannered, respectful. Didn't have the attitude a lot of my girls get. She was trusting."

Which was probably what killed her. "Did she do outcalls? For sex?"

"Not to my knowledge. That would be illegal, you know."

"Yeah, but did she do them?"

"I don't think so. She was a good girl."

"But she was working here. The night she disappeared."

"Yes, and two of my girls saw her leave with a customer. One of them actually referred her to him. She blames herself."

"She shouldn't. He picked his victim based on her name and her appearance, not any referral."

"Really?" For the first time, her mistress-of-pain façade cracked a bit. "I'll tell her that. I hope she takes some comfort from it."

"I'll want to talk to all the, um, employees who saw this guy."

"I'll assemble them. But you won't get much. They can't describe his face."

"Surely if they saw him right here—"

"But my girls are trained never to look a customer in the eyes. The entire face is to be avoided, as much as possible. We don't want attachments forming. It clouds the judgment. In this line of work, it's important to retain a certain professional detachment."

Just my damn luck. My only eyewitnesses are sex merchants who've been trained not to look at people's faces. "I'll still want to talk to them just as soon—"

I was cut off by a piercing scream from down the corridor. I raced past the mistress, fumbling for my weapon, remembering that I wasn't allowed to have one anymore. Damn!

Another cry, this one even more terrified than the first. I tracked it to a closed door, grabbed the knob, flung it open.

There were two women in the bed, both stark naked. The one on top, the one with the surgically enhanced knockers who was holding a huge dildo in her right hand, appeared to be the trained professional. The skinny girl who had pulled the covers up to her neck was undoubtedly the customer.

Darcy was on the floor at the side of the bed, hunched over in a fetal position, rocking back and forth. He was making strange nonsense noises, babbling, whimpering.

The mistress came in behind me. "What happened, Kimberly?"

The silicone princess dropped her equipment. "We were just—"

The mistress shot her a harsh warning look.

"—having a conversation," she continued. "And this simp comes rushing into the room."

Darcy looked as if he were having a total meltdown. I'd never seen him like this. He began pounding his head against the floor. I ran to his side and wrapped my arms around him. "Darcy—what happened?"

He flapped his hands, rubbed the sides of his head. "Did you think that one was in trouble? Because I thought she was in trouble."

"But why—"

He couldn't stop rocking. "She was screaming. Screaming real loud. I thought the big one was hurting her."

I closed my eyes. "So you rushed in to help?"

"And I saw she wasn't wearing any clothes, and I remember the bad man took all the girls' clothes away, and I tried to help, and she hit me with—with—that thing." He was hand-flapping with a frenzy. His voice was never well modulated, but now it sounded as if he was shouting. "Why did she do that? Why did she hurt me? I don't think people should hurt each other!"

I took his wrists and tried to get him under control. "It was a misunderstanding, Darcy. She wasn't hurting the other woman. She was just—"

Okay, where did I go from there? Even if O'Bannon had had that little talk with his son, would it have covered activities such as the one he'd just stumbled upon?

"Let's go back to the car, Darcy," I said. "We'll get a custard or something."

"Why would she scream if she wasn't hurting? I screamed last night when I stubbed my toe because it hurt and she was screaming and she didn't have any clothes on and—"

"Come on," I said firmly. "We're leaving."

I made a few excuses to the mistress and got him the hell out of there. Damn it all. I should have seen that coming. Maybe Granger had been right. Maybe I didn't have any business dragging Darcy to these horrible places. All kinds of traumatic things might be going on inside his head that I knew nothing about. I had enough problems without playing with fire of this magnitude. O'Bannon's autistic son. Christ, what was I thinking?

Those are bad girls and I know they are and they were doing bad things. Bad people go to hell and I don't want to go to hell. Mr. Strickland said that we have to behave ourselves and if we didn't we'd go to hell and he took me by the hand away from the others and told me he knew what I was thinking that I had these ideas and all the boys like me did and we couldn't control them but I had to or I would be a dirty boy and I would go to hell. Bad girls! And the smell was so yucky on the big girl with the mole under her right knee and the holes all up her arm. Like the smell of Mommy's dishwashing gloves when Mommy was still alive.

I hope Susan doesn't stop taking me places even though I had a fit and Dad told me to control myself but I couldn't help it and I wanted to rip my hair out but I didn't and I hope Susan doesn't stop taking me because I was bad but I'm afraid she will because she has been smelling really funny bad and it isn't funny and Dad wouldn't let me read the D. H. Lawrence books because he said they would be bad for me and I think this is all scary and I wish people wouldn't do those things to other people. Bad girls! Bad girls!

Midnight. Most of the operatives had gone home, but Dr. Spencer and several others were still in the hotel ballroom. The phone rang incessantly. He had an hour to go before his shift ended.

"This is really something, isn't it?" Harv said with his usual conversational panache.

"Did you have a specific **this** in mind," he replied, "or just a general **this**?"

"This. Everything." He waved his arm about. "The whole works. Can you believe this operation was pieced together by one woman? What a pistol."

"A . . . pistol?"

"Yeah, you know. A hot tamale. Proactive. Ballsy."

"I don't see that her efforts have produced much in the way of results."

"Give her time, Ernie. They will. Everyone knows it. She must have that sick son of a bitch quaking in his boots."

That might be something of an exaggeration, all things considered. "You seem to be enjoying this assignment." Which might explain why Herb was still hanging around, even though his shift had ended half an hour ago.

"'Course I am. Didn't I tell you I always wanted to be a cop?"

"Yes, but you weren't and you still aren't. You're a security officer temporarily assigned to a private room. No one here is a cop."

"I'm a lot closer than I was bagging pickpockets in the blackjack pit. I mean, you can feel the excitement in here. You can breathe it. Makes my whole body tingle. Hell, I'm having a moment as we speak."

That was really more information than I required, he thought ruefully.

"On this detail, we're a part of something that matters. The whole world is watching this investigation."

"The whole world is watching the police

investigation. This gang is little better than a well-financed vigilante squad."

Harv ran a hand through his russet curls. "You're pretty damn down on this operation. But I know you volunteered for it. Why? If you dislike it so much, why don't you go back to policing the slot machines?"

Well, there was a very good answer to that question, but he wouldn't be sharing it with Harv. "I need the money."

"That bonus in the pay envelope was pretty good, wasn't it? I may be able to take Elaine on that Halloween holiday she wanted." He took a handkerchief out of his back pocket and wiped it across his brow. "No disrespect to my Elaine, but Dr. Spencer looks pretty damn good for her age, doesn't she?"

He made a slight clicking noise with his tongue. "Too much hair. And the plastic surgery was a mistake."

"Yeah, like you'd kick her out of bed for eating crackers." He laughed. "The ladies are tough on you little guys, aren't they?" He gave his co-worker a gentle jab that was not returned.

A few minutes later, a trim black man with a cell phone in each hand approached them. "Which one of you two officers is in charge?"

"I am," Harv chirped.

He burned. Was that because you're so incredibly tall? "We're both of equal rank and stature on this security detail," he replied.

"Well, the doctor needs someone to drive her to the airport."

Behind them, Dr. Spencer approached with her usual no-nonsense deliberateness. "Hello again, Ernie. Car's parked out back, same lot you people use. These bodyguards can get me to the parking lot. But I need a driver. So which of you lucky boys is going to do the honors?"

He cut Harv off before he could speak. "I would be pleased to escort you, ma'am."

"Sure you wouldn't mind? It isn't an official part of your job description."

"That doesn't matter. I would be honored."

"Well, if you're sure you don't mind, let's be off."

"Maybe I should be the one to go with her," Harv cut in.

He felt his jaw clenching. Steady, old boy. Steady . . .

"Well, you're still on duty, aren't you?" Harv added.

"My shift ends at one."

"And we don't want to leave the door un-guarded."

"But if the good doctor is leaving now—"

"I got off half an hour ago. I'll take her."

"I could still—"

"No, he's right," Spencer said. She was looking at him, staring with an intensity he had not
felt before. Did she . . . see something? Was he
too anxious? Was it possible she suspected? "It
makes more sense for him to go."

"Yes, of course," he said, acquiescing as
gracefully as possible. "Take care of the good
doctor, Harv. You never know what might happen out there."

Infernal imp, he thought, swearing to himself
as he pushed his way into the break room. He'd
almost had the woman exactly where he wanted
her, where he needed her. A moment of vulnerability handed to him like a gift. Until Harv,
with his inveterate imbecility, pursuing his infinite dreams with his infinite ego, intervened.

He poured himself a cup of the hotel's
mediocre coffee. In truth, he did not feel overly
disappointed. Was it possible his heart wasn't in
this work? It had seemed important, but there
was no denying that it was not in the plan. And
for that matter, the plan had failed to produce
its desired results. Perhaps this was a signal that
it was time to rest and reconsider. Perhaps he
should take a leave of absence, at least until the
TV doctor lost her zeal. He could travel, read.
And then perhaps—

"Why have you betrayed me?"

The voice was deep and reverberating, shaking him to his core.

"Why have you betrayed me?"

"I—I don't understand."

"Why have you strayed?"

"I don't know what you mean."

"What did I tell you to do?" The voice came from nowhere and everywhere at once, from no one place. **"What did I tell you to do?"**

"I made three offerings. Just as the texts prescribed."

"And were you successful?"

"No. Nothing happened."

"What have you learned from this?"

"That—that perhaps I was wrong. Perhaps this is not the way."

"No!" The dark voice split his skull, knocking him to his knees. **"You failed because your faith was weak."**

"That's not true. I believed. I did everything I could to—"

"You failed because your offerings were unwilling. They withheld their spirit. You did not ascend."

"I've done everything I know to do."

"Why did you not take the doctor?"

"I didn't get a chance. Another man—"

"That is the answer of the weak! The dissembler. The betrayer."

"No! I—I—"

"Your faith is not strong. That is why Dream-Land did not accept your offerings. To succeed you must be strong."

"Please—"

"From this moment forward, everything will be different. You will act as prescribed by your destiny. You will be my Instrument."

"Yes. Yes!"

"Would you know the secret?"

He braced himself against the wall. The voice was so loud, so overpowering. "What—secret?"

"Would you know why you have failed?"

Tears came to his eyes. "Yes. Please!"

"Then I will tell you. But not until you have done what you know you must."

"But I—I—"

"It is your Destiny. Do this and I will give you the knowledge that you seek."

"I will. I swear to you. I will!"

It had taken almost half an hour to finish all the checks, sign the papers, and put the bodyguards at ease, but Harv and Dr. Spencer eventually entered the employee parking lot. It was ridiculously dark, Harv thought. Of course, he came out here every night and it had never bothered him before. But it was different when you were on the job. In this blackness, how well could he protect her? How could he know what lurked in the hedge beyond the north perimeter? How could he know who might be watching from one of the balconies? Maybe he should've asked those bodyguards to come all the way to the car. . . .

"Best to get right to it, ma'am," he said, trying to sound very official. Spencer pointed toward the far end of the third row of cars and they headed that way. "I've really enjoyed working with your team," he added.

"I'm glad," she replied, walking with determination and deliberate speed. "I'm grateful for your assistance."

"This is a great thing you're doing. A great thing. If you don't mind my saying so . . . you do your daughter proud."

"Well . . . thank you." They rounded the end of the third row and started down it.

"I just wanted to tell you, while I had the chance . . . and I hope you don't mind . . ."

"What is it?"

"Well, this security work, it's a fine job and all, but it isn't what I really want to do, you know? I mean, I'd hate to think of me ending up like one of those guys you see at the mall, gray hair and a paunch that stretches out a mile in front of the uniform. So old they don't let them carry a gun."

"We all get old, Harvey."

"Yeah, but you're doing work that's important. Not just this but that . . . that stuff back in New York, helpin' people find fulfillment and all. Anyway, I just wanted to say—after this is all over and you've caught the dirty bastard who took your daughter's life, if there's anything I can do for you—"

"If I ever need a security officer, you'll be the first one I call."

"Well . . . yeah. That'd be nice. Or anything. There's a lot I can do. I'm good with a wood lathe and I make these pillboxes that my wife gives all her friends at Christmas. They really love 'em. I even play a little banjo. . . ."

They reached her car. "You get in the passenger seat, ma'am. I'll drive."

"If you don't mind." She slid inside.

Harv walked around the back. Just as he came by the trunk, the headlights lit on a car at the far end of the row.

"Who the hell is that?" Harv muttered. He kept walking.

The car peeled out. Tires squealing, accelerating.

Heading straight toward him.

"Son of a bitch," Harv muttered. "Stop! You're under arrest!"

The car kept coming. Even faster.

Harv drew his weapon. "Stop!"

Despite the haze of the headlights, Harv realized—it was his own car.

And it was about to kill him.

He fired twice. Both shots hit the windshield. But the car kept coming.

Harv turned, trying to get out of the way. But he wasn't nearly fast enough. The car surged forward, engine roaring, till it smashed into the back of Dr. Spencer's car.

Bisecting Harv.

He unbuckled his seat belt and stepped out of the car. Then he paused, gazing down at what was left of his colleague. "Guess you're not so tall now, huh?"

He opened the passenger-side door. Spencer was conscious, but her eyelids were fluttering. The twisted position of her body told him she had not been wearing a seat belt. A streak of blood ran down the right side of her head. She was breathing rapidly, panting, cowering, her hands clutched to her chest.

"Come," he said simply. "We don't have much time." He held out his hand.

Spencer stabbed him with a pocketknife, ripping the flesh of his palm. Then she pushed him away and tried to scramble out of the bucket seat.

He grabbed her throat with his uninjured hand and squeezed. He knocked the knife out of her hand and shoved her forcefully back into the car, falling forward, halting his descent with a hand on the floor mat. She reached up and scratched the side of his face.

"Oww!" His face flushed red with rage. He pulled the syringe out of his coat pocket and jabbed it brutally into her neck. A few seconds later, the struggle was over.

His hand was bleeding. He had to be careful not to let it drip; the police would have a field day with a blood or skin sample and he didn't have time to perform a thorough cleanup. Even this time of night, someone must've heard the crash. He pulled a tissue out of his shirt pocket and wrapped the wound, wincing at the hideous torn mess she had made of his hand.

He put the pain out of his mind. It had been a brilliant stroke, using Harv's own car. Since the man had never been able to keep his mouth shut longer than it took to breathe, he'd known which car was Harv's and where he left his keys.

He could not fault Dr. Spencer for attempting to defend herself. But he could fault her for what she had done before, how she had publicly and brutally maligned him. He could not let this offense pass. He had been told he must be strong, and so, like it or not, he had to act. For his honor. And for . . . for . . .

For the love of God, Montresor!

Yes, he thought, as he lifted her body and carried it back to his truck. For the love of God.

CHAPTER SEVENTEEN

I saw him again. Standing at the foot of my bed, just like before. He was wearing pajama bottoms and no shirt. I always thought he was sexiest when he wore pajama bottoms and no shirt.

"Are you attracted to him?" David asked.

"I dunno," I mumbled, still barely awake, if at all. "Maybe."

"It's okay, you know."

"Well, yeah, we're both consenting adults, even if he is—"

"I mean with me. It's okay with me."

"It is?" I tried to pull my head off the pillow, but my body wasn't responding to commands.

"Of course." He looked so strong, so manly,

like when we were first married. Like a man who was capable of doing anything. "I don't expect you to become a nun."

"Well, sure, but still—"

"You have my blessing."

"That's damn straight of you."

His face dissolved into that smile, that silly, toothy smile that used to turn my insides into goulash. "Well, I love you, you know."

"You do? Even—"

"Even."

It felt good talking to him, so warm and comforting. I felt as if I could sleep forever after that, like I could smell him, right there next to me in bed. So you can imagine the shock I experienced when I blinked and saw Lisa peering down into my face.

"What the hell have you done to yourself?"

I tried to bring myself around, but my head was screaming and there are some levels of pain that are impossible to mask.

"You're hungover."

"Don't be stupid." Did I slur my speech? "I had a tough night."

"I can see that." And then the most horrible thing happened. Horrible and horrifying. She started to cry. "Damn it, Susan, you said you weren't going to do this anymore."

"I—I wasn't—"

"I'm supposed to be looking after you. God,

what a shitty job I've done. I mean, you've only been out of the hospital for—"

"Lisa," I said, concentrating on proper pronunciation, "it's not your fault. I was just feeling a little stressed."

"Oh, spare me your rationalizations." She pressed her hand against her forehead. Tears streamed around the palm of her hand. "I talked to Dr. Coutant yesterday. He told me you missed your appointment with him. That you haven't been going to IOP."

"I've been working."

"They have night sessions."

"I've been working nights, too. You don't want me to lose this job, do you?"

"Frankly, I don't care about your job, Susan. I don't even think this is a good job for you, not now. What I care about is you!"

And she did, too. I could see that in her watery eyes, not that I needed additional proof. I felt like something someone might scrape off the heel of their shoe. "Look, Lisa, I'm sorry. It won't happen again. Honest."

"That's such bullshit."

"No, I mean it this time."

She walked away from the bed and stared out the window. "It's just like they told me. You're an alcoholic. And alcoholics are liars. They'll say and do anything. Because deep down, no lover on earth can take the place of a chemical addiction. Addicts will lie, cheat, and steal to get their fix."

"Honey, please—"

"I'm moving in with you, Susan."

"Now wait just a—"

"Don't waste it. I should've never let you stay by yourself. That was stupid. I'll pick you up at work and we'll spend the evenings together."

"I don't need a damn babysitter."

"You don't know what you need. And you'll start going to IOP at night, too, no matter how many crazed killers are on the prowl."

"And supposing I don't agree?"

Lisa sucked in her breath. "Dr. Coutant has been asked by Chief O'Bannon to report on your progress."

"What?"

"So that O'Bannon can evaluate whether you're ready for reinstatement. And I talk to Coutant. Often. So you see, Susan, if I give you a bad report—"

"You wouldn't."

"I sure as hell would."

At this point in time, I think it would be fair to say I hated Lisa. She was my best friend and always had been—and I hated her. I knew that she was trying to help me, that everything she said was right. I knew how hard it was for her to play tough with me. But I still hated her.

"That sounds fun, Lisa. A sleepover. Maybe

you can paint my toenails. We can braid each other's hair."

My sarcasm was wasted on her. "Clean yourself up and get dressed. I'll drive you to work."

"I have a car."

"I'll drive you to work."

"Lisa, it's eight o'clock in the morning. I wouldn't—"

"I'll drive you to work."

I rolled out of bed, trying to pretend like I wasn't hurting, thinking maybe I wouldn't go into the office at all.

Then the phone rang.

I'd never expected this investigation to bring me back to the Transylvania. Thus far, the killer had been careful not to repeat himself. But I suppose he didn't have much choice. She wasn't coming to him. He had to take whatever chance he could get.

It wasn't hard to figure out what had happened here. Both cars were still attached to one another. The parked car was particularly damaged. Anyone who had been in there must've been injured, maybe seriously. Blood was everywhere. Maybe it was just the fact that I'd drunk all my meals for several days running, but it was getting to me. I was sick in so many ways I couldn't enumerate them all.

The press was there in force. Not surprising, given who the abductee was. The news was already blanketing the airwaves. This was now the biggest story anywhere, everywhere, all across the nation. Maybe even internationally. The reporters were demanding answers that we didn't have, acting as if it was our fault that we didn't. They shouted questions at me as I passed, which I ignored. O'Bannon was dealing with them, or trying. He looked like a drowning man facing a tsunami.

Lisa dropped me off at the outer perimeter of the crime scene, where Patrick was waiting to brief me.

"How did he find her?" I asked.

Patrick shrugged. "Everyone on earth knew she was at the Transylvania. It had been on the news. She even mentioned it on her show. She was doing live remotes from the ballroom. He may have known what car she was using. Possible that he scouted all the parking lots—including this private one for employees and VIPs—found her car, waited for his chance."

"Why go after the guard? He's never killed a man before."

"It was necessary to get to Spencer."

"And why did he want to do that so badly?"

"She practically put out a hit on him."

"Yeah, but so what? He likes attention. He's been craving a challenging opponent." I shook my head. "It wasn't the reward money. It was the character assassination."

Patrick didn't get it. "Is it possible to assassinate the character of a serial killer?"

"It is in his mind. Remember—he's a proper southern gentleman doing some kind of respectable, perhaps even sacred work. And then this woman goes on television and suggests that he's a pervert. It's an affront to his honor."

Chief O'Bannon walked between us, a grim expression on his face. "They're demanding a press conference, people. What can we tell them?"

"Stall," I advised. "We need more time."

"They're very insistent."

"Tell them to cool their heels."

"That won't cut it. In their view, we've let a serial killer snatch one of America's most beloved television personalities. One who recently suffered a great personal loss—thanks to the same killer. All the news reports have been critical of us."

"Okay, then promise them a conference—later. After we've had more time to sift through the evidence."

He grunted. "Can I at least tell them whether we think Spencer is still alive?"

"There's no corpse," Patrick said. "Why bother taking her if he's going to kill her?"

"He's killed all the others."

"But not right away," I insisted. "There's no reason to believe this will be different."

"So there's still a chance. If we move quickly."

"But I wouldn't say that to the press," Patrick quickly interjected. And we all knew why. Because we didn't want to be blamed if we didn't find the killer in time to save her. As things stood, we weren't even close.

"We've got to do something," O'Bannon growled. "You bring Darcy out today?"

"No . . . I thought it would be best not to."

O'Bannon nodded curtly. "He seemed pretty upset last night. Had to give him something to get him to sleep. Haven't seen him that anxious in a while. You take him to an espresso bar?"

"No. He . . . saw something that bothered him."

To my surprise, O'Bannon didn't ask any more questions. Sighing heavily, he headed back toward the press corral.

Over by the smashed Chevy, I heard a cry. Either pain or exultation, I couldn't tell. But a few moments later, I saw Tony Crenshaw running toward me.

"What?" I wasn't going to get my hopes up, but his eyes were like Christmas lights. "What have you got?"

"You are going to love me so much," Tony said, obviously pleased with himself. "You are going to fall down on your knees and kiss my feet. Perhaps even some more sensitive spots."

I saw Patrick giving me a sidewise glance. "Cut the fantasy and tell us what you've got already."

But he wasn't giving it up that easily. "Most forensics would've missed it, of course. You do the outside of the car, sure. The upholstery. But how many would've bothered to check the floor mats? Especially with a guy who has been so scrupulous in the past?"

I grabbed him by the lapels. "Prints? Are we talking about prints?"

"It's possible. . . ."

"I'm not your joytoy, Tony. Don't play with me. Have you got a print?"

"There's definitely something there. I'll take the mat back to the lab and try vacuum metal deposition. It's great for lifting prints off plastic. I'll get something for you."

I couldn't restrain myself. I pulled him closer and smacked him a big one, right on the lips. "But that's as far as it goes," I cautioned.

"Looks like there was a tussle," Tony explained. "We found a few drops of blood in there that didn't come from Spencer. I think she hurt him. He fell forward, his hand went down on the mat, he forgot to clean up. Maybe didn't have time. The rental company tells me those mats were washed just before Spencer rented it, so . . ."

I couldn't help myself. I kissed him again.

He arched an eyebrow. "Could we take this somewhere?"

I released his lapels. "Yeah, back to the lab. Now."

She must've heard him coming. The steps leading to the basement were wooden and creaked when he stepped on them.

"Who is that? Let me out of here!"

The basement was dark, but he liked it that way. When he first moved in, he had been down almost every day, oiling hinges, wiping the walls with mildew remover, but at some point he had realized that was futile and foolish. He was denying the basement its true nature, its essential basementness, so to speak. Certainly the prophet would not have approved. So these days, he let things be what they were. As a result, the basement had acquired a distinctive odor, not noisome, but a lovely evocative mustiness. The air seemed thick and earthy; the walls bore a thin filmy layer of green growth.

He found Dr. Spencer in the alcove on the far side, strapped to the table, just as he had left her.

"You can't get away with this," she shouted.

Her words echoed through the basement, reverberating off the stone walls. "I've had people following me everywhere I go."

"Then where are they, madam?" he replied, smiling sweetly. "I'm afraid I find that statement lacking a certain credibility. You see, I am intimately familiar with all your security precautions. I struck at a time when your protection entrusted you to the custody of the rather poorly chosen and recently bifurcated Harv Bradford."

Between the two of them, forming a partition between the alcove in which she lay and the rest of the basement, was a four-foot-tall brick wall.

"You're the security man, aren't you?" she said, staring at him. "Back at the hotel. The other one."

"What a memory you have. Spectacular."

"Let me tell you something, mister. You didn't know half the precautions I was taking. I had eye-in-the-sky copters watching me. There's a homing device in my shoe."

"I don't think so."

"As soon as they zero in on my position, your ass—"

"Madam, you have been here more than twenty-four hours."

She paused, her mouth sucking air. "But— I just—"

"You've had a nice long nap, courtesy of my favorite pharmaceutical. But I am forced to conclude that if anyone had the slightest notion where you were, they would have long since arrived."

She was silent for a while. "What do you want? Are you going to strip me naked and . . . do whatever it is you do?"

He struggled to maintain control. "I have not removed your clothing because you are not now, nor could you ever be, an offering. And may I add that I have never assaulted or in any way behaved inappropriately with any of my offerings. Your public accusations were offensive and ungrounded."

"You killed three girls!"

"That is correct, in a technical sense. But there was no sexual misconduct, my dear pseudo-doctor. I'm sure the police have conducted tests establishing that for a fact. They in all likelihood have shared that information with you. Nonetheless, you appeared in a public forum and made your vile accusations." He paused. "A gentleman's reputation is his stock in trade. You have impugned my personal integrity. For that, you must be punished."

He had prepared the mortar earlier. He added some water from the sink, loosening it. He stirred it with the trowel. It was ready.

"I can't believe this," Spencer said. Her voice

was hoarse from shouting and it had acquired an edge, but one born more of fear than of menace. "I've got a serial killer complaining that I tarnished his reputation."

He slapped mortar down atop the partial wall, then pressed a brick into place. It held.

"I mean—don't you see a certain irony in that?"

"I see that you understand nothing," he said, applying another brick, then another. "I see that you categorize me with the insane, or those who kill for pleasure or sexual gratification. Insult upon insult." Another brick. Then another. Then another.

"What are you doing?" she asked.

"Just finishing a little something I started. I'm a great devotee of home improvement." Another row finished. Then another.

Time passed. She watched him work. As each new brick fell into place, her voice became more strained. "Look . . . I never meant to offend you. I just—I loved my daughter."

"You did not, madam."

"How dare you—"

"Annabel talked quite a lot about you before she was offered. She told me that you never paid any attention to her, hadn't for years. That you were always absent, obsessed with your career. Your work, that was what you loved. Not her."

"How can you presume to—"

"I have it from the best authority, wouldn't you say?"

"Annabel was a child. She couldn't understand what a working single parent—"

"She knew whether her mother paid attention to her or not."

"Paid attention to her? I lavished every possible attention on her. Did she tell you she was going to MIT, for Christ's sake? Did she tell you what she was driving?"

"The checkbook, my dear woman, is no substitute for parenting." He slapped another layer of brick on the wall. It now reached two-thirds of the way to the low basement ceiling. He had to stand on a ladder to continue his work. "Could you perhaps name one of her friends? No guessing, now."

"What difference does it make? Friends come and go."

"Did you know she was pregnant?"

Her voice came back a little quieter. "The police told me."

"Did you know the name of her beau, before the police found him?" He smiled, stirring the mortar. "His name was Warren. He and Annabel were in love and wanted to marry. She came to Las Vegas to make some money playing blackjack so they could start their life together."

"She could've just asked. . . ."

"She felt she couldn't. She knew you would

be importunate and disapproving and would not give her anything, so she didn't bother. Because you were too wrapped up in your own world to be a part of hers."

Dr. Spencer was quiet for several layers of brick. When she spoke again it was with a sullen defiance. "So you're doing this to punish me for being a bad mother?"

"Not at all. You're the one who brought up your relationship with your daughter."

"Then why?"

"I cannot let you continue to interfere with my work. My plan."

"What are you talking about? What do you think you're doing?"

He slapped down another slab of mortar. "At the moment, I'm building a wall."

"Around me? Is that your sick idea? You're going to entomb me in your basement?"

"More or less."

"And I'm supposed to lie here till the end of time?"

"Goodness, no. That would be cruel and inhuman." He continued laying the bricks. "This is a small alcove, and the way you're breathing, you'll use up the air quite quickly. I doubt if you'll last more than an hour or two."

Her arms and legs stiffened, straining against the leather straps. It seemed her muscular control had returned. "Sadist!"

He made a **tsk**ing sound, then continued working. Barely half a foot remained between the top of the wall and the ceiling.

"Please don't do this." Her voice finally cracked. "I'll give you anything you want. Just let me go. I won't hunt you anymore, I promise."

He sighed a little as he slapped down the bricks. It was so disappointing. In the end, they all gave way to weakness.

"What is it you want from me?"

"Only your death. A slow and painful one. A terrifying demise." The wall reached the ceiling. There was only one opening remaining, one space he had left vacant at eye level. "I'm afraid this is where I must bid you adieu," he said, peering through the gap.

"Please don't leave me in here!"

"Dr. Spencer, you are wasting precious air. Instead of this useless caterwauling, may I recommend that you spend your remaining time coming to terms with your Maker? Use these last precious hours to commit yourself to your faith. If you have one."

"You'll pay for this!"

"And if not," he said wearily, "this might be an opportune moment to adopt one."

"For God's sake—"

"Yes. **For the love of God.**"

With a splash of mortar he wedged the final

brick into place, then plastered over the wall to ensure that it remained airtight. Not a bad bit of masonry, if he said so himself.

She did scream, of course, even though it was the stupidest thing she could possibly do. She threatened and pleaded and repeated the vile insults that had made this action so necessary in the first place. After a while, he realized he did not need to subject himself to this. He went upstairs, closing the basement door behind him, and waited for the screaming to end.

CHAPTER EIGHTEEN

"Explain this to me again," I asked Tony.

"My pleasure." His nose was pressed against the glass of the vacuum chamber as he repeated the entire exegesis. "We put the floor mat in there with a milligram of gold in the heating element, then sealed it. The pumps suck out the air and create a vacuum. The gold boils, almost into a steam. A thin invisible layer coats the plastic. The gold will sink into the oil from the print, leaving only the ridges uncoated. Then we do it again, this time with zinc in the heating element. The zinc vaporizes, then recondenses only on metal—in other words, the gold from the previous treatment. And the result?" He directed our attention to his nearby computer monitor. "A great big beautiful high-contrast reverse-image print."

"Nice little gizmo you've got here," I murmured softly.

"Glad you think so, Susan," he replied. "Because vacuum metal deposition costs a fortune, what with the gold and all. I'm telling Granger you authorized it."

I hunched over his shoulder, peering at his computer screen, but no matter how much I squinted, no matter which way I turned my head, no matter how long I let my eyes go fuzzy, I couldn't make out the print. "The lines all look the same to me," I said, admitting defeat.

"Don't sweat it," he replied. "Psychos all look the same to me."

What we were looking at was a computer enlargement of the print he had found on the floor mat in the car from which Fara Spencer was taken. It wasn't all there—a chunk from the upper left never came clear—but Tony assured me that was enough to make a match. And this time it was a forefinger, not a palm print. I was trying not to get my hopes up, but we were all hoping this would allow us to identify the killer. With Patrick's assistance, he'd already fed the print to FINDER, the FBI's automatic fingerprint reader and processor. If this print or anything like it had been recorded by any computerized law enforcement agency in this country or several foreign nations, they could give us the identification we so desperately needed.

"We've got mail," Tony said, pointing at his screen. "Three partial matches."

I watched as three more prints appeared on the screen in a vertical column opposite the original. Tony scrutinized each whorl and swirl.

"Well?"

"Give me a minute."

I saw that each of the match prints had a name beneath it with a hyperlink to a full FBI bio. If we could get a name, maybe even an address, this killer could be behind bars by midnight.

"No," Tony said, after dragging the suspense out for what I thought was an ungodly length of time. "None of these work."

"What do you mean?"

"They aren't him. There are similarities, sure. Enough to pass the computer software match threshold. But they aren't the same."

"You're sure?"

He was still staring at the screen. "Much as I wish I weren't. Besides, none of these guys comes close to matching your description. This one's a woman. The next is a guy in his seventies."

"But we were sure that print came from the man who abducted Fara Spencer."

He pushed back away from the computer,

rubbing his eyes. "So now we know that our guy has never been arrested. Never run for political office. Never taken the bar exam. He's managed to get through life without being fingerprinted. He's never done anything like this before." He slid out of his chair and switched the power off his monitor. "Or if he has, he's never been caught."

He ambled up the sidewalk outside Central Division headquarters trying to concoct a suitable conversation starter. As it happened, the young man sitting on the front steps eliminated the need.

"Are you a grown-up person?"

"Ye-es . . ."

"You must be kind of a short person. Are you kind of a short person?"

"I am as God made me."

"I'm six foot one. Do you know how tall the Sears Tower is?"

He tugged at his collar. All his initial impressions were correct. There was something strange and more than a little disconcerting about this man's demeanor. The way he struck up a conversation, albeit a nonsensical one, with a total stranger on a Vegas street. His voice was simple, almost childlike. And yet he was an adult, somewhere in his mid-twenties by appearances.

"No, I'm afraid I don't."

"It's one thousand four hundred fifty-four feet tall. One hundred and three floors. It used to be the tallest building in the world. Not anymore."

"Fascinating."

"Do you know how tall the Empire State Building is?"

"Not exactly."

"It's one thousand four hundred fifty-three feet. One foot shorter than the Sears Tower. One hundred and two floors. Have you ever talked to a midget?"

He stiffened. "I'm not sure what—"

"I saw a midget once and I talked to her. I got in trouble for talking to her but I don't know why because I didn't do anything to hurt her."

There was something wrong with this man, a discernible . . . vacancy. He didn't lack intelligence or language. His syntax was skewed, but there was a distinct legerity to his responses. At the same time, there was a profound oddness about him: the way he held his head when he talked, the curious inflection, the unvaryingly excessive volume.

"I'm Darcy O'Bannon the second. My dad named me for my uncle, he's dead. My uncle, not my dad."

"Please to meet you, Darcy." He extended his

hand, but Darcy did not take it. Instead he stared at it, as if hesitant to make contact. "My name is Ethan."

"Are you a jockey?"

"Uh . . . no . . ."

"Because I read that jockeys have to be short and they like jockeys to be short so you should be a jockey."

"No, I'm . . . I'm an accountant."

"How tall do you have to be to be an accountant?"

"I'm not aware of a height requirement."

"I think I'd like to be a jockey. I rode a horse once and I liked that. It went really fast and I like to go really fast. Do you think I could be a jockey?"

"Uh . . . probably not, given your height. But I'm no expert."

"Willie Shoemaker won eight thousand eight hundred thirty-three races, did you know that? He was four foot eleven. But he got rich. I think my dad would like me better if I were rich."

"Darcy . . . I'm looking for Lieutenant Pulaski. Do you know where she might be?"

Darcy cocked his head to one side. "Do you know Susan?"

"I've had the pleasure of meeting her, yes."

"You're not going to take her away from me, are you?"

"I'm . . . not sure what you mean."

"Whenever I really like someone somebody else takes them away or tells me I can't play with them anymore. I'll be sad if Susan goes away. I like her a lot. Do you think she's pretty?"

"Most striking."

"I think so, too. But she's not the prettiest woman ever. Some people say Cleopatra was the prettiest woman ever but did you know archeologists dug up a coin with her face on it and she wasn't pretty at all?"

"I didn't know that." He suppressed a smile. And he had worried that this harmless meshuggener might be a threat, a rival, that he might come between himself and Susan. Obviously, that was not going to happen. What was she doing with this boy? Was he some sort of charity work, a Good Samaritan exercise? Was this Susan's plan for worming her way back onto the force? Earning Chief O'Bannon's favor by babysitting his brain-addled son?

"Do you know what the tallest building in the world is?"

"Uh . . . the Sears Tower?"

"Wrong!" He made a honking noise and pointed. "Faked you out. It used to be the Sears Tower, but now it's the Petronas Tower in Malaysia. It's one hundred and ten stories tall. That would be two hundred and sixty-four of me stacked on top of each other."

"Imagine."

"Would you like to see the Sears Tower and the Empire State Building stacked on top of the Petronas Tower? I would. Do you know how many stories that would be?"

"Rather a lot."

"One hundred and two plus one hundred and three plus one hundred and ten. Know what that is?"

"Sorry, I've never been good with numbers."

Darcy's head tilted. "But I thought you said you were an accountant."

"I . . . I rely heavily on my calculator."

"Accountants are good adders. I read that in a book. My dad took me to an accountant once and he could add five-digit numbers in his head. So can I but he was the only other person I ever saw who could. Why can't you add three-digit numbers?"

"Well . . . of course . . . I wasn't really listening."

"Are short accountants not as good at adding as tall ones?"

He stepped onto the sidewalk. "I really must be going."

"Goodbye," Darcy said. "You might think about seeing if you could become a jockey. 'Cause I'm not sure how good you're going to be as an accountant."

He hurried back to his car, wrapping his jacket tightly around himself. That had been an unforgivably stupid mistake. He'd relaxed his guard, thinking this mental deficient could pose no danger to him, and as a result, he'd made a foolish error. If the boy were not so pitifully without guile, he would've become suspicious, perhaps conveyed his suspicions to Susan. And that could be disastrous.

At least he'd ascertained that there was no romantic affiliation between the two. Now that he knew he had a clear field, he would contact Susan again. Soon.

What bothered him was his inability to read the young man. The connections this Darcy's brain made were unpredictable. Illogical. There was no way of anticipating him.

If it became necessary, the young man would have to be removed. For Susan's sake. And his own. And that of the world to come.

By the end of the day, several more FBI agents had made the scene. In addition to our rent-a-behaviorist, we now had agents from CIU—the Critical Incident Unit. From the shadowed basement of the J. Edgar Hoover Building to the sunny Vegas strip. We also had some liaisons with VICAP—the Violent Criminal Apprehension Program—some of them pretty famous, names I recognized from the **Law Enforcement**

Bulletin. They were cataloging and analyzing data, comparing these crimes with others the feds had encountered. Patrick had them all gathered in a back room and was bringing them up to date on the case.

I saw a thick stack of paper on the corner of my desk—summary reports on all the confessions that had arrived in the last few days. We'd been getting them since murder number one, but they were skyrocketing now that a TV celeb was involved. If I worked this job till doomsday, I would never understand what it was about high-profile media cases that made perfectly harmless people crawl down to the station to give false confessions. Unless they were obviously bogus, they had to be checked out, at least a little, which diverted our already strained time and manpower.

I scooped up a stapled document that someone had dropped on my chair. Looked like the Feebs had been busy.

SECONDARY VICTIMOLOGY REPORT, BSS04-67
SUBJECT: EDGAR

I had to grin a little. I knew the feds always gave their serial killers a pet name. So this one was Edgar. Cute. I scanned the report.

VICT1—Helen Collier, Clark County Police Dept, homicide
WF, DOB 1-9-87, DOD 10-4-04
DEATH: Asphyxiation
WEAPON: Coffin
POD: Transylvania Hotel ballroom
BODY FOUND: Transylvania Hotel
No witnesses. Forced entry. No trace evidence attributable to assailant.

VICT2—Annabel Spencer, Clark County Police Dept, homicide
WF, DOB 8-15-86, DOD 10-8-04
DEATH: Exsanguination
WEAPON: Dental tools
POD: Unknown
BODY FOUND: McCarran Airport, retired aircraft field
No witnesses. No forced entry necessary. Only trace evidence attributable to assailant is a tire track and a partial palm print.

VICT3—Lenore Johnson, Clark County Police Dept, homicide
WF, DOB 7-13-85, DOD 10-13-04
DEATH: Decapitation
WEAPON: Axe
POD: Unknown
BODY FOUND: Neon sign graveyard

No witnesses. No forced entry. No
evidence attributable to assailant.

VICT4—Harvey Bradford
WM, DOB: 01-04-60 DOD: 10-17-04
DEATH: Massive bodily trauma
WEAPON: Automobile
POD: Hotel parking lot
BODY FOUND: Hotel parking lot
Security guard at Transylvania Hotel.
Killed by impact of his own car. Died
instantly.

VICT5—Fara Spencer
WF, DOB: 10-16-61 DOA: 10-17-04
STATUS: Unknown
Mother of Vict2. Abducted after car
incident with Vict4. No witnesses.
Unidentified partial forefinger print
possibly attributable to assailant.

Pretty damn thin, when you got right down
to it. I thumbed through the additional material
attached to the cover report. Not much there.
Was it any wonder we hadn't caught this clown
yet? About the only thing this report didn't
cover was the phone call I'd gotten from
Edgar—great, now they had me calling him
that—and his present. And I received a detailed
analysis on those barely an hour later.

"The lab found nothing useful on the box, the wrapper, or the teeth," Tony Crenshaw explained. "Neither did Latent Prints."

"Voiceprints?"

"Nothing. We have a pattern now we can compare against any future communications. But even maximum volume magnification failed to turn up any useful background noises. There were few clues in his language other than the obvious one—**neon.** No distinctive patterns. Southern accent, to be sure, but the experts think he was affecting that."

"Because he wants to be like Poe. But he isn't really from Virginia."

"That's our guess. Other than that, no real clues. He chose his words carefully. Probably rehearsed what he was going to say before he called."

That would be consistent with the organized sociopath I had in my head. "I'd like a copy of the tape of the phone call."

"Sure." Tony seemed hesitant. "You know he was trying to rattle your cage, right? Talking about your bad habits and all. Doesn't mean he knows anything. It was an easy shot. Everyone has some secret. He wants to scare you. Chase you off the case."

Did he? Maybe. But to me, it seemed more like he was trying to impress me. To win me over.

"But you're not going to let him get to you, right?"

My eyes lifted. "What's this? A trace of concern? For **moi**?"

His eyes darted to the carpet. "Granger doesn't speak for the whole department, Susan. You still have friends around here. Lots of them."

Well, that was cheering. "Thanks, Tony. I appreciate it."

"All the guys loved David. You know that. And we think what happened . . . wasn't right. The way you were treated."

"Tony, I really don't care to—"

"Just wanted you to know." He gave me a mock salute. "Back to the trenches."

I thrust my nose into my paperwork, trying not to be resentful. Of course, that was what it would be about. David, not me. Everyone had loved David. Everyone.

I'd loved David, too, damn it. But that wouldn't bring him back.

I was on the phone with my lawyer, which is about as unpleasant as life gets.

"If the judge isn't going to decide anything, why do I have to be there? I'm in the middle of a major investigation."

"Do you want custody of Rachel or not?"

"That's why I got this job! On your advice."

"Then you must be there. Dressed conservatively. Sparing makeup. You need to sit next to me and be untempermental, cool, and well mannered."

"In other words, exactly not like myself."

"Whatever."

"I can't believe this judge is so shallow he's going to make a decision based upon whether I wear red."

"He might not do it consciously. But judges are influenced by their subconscious impressions, just like everyone else in the world. The most important part is that you remain calm. NDHS will try to convince the judge that you're unreliable. You have to show him that you can be restrained and responsible, fit to raise your niece. You have to tell him you've sworn off booze and you're working to stay clean."

I felt an itching in my chest that wouldn't go away. "I can do that."

"Good. See you there."

Damn everything. As if I didn't already have enough on my plate. Now I was going to have to deal with the American legal system. The tenth circle of hell.

"Eureka!"

I glanced up. Darcy was standing at the edge of my desk, grinning like a sheepdog.

"Eureka!" he repeated.

"Okay, I'll bite. What are you talking about?"

"Eureka means 'I found it.' Did you know that historians say that's what Archimedes said when he discovered about the displacement of liquid? He jumped out of the bathtub yelling, 'Eureka! Eureka!'" Darcy giggled. "He was strange."

"Thanks for the ancient Greek perspective, Darce. Why are you telling me this?"

"It's the name of a thing by Edgar Allan Poe."

"What? I read his complete works—"

Darcy corrected me as gently as possible. "I think maybe you read his **Complete Stories and Poems.** That's what everyone reads. No one reads **Eureka.** Even my dad doesn't have a copy."

"Then how do you know—"

"I ran that code message that the bad man left with the teeth through the Internet." I swore silently. I should have thought of that myself. "Even Dad says I'm good with computers. Do you Google? I love to Google. You never know what you'll get. This one time—"

I cut in. "So what is it?"

"Poe called it a prose-poem."

"What the hell does that mean?"

Darcy's face reddened. "I don't know. It's like about stars and stuff."

"Stars?"

WILLIAM BERNHARDT

"Science. Where the stars come from. Planets. Heaven."

I was thoroughly confused, and Darcy wasn't making it any better. "Can you get me a copy?"

"I could not find the whole thing on the Internet, only some parts. Then I went to the library, but they don't have it."

"Keep trying. And Darce—I owe you a custard."

"When do you think that will be? Sooner than a blue moon, I hope, because a blue moon—"

"I remember. We'll do it, Darcy, promise. But first I think I need to read that book."

He left, and a few minutes later my phone rang, as it always seems to do at the most annoying and least convenient times. "Yeah?"

"You look lovely in a black turtleneck. You should wear that more often."

Him.

I stood up, waved at the boys on the lower floor. I pointed to the receiver, trying to get the message across. Men can be so slow-witted. Eventually enough ribs were jabbed and the tracing began.

"Uh, sorry. I was . . . distracted."

He laughed. "Have they instigated the trace now? Can we talk?"

I tried to concentrate. I had to learn as much as possible. And I had to keep him talking. "I don't suppose you plan to stay on long enough for us to trace the call, so why bother?"

"Oh, you never know, dear. I might give you a sporting chance."

Damn straight of you. "Look, I don't know what to call you."

"The FBI agents call me Edgar, don't they?"

And how the hell did he know that? "Is that okay?"

"It's as good a name as any."

"Is that who you are?"

Another pause. "I'm an acolyte. Not a prophet."

Oooo-kayyy. "Can you explain to me what that means?"

"I'd like to. Because you don't have to remain behind, mired in this miserable life you've made for yourself. I can help you. I have only your best interests at heart."

I knew my goal—not only to keep him talking, but to keep him off whatever prepared script he had in his head. The more he extemporized, the more likely he was to tell us something useful. "Have you hurt Fara Spencer?"

"I'm afraid I can't answer that question."

I tried something else. "I got your note. Tracked down the quote, too."

"Did you really?"

"Yeah. **Eureka,** right? I'm trying to find a copy."

"Don't bother, dear. I've brought you one."

At that point, I looked up and saw three Feebs standing in front of me, waving their arms. Meddlers. Couldn't they see I was trying to focus?

I covered the talk end of the receiver and mouthed: "What?"

One of them held up a note he'd scribbled furiously on a legal pad. WE'VE TRACED THE CALL.

Why the hell tell me? Just go already.

Then came the follow-up message. HE'S IN YOUR APARTMENT.

I felt my heart stop. I uncovered the receiver, breathless. "Edgar?"

The line was dead.

Of course, he was long gone by the time the police arrived. True to form, he had gotten in and out without leaving a trace of himself behind. All he'd left was a paperback Dover Press edition of **Eureka: A Prose-Poem** by Edgar Allan Poe, which the techs were treating to a microscopic scrutiny. I knew they wouldn't find anything— nothing useful, anyway. Although he'd left no evidence, we could tell where he had been. Footprints in the carpet. My underwear drawer left open. An indentation on my bedspread.

None of my neighbors had seen him. One

reported spotting a nondescript meter reader, so we were guessing Edgar had used that disguise. But he'd only seen the man from a distance, so he had no useful information.

"I don't get it," Patrick said. "He's been so careful before. So calculated. Why would he come here? Why take the risk?"

I thought about that. In the early days, all his actions had seemed well planned. Careful. But he was becoming increasingly impulsive, or at least more varied in his approaches. Acting on emotion. Kidnapping Fara Spencer, essentially for spite, even though she didn't fit his profile. And now this. How could burglarizing my apartment fit into his fabulous master plan?

Of course, there had been other cases of serial killers who became involved, even obsessed, with one or more of the officers trying to catch them. But just as there was something very different about this killer, there was something unusual about the attention he was paying to me. Like I'd told Tony before, I didn't get the sense that he was perpetuating a cat-and-mouse game for his own amusement. It was more like he was trying to . . . win me over. Seduce me. Even this in-your-face power play had an element of seduction about it. **I have only your best interests at heart.**

"You're getting round-the-clock security," Patrick said. "Don't bother arguing. Should've done it after those damn teeth arrived with your name on the package."

"Does this mean you think—"

"You already know what I think. He'll only be content with presents and phone messages for so long. He's working up his nerve. Till he comes after you."

He could almost pity her as she lay on the table, her eyes closed. If only he could forget all that she had said and done. Forgive. But he could not. That power was no longer his.

At last she awoke, blinking, a dumbfounded expression creasing her brow.

"Am I dead?"

"Of course," he said, leaning into her face. "Welcome to Hell."

She gasped. "You."

"Did you enjoy your nap, Dr. Spencer?"

"But I—I thought—"

"I know. You thought you were dead."

"I remember the wall. And . . ." Her words came slowly, as she retrieved them through a dense fog. "It was hard to breathe. And then—hard to think." Lines formed around her eyes. "Then I don't remember anything."

"You passed out," he explained. "All but asphyxiated. Yes, you were a goner, as the moderns say." He opened his black bag and began laying out the instruments. "But I rescued you. Am I your hero?"

She tried to struggle but soon realized it was useless. She had regained control of her body, but she was firmly affixed to the table. "Why?"

"What fun would it be simply to kill you? A mere two hours of torment. When you deserve ever so much more." He held the instruments up before her face. They glistened in the light from a large overhead lamp. "Do you recognize these?"

She squinted. "Are those—surgical instruments?"

"Indeed. Have you ever seen a straight razor?" he asked, swishing a scalpel in the air. "One sometimes reads about them in books—an orangutan did great damage with one in 'The Murders in the Rue Morgue.'"

"What—what are you going to do with that?"

"Don't you know? You're the doctor." He smiled. "Ah, but you're one of those odd television doctors who aren't actually doctors."

"I want to know what you're planning to do!"

"Apologies in advance. I don't have a hospital gown for you."

She craned her neck, realizing for the first time that she was naked. "Why have you taken my clothes?"

"Standard pre-op procedure," he replied.

She closed her eyes tightly. She was trembling, but despite her fear, she kept her voice remarkably strong. "Is this another pathetic attempt to scare me?"

"Alas, no. I have to move on to other responsibilities. This time you're going to die."

"Of course you have to say that. To terrorize me."

"Believe whatever makes you happy, Doctor."

"Listen to me—you're a sick man. Ill. You're—"

He pressed the razor against her throat. **"Stop it!"**

She quieted. But her eyes continued to peer at him, refusing to look away.

"I've always been fascinated by the idea of open heart surgery, as I'm sure was that orangutan," he said jauntily.

"Please don't do this."

"I must admit I have butterflies in my tummy. I've done a lot of reading on the subject, mind you. But this is my first attempt."

"Please."

"Tell me if I have this correct, **Doctor.** Are you knowledgeable about cardiopulmonary bypass? Percutaneous transluminal coronary angioplasty? Can you say that three times fast?"

The doctor did not respond.

"I gather the typical heart operation begins

with the all-important opening of the chest to expose the heart. Is that right?"

"God, no. Please."

"And the most common way to do that is to slice down the middle of the chest, dividing the breastbone. Am I going to need a bigger knife?"

"I'm begging you."

"Then I expose the heart by dividing the protective covering—the pericardium." He clapped his hands together. "This is going to be delightful."

"At least put me out. Show me that mercy. I know you have the drugs for it."

"Ah, but that would spoil the fun. Tell me, Doctor—do you use a pump oxygenator? I'm fascinated by those little machines."

"This is wrong. You're not thinking rationally or you wouldn't want to do this."

"I'm not sure where to make the first incision. My books don't show. Do I go through the rib cage? I think I'll try. I'll start here. Then here." He stair-stepped the scalpel down her rib cage, stopping to press in at the valley between each rib. "Then here, then here, then here. And when we're done, your lungs will be thoroughly punctured. Will your heart stop? Because I know it's important that the heart stop before we take it out."

"Take it out?"

"Come now, Doctor—you didn't think I'd go to all this trouble and not come away with a souvenir, did you?"

"Please listen to me. You need help."

"Don't presume to psychoanalyze me. You're the one on the couch."

"I'm not qualified to psychoanalyze you, and I don't really believe in all that bullshit anyway. But you should see a professional."

"Doctors. Always making referrals."

"I can't believe anyone wants to live as you do. I know you must be tormented. Do you have hallucinations? Do you hear voices?"

"I've had about enough of—"

"We can block out those voices. We can suppress the irresistible impulses. We can help you." She strained against her bonds. "I will personally ensure that the finest doctors are—"

"Stop it!"

He poured a drink down her throat and then, when the convulsions ceased, he raised the blade of the scalpel and thrust it downward, cutting between her top and second ribs. A terrible hissing sound followed as air escaped from her lungs. Blood rushed up her throat and out her mouth.

"Where is that heart? **Where is it?**"

The razor plunged again, this time between the second rib and the third.

Her body rocked. Gases seeped out of the gaping wounds. Despite the restraints, she jerked and spasmed as if she were in seizure. Blood gushed from the openings in her chest, her mouth, even her ears.

"Where is it?" he cried. "Where is it?" He stuck the blade into her body again and again, until blood streamed from more than a dozen places. " 'Dissemble no more!' " He slashed wildly with the knife, cutting her arms, her legs, her torso, slicing open her chest, drenching himself, staining everything in sight. **" 'I admit the deed! It is the beating of the hideous heart!' "**

CHAPTER NINETEEN

I didn't get free of the cops till midnight, and even then, since my apartment had turned into a crime scene, sort of, I was going to have to stay at a hotel for a few days, with security detail in tow. Which was all right with me. As long as it wasn't the Transylvania.

Thank God, Patrick agreed to meet me at The White Feather. I made some excuse about why we should go separately—the real reason, of course, was so I could leave the security guys posted outside the front door, dash to the bar in the back, grab a fifth, then down it in the ladies' room. I knew I'd promised Lisa I wouldn't, but these were pretty damn extenuating circum-stances. I mean, the man had been on my bed, for God's sake. He'd gone through my drawers. When I thought about this psycho pawing my underwear, I got physically ill. I felt like a rape victim, even though he hadn't laid a finger on me.

Patrick was very good about it, very sweet. I knew he was tired and probably wanted to go home, but he stayed with me just the same. God, I wanted his arms around me. I just wanted to feel safe. I just wanted to feel.

The waitress came by. "Another whiskey?"

I stiffened. "I'm drinking club soda."

"Okay. Want another one?"

I shook my head. Patrick got another beer. Half an hour later, we were still talking.

"You were pretty tough on the boys," I said. "Back at my place."

"With good reason. Someone does a home invasion on a member of the team, that's serious business. We have to take care of our own."

"Thanks for sticking up for me."

He shrugged. "It's what partners do."

God, he was handsome. I felt an itching I couldn't scratch and suddenly I didn't want to be in this bar anymore. "Patrick? You did tell me you were unmarried, right?"

"Ye-es."

"Do you think you could get rid of those security guys for a while?"

"I could, but why on earth—"

"Tell them you're going to stay with me."

He raised an eyebrow. "I am?"

I gave him my best big long lusty. "Unless you still think it would damage our working relationship."

"Probably would. But at the moment, I'm not sure I care." He pushed himself out of his chair. "I'll go talk to the uniforms."

I'm sure he thought we were going back to his motel room, but we never made it that far, at least not at first. I led him by the hand to his car out back, slid onto the hood, and reeled him in.

"Now, wait a minute," Patrick protested.

"What?" I said, grinning in what I hoped would seem a lascivious expression. "Don't you wanna make a girl happy?"

"We're professionals. We shouldn't—"

"Don't be a spoilsport."

"But someone might come. . . ."

"Who cares?" I bit him on the side of the neck.

He pulled away slightly. "It would be wrong of me to—"

"Oh, don't be so damn good. Just this once." I unbuckled his belt and reached inside. After that, I knew I had him. He didn't care who was watching. I pulled him inside me and felt the warmth, felt the glow, felt good, felt safe. For a little while.

Oh, Susan. Oh, my dear, sweet Susan. I wanted so much for you. I wanted to elevate you, to cherish you, to escort you through the gates of Dream-Land. I tried to win you over, to help you see the light, to seduce you with the truth.

But now I see that you have been seduced by another master altogether.

I followed you because I wanted to help you, to learn more about you. Because I cared for you. And I was concerned, genuinely desperately concerned when I saw you enter that bar, knowing your weakness as I do. But that was nothing compared to the abject horror I experienced when you emerged. How could I know you had an addiction worse than alcohol, an addiction to decadence, to evil? I could never have believed it—until I saw you roll onto your car like the most debased jezebel, like the village harlot, an impure woman less worthy than the dust. Yes, I know you've been drinking again. But that is no excuse. There is no excuse.

I know now what I must do.

I must show you the error of your wanton ways. I must show you the result of indulging your passions, let you see your ultimate destiny if you continue on this wicked path. I must crush the spiritual depravity, modify your behavior with an experience so ghastly those old instincts will be dissipated, now and for all time. You must hit rock bottom before you can be cured.

I know you will not come of your own accord. You are willful, stubborn, eternally contumacious. But I can break you. And I will. Not because I want to. Not because I will enjoy it. But because it must be done.

I have only your best interests at heart.

CHAPTER TWENTY

I was used to waking up groggy, disoriented, not knowing where I was. I was used to a throbbing head, pulsing temples, dry cottony mouth. I was thoroughly familiar with finding I had forgotten to put on my jammies. And I was not altogether unaccustomed to finding myself in a strange bed.

But being handcuffed to it? That was different.

"Wha . . . tha . . ." My eyes felt as if they had been pasted shut, and I couldn't wipe them clear since both wrists were cuffed to the headboard. What the hell had happened to me? Could I have been abducted by—

That's when I felt it—the cold clutching at

my heart. The paralyzing, stabbing pain in the chest. Shortness of breath. Panic.

Edgar. Had he found me? Had he given me his drug and chained me here, waiting for the right moment to begin whatever sick Poe-derived deprivation he had in store for me? I pulled at my bonds, but they were secure. I was chained down like a dog on a leash, utterly at his mercy, powerless to help myself. Any moment, he would return with his axe, his dental implements, his—

"Ready for some coffee?"

Patrick appeared in the doorway, carrying a small tray with two cups. "Maybe I'm wrong, but you seemed less the tall-glass-of-OJ type and more the stiff-cuppa-joe type."

"Why the hell am I chained up?"

He looked up absently. "Oh. Right. Sorry about that." He put the tray down and fumbled in his pockets for a key.

"You forgot? Is this some twisted power trip for you? You get your jollies by chaining up women with your big stud FBI toys?"

"I didn't want to do it."

I quieted. "You didn't?"

"Do you remember anything about last night?"

Thinking hurt, but I made myself do it anyway. I recalled the phone call from Edgar, of course, the bar, the thing on the hood of the car.

After that, it got a little hazy. Well, actually, it was a void.

"Maybe you're used to, um, this sort of activity, Susan, but I have to tell you—I'm not."

"Look, just undo the cuffs, okay?" He reached over and freed me. He smelled good. He was already scrubbed and dressed and aftershaved and ready to tackle the day.

I didn't realize how stiff my arms were until I could move them again. They ached. I managed to work them back down to my side. They tingled as if they had been asleep for a thousand years. "Where are my clothes?"

He pointed. I crawled out, clutching the sheet to me, and started dressing. "I hope I didn't—"

"No. You were great."

"I . . . was?"

"Unpredictable. Intense. But great. Really." He grinned. "Something like that is good for you every now and then. Shakes things up a little."

"Yeah. I feel the same way," I said, wondering what the hell had happened.

"I got some food from the diner downstairs if you want it. But my hunch is—" I made a gagging face. "Yeah. That was my hunch." He smiled. "I'll be in the next room. When you're ready, I'll drive you to work. You don't have a car, remember?"

"Okay." It went against the grain, but damn it, I had to say it. "Patrick?"

"Yeah?"

I tried to smile. "Thanks."

I actually ventured a slice of toast as we drove to the office. And even after we arrived, I wasn't quite ready to say goodbye. We walked together to my desk.

"What's this? Another package?" I picked it up. It was about the size of a bowling ball, wrapped in brown paper. "It has my name on it."

"Susan! Get rid of it!" Patrick cried. He shouted for assistance, but I was already unwrapping it. "Susan! We need to have it—"

"It's not a booby trap. He wants me alive."

"Not again! For God's sake—"

Too late. I lifted the lid.

The stench emanating from that box was unlike anything I had ever smelled in my life. And I've been around corpses, sickness, all kinds of filth.

"My God!" Patrick cried, covering his nose and mouth, staring at the wet, viscous, blackish red lump in the box. "What is it?"

There was a card, hand-lettered in block print. He hadn't bothered to encode it.

DR. FARA AND I HAD A NICE HEART-TO-HEART. SEE?

BEHAVIORAL PROFILE—
EDGAR

BY SUSAN PULASKI, M.A., LVPD, AND
PATRICK CHAFFEE, BSS, FBI

Based upon what is generally accepted about serial killers and their crimes, Edgar is probably a white man, between twenty and forty. He is more likely a book-reader than an athlete. He may have some physical deformity. He is literate, perhaps highly so. He is intelligent, as evidenced by his familiarity with and adoption of the works of Poe and his proficiency with ciphers. Various witness statements have described him as both tall and short, thin and wide. Although this could indicate that Edgar is in fact two people, it is more likely that some of the descriptions are inaccurate. At this time, we have no way of knowing which reports are erroneous.

Although he has used a southern accent in his telephone communications, that is probably an affectation associated with his idolization of Poe. If he has any natural accent at all, it is more likely that his origins are in the western United States, Nevada or the surrounding states. Although he has used many Vegas-area locations for his crimes, we cannot assume that he is a native or even that he currently resides here, especially given the propensity of serial killers to move from one place to another. It is possible that the Sin City reputation attracted him. Many of his actions—punishing strippers, removing body adornments or nail paint, dyed hair, etc.—evidence a desire to enforce old-fashioned values.

There are no indications of great wealth, but he must have some income flow. Several of his crimes have required unusual props or equipment. All have involved a drug that cannot be obtained legally in this country without a prescription. Tire tracks suggest that he drives a truck.

Serial killers commonly bear great hostility toward women, often triggered by a negative early female influence. In this case, however, despite the fact that he has murdered at least four women, there are some indications that he holds women in an almost Victorian-era reverence. His background may reflect the conflicted influence of both females he adored and females who abused him. In any case, he likely had a violent and chaotic childhood with little stability. Broken marriages, domestic violence, and early exposure to death are all likely. It is also likely that the male head of his household was absent for a protracted period during his childhood.

Given this rather bleak upbringing, detectives should look for an adult who as an adolescent, or even earlier, was lonely, isolated, withdrawn, angry, and violent. He likely had an active fantasy life in which he imagined himself an important or powerful personage. His fantasies may have involved domination and retribution against those who he felt wronged him. He was probably preoccupied with sex, even more so than most adolescent boys, and had no close friends, much less a girlfriend or sexual partner. During these years, his psychological disorder would have become progressively more apparent, making interpersonal relationships more unlikely. Sports, extracurricular activities, and hobbies would not have appealed to him. He may well have developed an interest in pornography, possibly involving young girls.

The psychological portrait of Edgar that emerges from all the information we have gathered is that of a narcissistic, self-absorbed, antisocial individual. He has an insatiable desire for attention. Despite his antisocial tendencies, deep down he wants to impress, wants people to be appreciative of his work. The crimes Edgar has committed evidence an ability to compartmentalize and rationalize extreme behavior. Thus far, he has acted in conformity with a preestablished pattern, but his recent variation from his previous victimology model—in order to wreak revenge on Fara Spencer—suggests that his innate psychological controls may be slipping.

Edgar's demands for attention—the coded messages, the gifts, the phone conversations, depositing corpses in clever "theme" locations where they are certain to be found—are all classically infantile. Presumably his basic needs were not met early in life and he is psychologically overcompensating for that deficiency now. He has not progressed beyond the self-absorption that characterizes the infantile stage. Although he justifies his acts with some purpose we do not as yet understand, fundamentally he is trying to give himself the psychological nutrients he did not receive in youth.

A sense of superiority and a desire for control characterize the antisocial personality disorder and paranoid personality disorder. The **DSM-IV** does not require us to choose between the two diagnoses, and indeed, Edgar shows traits of both. Because Edgar is afraid of being controlled by outside forces, he will increasingly attempt to control others and subjugate them to his will.

Another disturbing possibility is dissociative personality disorder—what is commonly called multiple personality disorder. Although this has been used in the past as a legal defense by multiple murderers who showed no true pathology of it (Bianchi, Gacy), there are instances of it being a bona fide aspect of the psychological makeup of a serial killer. Of course, even normal personalities can develop imaginary friends and playmates, talk to themselves, etc. But for those suffering from the disorder, one or more alter personalities acquires a specific sense of self. The alter personality can become an outlet for the individual's worst instincts and desires. Should such a personality emerge, the scale of Edgar's activities could escalate to a horrifying degree. . . .

O'Bannon looked up from the thirty-page document he held in both hands. "Good report, Susan. Damn good."

I fluttered my eyelashes. "Well, I try. Do you mean you've actually read it?"

"Twice. And I plan to read it again tonight. I

get something new out of it each time. I'm giving you a special commendation for it."

"Well, be sure to give Patrick credit, too. He came in late, but he's been a huge help."

"Whoever did it, it's brilliant. I think you've nailed him."

"I think so, too."

"Has the lab said whether that heart belonged to Fara Spencer or not?"

I sat on the opposite corner of his desk, facing him. "At this point all they can say for certain is that it came from an adult female of approximately her age. But they're planning a DNA analysis—compared against a sample taken from her daughter's corpse—as soon as possible. And of course it was pretty sliced up. In addition to all the other exclusionary factors in Edgar's profile, I think we can rule out the possibility that he's a trained surgeon."

"And the coded message? The one in the bottom of the box."

"To my astonishment, Darcy wasn't able to solve it instantly. But he's working on it. Apparently Edgar made this one even more devious than the previous ones."

O'Bannon folded his hands in his lap. "The boys tell me you're seeing Patrick Chaffee. Socially. True?"

I squirmed. "Sorta."

He nodded. "Fine man. Solid. Far as I can

see. He'd be good for you." He nodded again, then turned his eyes toward the window. "Don't hurt my boy."

I rose to my feet. "I'll take care of him, Chief. Promise."

We were in a classroom setting—a private conference mandated by O'Bannon between me and all the detectives on Granger's team. I didn't know what the point was, with Granger so openly hostile to my work. When he was with his boys, at any rate. O'Bannon told me he'd seen Granger after hours marking up a copy of my report with a yellow highlighter.

"So we're looking for some freak who's talking to himself?"

"Well, perhaps," I said, with a degree of tolerance that startled even me. "And there are other markers, too. The fake accent. The assumed Victorian sensibility. The obsession with the works of Poe."

"How could we search for any of that?"

"Well," said one of Granger's new lieutenants, "we could check the libraries. See who's been reading Poe."

"Or the video stores," suggested another. "Aren't there a lot of Poe movies?"

"Both good ideas," I said, giving them the verbal pat on the back I knew they'd never get from Granger. "And don't forget this little prank he's playing with the bodies, depositing them in faux graveyards. How many of those can there be?"

"A good Internet search could tell us," said the first lieutenant. "I'll get on that immediately."

"Even if you don't find him, any action that disrupts his usual patterns could be valuable. Remember—we've gotten more information from his last little escapade with Fara Spencer than all his previous murders put together. Why? Because that crime wasn't part of his plan. For once, he acted impulsively. He saw an opportunity and he took it. If we can get him to do that again, he may make another sloppy mistake. He may be smart, but he's still working under some handicaps."

"Like what?"

I gave the class a little smile. "He's nuts."

CHAPTER TWENTY-ONE

If I wasn't mistaken, my lawyer's office was in one of the high-rises Howard Hughes used to live in while he was hiding out in Vegas, before he took up semipermanent residence at the Sands in 1966. Everyone seemed to think he'd lived here forever, maybe even died here, but in fact he was only in Vegas about four years, made some bad investments, split. From publicity hound to Vegas recluse—although I suppose the hermit routine was another way of generating attention. But while he was here, he influenced world politics—and football games—consorted with (and according to some, bribed) both LBJ and Nixon, got progressively balmier, and tried to buy ABC to prevent miscegenation on **The**

Dating Game (true!), all the while protected from the world by his bubble of loyal attendants. Until he died. But hey—he got a parkway named after him, one you just about had to use to get to the airport. Could be worse.

When we arrived at the courtroom, I saw that the Shepherds were looking their usual saintly selves. He was wearing a plain-vanilla suit and tie; she was wearing a cotton print maxi. Did they always dress like that, I wondered, or was this a courtroom ploy to show how different they were from me? Particularly in dullness. I would've preferred to avoid them altogether, but I didn't want to be rude. The judge's bailiff or someone might be watching.

"Nice to see you again," I lied. "Rachel couldn't come?"

"The judges prefer not to have the minors present at these hearings," Mrs. Shepherd explained. "If the judge wants to talk to her, he'll call her to his chambers. Besides, she has basketball practice."

"Rachel?"

"Yes. She's joined the school team."

"Rachel is playing a team sport?"

The woman was so tiny she seemed to bob when she spoke, like one of those mechanical storks you saw at truck stops poised over the rim of a glass. "She's enjoying it. Making new friends."

"Is she any good?"

"Well," Mr. Shepherd explained, "she's inexperienced. She hasn't played as long as most of the other girls. But she has the height, and she's not without talent. I think she has some natural athletic gifts. I'm surprised you didn't encourage her to play."

"Well, I . . . didn't . . . I . . . thought it best to focus on academics."

"Her first game is Monday night. You should come. I think she'd like that."

"I'll try. I've been busy with this investigation."

"Of course."

Delacourt shot me a look, and I amended, "But I'm always ready, willing, and able to spend time with Rachel."

Goddamn those Shepherds, anyway. Did they do it on purpose—always making me feel inferior to their pedestrian middle-class blather? I threw myself into my chair. At least they hadn't turned her into a cheerleader. Yet.

"You know the judge will be watching you," Delacourt said to me quietly.

"Is it my hair or this new Wonderbra?"

"He'll be watching your demeanor. Trying to judge whether you're capable of raising Rachel. I told you this already, remember?"

"You also said nothing would be decided today."

"That doesn't mean he can't start thinking about it."

"And he can tell what kind of parent I'd be from looking at me?"

"He can tell a lot. He's been doing this for thirty years. He can tell if you're drunk, which thank God you don't appear to be. He can tell if you're able to control your temper."

"So I will."

"Then we have nothing to worry about."

The first fifteen minutes of the hearing were boring beyond belief. Lawyers talking lawyer-speak to other lawyers. Occasionally I'd hear my name and my interest level would increase. But after another ten seconds or so of **parens patriae** and **guardian ad litem** my head would be in another place.

"Ms. Pulaski?"

I was pretty stunned to realize the judge was talking to me. I rose to my feet. "Yes, Your Honor?"

"Do you agree with what the counsel for NDHS said?"

I hated these memory tests. Especially when I hadn't been paying attention. But I figured if the lawyer who wanted to give Rachel to the Shepherds had said it, it couldn't be good. "No, Your Honor, I certainly don't."

"Good. Neither do I." I sat back down. Judge Gaynor was in his late fifties, but his hair was still jet black and his face relatively unlined. He had a clipped tone to his voice but seemed to make a point of avoiding rudeness to anyone. "In fact, I'm rather disappointed to hear the state make the argument."

"Your Honor," the other lawyer protested, but the judge waved it away.

"We need public servants. Now more than ever. We are perhaps only beginning to appreciate the enormous benefits provided to us on a daily basis by the law enforcement community. Their job is difficult and the hours are long. We should honor their dedication, not use it as a weapon against them. I've never heard of anyone losing custody because police work was inherently demanding. Or dangerous. And we're not going to set a precedent in my courtroom."

I only half understood what was happening. But I had the sense to know it was good. "Thank you, Your Honor."

"I am aware that Ms. Pulaski is a behaviorist and that she is working on the current spate of killings that have plagued our community. I commend her for taking on this challenge."

My God—was it possible? The judge actually liked me?

"The state's concerns about her income and employment status seem to me totally without merit. I also note that you have found a new place to live."

"Yes, sir. Although my job recently forced me to make yet another move. It's small, but—"

He nodded. "We like our parents to have homes, but we're certainly not going to evaluate their worthiness based upon square footage. Especially not for a dedicated public servant."

For the first time, my spirits swelled. Maybe, just maybe, I had a chance to win this thing.

Of course, it couldn't last. "I am, however, concerned about the state's allegations regarding the personal problems that arose after the loss of your husband. According to the Human Services' brief, you're an alcoholic. Is this true, Ms. Pulaski?"

What to say? I didn't like being labeled, and I didn't think it was fair or accurate, but if I quibbled with him, they would say I was in denial. As I peered into the judge's eyes, I realized that he already had all the factual information he needed. He had asked the question to see how I would respond.

"I have problems with alcohol, Your Honor. That is absolutely true. But I'm dealing with it. I've given up drinking. Totally."

He looked at me intently but didn't say anything.

"I've completed a detoxification clinic. I'm attending Intensive Outpatient classes downtown."

He shuffled some papers. "I have a report

from a . . . Dr. Coutant, who treated you at the detox center."

I felt as if my heart had been stabbed with a dull pizza knife.

"According to him, you haven't been attending the IOP classes. Is that true?"

"I . . . uh . . . I have been absent for a while. This case takes up so much of my time."

"Surely your recovery comes first."

"I plan to start up again, just as soon as—"

Judge Gaynor cut me off. "Alcoholics always plan to do something in the future. Just as they always say they're not going to drink anymore. It's part of the disease."

"But—"

"I admire your work, Ms. Pulaski. Truly I do. But unless and until you've dealt with this problem, no court on earth is going to grant you custody. It would be irresponsible. And certainly not in the best interests of the child. Quentin?"

My lawyer rose. "Yes, Your Honor?"

"At our court date, I'm going to want full and complete medical records on your client."

"Yes, sir."

"I'll want attendance records from the IOP classes. And evidence of enrollment in a certified AA program. And I want periodic blood tests."

He breathed heavily. "Yes, sir."

The judge gave me one last look. "If those tests show alcohol in your bloodstream, Ms. Pulaski, you might as well not bother coming to court."

The rest of the hearing was a blur. I don't remember what happened. I know Delacourt got me to a car, made some inquiries about my state of mind, and entrusted me to the care of my security detail. Meanwhile, my brain stayed on one topic. What the judge had said. How he'd built my hopes up. Then cut them out from under me with a single swath of his vicious scythe.

The hardest part was not the embarrassment, not being called a drunk in open court. Nor was it the judge's demands and requirements. Not even the blood test. Damned intrusive, but in my heart I knew it was a perfectly reasonable request under the circumstances. No, my problem was not the fact that the judge was trying to force me to give up drinking.

My problem was that I knew I couldn't do it.

Why won't the letters do what I want them to do? Normally they dance around and they tell me what they mean and I get it and I can tell Susan but this time I can't tell her anything. I know the Bad Man made it harder because he knew I was good at this just like that teacher in the tenth grade who was mad at me because I showed him that he was working the quadratic equation wrong and so he made me stand at the front of the class and gave me calculus problems and he was trying to make me sad because I hadn't read any calculus books and he made me stand there the whole time and work on it and I did get it eventually I did but by then everyone had gone home and when I showed the teacher the next day he said that I had cheated and I got in trouble. I don't know why I always get in trouble and I'll probably get in trouble if I solve this puzzle but I want to do it because Susan wants it and if Susan wants it then I have to do it.

Talk to me!

He's trying to fool me he's using the same letters over and over again but changing what they stand for like before but more often it's like the letter only appears once and then it's something else and that's why the letters can't talk to me he won't let them. But I can sorta see the words even when he keeps changing everything and he won't tell me where one word ends and the next begins and I think he messed it up in a few places but there's still a pattern and I can trace that letter that keeps coming over and over again I thought it must be **E** but it isn't **E** and if it isn't **E** maybe it's **S** and if it's **S** why does it keep coming up again and again like one word with two **S**'s close together like he's talking to someone and—

Susan.

This was a letter to Susan like maybe they were all letters to Susan but this one really is because her name is in it. **Talk to me!**

Susan oh no no no no no Susan I have to call Dad or someone or that Patrick and get them to get to Susan oh no quickly Susan oh no oh no oh no no no no no no . . .

DAM YOU IM ACELERATING YOUR EDUCATION YOURE NEXT SUSAN

I felt like death on a soda cracker, to use one of David's favorite phrases. I felt as if I had wrapped Rachel up in a box and gift-wrapped her for those narrow-minded prigs she'd been living with. I'd been kidding myself, pretending that I might be smart enough to catch this killer when I knew damn well I wasn't. Not now. Probably not ever. I was as depressed as I ever remembered being in my entire life. And the worst part of it—I wasn't even free to drink. Not in a public place, anyway, not when I knew spies might be watching me at any time.

Why did they have to make everything so hard? Why couldn't they understand? I'm try-

ing, but I'm not Wonder Woman. I'm not perfect. But Rachel wants to live with me, and I
want to live with her. Why isn't that enough?

Just to make matters worse, Lisa was out with
some new kisser of the week, and Patrick was
too busy babysitting the new feds to step out
with me. Not that I really wanted to wake up
handcuffed to the headboard again. But I didn't
want to be alone, either. So instead of chatting
with a handsome FBI agent, I was in The White
Feather wondering if one of the security guys
posted outside could be lured in for a club soda.

Was there anything I hadn't screwed up?
Would there ever be?

David could answer that question. Yes, he
certainly could. But I might not like the answer.

"Susan? Is this chair taken?"

You can imagine my relief when I saw that
accountant-informant guy, Ethan, standing at
the other end of the table. He was a small guy,
but still reasonably attractive. He wasn't Patrick,
but now that I looked at him, I realized they did
have a similar look about them. And Patrick
had given me a pass. So a girl could hardly be
faulted for exploring alternatives.

I invited him to have a seat. He ordered a
Coke. I continued nursing my club soda. We
talked about nothing in particular for a while.

"I know you've been buried in that case," he

commented after a while. "But you haven't said anything about it."

"And I'd like to keep it that way, if you don't mind."

"What do you think that guy wants?"

"Who? The killer?"

"I can't help being curious. After all, I saw the man."

"He doesn't know what he wants. He's delusional. Psychos of his caliber work up these grandiose schemes that only make sense in their own minds. If there."

"Are you sure? I'm no expert, but it seems to me as if he might be . . . working toward something."

"And this is based on seeing him in the parking lot?"

"And everything I've read. You don't think he has a greater plan?"

"Not one that makes any rational sense."

"Do you think you're close to catching him?" He seemed awfully interested in this killer. Didn't he get that I didn't want to talk about it? "I mean, I'm wondering if I might have to come in and pick him out of a lineup or something."

"It's possible. I can't talk about how close we are."

"Sure. I understand." Finally we moved on to other topics. A few minutes later he got around to asking if I was married.

"Widowed. You?"

"No. Wanted to. But never met the right girl."

"You wanted to be married? Why? Just for the pleasure of sharing a bathroom?"

He smiled shyly—almost boyishly. "A stable lifestyle is the key to harmony. A family. You have any children?"

I felt my buzz fading. "No."

"Pity. You'd make a great mom."

"Tell it to the judge." He couldn't possibly know how sensitive a nerve he'd just struck. "I'm sorry, long story. Stupid."

"No, not at all." To my surprise, he put his arm around me and held me. Warmly. There was nothing sexual about it. He was just . . . comforting. "Best to let it out."

"No. I just . . . oh, God."

The bartender came by, obviously wondering if something was wrong, if he was a masher trying to overpower me or something. "She's just not feeling well," he explained, and now that he mentioned it, I realized I wasn't feeling well. My eyesight was getting fuzzy. My limbs were stiffening.

"I—I think I may need to go to the bathroom."

"That's okay," Ethan said. "Let me help you."

"I—don't—need—" All of a sudden, I could barely move. Or speak. He helped me off the stool and all but carried me back to the ladies' room. To my surprise, he went in with me.

And locked the door behind us.

"Is your head feeling heavy, dear? You're starting to slur, and for once, it isn't the copious quantities of booze you've imbibed. I put a little treat in your drink."

I tried to do something, but it was impossible. I was alert and fully cognizant of what was happening. But I couldn't move.

"I didn't want to do this, Susan. I wanted you to come willingly, eagerly. You made this necessary."

He opened the window in the back of the bathroom and stuffed me through it. He was stronger than he looked.

"We're going back to my place now. I've got my truck parked in the alleyway. You're familiar with that alleyway, aren't you? Your security detail is taking a nap, but we'll use the back way just to be careful."

As promised, his truck was right there. He lifted me into the cab, pulled a blanket over me, and started the engine.

"I'm going to give you something to help you sleep now, Susan. You'll wake later. We'll talk. You won't believe all the preparations I've made."

Noooo! I wanted to scream. **Someone help**

me! But I couldn't do it. Couldn't do anything. I was worse than putty in his hands.

The syringe descended toward my neck, a silver drop dangling from the tip. I didn't feel it penetrate, but I knew it had. And a few seconds later, I was gone.

Granger didn't even wait for the car to stop. He leaped out the passenger side door, stumbling, recovering, racing. Darcy followed close behind. Despite repeated efforts, they'd been unable to reach Susan or any of her security detail on their cells.

Granger raced into the bar and flashed his badge. "Susan Pulaski. Tall, dark hair. Tough. You know her?"

The barkeep shrugged. "Sure. Seen her on TV."

"Where is she?"

"She's over—" He turned and almost pointed before he realized the chairs were vacant. "That's funny. She was sitting right there."

"Was she by herself?"

"At first. Then some other guy joined her."

"Who?"

"I didn't know him."

"And this didn't concern you?"

The barman's eyes crinkled. "I thought he

was trying to pick her up. My only concern was that she might wipe the floor with him."

"What did he look like?"

He pondered. "Kind of nondescript. I didn't really notice."

Darcy stood by the empty chairs. "Did you know that she left her purse? Do you think Susan would go away but leave her purse?"

Granger gripped the bartender by the shoulders. "Did you see where she went?"

The barkeep shook his head. "No."

"I did." It was one of the waitresses. "She went to the ladies' room. Her friend was helping her walk. She looked kinda sick."

"Sick? As in ill?"

"Well, I've seen that look on her before." She winked.

Granger plowed through the crowd, carving a path to the ladies' room. Darcy followed. "Clear out!" Granger shouted. And then he kicked the flimsy door to pieces.

The ladies' room was empty. But the rear window offered a view of the alley behind. And it was open.

"Goddamn it. Goddamn it!" Granger shouted. He pushed his head through the window. Nothing there.

"Do you know where she is?" Darcy asked. He was pacing in a small circle, running his fingers through his hair. "Did she go through the window? I think she could fit. Do you think Susan would crawl through the window?"

"No," Granger said bitterly. "Not on her own."

"Then . . . then . . . what . . . what do you think happened to her?"

Granger didn't respond. Because as strange and stupid as Darcy seemed at times, he already knew the answer to that question.

He sat patiently by her bedside throughout the night, wiping her brow, stroking her face, brushing her hair. He could not have been more tender, more loving. Lying quiet like this, freed from the stress of the world, from the demons that plagued her, there was something almost angelic about her countenance. She wore no jewelry, no finger paint, no hair dye, not even makeup. Pure as the day she was born.

He felt an aching yearning for her. **With a love that the winged seraphs of Heaven coveted her and me . . .**

When at last she woke, the face she saw first was smiling.

"Good morning, sweet Susan."

"W-W-Www . . ." She licked her lips, stretched her jaw as if breaking it in for the first time. "Where . . ."

"You're with me, my darling. In my safe-keeping."

"I'm alive?" She looked around as much as possible, given her restraints.

"I wanted to talk with you. Before . . . I'm forced to proceed."

Her eyes darted about the room, obviously trying to learn as much as possible about her location. "What's that noise? Sounds like a waterfall. Where am I?"

"I can't tell you that."

"Why am I strapped down?"

"I couldn't very well let you run free. I did leave you your clothes, and I left the restraints as loose as possible—"

"Let me out of here!" Her voice was finding its strength. "Now!"

"I'm afraid I can't do that, Susan."

She bucked and heaved, straining against the belts that held her to the table. "Let me . . . go!"

"Susan . . . please remain calm. We don't have that much time. I need to tell you about my work."

"You don't have any work. You're a psychotic killer."

"Just let me talk to you a few moments."

"Let me go. Then I'll listen."

"Be reasonable. I know what I have to say may seem . . . unconventional at first, but I'm confident that you're capable of assimilating it."

"I want out of here!"

"We could be such a team, Susan, you and I.

There is another world, Susan, a better world. And we can go there together. I can make it happen. Give up this mortal plane that has so ill-used you and join my quest! We'll meet Virginia—"

"Who?"

"My dear late sister. We could all live together in peace and—"

"Listen to me!" Susan took several deep, invigorating breaths. "I know this will be hard for you to understand, but it's the truth. You are not well. You don't do these hideous things because you have been chosen or because a prophet is speaking to you. You do them because you are ill."

"No, Susan, no." His eyes became clouded. "Please don't."

"This is something I know about. I also know that people like you can be helped. With invasive drug therapy."

"Chemical emasculation."

"Or intensive behavior modification. Or a combination of the two. If you let me, I will try to help you. But if you go on killing as you have been, you're going to end up dead. Do you hear me? They will catch you in the end. And they will kill you."

Was it possible she was right? She seemed so earnest, so good, and her dark eye shone as clear as the—

"You know what you have to do."

"No!" he shrieked, hands pressed against his ears. "Go away! I'm not ready."

Susan's brow creased. "What? Are you talking to me?"

"You know what you have to do."

"There's still time. I think she's beginning to see, just a little. . . ."

Susan strained futilely against her restraints. "I don't know what you're talking about."

"You have strayed. You have allowed this witch of Endor to seduce you."

"No, you don't understand. I just—"

"I am the Raven!"

"I . . . know . . . I—"

"Then you know what must be done."

"I don't want to hurt her. If there's any chance—"

"No more chances! She must be broken! She must be shown the grievous error of the path she has chosen." The voice thundered in his head, knocking him back against the table. Susan stared at him, brow creased, lips parted.

He stumbled to his feet, wiping the water from his eyes. He staggered until he found the black bag, then withdrew a syringe. "I'm so sorry, Susan."

"You don't have to do this."

"I do. I don't want to hurt you. But I have no choice."

Susan twisted back and forth. "You always have a choice. It's never too late."

"It is," he said, his voice cracked with pain. He clenched the syringe in his fist and thrust it into her neck. Almost immediately, her eyelids fluttered closed.

"Goodbye, Susan," he choked. "Goodbye and farewell. Please remember that I loved you."

After that, there was only blackness. For both of them.

BOOK TWO
THE ARABESQUE

I was a child and she was a child,
In this kingdom by the sea:
But we loved with a love that was more
than love—

—"Annabel Lee"
EDGAR ALLAN POE

CHAPTER TWENTY-TWO

"Damn it, Boss, it's been five days."

"I know how long it's been, Granger."

"The press is asking questions. A lot of questions."

"The press can go screw itself."

"Did you see those pictures?"

O'Bannon stiffened, like a metal rod had replaced his spine. "Yes."

"I have to assume we're not the only recipients. I'll bet they went to all the papers, all the TV stations. They're going to want to know what happened to our behaviorist."

"Who the hell doesn't?"

Granger's face twisted up. "Boss—those pictures. They're—we have to tell them something! Try to explain—"

"Why?" O'Bannon pushed away from his desk, matching Granger bellow for bellow. "It would be different if we knew something. But let's face it—we don't. We don't have the slightest idea where she is or whether—" He stopped short of saying it.

"Face facts, Boss. Five days. None of this guy's previous victims lasted five days. All of them were killed within a day or two of their capture."

"Shut up."

"I'm telling you, we've got to face up to it."

"And I told you—"

"Susan is dead."

O'Bannon froze.

Darcy sat behind him, in a chair in the corner of his office, not saying a word. Listening to everything.

"Darcy," O'Bannon said, lowering his voice, "would you leave us alone for a moment?" He fumbled in his pocket for change. "Run across the street and get yourself an ice cream. Get us both an ice cream. Okay?"

"No."

The response was so startling that both O'Bannon and Granger were thrown. "Excuse me?"

"I think I would rather stay here." As if a

sudden chill had come over him, Darcy's hands rose and flapped against themselves. "Did you know there was a woman kidnapped in Vancouver in 1979 who was held for sixty-seven days till she escaped? She overpowered her kidnappers and ran away. She hadn't been harmed."

O'Bannon and Granger looked at one another. "Darcy . . ."

"In Omaha, in 1984, a teenage girl was kept in a basement for over six months until she was found by the police. She wasn't hurt, too."

O'Bannon felt as if he had gained a hundred pounds in the space of a second. "Darcy, we have to be realistic about this."

"Elizabeth Smart was gone for eight months, but she came back. Patty Hearst was held for a hundred and twenty-four days until she was found by the FBI, but she had been brainwashed into joining their cause. Do you think Susan could be brainwashed?"

"No," O'Bannon grunted. "I think anyone who tried to play mind games with Susan would probably end up in the loony ward himself."

"Actual brainwashing in the post–World War II era has been quite rare and mostly ineffective," Darcy recited. "Several instances of the Stockholm syndrome have been documented, but it is still uncommon."

"What have you been reading?"

"Unless there's torture involved. Do you think Susan might be tortured?" His voice remained as loud and expressionless as ever, but the flapping of his hands accelerated.

"No, son." He took the boy's hands and brought them to rest. "I don't think so. But we have to accept the fact that Susan is prob—is— may not be coming home."

"I think that I should have figured out that message sooner. Do you think that I should have figured out that message sooner? Should have should have should have. That makes it my fault that the Bad Man got Susan."

"Of course it isn't."

"For that matter," Granger said, "I wish I'd reacted faster."

"There was no way anyone could have predicted what this bastard would do. He took out three security officers, for God's sake, with that magic drug of his." O'Bannon pressed the heels of his palms against his forehead. "Darcy, please go get some ice cream."

"No. I will stay here."

"Darcy, we have our best officers working on this case. The best thing you—"

"I am not going for ice cream. I am going to help."

"Darcy, you're not a police officer."

"I could be!" He turned, and although he did not quite make eye contact, he looked in the direction of his father. "You—you—you always w-w-wanted me to be a policeman. So I will be a policeman."

"Darcy . . ."

"You—you d-d-don't think I can do it."

"These men have been through years of training and—"

"I can do it. I can do training."

O'Bannon turned for help to Granger, who was pointedly looking away as if he were not paying attention. "You have some . . . special challenges, Darcy."

"Everyone has special challenges."

"But we have to be realistic and—"

"Do you think that any of your officers could decode the Bad Man's messages? Because I do not think any of your officers could decode the Bad Man's messages."

O'Bannon craned his neck. "That was a special situation. You need to go home, Darcy. When I get back tonight, we'll talk more. Maybe we can make popcorn."

"No!" Darcy threw down his hands. "I do not need popcorn or ice cream or going home. I will help on this case, even if you don't think I can. Susan thought I could help and I did help. I did!" He marched to the door, his eyes watering. "I m-m-may be an idiot, Dad, but Susan needs me. And I am going to help her."

Am I dead? I wondered as the light streamed into my eyes. It wasn't a warm sensation—more like the grinding of gears against metal, brakes after the brake pads have worn. I should've been surrounded by darkness, I remember thinking, but instead I was immersed in light, too much light, white hot and blinding. I wanted to turn away from it but found that I couldn't move.

"Hello, sugar bear."

David again. I wasn't surprised. Wasn't exactly relieved, either. But he was something to look at. As always.

"What are you doing here? Do you know what happened to me?"

He didn't have to answer. He gave me that soft, knowing look, the one he always used to disarm my wrath.

"I feel so . . . stupid. So ashamed."

"You shouldn't. It wasn't your fault."

"Wasn't it?" A thought occurred—I should try to open my eyes. I needed to orient myself, separate the real from the imagined. "I think I'm . . . broken."

"You did before."

"But this is . . . different. This seems . . . I don't know. Final. Unrecoverable."

"I've felt like that."

I looked at him unflinchingly, peering into

the depths of those overwhelming blue eyes. "I guess you must've."

"But here's what you need to remember, Susan."

"You're giving me advice?"

"This is what you already know. What you've always known. What I could never figure out. When you forgive others, you're not doing them a big favor. You're doing yourself a big favor."

"David." All at once I wanted to reach out, wanted to hold him, wanted to bring him back to me and never let him go. "Am I dead?"

"What do you think?"

"I think . . . I saw someone. Something. Before you. It was beckoning to me."

"And you think it was . . . ?"

"You know what I think it was."

"You think it was Death."

"Can you tell me what to do?"

He smiled that goddamned irresistible grin. "Well, if he wants to play chess with you, don't."

"How long has he been in there?" Lisa asked.

"Days," O'Bannon replied. They both peered through the window of the door to the small police library where Darcy had taken up residence. He had his books, an evidence file, and an Internet connection. "I've been sending in food—pizza and stuff—and sometimes he eats it. I don't know when was the last time he slept."

"What does he hope to find?"

"I don't know. I've asked, but he can't really explain it. He just starts stuttering and flapping his hands. I think maybe he has some crazy idea that if he punishes himself enough, it will bring Susan back."

"What do you think?"

O'Bannon looked away. "You know what I think. What everyone thinks."

Lisa's face crumpled. She pressed a hand against the wall to prop herself up. "I should've been with her that night. She called me, but I was off on a date with some loser I didn't even know. If I'd been with her—"

"He might've taken you both."

She shook her head, brushing away her tears. "No. I could've stopped it. It's my fault."

O'Bannon walked to the water fountain and splashed cold water on his face. "You sound like Darcy. He says the same thing." He used his shirtsleeve to dry himself off. "Susan had been so depressed, felt so isolated. I think she thought she had lost everything, that no one loved her anymore." His teeth clenched. "My God. She had no idea."

"Is there anything more you could be doing?"

Lisa asked, her voice cracking. "Anything I could be doing?"

"Believe me, we're trying everything possible and then some. We've reassigned all available manpower and borrowed more from neighboring jurisdictions. We're tracking down every lead we get, every sighting. So far, they've all been bogus."

Lisa covered her face. "I've—I've seen the pictures."

"Damn! What irresponsible—"

"I made him. This reporter I know at the **Courier.** He showed me." She pushed herself into the corner, eyes wet and wide. "My God, do you think it's even possible? Could she still be alive?"

"I don't know," O'Bannon said, swearing under his breath. "And at this point, I don't know if she'd want to be."

The first sense to return was my sense of smell. There was an acrid bitterness in the air, kind of like coffee left too long on the burner. And there was something else, something fouler. Sour milk. No, that wasn't it, but it was like that. Stale, stinky. Something I didn't want to be near.

Then I heard the sounds. Wind whistled in my ears, and I felt cold. And a pounding, crashing sound, an auditory sense of motion. It was that rushing water noise, same thing I'd heard before. A forceful sound, the kind that could sweep me up and wash me away.

I wished it would.

My eyes finally opened on a bleak field of gray. Was I in the desert? I wondered. On a mountaintop? Took me more than a few moments to realize what I was staring at had to be an overcast sky, since I was lying flat on my ass. Literally. Because I was naked.

I suppose that shouldn't have been a big surprise, all things considered. I was on something hard and flat and grainy. Dirty. It was in my skin and under my fingernails. I wondered how long I had been there. A long time, I thought.

I tried moving and was amazed to find I actually could. My joints were stiff, stiff to the point of near immobility. My skin hurt. But I forced myself. I sat up, and it couldn't have taken more than half an hour or so.

I surveyed my surroundings. I was in some kind of gravel pit, white and chalky, no one else around as far as I could see. The crashing sound I'd heard was water, huge tumbling quantities of water, tumbling down not far from where I lay.

Eventually I had to turn my attention to myself, in all my glory. My skin was red and scorched, except for the bruises, which were many. I was exposed, floppy, veined, dirty, about as unattractive as it was possible for a woman to be. I repulsed myself.

What the hell had happened? I tried to recall, but the effort made my head pound. I remembered being captured. I remembered lying on his table. I remembered being scared, so scared, like I haven't ever been before, not even when I found out about David. I remembered hating myself because I was helpless. I should've figured a way out. I should've pulled some clever last-minute trick that saved the day. Instead, I became a victim. Another pawn in the hands of a psycho who had proved himself a thousand times smarter than I was.

I had no sense of time and no timepiece. I'd forgotten what little I ever knew about telling time with the sun, so I can't possibly say how long it was before I noticed the boxes. Seemed like an eternity that I sat there thinking, crying, cursing, not able to move, not wanting to move. But eventually that passed, or at least subsided. And I turned my attention to the shoe boxes he had left at my feet.

There were two of them, each with a message scribbled across the top in indelible black marker. The first box read: TO HELP YOU REMEMBER.

Like Alice in Wonderland, I slowly opened the envelope inside, not wanting to know what it contained, but unable not to look.

The envelope contained pictures, lots of them. Polaroids, amateur stuff, obviously taken by Edgar himself. They all had the same subject. Me.

They must have been taken while I was under the influence of his drugs. My eyes were open, but there was no one home. I could tell. There was no me in there. Only my body. My naked body.

I had been posed, over and over again, different for each picture. He had . . . made me do stuff. He had me playing with myself. Touching myself. Sexual poses, me on all fours, me with my legs spread, me dry-humping the furniture. One nasty pose after another. In some of them, he'd given me props. A broomstick. A Coke bottle. A dildo stuck in my mouth. A dazed, zoned expression on my face, like I liked it. Like I was drunk and I liked it.

I fell forward on my hands, heaving. He must not have fed me, because nothing came up, much as I tried. I hurled so hard I expected the lining of my stomach to spew out. I felt sick. Betrayed. Abused. Raped.

I wanted to throw the pictures away, to lose them, to forget they ever existed. And then I saw the sheet of paper in the bottom of the box. It was a mailing list. All the places he had sent copies of the pictures. All the local television stations. National news agencies. Local radio shows. Police headquarters. The FBI. Chief O'Bannon.

He'd sent the pictures to Chief O'Bannon's home.

Darcy.

I fell forward, scraping my breasts against the gravel, wanting to hurt myself, wanting to die, wanting this to all be over, just please, please let it be over. I pounded the box with all the force my fists could muster, which wasn't enough to dent cardboard. Look what he's done to me, David. Look what I let him do to me.

Of course it was just a matter of time before I opened the second box. It had been labeled, too: TO HELP YOU FORGET.

Only one thing inside that one. A quart bottle of scotch whiskey.

I ripped the lid off the bottle and pressed it to my lips. I was hungry, starved, thirsty, desperate to forget. I opened my mouth and let the liquor course down my throat.

I gagged. The booze spilled everywhere, all over me. I bathed in it. As soon as I'd stopped choking, I tried again. I would use more restraint this time, I told myself. Just take a sip. A little sip, then another. Sip myself into oblivion. I raised the liquid salvation to my lips.

This is what he wants you to do.

I stopped. Where had that come from?

This is what he wants you to do. Why do you think he gave it to you?

I pulled the bottle away and stared at it, as if I had never seen such a thing in my life. He was manipulating me, just as he had done from the start. As I had allowed him to do. This is why he let me live. This is why he gave me the bottle. Because he knows I won't be able to resist.

And he was so right. So bloody goddamn right.

He was trying to break me, to destroy what little was left so he could scoop up the pieces and reshape me into whatever he wanted me to be.

I pushed up to my feet, amazed that I could do it, and walked toward the noise. I stood naked before the god of the waters, staring down from the precipice. It had to be a hundred feet down to the basin, maybe more. I didn't even have to climb over a barrier. Just one simple step. That's all it would take to end it, to find peace. Hell of a lot simpler than slashing my wrists with a shard of glass. No one would care. Not after they saw those pictures. And everyone would see those pictures.

The thundering crash of the water crescendoed in my ears.

That's what he wants you to do.

I stared down into the maelstrom. And saw something I had never seen before.

That's when I made up my mind.

First, I got the goddamn pictures and tossed them in. The next bit was harder, a lot harder. But I did it. I turned the bottle upside down and let it pour out into the abyss. It would've been simpler to just toss in the bottle, but this was more satisfying. It occurred to me that I might be spiking the Vegas water supply. Well, tough.

The booze was gone. The photos were gone. The need to destroy myself was gone, at least for the moment. I was naked, and I didn't know where I was, and I had no idea how to get back to civilization. Or even if I should.

I fell back onto the gravel as if I were a bag of boneless meat. And stayed there. In time, I fell asleep. Not unconsciousness, not drug-induced stupor, but the real thing.

And I even dreamed. Or something like it.

CHAPTER TWENTY-THREE

Patrick marched into headquarters, his face taut and lined. He threw his coat at the nearest hook on the rack. It missed, fell in a crumpled heap on the floor. He didn't notice. He slid behind Susan's desk and started reviewing all the reports on Susan's disappearance. Just as he had every day this week. Over and over again.

"You've got messages," Madeline shouted from the lower floor, waving pink slips in the air.

"Give them to someone else," he said, his face buried.

"They want you."

"I don't have time for crackpots and false confessions."

"Some of them say—" She paused, lowered her voice. "They've seen Susan."

"I've followed up on twenty-two Susan sightings. Granger has done more than that. Not a damn one has led to anything."

"You got a problem?"

Patrick whipped his head up. Somehow, O'Bannon was right in front of him. "Sorry. I've been . . . immersed."

"So I hear. Obsessed, some say."

Patrick craned his neck. "Sir, when an officer is down—"

He waved it away. "You don't have to tell me, Chaffee. I've known Susan all my life. I used to diaper the girl's bare bottom." O'Bannon's eyes briefly closed. He looked tired, aged. "Madeline says you were making a stink about the files."

"I was trying to find out everything I could about Susan. Her background, personnel file, police record."

"You think the key to finding her is in her past?"

"I don't know. But profilers are supposed to absorb all the data, collect every scrap of evidence, then come up with some brilliant conclusion. And I've read everything else." He paused. "Except one file. It was logged into the computer index. But I couldn't find it. Madeline thought maybe you had it."

"She was right. It's restricted."

"I don't know why you pulled it, but if there's any possibility that it could help us find her—"

"It's not about Susan."

Patrick stopped, thought a moment. "I found it listed in her directory."

"A cross-reference. It's about her husband. He was a cop, too."

"David."

O'Bannon frowned. It was obvious that this was a subject he preferred to leave alone. "How much do you know about him?"

"Not much. Except that he's dead. And his loss seems to have really hit Susan hard."

"It did."

"Started her alcoholism."

He shrugged. "Certainly a contributing factor."

"I know he was a detective. Worked with Granger."

"Know anything about his death?"

He shrugged. "Police work is dangerous. I assumed he was killed in the line of duty."

O'Bannon drew in his breath, then slowly released it. "The first part is right. The last part is wrong."

"He didn't—?"

"They'd been married eight years. Susan probably wasn't the easiest person on earth to live with, but then David had a temper on him, too. They fought, but no one thought much about it. In a lot of ways, they were perfect for each other."

"Chief, are you saying—"

"They had a big fight that day. Right here at headquarters. Everyone watching. He stormed out. And that was the last time we saw him."

Patrick's lips parted. "No."

"Yeah." He handed Patrick a thin file. "Put his weapon in his mouth and blew his brains out." O'Bannon shook his head. "I guess he won that argument."

I was sitting at a dinner table lit with candles. The soft, rosy glow cast a warm aura across the sumptuous spread. I felt all warm and snuggly.

"What happened?" I asked.

Rachel answered. "We found you, remember? In the desert. The police brought you back here."

I turned my mind back, a mental process that produced physical pain. I remembered wandering around the desert, or trying. But my legs still didn't work well and could only move a few feet at a time. Something had happened to my right leg, or maybe it was the lingering effect of the drugs. I couldn't seem to remain conscious long enough to focus my thoughts. I was hungry. And thirsty. I had thought myself very noble when I poured the booze into the brink, but I later came to regret it. I needed to drink. I didn't need a drink. There was a difference. I kept telling myself.

"I told you I was going to prepare a very special dinner," Rachel said. "Don't you remember any of this?"

"I—I—"

Another voice from down the table. "Surely you remember the kiss I gave you when you got home."

It was Lisa. Lisa!

"I mean," she continued, "I don't normally go in for kissing chicks. But when my homegirl has been lost in the desert for damn near a week, that's different. I kissed with wild abandon."

"I hope this doesn't mean you're going to give me a nickname."

"Well . . ."

"Or if you do, I want it to be Goddess."

Lisa laughed. "Goddess it is." She held up a platter. "I made my artichoke dip."

I gasped. Lisa made awesome artichoke dip. Three different cheeses, mayonnaise, and oh yes I think there's some artichoke in there somewhere. It is to die for. She hadn't made it in months. I'd almost forgotten how good it was.

Rachel held out yet another platter. "Don't forget the buffalo wings."

I gazed down in ecstasy. Another favorite. With bleu cheese on the side, not ranch dressing like some lame-o joints served. "Did you make this?"

Rachel squirmed. "In a sense."

"In what sense?"

"In the sense that I drove to Chili's and picked it up."

I laughed and pushed six of them onto my plate.

Lisa chirped up again. "Don't forget the potato skins."

"Potato skins? What kind of a meal is this, anyway?"

"All your favorite junk," Rachel explained. "You deserve it."

It was too good to be true. "What about the Shepherds? Will they be joining us?"

She shook her head. "They've given up the battle. NDHS, too. It's sad that it took your being kidnapped for them to realize what a wonderful guardian—parent, really—you've been to me. They've all agreed that you should have custody." She giggled. "I'm so glad, Susan. It's what I've wanted all along. I'm coming home."

"And . . . and the basketball? And that church group?"

"Oh, the Shepherds made me do that stuff. All I want is to be home with you."

The flickering glow of the table filled me. I felt a warmth inside, a contentment. Something I couldn't remember having felt for a long time.

Granger cleared his throat. "Susan, would this be a good time to tell you something I've wanted to say for a good long while?"

"Well, that depends . . ."

"I'm sorry. About the way I've behaved."

"Oh, you haven't—"

"Sure I have. I've been a regular bastard and I know it. I knew it when I was doing it. But I just—I just—"

"I know. David."

"It's not that. Not just that." He sighed. "It's because you're such a good cop. And I know it. Hell of a lot better than I am. Smarter. I feel inferior around you."

"You shouldn't. Let it go."

At the end of the table, one chair was empty. The place had been set. "Why isn't someone there?" I asked.

"Because you haven't decided," Rachel said.

I gazed about the table. "Surely all this food isn't for me."

"Of course not." Rachel laughed, then pointed.

David was sitting at the other end, facing me.

"You're back," I whispered.

"Surely you knew I couldn't stay away for long."

I nodded. "Thank you."

He seemed puzzled. "For what?"

"For helping me. Back in the desert. Helping me survive."

"Oh. Well, there's a problem with that."

"Problem." My heart raced. All of a sudden I couldn't catch my breath. "What problem?"

"You see, Susan . . ." I knew he didn't want to go on, but he did. He was always braver than I was. "You're still in the desert."

"I—I am?"

"Yes, honey."

"But I can see you. And Rachel and Lisa. And all this food."

"Because you're starving." He laid his hand gently on mine. "You're dying, sweetheart."

I opened my eyes. The sun blistered. I didn't know where I was, found it painful to move. My naked skin was burned and scratched and bleeding. I had chills and sweated and shook.

I had never left the desert. I could hear the crashing of water, but it was more distant than it had been before. Why weren't there any people around? Shouldn't there be people? How long had I been wandering? Weak, exposed, lost. Broken.

Had David said I was dying? But I was already dead. Surely I was already dead.

CHAPTER TWENTY-FOUR

She isn't dead she isn't dead she isn't dead I don't believe that she is dead Mom Mommy is dead and they wouldn't tell me and everyone looked at me so sad and I didn't know why and Uncle Braden smelled like rosewater but she couldn't be dead because if she's dead then it's my fault and we won't have babies and I won't get to be a policeman and most of all I won't get to see her and I like her I really really really like her she's nice to me.

Why couldn't I have read that message sooner?

DAM YOU IM ACELERATING YOUR EDUCATION YOURE NEXT SUSAN

Dad says I shouldn't use words like that and

I should forget I ever heard them and so I did forget and it took me longer for the letters to talk to me and the Bad Man took Susan. It's my fault because I'm so stupid stupid stupid I'm a retard just like they say at Dad's office I'm a stupid stupid retard. **Your mother can't be with you anymore, Bambi.** This Bad Man is playing with us he likes to give us clues but we don't know what they mean and he took Susan and we don't know where and please let her still be alive please please please Mr. Strickland said that Jesus saves and Jesus protects so please take care of Susan and keep her alive.

DAM YOU IM ACELERATING YOUR EDUCATION YOURE NEXT SUSAN

Also if he spelled better it wouldn't have taken so long and he made mistakes translating the words into code, too. He left out the apostrophes and he didn't put a period at the end of the sentence and Mrs. Calloway in first grade said I should always put a period at the end of the sentence but I don't think that way and she smelled moldy like she didn't brush her teeth enough and he put in the wrong kind of **dam** I would've gotten it sooner if he checked his spelling.

Unless that's the trick.

Dad! I need my dad or Patrick or someone I hate it when they make games with words I never get those stupid jokes because words just say what they say and he used the wrong one unless he meant to use the wrong one because he thought it was funny and maybe we can still help Susan maybe it's not too late for Susan please don't let it be too late for Susan please please please please please.

Why does everyone who's nice to me have to go away?

"Paaaa-trick!" Before he could look up, a body fell across the desk, almost head-butting him in the process. It was Chief O'Bannon's son, Darcy.

Madeline came running up behind him. "I'm sorry, sir. I told him you didn't want to be disturbed."

"It's okay." He helped the young man off his desk. "Haven't seen you in days."

For once, Darcy's conversation was remarkably direct. "I know where she is."

Patrick felt a deep sadness in his heart. He knew the boy had a crush on Susan. Even if he wasn't physically demonstrative, his devotion couldn't have been more evident. Given his pre-existing emotional fragility, her disappearance must be tearing him up. "Did you have a dream about her?"

"I know where she is! I figured it out."

"I'm sure you did."

Darcy grabbed his shoulders and shook him. "Did you know that in World War II the Allies invented a code that could only be solved if you had a special machine because they used hidden cells and multiple substitutions and—and—" His voice began to break up, like it was tumbling into a funnel. "Did you know that these codes are impossible to solve and that must be why the Bad Man used it when he wanted to say something that we wouldn't get until it was too late?"

Patrick didn't know what to do. If this were a normal man, he'd think he was on the verge of a mental breakdown. With an autistic, he didn't know what it meant. Except that he needed help. "I know you're good with codes. You figured out what Edgar's warning said—"

"But not what it meant!" Darcy flapped his hands, rocking back and forth. He broke away from Patrick and circled around the desk, again and again, with increasing speed. "My dad says I don't get jokes."

"Well, sometimes I'm not the quickest—"

"But I do! I do get jokes. Maybe I don't think they're funny, but I know when people are kidding, some of the time. I knew when the other kids were making fun of me."

"Darcy—"

"But I hate puns. Why should one word have more than one meaning? It's confusing and it doesn't make any sense."

His agitation was intensifying. Half the office was watching now. Out of the corner of his eye, Patrick saw Madeline go for Chief O'Bannon, probably thinking he was the only one who could get the boy under control. "Darcy, I think the best thing would be for you to go home now. Get some rest. If anything happens—"

"You thought he spelled it wrong!" Darcy shouted. "But he didn't spell it wrong. He's too smart for spelling wrong. It was a clue."

"What?"

"About **dam.** 'Damn you.' But he left off the **n.** Because he didn't mean that kind of dam."

"As I recall, he misspelled a couple of words."

"To fool us. He's smart and tricky. You said so in your paper. 'The subject is possessed of extraordinary intelligence and imagination.' So why would he misspell words?"

Despite Darcy's convoluted, histrionic manner, Patrick was beginning to grasp his point. "Are you saying—?"

Darcy climbed up on the desk chair and began jumping up and down. "She's at a dam! He took her to a dam!"

O'Bannon appeared at the top of the stairs. "Come on, Darcy. Let's go home."

"She's at a dam! You have to go and find her!"

Somehow, O'Bannon managed to drag his son away, apologizing to everyone as they passed. Darcy kept on screaming. He looked back, his hands stretched toward Patrick.

"Go to the dam! Go to the dam!"

Patrick fell back into a desk chair. Was it possible?

Hoover was the closest and most famous dam, but hardly the only one. How could they know? It was probably nonsense. He couldn't take tips from a hysterical autistic boy. Surely they weren't that desperate. If there was any chance of finding her, it would only come from good solid detective work. Surely.

"You aren't real," I said as I ran my fingertips down David's perfectly sculpted chest.

"Does it matter?" he replied. "I'm the only game in town."

I laughed and pulled him closer. "Do that thing."

"What thing?"

"You know. That thing you do."

"With . . . what part of my body?"

"Your nose, silly." I laughed. I loved it when he was like this, all tender and attentive. Happy. No moods, no complaints, just him and me. "The way you crinkle it."

"I do not crinkle my nose. That's a girl thing."

"You do. Sometimes."

"I do not." He pressed against me, letting me feel the ripple of his rib cage, his strong thighs pressing between mine. Letting me remember how it was before . . .

And then he took me. All in a rush, the way I liked it best, the way that always gave me goose pimples. Orgasm was nothing compared to the creeping, dizzying head rush that hit when he came after me like that. It was all I could do to breathe, to prevent myself from perishing from a surfeit of pleasure.

"Susan?"

I blinked rapidly. That wasn't David.

A shadow fell across my face. "I'm sorry it took us so long."

"Patrick . . ." I grinned a little. "Could you wait a minute? My husband and I were having a thing. . . ."

He put his hand on my forehead. "Why didn't you stay where Edgar left you?"

"I wanted to stay. David told me I should go."

"David?"

"That's what Edgar wanted, you know. He wanted me to stay at that place and he wanted— well, he didn't get it. I wouldn't give it to him."

"You're delusional, Susan. Which is no surprise, given your condition." He shouted over his shoulder. "Can I get some help?"

I laughed. "Whatever. You're not real, anyway."

He kept on shouting. "Get a stretcher! Start the IV! She's dehydrated and starved, with a serious case of exposure."

"You shouldn't be looking," I said, giggling a little. "I'm naked."

"Not anymore." He spread his coat over me. It felt warm and scratchy. "We'll get you to a hospital."

"No, you won't. I'm just dreaming you. But it's a good dream. Nice of you to come."

"I didn't come alone."

A moment later, I saw Darcy rush forward, hovering behind Patrick. "Susan!"

Good grief, who let **him** into this hallucination? "Darce." I tried to wiggle my fingers but couldn't. "Nice to see you too."

His face was weird, eyes wide and kinetic, as if he were being pulled a thousand directions at once. Just as well that he was a stoic sort who wasn't comfortable with human contact, because—

"Ooof!"

Darcy threw himself on top of me, squeezing me in his arms. "Susan! Susan!"

Well, I couldn't dream this, could I? "Darcy?" I said weakly.

He was screaming and crying all at once. The volume made me wince, another element I couldn't be dreaming. "I told them it was a dam. I told them it was a dam."

"All right, son, please move aside. Let us get her into the ambulance."

I could tell he didn't want to let go. Funny thing was, I didn't really want him to let go. But they pried him away and hoisted me onto a stretcher. Darcy insisted on riding in the ambulance with me. I could tell Patrick didn't like the idea, but he didn't want to take the time to argue about it.

It was a pleasant little ride to the hospital, my friends all around me. I slept a little, listened a little, maybe both at the same time. It was nice. Darcy held my hand the whole way.

CHAPTER TWENTY-FIVE

She's alive! She's really alive and I knew she would be except I didn't know but I hoped and she is she's alive alive and we found her and I guess Jesus does save because I prayed and I prayed and there she was she's all beat up and she lost her clothes but she's alive and I'm so happy I was so sad and scared but she's alive and she let me hold her hand in the big car on the way to the hospital.

Her hand felt nice.

The next time I opened my eyes—at least, the next time I opened my eyes and remembered it—I felt much better. Which was not to say I felt good—I was feeble and tired and had trouble speaking. I felt like hell, like I still had one foot in the grave. But definitely better than before.

"It's because they've been force-feeding you," Lisa explained. "Through the tubes."

I made a purring sound. "Must be yummy stuff. Could I get some to take home with me?"

"You don't want it." She was sitting beside my hospital bed, her arm snaking through the steel bars and resting on mine. "May be good for you, but it makes your skin cold as ice. You'll never get a date."

"Might be better for everyone." Rachel was also there—really, truly there. I don't know how she'd managed to slip away from her keepers, but I was grateful they'd allowed it. "Help me out, Rache—have I given you a hug yet?"

"Yes, but here's another." She leaned across the bed and gave me a squeeze I could feel through the sheets. God, but that was good. What had I done to merit this attention, this warming affection? It reminded me how pathetically I'd abused their friendship, lying, hiding, them trying their best to help me while I acted as if my only friend was that revolting bottle. I didn't deserve them. "I love you, Susan."

Damn it if I didn't start to cry. Must be the medication. The tears just welled up in my eyes and there wasn't a thing I could do to stop them. I choked, couldn't speak. I was going to start earning this friendship, this affection. I had to do better, for them if not for me.

"Love you, too," I snuffled, wiping water from my eyes. "So this is real, right?"

Rachel and Lisa exchanged a look. "As far as we know."

"And you're real. This is actually happening."

"Are we delving into existentialism here?" Lisa asked. "Because if so, I need to go home and reread my Kierkegaard. Then I'm sure we could have a very deep and profound metaphysical conversation."

"Please don't." I squeezed Rachel's arms. "Did I mention that you look great?" Very fresh-faced and healthy—the picture of an all-American teenage girl. She was wearing a little makeup, which she'd never done before. But I had to admit it looked good on her. She was dressed well, too, in a skirt and some kind of fancy pastel T-shirt. The jeans I was accustomed to seeing her in didn't show off her legs, which were truly excellent legs. And it appeared that Mrs. Shepherd, unlike myself, knew the current location of her ironing board.

Rachel laughed, obviously pleased. "I think it's the basketball. I've been getting lots of exercise."

"Heard you were quite the defensive player."

"Yeah, I do the pick. I mean, they give me

that because I can't shoot. But maybe next year . . ."

"I have no doubt." I gave her another squeeze. "You can do anything you want to do. You know that. Why don't we get together, soon as the warden releases me. Maybe even this weekend."

She winced. "This weekend?"

"Uh-oh. Big game?"

"Actually . . . it's the science fair."

"You're in the science fair?"

"Yes!" she said, bubbling with enthusiasm. "I made this cool automated mini-cyclotron thing that demonstrates the principle of torque. Do you know what torque is?"

"Will you think less of me if I say no?"

" 'Course not."

"No."

"Well, then. You need to come see my exhibit."

"Engineering . . . that's Mr. Shepherd's field, isn't it?"

"Yeah, before he retired. He's been a big help. I mean, it's my work. But he was able to, you know, give me some assistance. . . ."

That I couldn't have given you in a million years.

There was a knock on the door. Patrick poked his head in.

"Come on," I said. "We're having a party."

He did, and Chief O'Bannon came in behind him—with Darcy. Darcy hung back and didn't say a word. But he seemed pleased to see me. And I was pleased to see them.

And then I remembered the pictures, which Patrick and the Chief had seen—I could tell just by looking at them. And I wished I could crawl into a coffin and close the lid behind me.

Patrick gently laid his hand on my shoulder.

"Are you feeling any stronger?" he asked.

There were times when I wished I didn't have this empathic gift. "Oh, God, you want to talk business, don't you?"

He squirmed slightly. "If you're up to it."

Lisa jumped to her feet. "If you guys are going to start talking serial killer, I'm out of here." She looked at Rachel. "Give you a ride home?"

Rachel nodded. I waved at Lisa on her way out. "Call me tonight."

"Okay. It'll be late. I've got a date."

Of course she did. "Don't kiss anything I wouldn't."

"That—" She stopped, made an erasing gesture with her hands. "Too easy."

After they were gone, Patrick began his subtle probing. Apparently he had been chosen as point man. Darcy and the chief sat quietly behind him.

"I know no one has specifically asked you about what happened yet," he said.

"True."

"And I'm sure it's the last thing in the world you want to talk about."

"True."

"But the doctors say you may be here for weeks, and we just can't wait that long. What can you tell us about him?"

"He was very weird, Patrick. Babbling. I think our theories about multiple personalities must be right. He was talking to a voice I couldn't hear, acting as if it were controlling him."

He pondered a moment. "We've neither seen nor heard any trace of him since you were kidnapped. There've been no more killings or abductions. No letters or phone calls or packages." He smiled a little. "We were wondering if maybe you'd killed the bastard."

"I wish."

Patrick grew quiet. I knew what was on his mind. "Susan . . . we've seen the pictures."

"I know," I said quietly.

"The media got them, too. But to their credit, they haven't run them, not in the papers or TV. But they have . . . talked about them."

I closed my eyes. I felt even more naked, more exposed. More raped. But what did I expect? Deference from the media? Right, and a Corvette for Christmas.

"Does Rachel know?"

"She hasn't seen the pictures, but . . . she must've heard or read something."

And the custody judge who already thinks I'm unfit, too, no doubt.

I looked across the room at Darcy. Had he seen those lovely glamour shots? Would he understand them if he did? Impossible to know. But when I peered into those expressionless eyes, I was sure I saw something. If not a total comprehension of how I had been compromised, then at least a knowledge that I had been hurt. And a sorrow. For me.

"I want to assure you," O'Bannon said firmly, "that this will not in any way affect your consulting relationship with the LVPD. As soon as you're released, if you want to continue working, we want you."

"Thanks, Chief."

"Although I think it might be best if we took you off this case."

"No way in hell."

Silence.

"Look, I wasn't drinking. I don't care what it looked like in those pictures. I wasn't drinking." At that time.

"Susan—"

"I'm telling you, I didn't drink!"

Patrick grinned, damn him. "I know."

"You—do?"

"Blood test. Your blood alcohol was a big fat zero. If you'd been drinking, we'd have found a trace, even after all the time you spent out in the desert. He used his drug on you."

Thank God I managed to resist Edgar's little bottle of temptation. "So I can stay on the case, right?"

I could see O'Bannon wasn't happy, but he wasn't going to argue with me. While I was stretched out in a hospital bed with an IV in my arm, I had the upper hand. Momentarily.

Darcy was the one who broke the silence. "Why didn't they bring you ice cream? When you're in the hospital, they're supposed to bring you ice cream."

I couldn't help but grin. "As soon as I get loose of this joint, Darcy, you and I are going on a custard binge. We need to make up for all those potential Very Excellent Days I missed."

"Is there anything more you can tell us?" Patrick asked. "Did you see his face?"

"Yes. And as it turns out, I've seen him before. But he was disguised. He's smart, Patrick. Smarter than we ever realized."

"I think that has become abundantly clear. It's just unfortunate that you were drugged. I wish to God we knew where he took you."

I drew in my breath, wriggled up against my pillow. I had to seem strong for this. "I know where he took me."

"What?"

I let the memories trickle in, unwanted as they were. The rushing of water, even when I was flat on my back on his table. We were near the dam, even then. And I saw enough of the interior to make a pretty good guess about the exterior. "Approximately. I can find it, anyway. But I want to go with you."

"Susan—he could still be there."

"No. He's smart, remember? He's gone somewhere else."

"But you can't be sure—"

"Oh, yes," I said, hoping my resolve was evident. "I can be sure. But we still might find something of interest. Now how fast can you get me out of here?"

"Susan, the doctors say—"

"I don't care. We have to act fast. And no, I can't give you directions. I have to go."

"Susan, you've been through a horrible ordeal."

My eyes narrowed. "And I want to make sure Edgar never has a chance to do that to anyone else. Ever."

The doctors pitched a fit, but I lied through my teeth and told them I felt fine, and eventually the need to track down this maniac won out over medical prudence. They gave me some pills to help with the pain and a few hours later I was in a car with Patrick trolling around the dam, searching for something I recognized. I knew I could find it. And I did.

"This is it," I said.

I was certain I was right, even though I'd never seen it from the outside. It was a small cabin, a shack, really, stuck in some of the scrubbiest country you could imagine, not far from the Hoover Dam. The spindly trees and faint vegetation weren't enough to make anyone forget we were in the desert. The joint was probably intended as a weekend retreat for boat or fish fans. "Let's go."

"We need a warrant," Patrick cautioned.

"You're a fed. Don't you carry them around in your back pocket?"

"No. But I can send a fax via my cell phone. And my address book has the numbers of a lot of judges."

Well, that wasn't too shabby. Granger put a phalanx of officers around the perimeter, and we waited.

An hour later we were inside.

The ground level was perfectly ordinary. Tacky furniture, no food, a dinky television. But I knew there had to be more. It didn't take me long to find the basement door. It was locked, not that it mattered.

The light switch didn't appear to work, so we

had to resort to those cool pencil-thin flashlights like you see cops use on television. It was dark and dank, stereotypically basement-like. There was no wind, but I felt a chill just the same. I usually got my impressions from people, not places, but this little dungeon had a palpable ambiance. It was terrifying, threatening, oppressive. Insane.

"Maybe you should stay upstairs," Patrick whispered to me.

No. In truth, I still felt weak, nauseous, barely able to stand, but I wasn't going to let them shut me out. I inched forward, shining my light ahead. The more I saw of this room, the more I recognized. The warped wooden walls. The high window, probably the only source of exterior light—and the passageway for the sound waves that brought me back here. The table. His goddamn table with the restraining straps. And there was a stench. A putrid, almost unbearable stench.

I heard a sound, sprang around. The beam of my flashlight crisscrossed the room. Just Granger, creeping up behind me. This was a big basement, I saw now. Maybe it was just an illusion, but it seemed as if it was bigger than the house. Like it stretched on forever.

Then I jumped. Way up in the air, like a human bottle rocket. Dropped the flashlight and everything. And I had practically been expecting what I found. But that isn't the same as seeing it.

There was a body hunched behind the table. A corpse. My God—had she been there the whole time I'd been held down here? The whole time he'd been playing with me?

It was Fara Spencer. Her eyes were wide open, her face frozen in an expression of fear or panic or whatever her intense final horrific emotion had been. Her skin was gray and seemed stretched, barely covering the prominent bones of her chin and cheek. She was naked, with a huge blood-caked cavity in her chest. She'd been decomposing for more than a week, but you could still tell who it was. Even if you wished you couldn't.

I clamped a handkerchief over my mouth. The nausea was almost overwhelming. "Call the coroner," I muttered.

"Already on it," Granger said, and I guessed he stopped to dial his cell, and Patrick was getting a close-up look at Fara, which explains why I was the first lucky devil to see the really big surprise Edgar left for us.

For me.

At first I thought it was plowed soil. Had he been gardening down here? I wondered. Potatoes, maybe? But my first impression was wrong. There was dirt, and evidence of digging. Two spades were propped up against the far wall.

Not a garden. A graveyard. A real one, this time.

The mounds went wide across the floor and deep into the background. But they weren't buried. Not entirely. As if to create a memorable tableau, he'd left parts sticking up out of the ground. A decayed arm. A rotting leg. Sometimes a face. And at this stage of decomposition, they all seemed sadly the same. Small. Young. Female. Dead. Long dead.

My God, I thought, as the aching in my gut, in my heart, intensified to unbearable proportions. Must be more than a dozen of them.

We thought Edgar had five victims. We thought he began with Helen Collier.

We were wrong.

My head became unbearably heavy. My legs began to ache, pinpricks running up and down them. I remember thinking, I ought to get to a chair. But there was no chair, and I sure as hell wasn't going back to that table. I heard Patrick scream out my name. I saw the dirty ground, the corpse-strewn soil rushing toward me.

And then I was out.

So they finally found it, he observed, smiling to himself. The audition. The warm-up act. It seemed more impressive, viewed from this height. Almost disturbing for its . . . wastefulness. But this had been the work of his previous incarnation. Not him. Another person altogether.

He had expected them two days ago, and was startled to see not only that they finally arrived, but that they had brought Susan with them. She must've insisted.

She had not been drinking. Had she resisted the temptation he'd laid before her? Had he broken her, or had she somehow managed to reassemble herself? He would have to wait quietly and watch. Proceed with the new plan, with the implementation of the secret he had been given. And when the time came, hope that Susan was ready for him.

No wonder he had found himself attracted to Susan. It was all so clear now, now that he knew everything.

She was the Vessel.

He put the binoculars back in their leather case. It would be so easy to pick them all off, one by one, leaving nothing but a few more corpses littering this potter's field. And why not? He could do anything now, anything at all.

He'd had to isolate himself these past few days, return to the texts, meditate. Commune with his totem. He eventually realized that his flaw was not so much in his actions, nor in his plan—but in himself. He could not force the

offerings—they had to come willingly. These
paltry reincarnations were woefully insufficient;
something far greater was necessary to merit the
meed he desired. And he had to secure a Vessel
worthy of the soul with which he sought re-
union.

He was a new person now, a new man with a
new plan.

He was ready to Ascend.

His long days in the xeric wasteland had been
fraught with temptation, but he had resisted
them. His passage had been filled with tor-
ments, but he had weathered them. His last
night in the Spring Mountains had been the
time of his translation. He had offered his very
essence, everything he had. He had gone without food, without water, re-creating the vision
quest that first revealed his true destiny. He'd
stripped and pounded himself with sand,
abused himself with the cactus flower. He'd bled
and he'd wept. And when at last he'd fallen
down on the rocky crag, exhausted beyond
reckoning, he believed he had failed.

The truth had come to him in a dream, as
did all knowledge of that other blessed world.

"You have done well," said the voice, the
one that could not be ignored. **"You have
pleased us, and so you shall become one with
us. The time of your Ascension is at hand."**

And so the voice which he had once heard in his head became his own. He became the totem. And the totem was he.

He looked down now upon those pitiful fools, scurrying about like infantile ants. He laughed, and even his laughter was filled with power. He was the mountain now, and they but grains of sand, a part of him, but not of him, in his world, but not of his world. He was invulnerable, indomitable. He had slipped beyond the boundaries of time and space—**By a route obscure and lonely, / Haunted by ill angels only, / Where an Eidolon, named Night, / On a black throne reigns upright, / I have reached these lands but newly . . . / From a wild weird clime that lieth, sublime . . . / Out of Space, out of Time . . .**

He stretched his arms toward the sky, letting the stardust settle all around him, feeling at home and at one with the cosmos. I am larger than death, he knew, and greater.

The man I once was is no more.

I am the Raven.

CHAPTER TWENTY-SIX

After I came to, I stayed outside the basement while the crime techs did their work. There was nothing I could contribute at this stage. Better to let the experts work unimpeded. I took another pill, rested in the backseat of Patrick's car. I still felt drawn, unsteady. And I'd be lying if I didn't admit I was embarrassed. Fainting was so amateurish, and worse, so . . . girlish. Even if I did just get out of the hospital. It was exactly what the old-guard grunts expected someone like me to do.

After another hour or so, I got bored and slowly made my way inside. I saw Amelia Escavez outside the house. She had a football-sized metal frame on the ground and was pouring plaster inside it.

"Another tire track?"

"Footprint. Wanna see?"

I did. "Think it's him?"

"A definite possibility. There are several of them around the place."

"Anything that might help us find him? A distinctive tread, maybe?"

"I don't think so. But it'll be good for confirmation if you do catch him." She quickly corrected herself. "When. I mean—after—"

"I know what you mean."

I entered the house. Crime lab guys in coveralls were working over the shack, upstairs and down, hoping against hope for any trace of a clue that might tell us where this man was now. Using something called gentian violet, which stained skin cells left behind on adhesive surfaces, they'd managed to lift prints off a piece of masking tape. But since Edgar didn't appear to have a record, that wouldn't get us far. Ditto for the hair and fiber traces. As always, Edgar hadn't given us anything that would help us find him. Didn't even have the courtesy to leave a forwarding address.

When I got to the basement, I found Darcy hunched over the remains of Fara Spencer. Now that was a bizarre sight. Here was a kid so innocent, so gentle, he literally wouldn't step on a spider. Terrified of puppy dogs. But he had no difficulty working around a corpse. Of course, the corpse could do him no harm now, but that wouldn't comfort most people. Only Darcy's brain was free from those irrational emotional associations we have about the dead.

"Did you ever eat bugs?" he said when he saw me approach.

I don't know. Maybe it was the combination of that horrible corpse—which was crawling with bugs—and the suggestion of eating them that made me certain I was going to heave, the only thing that would be even more embarrassing than fainting. I placed a hand against the wall to steady myself and willed my stomach to behave. Most importantly, I kept my eyes locked on Darcy—not the corpse he was scrutinizing, and not the field of corpses that lay beyond.

"No, my tastes run more to meat and potatoes."

"Did you know that some people in some countries eat bugs all the time? I don't like eating bugs. When I was in grade school, some of the other kids told me to eat bugs and I did. But then they laughed at me."

I'd wager he got a lot of that in school. "I don't blame you for not liking bugs."

"But I do. Bugs are cool. Except for spiders. Just not for eating." He grinned guilelessly.

Well, of course—what little boy didn't like bugs?

"I used to collect them, but my dad made me throw them all out."

"Spoilsport."

"Then I started reading about them in the library. Did you know that blowflies love dead bodies?"

"I, um, think I heard that mentioned at the academy."

"They love to lay their eggs in dead people. This body has bugs all over it."

"Yup." I didn't look.

"Do you know how long it takes a blowfly to go from egg to larva to pupa to adult?"

"Oh, the answer's on the tip of my tongue. . . ."

"When it goes from egg to first instar larva, it's about this big." He held his fingers only a few millimeters apart. "Then it sheds its skin and goes to second instar larva—this big." The fingers widened. "Then it sheds its skin again and does the third instar." His fingers were more than ten millimeters apart now. "After that, it becomes an adult."

"That is so cool. You know, I should go to the library more often."

Darcy pointed at the squirmy, whitish bits crawling out of Fara's nose. "Those are third instar. She died ten days ago."

I did a double take. "But how could you possibly—"

"It takes eight days to get to the third instar."

"But you can't know when it was born."

"Blowflies like to lay their eggs in dead people two days after they die. Eight days later, these bugs are third instar. So she died ten days ago. Right?"

The things that emerged from that wild gallimaufry brain of his. I wondered if maybe he was just talking through his hat, trying to impress me. But I really didn't think he possessed the slightest instinct for deceit.

"He's right."

I turned and found Jodie Nida, the coroner's assistant, standing behind me. "You know the five stages of decomposition?"

"Um, gross, grosser, more grosser . . ."

"No. Initial decay, putrefaction, black putrefaction, butyric putrefaction, and dry decay. Each is associated with a different type of insect infestation. Your young associate was describing the putrefaction stage—that's when blowflies like to join the party. The gas formed by bodily organisms causes the body to swell. And smell. Blowflies groove on that. Which is why the body has those larvae crawling in and out of every available orifice."

"Except her mouth," Darcy said, not looking up.

Jodie examined the body. Bugs all over the nose, the eyes, the ears, the cavity in the middle of her chest. But not the mouth. "You're right, kid. Guess they didn't like her lipstick."

Darcy tilted his head to one side. "Which do you think would be grosser—her lipstick or that big hole in the middle of her chest?"

Jodie chuckled. "Blowflies have different tastes than you and me."

"I had this teacher once, Miss Overton, who tried to kiss me on the forehead every day. She wore lots of lipstick. I thought it was yucky."

We all laughed, which was pretty amazing, given the circumstances and surroundings. Here we were, standing in a field of corpses. And what does Darcy think is gross? Lipstick smooches.

And you know what? He's right.

"Twenty-two corpses, total," Patrick announced.

My eyes closed. "Jesus God. All young girls?"

He nodded. "Brace yourself. You're about to be inundated with white shirts." So he knew how respectfully we locals spoke about his brethren. "No question now but that this case is federal. And major."

Just as well, much as I hated to admit it. It wasn't as if we were closing in on him. "Anything new from forensics?"

"No. But they have instructions to copy us

on all reports. And there will be a lot of them."
He looked at me, and his eyes seemed to soften.
"I'm thinking we need to spend the night to-
gether."

Could he possibly mean what he was saying?
After what happened to me? "Are you saying—"

"Pull an all-nighter. Like we were in college.
Rework the profile from top to bottom, incor-
porating all this new information."

I stared at him. "That won't take all night."

He looked back at me. "Then we'll have to
think of something else to do."

My cell phone rang. I opened it up, not even
thinking.

"Hello, my dear. Glad you made it home all
right."

I tensed up, my back rigid. Bugs were crawling all over my skin, sending prickles of fear
coursing through me. I could never mistake,
never forget, that voice.

I mouthed to Patrick, "It's him."

"I made it, all right. No thanks to you."

"Susan, you wound me. Did I hurt you?"

"Damn straight." I realized this probably
wasn't the psychologically soundest technique
for extracting information, but I couldn't help
myself. I hated the bastard. I hated him. I could
never forgive what he did to me.

"I caused you no physical injury. And I gave
them a fair clue so they could find you."

"So what do you want? A medal?"

"You."

My heart stopped. I almost couldn't speak. "You—had me."

"Not your body. Your mind. I want you to see what I see. I want you to join the enlightened. The name Pulaski is etched on the rolls of Dream-Land. You are to be the Vessel."

"What about the other girls? The twenty-two we found in your basement. Were their names etched, too?"

"I haven't given up on you, Susan. You're very special to me." He paused. "I slept with you, Susan. Did you know that?"

"I—I—" The gorge rose in my throat. I felt physically ill.

"While you were sleeping. I held you close, pressed up tight, your naked body against mine."

"You—"

"It was meant to be, Susan. I knew that. Every time I touched you. Our destinies are intertwined."

I screamed into the phone. "You had no right to—"

"I did what had to be done. Just as I do now. You will come to understand this, Susan. Soon. The Day of Ascension is almost upon us."

"What's going to happen? What are you planning?"

He sounded rapturous. "Something im-
mense. Something spectacular."

"Could you be a little more specific?"

"It starts tonight. The new offerings will be
chosen. And it ends as the prophet would've
wanted it."

"What? What are you talking about?"

"The end of the world, Susan. The end of
this world. The start of the world to come."

And on that note, he hung up.

"We have to put our plans on hold," I told
Patrick. "I mean, for the—the—you know." I
stuttered like a stupid schoolgirl. "We should go
on patrol. Even if it's hopeless and futile. We
should try. Tell Granger to get every man he has
out on the street."

"You think Edgar is going to do something
tonight."

I felt a chill spread through my entire body.
"I'm certain of it. I don't know what. But he's
starting something. Something new, something
horrible. Something worse than anything he's
done before."

Judy and JJ and Tiffany waited until they were
sure no one was watching, then tiptoed past the
PARDON THE INCONVENIENCE cones and slipped
behind the door.

"I can't believe we're doing this!" JJ squealed.

"Me neither," Tiffany said breathlessly. "Wait till we tell the rest of the squad. They'll die!"

The three girls clung to the shadows draping the walls, then crept through the cobwebs and pumpkins and papier-mâché ghosts.

"Do you think he's been here?" Judy whispered.

"You know he has," JJ replied. "I mean, how could he not? That's where they found the first one. It's probably why they've shut it down."

"Shhhh," Tiffany said. "We can't stay long. Mrs. Cross will miss us. I just wanted a little souvenir. Maybe get my picture taken in the graveyard."

They were wearing matching uniforms, V-neck sweaters and short pleated skirts, both in orange and black. They were all three teenagers, all three blond, all decked out in makeup and sports bras.

"All right," Tiffany said, passing a palm-size metallic object to JJ. "Here's my Advantix. Take me on the porch with the graveyard in the background. I'm going to try to look scared. Does this look scared?"

"More like you're having an orgasm."

Tiffany knocked her on the shoulder. "You whoredog."

"I'm not a whoredog."

"Are."

Not much of the haunted house façade was left. The hotel appeared to be in the process of creating a new decorating scheme.

"Stop!" she hissed. "Did you hear something?"

They sneaked back into the shadows, stopped, listened intently. JJ wished she had thought to bring a flashlight as well as a camera. The atmospheric darkness, while useful for avoiding detection, became oppressive when she suspected someone else was in the room.

Suddenly, just at the edge of her peripheral vision, Tiffany saw a flicker of movement.

"Over there!" she hissed.

The others turned just in time to see the approach of a slight dark figure, hair wild, arms waving, running toward them. "Nevermore!" he bellowed.

The girls screamed. "It's him! It's him!"

One after the other they ran toward the front door—only to find it securely locked. They pounded with their fists, but it would not budge, and no one came to their aid.

They could see him more clearly now. He was wearing a black waistcoat with a ribbon tie. He had a small mustache and a furrowed brow and eyes that peered at them like daggers. He spoke again, an evil smile playing on his lips. "'Once upon a midnight dreary, while I pondered weak and weary . . .'"

"Help! Please! Someone!"

The dark figure held his arms over his head like a monster and shouted: **"Boo!"**

And then he began to laugh.

A moment or two later, the girls stopped pounding. They stared at the formerly menacing figure, now prostrate on the floor, giggling at them.

"S-S-So—you—thought—" It was difficult for him to speak, he was laughing so hard. "You thought I was the guy?"

JJ felt foolish and annoyed. "Well, you look like him."

"And how would you know what he looks like?"

"You've got that whole Poe thing going on."

"Ah. That would be a clever disguise." He pushed himself up off the floor, brushing the seat of his pants. "My name is Elliot Barnes. I'm an actor. I used to work here till they shut down the Poe display. And you are . . . ?"

With some reluctance, JJ introduced herself and her two friends. "We're here for a cheerleading competition. We had some spare time, and we're not old enough to gamble, so we thought . . ."

"That you'd come see where the first body was found? The parking lot where Dr. Spencer was kidnapped?" He shook his head. "Rather morbid bit of spectating."

"But this story is huge! And it started right here," Tiffany said. "It's all they talk about on the news!"

"And isn't that a sorry statement. On a slow news week a celebrity hangnail could command national attention."

JJ cleared her throat. "Can you tell us why they're shutting down this room? I think it's kinda cool."

"Well, after the body was found here, it seemed in bad taste, even by Vegas standards. There was some thought of simply eliminating the graveyard, but now, with all the attention this case has been getting, Poe has lost his fun factor. We're going to remodel the room. This haunted house will become the cathedral Notre Dame de Paris. Should be ready by Halloween."

"Bitchin'."

The man stopped, tilted his head, looked at her strangely. "Would you mind saying that again?"

JJ gave him a look. "Why?"

"Humor me."

"Oooo-kayyy." She glanced at her friends and shrugged. "Bitchin'."

"Perfect delivery." He snapped his fingers. "Has anyone ever told you that you resemble Britney Spears?"

"Me?" She pressed her hand against her chest. "No."

"I'm surprised. Are you familiar with our Legends show? It's an impersonator gig. They're all the rage right now—hotter than the buffets. Everybody's got one, but ours is the best. We've been looking for a Britney Spears."

"Serious?"

"Dead. If you're interested, I could set up an audition."

She hesitated. "I can't sing all that well."

"You don't have to. We play records—all you do is move your lips. Well, for a Britney Spears show, I suppose you move everything. But you don't sing."

"I can dance," JJ said, bubbling. "I'm a cheer-leader. I know how to move."

"I'll bet you do."

"What do you think, girlfriends?" She turned to her cohorts, then back to him. "You got any parts for my friends?"

"I can't guarantee anything. But Britney usu-ally performs with backup dancers, doesn't she?"

"Cool! What would I have to do?"

"Just audition." He handed her a card. "Here's my address. If you could come by tonight around midnight—"

JJ's brow furrowed. "Is this your place?"

"Yes. I just moved in. Why?"

JJ stared at the card pensively. "I don't know. . . . I'm not sure I'd feel right going to a stranger's house alone. I mean, I'm sure you're a nice guy and all, but what with . . . you know. All that's been going on."

"I can assure you I'm perfectly safe."

"Oh, yeah, sure, but—"

"I'm not really Edgar Allan Poe, you know. I just play one on TV."

She giggled. "Well . . . could we all come? Together?"

He clasped his hands together. "I think that would be lovely. Strength in numbers, right?" He beamed. "I have a very good feeling about this audition. I have something marvelous to show you."

"Freeze!"

The girls jumped. From behind the crumbling haunted house façade, a man in a uniform came running toward them.

"Elliot, you're under arrest."

The man in the Poe getup threw up his arms. "Damn! What are you doing here?"

"Protecting these foolish young ladies from you." He grabbed the man's wrists and handcuffed him. "Hotel security, ladies."

Judy took two steps backward. "But—doesn't he work here?"

"No, he doesn't, and if you don't mind my saying so, miss, you were foolish to think he did just because he's in a Poe getup. I've been listening, waiting until he solicited an illicit rendezvous with minors. This man is a known exhibitionist."

"A—what?"

"He had something marvelous to show you, all right. But it wouldn't have gotten you a part in a show."

JJ gulped air. "Oh, geez, yuck. I feel so stupid."

"You should. Do you girls understand that there is a sadistic killer on the loose in this town? This isn't the time to go sneaking away from your teachers to see if you can get a souvenir from a crime scene. Young women are being tortured and killed. And the way you were acting, you could well have been next on the list."

"I'm sorry, sir," Tiffany jumped in. "We weren't thinking."

"Yeah," Judy said. "We'll go back where we're supposed to be. We promise."

"As if that was worth anything." He pushed his arrestee toward the door. "You just stick with me, young ladies. I'll drop him off at our holding facility. And then I will personally escort you back to your sponsor."

"You don't have to do that. We can just—"

"With all due respect, miss, I'm not offering you a choice. I'm in charge of security here, and the hotel doesn't need any more young corpses turning up. You're sticking with me."

Tiffany gazed at him with admiration. "He's right. He's got a job to do. Let's go with him, girls."

They followed the guard out of the ballroom.

The irony, he realized, a few minutes later as he led them out to his truck, was that all the publicity about the mad Poe killer had made it not tougher but easier to obtain offerings. When people are afraid, they put their trust in authority figures. A little too much so, as it turned out.

He could hardly contain his delight. This was so perfect, and so much simpler. Why not do all three at once? Now that he knew the truth, knew all the secrets, everything was so clearer. But those cheerleader outfits would have to go. Garish colors, preposterously provocative short skirts, even matching colored underwear. They looked more like streetwalkers than schoolchildren. Shocking. And the makeup would have to come off, all of it. The jewelry. And God knows, the studs. He just hoped none of them had tattoos. That could be time-consuming. And painful.

He smiled with the sweet contentment of a man who enjoys his work, who knows that his endeavors are worthwhile. There was so much to be done. So much wonderful work to be done.

The Raven never rests.

"We're not going to find him, are we?"

It was two in the morning, and I suppose Patrick was tired of humoring me. "Did you think we would?"

No. Of course not. Catch a killer before he strikes when you haven't got the who or what or where, only a deadly certainty that it will happen? Not likely. But I needed to try. If there was any chance of preventing a girl from experiencing what that man did to me, I had to try.

"We can pack it in," I said, trying to be charitable. "If you want."

"I can take it as long as you can," he replied. "I'm a fed, you know. We're invincible."

"I've heard that. But I've never had a chance to prove it."

"You came damn close the other night."

Ouch. Me and my smart mouth.

I looked out the window again, searching for some basis—any basis—to change the subject. Barry Friedman, my favorite comic, was playing at the Excalibur. What a treat that would be. Put all this misery aside and just laugh for a while. But I knew that wasn't an option. Didn't matter where I sat—I wouldn't be thinking about the jokes.

Patrick's face was a study in chiaroscuro as the car oozed down the street, segueing from one bright light to the next. A handsome, strong face. One I'd never taken the time to sort out my feelings for. Oh, sure, I'd had sex with him. I think. I'd yelled at him, bossed him around, been rude as hell to him. But how did I actually feel about him? How did I feel about anything? Why didn't I know? Had the booze deadened me? Or was I just dead and using the booze to hide the ugly truth from myself?

Hadn't had a drink all day. Hadn't had a drink since Edgar grabbed me. Another good thing about wasting the night trolling the streets of Vegas with Patrick. No opportunity. Of course, I felt hellish, but there were extenuating circumstances. Patrick had wanted me to check myself back into the hospital, and I have to admit that I was tempted. But I couldn't let this manhunt go on without me. I was needed here.

On the left, just past Circus Circus, I saw the Transylvania, where the killer had dumped his first victim. Where he'd taken Fara Spencer. I was tempted to pull over and check the joint out. But why? Edgar was much too smart to go there again.

"Maybe it is time to call it quits," I said.

"Want me to come back to your place?"

"Nah. I'm pooped."

"I can sleep on the couch."

"Not necessary. But thanks." A nice guy. Which no doubt explained why I still felt ambiguous toward him. God forbid I should get hooked up with someone nice.

Except that David had been nice, hadn't he? Once upon a time. Before the troubles started.

My God, David. Was that the real reason I was ditching Patrick tonight? Because I was still hung up on my dead husband? Or more accurately, because I still hadn't forgiven my dead husband?

Funny how much clearer you can see things when you're sober.

"Just drop me out front," I told him. "They've got so many people watching my place now, Houdini couldn't get in." I leaned over and kissed him on the cheek. "Night, Patrick."

"Night."

And I headed back to my boozeless, snoozeless, antiseptic hotel room, a yearning in my chest, my body complaining because I wouldn't give it what it wanted, my heart aching because even if I didn't know her name, I knew there was a girl out there dying tonight. One more person I had failed to save.

I pressed up against the door, eyes clenched shut. So this is what life is like sober? Wonnnnnnnnderful.

CHAPTER TWENTY-SEVEN

You'd think nothing on earth could be more innocent and stress-free than a stroll through the forensic lab. You don't expect screaming and shouting—that happens upstairs, where we high-IQ detectives hang out. And you certainly don't expect to see your toxicology expert getting into it with the boss's son.

"Please please please please please please please please please please please," Darcy said, over and over. He wasn't exactly shouting. His voice was always loud. Near as I could tell, his theory was that if he didn't give his opponent a chance to argue with him, then he won the argument. An approach I have to admit I've used once or twice myself.

"Listen to me!" Jennifer Fuentes (yes, now I knew her last name) was trying her best not to lose it. "There's no poison!"

"Please please please please please please please please please please please."

Jennifer was totally losing that cool detached scientist thing.

"What's going on?" I asked.

"This guy is making me crazy!" Jennifer said. "The chief asked me to humor him. He didn't say I had to take orders from him. Especially not stupid ones."

Darcy looked at me, his face brightening. "Did you sleep well?"

"As a matter of fact, I did. Why do you ask?"

"Your breath." And then he started right back up again. "Please please please please please please please please please please."

"Would you make him stop that?" Jennifer begged.

"Sorry. I work with him, but I don't control him."

"Try!"

I shrugged. "Darcy, lay off already. Before you get carpal tongue syndrome."

He did. Instantly.

Wow. Feeling more powerful than a locomotive, I asked Jennifer, "What does he want?"

She rolled her eyes. "He's got this crazy theory that Fara Spencer was poisoned."

"Poisoned?" I winced. "Darcy, I think we all know how she died. You may have noticed that big hole in her chest?"

Darcy flapped his hands. "Did you know that one in five domestic murders are committed with poisons you can obtain without a prescription?"

No, and I was happier not knowing. "Any chance he's right?" I asked Jennifer. "I mean about the poison."

"None."

"You did a tox screen?"

"Of course. Came up dry."

"But as I recall, your previous tox screens didn't detect the drug Edgar was using to paralyze his victims."

"That was a totally different situation. We couldn't miss the cause of death."

You wouldn't think. Still, Darcy had been right before. . . .

"You know, Jen," I said, slow and cautious, careful not to bruise any egos, "Fara Spencer was killed a good ten days before we found her. Any chance the poison might've broken down in the body? So it wouldn't show through normal toxicology tests?"

"Yes, it's possible, but we have no reason to believe that happened. Anyone can see how the woman died."

"Would you mind testing a tissue sample?"

"For what reason?"

"To make me happy." Seemed like a better answer than **Because I said so.**

"This is very irregular."

"Story of my life."

She fidgeted with her rubber gloves. "I suppose I could cut away a little something near the exposed chest. . . ."

"Mouth," Darcy said.

"Huh?" we replied in unison.

"Do you think that maybe you could take the tissue from her mouth? Because I think you should take tissue from her mouth."

"Why?"

"Did you notice that there were no blowflies in her mouth? I bet blowflies don't like poison. I don't think I would like poison. Do you?"

The toxicologist and I exchanged a look.

"Jen, do the test. I want the report on my desk ASAP."

He held the tip of the pendulum delicately between two fingers. He had honed the blade until it was razor-sharp, and he did not want to cut himself. He pulled it back to the height of its arc, then released it.

JJ screamed.

"I suppose you know how this works," he said, reclining in a chair near her table. "Everyone does. Even those who have never read the story. Have you read the story, JJ?"

"N-N-No."

"Seen the film, perhaps?"

Her voice was choked and broken. Her eyes were fixed on the steel blade swinging back and forth only a few inches above her chest.

"Maybe. I—I'm not sure."

"No matter. I just didn't want you to have any erroneous misconceptions. You see, in the original text, the narrator escapes. Oh sure, he's sliced once or twice across the breast—"

JJ's face turned ashen.

"But he survives. My dear JJ—" He took her hand and squeezed it. "You will not."

"W-W-Where are my clothes?"

"Burned. Nasty provocative little things. I'm astonished any reputable high school would allow you and your raffish companions to wear them—much less make them an official uniform."

"Did you . . . do stuff to me? While I was out?"

"Like what?"

Tears welled up in her eyes. "Like . . . sex stuff?"

"Would it bother you if I did?"

"I'm only seventeen, and I'm still a virgin and—"

"Liar."

"I am!"

"My dear, I can assure you I conducted a most thorough examination while you were unconscious." He looked at her sternly. "You are no virgin."

Her eyes were trained on the pendulum. "How—how high up is that thing?"

"At present, it swings about four inches above your lovely chest, but it is descending at a rate of an inch every minute. So you see, you still have a little time to enjoy the lovely mesmeric swinging—before you feel its cold blade slicing your flesh."

Her head whipped back and forth, her face contorted with fear. "Why are you doing this to me? I haven't done anything to you."

"Oh, my sweet thing. Please listen." He scooted his chair closer to the table—though careful to stay out of the arc of the pendulum. "I know this will be difficult for you to comprehend. So much of what we are told in life is simply . . . wrong. The emphases are put in all the wrong places. Look at you. Devoting yourself to cheering for the accomplishments of others instead making accomplishments of your own. Dressing up in that blatantly objectified costume that can serve no possible purpose other than the titillation of the dominant male hierarchy. Painting your lovely face."

He reached forward and stroked her cheek.

"You have fine features, my precious. Why would you smear paint all over them? Because society has taught you that your God-given looks are insufficient. In order to be attractive to men—and of course that is your principal function in life—you must add artificial color. It's a shame."

JJ licked her lips. "If—if I promise not to wear makeup, would you please stop that—swinging thing?"

"I merely use this as an example of what society has done to you. Just as it has taught you that because I take lives I must be some kind of monster. Just as it has taught you that your ephemeral life here on earth is so precious you must cling to it even when it is perfectly evident that your time is coming to an end."

"I—I don't want to die!"

"Darling," he said, leaning close and whispering, "your life on earth is over. But because of my work, because of your sacrifice, we will all be translated to a better world, a happier one. We will leave behind this earthly plane of disappointment, discontent, and disillusionment. We will usher in a Golden Age."

She trembled so much it was difficult for her to speak clearly. "Is—that—why I'm strapped to this table?"

"I would like to believe you have the strength to remain in position when the pendulum begins its final descent. That you would not run or attempt to save yourself. But the flesh is weak, even when the spirit is willing. And so much is at stake. I felt a few precautions were in order."

"Where are my friends?" Her eyes followed the blade, back and forth, back and forth. It was so close now it never escaped her line of sight.

"They are in other rooms. Enjoying similar experiences I've devised for their delectation."

She stared at the blade, barely an inch away now. "Is it going to hurt very much?"

"Yes," he said, stroking her brow, "I'm afraid it is." He pushed to his feet. "It's almost time. I'll leave you alone now."

She quivered, then rocked hysterically, crying, wailing. And the pendulum kept swinging. She screamed hysterically. "Stop it! Please help me! Please!"

The pendulum swung again and this time she felt it crease her exposed flesh. She cried out. But it did not stop. Again it swung and again it cut her. A thin line of blood trickled to the surface. She cried out uncontrollably, insanely, crazed, her eyes wild with frenzy. The next pass would be the one, she knew. The next swing of the pendulum would kill her.

"Please, God! Someone! **Help me!**"

The pendulum descended even lower, sweeping toward her chest—

Then stopped.

She was so hysterical she couldn't hold still. She arched her back and twisted, flinging herself from one side to the other, straining against her bonds, as if she'd lost all sense of time or place, all reason, all sanity.

Above her, holding the pendulum barely an inch from her breast, the Raven smiled.

CHAPTER TWENTY-EIGHT

The only thing more frustrating than knowing a killer is on the loose and not being able to do anything about it is knowing a killer is on the loose and not having anything to do. I was totally stymied. Waiting for reports. Waiting for lab results. Waiting for someone to give me the magic piece of information that would allow me to catch the miserable table-strapping picture-taking bastard once and for all. But that magic bullet was not forthcoming.

I thumbed through the stack of information that had trickled across my desk. They still hadn't gotten a fix on who owned or had built the cabin out by the dam. Speculation was that hunters or fishers had slapped it together, maybe dug the basement to store or cure fresh kills. Edgar found it and took it over. Maybe killed the original occupants, who knows? There were few other dwellings in the area, and they had found no one who had any knowledge of who lived there. Some of the new FBI personnel working the case had managed to track down the identity of two of the girls found in Edgar's basement—two out of twenty-two—by comparing the physical remains against old missing-persons reports in the FBI database. They were both runaways, both last seen in small towns in northern California about six months before. Although it was difficult to make reliable determinations about bodies so decomposed, the coroner believed they had been killed first, then brought to the shack sometime afterward. The logical conclusion was that our Edgar had a previous life—one in which he buzzed up and down the coast killing helpless girls, then dumped their corpses back here. All before the Poe motif fully developed.

I was feeling better. Not 100 percent, not even close, but given what that bastard put me through, I was pretty damn solid. I called Rachel, but she was out. Basketball game. Seems the team was still undefeated and if they won another game would be guaranteed a spot in the play-offs. Bully for them.

Called Lisa, too, but she was not at home.

Found a book on the corner of my desk, one I'd forgotten about in all the turmoil following my abduction. Edgar Allan Poe's **Eureka: A Prose-Poem.** The only Poe I hadn't read yet, as far as I knew. And weird as all get-out.

I opened the book and started to read. It was hard going. Strange. Poe as writer qua astrophysicist. Lots of cosmological theorizing, but couched in unscientific, poetic language that made it extremely difficult to follow. I'd read Poe's bio—he was no scientist. Why had he written this? It was like Carl Sagan on an acid trip.

I had to reread a passage three times—some babble about irresistibly attractive forces—before I got any sense of what he was talking about. Then it occurred to me that what he was describing, an enormously powerful force in space sucking everything toward it, sounded a lot like a black hole. Did we know about those in Poe's day?

Then there was the passage in the coded message Edgar sent us: **From that one Particle, as a center, let us suppose to be irradiated spherically—in all directions—to immeasurable but still to definite distances in the previously vacant space—a certain inexpressibly great yet limited number of unimaginably yet not infinitely minute atoms.**

Which, placed in context, sounded for all the

world like the big-bang theory, once I read it over about six times and decoded some of the nonscientific terminology. My history of science was sketchy, but I thought that idea came later, that in Poe's era people were still mostly buying into the Adam and Eve bit. How could Poe know this?

Normally, I tried to empathize with a living, breathing person, but this time, I let my mind wander into the psyche of this writer, long dead, who had penned this bizarre work. What was he trying to accomplish? And what did Edgar— our Edgar—get out of it? Why was this book so significant to him that he led us to it? It was baffling.

Until I started to see a weird sort of pattern emerging, a secret latticework woven between the sentences. And some disturbingly familiar termi-nology. Dream-Land. Ascension. Golden Age.

That was when I started to get it.

I was so absorbed in my reading I didn't even notice the woman standing at the other end of my desk. She had to clear her throat, then drum her fingers.

"Thallium."

I looked up. It was Jennifer Fuentes, the tox-icologist.

I squinted. "You're saying I need Valium? Do I seem stressed?"

"Not Valium. Thallium. A deadly poison."

I pulled my head out of the book. "And the reason you're saying this is . . ."

"I found it in Fara Spencer's mouth, just like the O'Bannon kid predicted. I used a wide range of reagents for different hard-to-detect poisons. Thallium clicked. The spectrophotometer confirmed it. It had broken down, as any poison would over that period of time. So to double-check, I put the sample in a graphite tube and heated it to vaporize the poison. Put it under the blue light. Voilà. Thallium. Judging from what was left more than a week after her death, I'd say it was a significant dosage."

"Enough to kill her?"

"Oh, yeah. Instantly."

"So he took the heart out after she was dead."

"I think so. Immediately thereafter, before the blood had a chance to coagulate."

"But she wouldn't have felt the pain."

"Not if she was dead."

Of course not. He'd captured her, sure. Probably terrorized her, just like he did me. And he'd taken the heart, because that's what Poe wanted him to do, and that's what he wanted to mail to me. But he couldn't do it while she was alive. She wasn't an offering, and outside of his twisted plan for redemption, he lacked the requisite cruelty. Or at least one of his personalities did.

And Darcy had known it all along.

"Tell me about thallium, Doc. Is it hard to get, like that voodoo zombie stuff?"

She shook her head. "Rat poison, most likely. Contains thallium sulphate. Half the people in Vegas probably have it in their garage, never suspecting how deadly it can be."

"But Edgar would know. Edgar knows everything."

"I feel like an idiot. I would've missed it altogether if it hadn't been for that kid."

"Don't feel bad, Doc. You were meant to miss it."

Jennifer walked humbly back to her office and I returned to my reading.

I'm getting close to you, Edgar, I thought. I was still missing a few key pieces of information, but it was starting to fall into place, like snowflakes on a Colorado mountaintop. And the few things I didn't know yet, I knew where to find.

In this book.

There was a reason why Edgar was who he was, why he did what he did. And I was going to discover it. Before his damned Day of Ascension. Before it was too late.

Who are you? Where did you come from?

CHAPTER TWENTY-NINE

"Please, Nana, please. We'll be careful."

"No. You're too young. You children should stay near the house."

"We're old enough. Honest."

"Ernie, I've given you my answer."

"But Nana!"

The twins had lived with their grandmother for almost a month before she relented, on a bright summer morning when the California air was so cool and the sun so warm even she must've found the temptation irresistible. Her small rural house backed up against a forest full of brush and hidden dangers, maple and oak and tall pines, redwoods and relics of redwoods. Even better, not a quarter mile beyond the forest was a vast expanse of beach, a private access road to the Pacific Ocean. Nana's family had bought this choice land not far from Salinas at the turn of the century and never let it go, even though they were poor as dirt and it came to be worth a substantial sum. But what good did it do the twins if they weren't allowed to leave the house?

"I want you children where I can see you. No telling what kinds of mischief you might get into." She had a cat in her arms, a huge peach-colored Maine coon that stared at Ernie with eyes that never blinked. "I know what you were up to when your parents weren't watching and I won't have any of it. You just stay put."

"But there's nothing to do in the yard!"

"And what is it you think you're going to do in the forest? Don't you know that place is full of ticks? Poison ivy? Do you know what poison ivy looks like? I'll bet you don't. You get a dose of that and you'll be miserable for days. Snakes out there, too."

Ernie was unconvinced.

"Did I tell you about the wild boars? My mother saw one, just before the Lord took her home. Teeth like razors. Could eat little things like you two in a single gulp."

But Ernie did not relent. To him, the forest was an unexplored wonderland teeming with adventure. Even from a distance he could see its dark and foreboding corners, and the mystery made it all the more alluring.

"We could play lots of games in there. We could build forts and play hide-and-seek."

"You can do all that in the yard."

"Not good. Not like we could there."

Nana's eventual surrender was inevitable, given how both Ernie and Ginny pounded her with the relentlessness only eight-year-olds can muster. "But just for one hour. And I want you to carry this tin whistle. You get in any trouble, meet up with a wild boar or something, you blow on it, hard. And when you get back, I'll be inspecting you for ticks."

"All right, Nana. We will, Nana," he said, throwing himself up against her and hugging her tightly.

"That's enough of that," she said, pushing him away.

"And what about the beach? Can we go there, too?"

"Under no circumstances are you to go near the beach. I couldn't hear you out there even if you did blow that whistle. Now get along, before I change my mind."

"Yes, Nana," he said, already running.

And so the revels began. They were like pagans, Ginny and Ernie, romping through the forest, worshiping each other and secret gods known to no one but themselves. They would pretend to be astronauts on another planet searching for new life-forms and alien civilizations. They would play endless games of chase. There were no other children living anywhere near them, and they never minded in the least. They were a world unto themselves.

On some afternoons, Ernie's favorite ones, after the running and chasing were done, they would sit together on their makeshift table, a huge stump of a tree that had been logged a generation before. Hidden amidst the maple and second-growth redwoods, they would tell each other everything. They had no secrets. Why would they? Each was an extension of the other. As far as they were concerned, they were two parts of the same person.

"Do you ever miss Mom and Dad?" Ginny asked, one such afternoon.

"I dunno." He stretched out, sunning himself. "Kinda sorta. You?"

"Maybe. Sometimes."

"I don't miss Mom yelling all the time."

"No."

"And I don't miss Daddy's spankings. Which really weren't spankings because they weren't on my butt."

"He never spanked me."

"That's 'cause he liked you. He spanked me all the time. He just liked you."

"Yeah," she said, drawing her arms inward as

she spoke, staring at the leaves. "He sure did like me."

"I hated it when they acted all weird and crazy and couldn't hardly walk."

"Me too. But that was when Daddy liked me the most."

"And Nana's pretty nice. Even if she is old and kinda strange."

"Yeah."

The breeze blew a trace of honeysuckle between them, rustling the leaves and giving them both a slight chill.

"But I still miss Mom and Daddy. Sometimes," Ginny said quietly.

"Yeah. Me too, I guess."

True to her word, when they returned from the forest each day, their grandmother performed full and thorough inspections.

"Those ticks are insidious. They dig down deep and they never let go. Strip!"

And she meant it. The inspection did not begin until both children were standing before her starkers. "No underwear. Nothing." Now they really looked like wild animals, primordial wood nymphs, hair tangled and full of leaves, even bugs, dirt sweat-stained to their skin. Their grandmother checked each nook and cranny, every fold and orifice. The children didn't much enjoy this assessment. But it did not deter them. Next day, they were back in the forest.

"Do you want to touch it?"

He had seen her looking at him while he went to the bathroom behind a tree. It was not the first time.

"No way. Gross."

"Isn't gross. It's just me."

"Well, I don't have anything like that."

"That's 'cause you're a girl."

They sat on the stump in silence for a few moments. He knew what she was thinking. It was always like that, and not just with her. He could tell what anyone was thinking, sometimes before they knew themselves. And he knew Ginny's mind as well as he knew his own.

"Okay," she said, something like fifteen minutes later, out of the blue.

"Okay what?"

"Okay I want to touch it."

He considered. "You'll have to let me touch yours."

"I don't have one."

"Well, whatever you got, I want to touch it."

"Okay."

Ernie dropped his shorts. And his Sears-bought Underoos, which drooped over his shoes.

And she touched it.

"That wasn't so much," she remarked, then giggled. "It's all sticking out now."

"That's not funny."

"Why's it doing that? Just 'cause I touched it?"

"You didn't do it right," he said defensively. "You're s'posed to kiss it."

"How would you know?"

"I saw it in one of Dad's books. You kiss it and it makes people happy."

She obliged. Afterward, he did the same to her. It was weird and gooshy.

Later that day, when the inspection was done, their grandmother kept Ernie after she let Ginny get dressed and go up to her room.

"I saw what you did," Nana said. "You nasty little boys with your nasty little things, you're all alike. Well, I won't have it. You understand me? I won't have it."

"Y-Y-Yes, Nana," he managed to squeeze out.

The cat curled around his grandmother's ankles, staring at him with large accusing eyes.

"There will be no nastiness on my property, hear me? Your father may have gone in for that sort of thing, but I most certainly will not. The Good Lord doesn't like it. And neither do I."

"Okay, Nana."

"Nasty. Nasty, ugly boys. Here. Put this on." She held out a sky-blue pinafore, one of Ginny's.

"But—that's a dress—"

"Put it on!" she commanded. He obeyed. She did up the buttons in the back, tied the bow, and spun him around a few times, admiring him. "There, that's better. Not so nasty now, are we?"

"But Nana—"

"Since you're so interested in girls, we'll let you be one from now on."

"Nana—"

"Go to bed now. And leave the dress on. You are not to remove it until I give you permission. Understand?"

He did as he was told, but the dress was scratchy and uncomfortable and he had a hard time sleeping. She made him wear it forever, days, weeks, including the night one of Nana's lady friends from town came over. Nana thought the children didn't know because the lady came after bedtime, as she had come many times before. But the dress bothered Ernie so much he couldn't sleep, and when he heard screaming, it scared him. Scared him so much he ran into Nana's bedroom.

"What the hell is this?" the lady said, sitting up in the bed.

Nana leaped out of her bed, wrapping a sheet around herself. "Nasty little boy! Nasty little boy!"

"Nana, I was scared—"

"Did you think you might see something? Is that what you were hoping for? That you might see something nasty?"

"No—I—I—"

"I tried to help you. I tried to make you not be such a dirty little boy. But I can see this dress wasn't enough. Not nearly enough." Enraged, she ripped it off him, her nails like claws, then ran to a sewing kit resting on her dresser.

"Nana, please—"

"My last sewing needle," she said, holding the silver shaft between thumb and finger. "Shame to have to use it like this. But what's got to be done's got to be done."

She lowered the needle and jabbed it into his little penis.

Ernie screamed. He tried to squirm away, but the old woman's hand held him firmly in place. Only after an eternity had passed did she yank the needle out, leaving a trickle of clear fluid in its wake.

Ernie clutched himself. He fell to the floor, curled up, hoping if he squeezed hard enough it wouldn't hurt anymore.

"I don't want you playing with Ginny. Not in the forest. Not anywhere."

His eyes widened with horror. This was even worse, the most horrible punishment possible. "B-B-B-But—"

"You heard me, boy." She held the dripping needle between her fingers. "Do I need to tell you what will happen if you disobey me?"

"N-N-N-No, ma'am."

She would not help him or allow the lady in her bed to help him. Ernie had to crawl to his bedroom, holding himself, biting back the pain. He lay on his bed for hours, not sleeping, empty, devastated, in every kind of agony. A swelling began and he didn't know what to do about it. He started to cry, and once he started, he found he could not stop. His whole body shook with the force of his tears. He did not cry so much for the aching, although that was great. He cried for Ginny. Because she was his life. And now his grandmother had taken his life away.

The next few weeks were torturous. The swelling eventually subsided, but in its wake the shaft of his penis turned an odd mottled color and bent to the left as if it were permanently broken. He was not allowed to play with Ginny or even to talk to her. He sat at the opposite end of the breakfast table and if he so much as glanced her way his grandmother made a motion toward her sewing kit. He learned to stare at his cereal bowl. At night he would lie awake in his bed, sleepless, thinking of nothing but her.

"Ernie?"

He sat bolt upright, on that memorable night so long into their forced separation.

It was her.

"Come outside."

It was dark as a cave in his room. What time was it, midnight? Later?

"Hurry!" He heard her tiny footsteps scampering down the stairs.

He followed, feeling his still broken member as he climbed out of bed, knowing all too well what he risked. But Ginny was calling, and he could not resist following her.

The floorboards creaked as he entered the hallway. He could hear his grandmother snoring; she was sound asleep. But he also knew how quickly she could rouse herself, given sufficient motivation.

Down the stairs and out the door. He found Ginny by the clearing at the edge of the forest, waiting for him.

"I'm not sure we should be in the forest at night," he said, even though he desperately wanted to go. "It could be dangerous. The ticks and boars and stuff. We might not see them."

"We're not going to the forest," she said, her eyes sparkling like a gift. "We're going through it. To the beach."

The beach! He felt a clutching at his heart. Their grandmother had expressly forbidden it. "Nana won't like this. If she finds out—"

"Nana won't find out." She took his hand. "If she does, we'll run away together."

She led the way through the edge of the forest on a worn path that seemed safe even when they were traveling with only the moon for a flashlight. Perhaps fifteen minutes later, they arrived at the beach.

Ernie was stunned. He had seen it from the road, of course, but never like this, never this close. Even from the edge of the forest, he could feel the spray on his cheeks. He could hear the thunderous roar. It was so loud—how could they not hear it back at the house? The waves crashed against the surf with a shuddering violence. The ocean seemed to go on forever and forever, receding into the horizon.

"Better build a fort fast," Ginny said, racing barefoot across the sand. "You're about to be under attack."

They played together like they had never played before. In retrospect, they were probably not there more than an hour or two, but it seemed a glorious eternity, a Golden Age. They built forts and lobbed sandballs at one another. They fashioned castles and dug tunnels between them. They played chase and ran like the sea breeze, squeezing the sand between their toes. Ernie caught her and they both tripped; he fell down on top of her.

"Do you think I'm pretty?" she asked as he lay against her, sand skimming her hair.

"Of course you are."

"I think my nose is too big."

"Is not. You're pretty."

"Then how come you never kiss me?"

"I—I didn't know if—if I—"

"It's okay."

If she said it was okay, then so it must be. He pressed his lips against hers, hard, like he'd seen his father do it to that woman in the drugstore. It didn't feel very warm, but it made him go all tingly and stiff just the same.

"That wasn't very good, was it?"

"Don't worry," she said, laughing. She pushed him away and ran free. "You'll get better."

And she was right. They came out to the beach every night that week, running and playing, hugging and kissing, happier than they had ever been before, in their kingdom by the sea.

They were always quiet when they left, always careful to brush the sand off themselves before they returned home. They gave their grandmother no cause for suspicion or alarm. Ernie was deliriously happy, and each night seemed more intense, more momentous than the one before. But he could never entirely shake his sense of foreboding. He knew that what they were doing was wrong, or at least that their grandmother would think so. Didn't that mean they would be punished? Would she return to her sewing basket? Would she hurt him again?

What he did not realize was that his punish-

ment, when it came, would be ever so much
worse.

"Ginny, look out! It's a big one!"

The wave crashed down on them, huge and
impenetrable as a wall, knocking Ernie off his
feet. "Ginny!"

He scrambled up, fighting the pounding of
the water, but his feet sank into the sand.
"Ginny!"

She had been digging a tunnel when last he'd
seen her, burrowing through the sand, connect-
ing his castle to hers. He called and called for
her, but she did not answer him.

"Ginny!" Another wave crashed down on
him. Ernie choked on the stale salt water,
coughing and spewing up something gray and
bitter. He had been daydreaming, not paying
attention, still tasting his sister's salty kisses on
his lips. Now he was soaked, mired down in the
sand. And she wasn't answering.

"Ginny!"

He struggled to make his way to the two castles and found a half-dug tunnel between them.
Ginny's feet were sticking out of the sand. Her
head was buried somewhere beneath.

The tide had come in while she was burrowing. The tunnel had collapsed and she'd been
buried, unable to escape.

He began digging as fast as he could, pulling out great clumps of wet sand, trying to find her head, but it was slow work for little hands. He knew every second counted. He called out her name again and again, crying into the night wind, but there was never any response.

He didn't know how long it took, a minute, twenty, he couldn't tell. He excavated her head and finally managed to roll her out of the muck. He brushed sand from her mouth, her nose, her eyes, all the while screaming out her name.

Her eyes remained closed.

He opened her mouth and blew air into it like he'd seen people do on television, but she did not respond. He was scared and alone and he didn't know what to do. He raced back and forth on the beach, the death clock ticking away in his brain.

He had to get help. Grown-up help. He started running toward the house, racing reck-lessly through the forest. His legs and feet were cut in a dozen places but he never stopped, never for a second. What would he do when he got there? If he told Nana what he had done, what they had been doing—he knew what would happen. But Ginny wasn't moving. He had to do something. He had to do something.

As soon as he arrived at the house, he called the police. They were the ones best able to help

Ginny—and perhaps to protect him. Nana heard him talking and came downstairs, but the police arrived before she could do anything to him.

Ernie found it difficult to function, to perform even the simplest tasks. He was weary and heartsore and scared and confused. He answered the policemen's questions as best he could and took them out to the beach.

"Dear God," the cop said when they finally arrived. "Why didn't you call us sooner, son? We might've saved her."

The rest of the night was a hideous blur. There were questions and questions and questions. He was still wet and cold and miserable. And all the while, his grandmother stared at him, her eyes dark as coals and cold as night. He knew what she was thinking.

Around three A.M., they took Ginny's body away. They would not let him kiss her goodbye. He would never see her again.

Ernie didn't know who all these people were. He'd never known Nana had any friends; only her nighttime lady friends came to the house. But at the reception after the funeral, the place was packed with strangers.

No one would talk to him, not at the funeral and not now. He knew why. Some of them thought maybe he'd done it on purpose. They thought he was a bad seed, a chip off his father's block. They blamed him not only for Ginny's death but for his grandmother's sudden decline. Everything.

Someone had brought food, a couple of casseroles and some bean salad, but he didn't eat much, even though he'd taken nothing all day. The first bite died in his throat; it seemed tasteless.

The minister was the only person there who didn't have wrinkles. He was new, maybe thirty. Ernie knew his grandmother didn't like him. Ernie didn't like him much, either. But he was the only one in the house who would talk to him.

"You mustn't blame yourself," Reverend Barton said. "God called her home, that's all. She's in heaven now, with the angels. We should be so fortunate."

"It doesn't seem right," Ernie mumbled.

"It never does. We think, why did it have to be her? But remember—she went to be with Jesus. That's a good thing, not bad. The Lord God moves in strange and mysterious ways. There is a plan, even if we have not yet discovered it. Evidently, God needed her more than we did."

Ernie looked up at the minister, his eyes

pleading. "What I don't understand is, why didn't God take me, too? We belong together."

"You will be together again one day, God willing."

"But why not now? I feel so—awful. I never should've gone out there with her."

Reverend Barton knelt down and took the boy by the shoulders. "It's not your fault, son. You were God's instrument. You helped Him fulfill His plan."

That night, she came for him.

"Ernie," she said, standing in the dark at his bedroom door. The cat was curled between her ankles. "Wake up."

"Can't . . . ," he moaned, pretending he had been asleep.

She grabbed his head by the hair and jerked him upright. Ernie sputtered, wild-eyed, drool spilling from his lips.

He looked down at her other hand. She was holding the needle.

"Thought those damn fools would never leave."

"Please don't hurt me, Nana. It was so bad last time. Please don't do it again."

"You're all alike," she said, her eyes glistening like the silver dagger she held in her hand.

"Your father took my first little girl away from me. And you took my next one." She grabbed him by the collar of his pajamas, shaking him. "Did you do anything to her before you killed her?"

"No!"

"You disgusting men with your disgusting little things." She shook him even harder. "Tell me the truth. What did you do to her? So help me, I'll—"

"No!" He broke away, scrambling across the bed. He dove through the doorway but miscalculated in the darkness, banging his head on the wall. He leaped to his feet, stubbing his toe in the process. She reached out just in time to grab his leg.

"Gotcha!" She jabbed the needle into the soft underside of his foot.

Ernie shrieked, then tore himself away from her. He pushed ahead, but the cat raced in front of him and made him stumble. He collided with the banister, headfirst. She came after him, her teeth bared, her needle shining in the reflected moonlight.

"Please don't hurt me," he whimpered. "Please don't."

"You'll take your punishment, Ernie. If I have to chase you to the ends of the earth. God punishes sinners. God and me."

She reared up before him, her needle poised like a dagger.

Ernie kicked her in the stomach.

For a long moment, she seemed suspended in air. He could have grabbed her hand and pulled her back onto the landing. But the needle was in that hand.

He let her fall.

When at last her body stopped, the tumbled heap at the foot of the stairs did not stir.

Ernie moved quickly. He gathered together everything he wanted to save, threw it in a bag, and hid it in the forest. Then he killed the cat. He took his time about that, releasing much that had been pent up for so long, in a slow, protracted, highly gratifying dissection. Then he burned the house down.

The books he'd read had given him a good idea how to do it in such a way that it would not be obvious that he had done it, at least not to the rural cops he'd met a few days before. He left the gas burners on for a long time. He tossed a match. Then he went outside and watched it burn.

There was nothing they could do to him that wasn't going to happen already. This way, no one would ever know for certain what happened. No one but him. And Virginia.

He was the Instrument, he murmured to

himself as he watched the shutters and shingles turn to ash. Now he needed to find his God.

In and out of foster homes and reform schools all his teen years, Ernie never stayed in one place for long. Soon after he left his grandmother's house he developed a stutter that plagued him until high school. The permanent deformity to his private member made gym class a nightmare and sports an impossibility. But he continued to search for some explanation, some meaning in his life, in the tragedy that had visited him. Which was what led him, during his sophomore year of college, to journey out into the desert to attempt a vision quest.

He had never seen such a desolate environment—flat, barren, bleak. Heat rose from the pavement creating miniature mirages, smoothing the road ahead. A man named Ralph Studi acted as his spiritual guide and instructor. The first three days, he learned, would be spent in preparation. The last four days he would spend in the desert, alone. "All this training will be geared toward one central objective—your spiritual growth. At all times, the emphasis will be on grounding you in the Spirit. Not just absorbing but owning the lessons learned. Because the true work of the vision quest begins when we return to our people."

———

The first day on his own, out in the wilderness, he was bored to tears. The second day, he was starving—and bored to tears.

The third day, he saw the Raven.

He had fallen asleep, or thought he had. His legs were aching from the stiff sedentary drain of remaining in the sacred circle for so long. He kept the fire burning, even though the air was hot and oppressive, even at night. He longed to stretch his legs, to partake of the tiny ration of water he had been permitted. Sweat dripped down the sides of his face. His eyelids closed and he drank in the heady smell of smoke and whatever was in that wood they gave him to burn. He thought he was asleep. But when the Raven spoke to him, he was wide awake.

He couldn't move. Somehow, the Raven had imparted a paralysis that he couldn't shake.

"Why have you strayed from the Path?"

Ernie didn't know what to say. He couldn't believe he was talking to a raven, but there it was, perched on his shoulder. It wasn't like other birds. It was larger, its face more expressive, more human. Its eyes terrified him.

"I—I didn't know—"

"The Path was shown to you. But you have not followed it."

"Well . . . I've been busy with classes and—"

"There are no excuses."

"Look, just—just tell me what to do. I'll do it. Really I will."

"You know what to do."

"I don't. But if you could give me a little hint—"

"Nevermore!" The coal-black eyes flared, angry and intense. Ernie tried to inch away, but he was still unable to move. **"I have been with Virginia."**

Ernie's hunger was supplanted by an aching in his chest, a new emptiness. "You've seen her?"

"I have been with Virginia. And so could you."

"But how—"

"In my realm, all are reunited. All are one."

"I don't know what that—"

"You have the potential for greatness. You could be what I am."

"I—I'll do whatever I must. Whatever you want."

The Raven unfolded its wings and the span was endless, a dark umbra that spread from one perimeter of his vision to the other, swallowing him. He screamed, and somehow, the act of screaming ended the visitation. He was wide awake, able to move, fully conscious that he was alone in the middle of the desert.

But he was certain he had been visited by his totem, and that the visit had meant something. What was he was being called to do?

The sweat on his brow had vanished, replaced by a fevered chill. He rubbed his hands up and down his arms, trying to warm himself. Something had changed, something inside him. He didn't know how or what exactly. But he knew he would never be the same.

It was hard to avoid the sorrowful look in the eyes of all who shook Ernie's hand as he left the questing headquarters. Word had gotten out. They all were aware that he had been visited by the Raven, the totem of death, and they all believed that meant he would soon be dead.

But Ernie knew differently. The Raven might be the totem of death, but not his own. This visitation had a different meaning.

He returned to school, ostensibly focusing on his studies, but obsessed with the Raven's words, trying to uncover the mysteries of his path. He graduated with honors and became a teaching assistant while pursuing his Master's in American Literature. But although he performed his appointed tasks with excellence, his heart was no longer in them. And his soul was in another place altogether.

He had not wanted to revisit the works of Edgar Allan Poe. He remembered those stories from his childhood as dark and gruesome, obviously the product of an unstable, demented mind. But he was TA-ing an American Lit survey course, and of course he had to grade the exams, and he couldn't do that unless he refamiliarized himself with the texts. So he sat down in his room late one evening, alone as always, with a thick volume of Poe.

He had not intended to read the entire book. A few of the major works would do, surely. He started with the poems, lovely things, sonically immaculate, if rather syrupy. But so much of it reverberated in strange and unforeseen ways.

She was a child and I was a child in that kingdom by the sea. . . .

Such love that the winged seraphs of heaven coveted her and me. . . .

Had Poe really written that about his lost child bride? Could anyone but Ernie himself have written that?

It was only a short while before he reread Poe's great masterpiece, "The Raven." Eighteen immaculately rhymed quatrains, with the Raven as the harbinger of death. Could this possibly be a coincidence?

And the raven, never flitting, still is sit-

ting, still is sitting . . . just above my chamber door. . . .

Ernie felt as if his brain had been opened wide. As if the sun had dawned for the first time. After the poems, he pored through the stories, over and over again. It was only after he had read them many times that he began to see beyond the superficial entertainments and realize that there was something important buried within them. The similarities, the points of correspondence, were too great to be coincidental. Just as the Raven had spoken to him, so it also must have spoken to Poe. He found a tantalizing clue in one of the worst of the tales, "Ms. Found in a Bottle": **It is evident that we are hurrying onward to some exciting knowledge—some never-to-be-imparted secret, whose attainment is destruction.** Yes! And another story—"The Premature Burial": **To conceive the horror of my sensations is, I presume, utterly impossible; yet a curiosity to penetrate the mysteries of these awful regions, predominates even over my despair, and will reconcile me to the most hideous aspect of death. The boundaries which divide Life from Death are at best shadowy and vague. Who shall say where the one ends, and where the other begins?**

That was what the Raven was trying to tell him. Death was not an ending but a translation, a passage from one borderland to another. But this wasn't a Christian fantasy, a heaven up in the clouds such as they spoke about in Sunday school. This was something real. The Dream-Land Poe described in his poems existed, and his sweet Virginia must be there. The narrator in "Ligeia" brought back his love. Could Ernie not do the same? But what was the mystic formula that the prophet hinted at but never described? How was this magnificent end to be accomplished? How could he enter Dream-Land? How could he make Poe's Golden Age a reality?

The answer came to him in the December of that year, not from his intensive studies, not from his work, but from a purely adventitious discovery in a small coastal California town. In a used-book store, he found an obscure Poe work, something that hadn't been in any of the anthologies. It was titled **Eureka.**

He had seen references to this work in some of the biographies he had consumed, but they were all brief and dismissive. A failed effort, they called it. A hopeless mishmash. It seemed useless and irrelevant, and for that reason, and because it wasn't in any of his books anyway, he had never bothered to read it.

When he did, it gave him the answers he had so long sought. The path.

Poe believed in dreams, not just sleeping

dreams but waking ones, believed they were glimpses into another world, a better world, one to which we could all be translated. He limned a memorable, if enticingly vague, portrait of this world in his poem "Dream-Land": **All that we see or seem is but a dream within a dream.**

Much of **Eureka** was concerned with Poe's efforts to create a new cosmology, which was rejected by contemporaries because of his lack of scientific training, and yet in retrospect, some of what Poe wrote was positively prescient. Poe solved Olbers's paradox—why the sky is dark at night—envisioned black holes, and was the first to describe the universe as expanding, then contracting. He proposed the big bang theory, which would not be formally discovered until seventy years later, by Alexander Friedmann, a Russian mathematician who was very fond of the works of Edgar Allan Poe.

How had Poe known, long before the scientific observations had been made that could prove it?

The Raven told him, of course.

Poe believed that man was a mere extension of the Deity. He believed that as man shrinks into spatial nothingness he will regain his lost harmony and become absorbed into a perfect, mystical unity. He wrote: **The pain of the consideration that we shall lose our individual**

identity [in death] ceases at once when we further reflect that the process, as above described, is neither more nor less than the absorption, by each individual intelligence, of all other intelligences (that is, of the Universe) into its own. That God may be all in all, each must become God.

After he read that passage, Ernie wept. He threw his hands up in the air, ecstatic, euphoric. He had wondered for so long, had needed to know. And all the while, the prophet had been trying to tell him.

These were not mere stories, mere poems. They were blueprints.

"I'm sorry, but I just don't get this Poe stuff. I mean, I know he was great and brilliant and all, but to me, it just seems gross."

Ernie was in his tiny TA's office, opening his mail, trying to appear interested.

"I guess, I grew up in the suburbs, you know what I'm saying? We didn't have guys sealing each other up in the basement or swinging big pendulums over their chests. And what was the deal with that story where the guy yanked out that woman's teeth? I mean, this Poe guy had issues, if you ask me."

Ernie tried to smile. She was a tiny thing, presumably eighteen, but she looked younger.

She had a round face and large eyes and long, straight blond hair. He knew she had a reputation as a partyer. She wore far too much makeup. "So what, pray tell, can I do for you, Miss Swanson?"

She shifted from one side of the chair to the other, crossing her legs. "See, I know the final is supposed to be like, final, but I think I didn't do so hot on it."

"Why do you believe that?"

"Well . . . I never finished the reading. I mean, I'm sorry, but those stories were just so **wrong.**"

"That's a pity."

"Yeah, but my sorority is counting on me to keep up the academic average, and I wondered if there wasn't some way I could . . . make it up."

"I'm afraid Professor Levy doesn't give second chances."

"Would he have to know?"

"I could hardly offer a makeup exam without his authorization."

"I wasn't really thinking about another test." She slithered off the chair and onto her knees, just before him. "I was hoping I could make it up . . . some other way."

"Miss Swanson, I'm sure I don't know. . . ."

"Come on," she said, rubbing her hands up and down his pant legs. "I know you pretend to be above it all with your big words and your old-fashioned suits. But I'll bet there's a real man in there somewhere."

"Miss Swanson, this—this is most inappropriate."

"Sure?" She unzipped the fly of his pants.

"Miss Swanson!"

"Come on. I'll do you a favor, you do me one." Her hand reached inside his pants. "And I'll bet—" She stopped, choked. "Oh, my God! What's wrong with you?"

Ernie hurriedly tucked himself back inside. "It's nothing."

"Nothing! It's gross!"

"I had an accident. When I was a child."

She stepped away from him, her face stricken. "I'm sorry. I don't mean to be cruel. I was just—startled." She waved her hand back and forth, as if fanning the air. "Look, let's just forget it."

"But—you said—"

"I can do a lot, but I can't do that. I'll just take the D."

"Nevermore?" he whispered.

He wasn't sure how it happened. But he heard the Raven speaking to him, loud, insistent, and he saw the girl, so like Poe's own, and he felt his shame and embarrassment, and he was desperate to find the path, to know what it was he was supposed to do. And a moment later, the letter opener was jutting out from her left temple. She was dead in seconds.

"You have done well," the Raven intoned. **"You have begun your journey. But there is still much to be done. Much to be discovered."**

And so Ernie quit his position at the college and trolled up and down the coast of California, through Montana, then Nevada, refining his prowess and technique as he traveled, finally making his way to Las Vegas, where the final secrets were revealed to him, and the countdown to Ascension could begin at last.

CHAPTER THIRTY

"So what you're basically telling us is, Edgar is Jesus Christ?" Granger wheezed.

"In his mind, yes." I was back in the classroom again, except this time it was packed beyond capacity, not only with Granger's increasingly sizable team, but with all the new FBI agents on the case, most of whom I hadn't formally met. And here I was lecturing these feds, debriefing them as if I were some kind of behavioral genius. Patrick had gracefully allowed me to take the lead, thereby ensuring that I would be kept in the loop and given a decent modicum of respect. But this case was federal now. We were still allowed to play. But they owned the sandbox.

"This stuff is all fine for the college professor crowd," Granger said, "but how is it going to help us catch the guy?"

"If you don't understand who he is, you'll never get him. You spent valuable man-hours last week having your men blanket all the S&M clubs and similar places Edgar would never dream of visiting."

"One of his victims worked in an S&M club!"

"He went there because his victim of choice was there. That's no indication that he liked it. I'll bet he hated it and left as soon as possible."

"Excuse me." This came from one of the agents in the front row. "In your opinion, will he continue to abduct only girls with given names found in the works of Poe?"

"Frankly, no." I saw their looks of disappointment—one of the few useful leads lost. But I had to give them the straight scoop. "Too restrictive, now that everyone knows. He won't be able to find an Annabel this side of the Rocky Mountains. And let's not forget about his last victim—there are no Faras in Poe. I think we have to assume he's over that, or that he's taking different instructions from whatever voice is talking to him now."

"I read your report on the **Eureka** book," he commented. "Fascinating. Do you have any idea what he might be planning to do? To bring about this Golden Age?"

"I'm afraid I don't. Except that it will have something to do with Poe. The connection may be mostly in his mind. But there will be one."

"And do you have any theory about when this might happen?"

"According to that last phone call, he's already started."

He scribbled something into his notepad. "I assume someone has reviewed the missing-persons reports?"

"Yes, but remember, this is Vegas. There were eighteen missing-persons reports filed last night. Four of them concerned teenage girls."

"Any likely suspects?"

"A group of three. Wandered away from a cheerleader clinic. No one has seen them since."

"Three? At one time?"

I nodded grimly. "As I said, Edgar's actions will escalate. Until his plan is completed. During the phone call, he spoke of a day of ascension—when something big was going to happen, something that would change everything. I called some of the local Christian churches. They say Easter is generally considered the day of ascension. But since this is October, I doubt if that's Edgar's target date. He's planning his own ascension, on his own timetable. Like any other self-respecting savior."

The Feeb almost smiled. "Does this put us in the role of Judas Iscariot?"

I returned the expression. "I'll be happy to kiss the man on the cheek. Next time I see him."

During the drive to Carson City, Darcy read police reports to me. It was funny listening to him, and not just because of that uninflected voice. His vocabulary was incredible; we never hit a word he didn't know. But his pronunciation was often far from the mark. I got the impression he had done a good deal more reading than he'd done talking. I suppose he wasn't the first person to find books more comfortable than other people. But I still liked being with him, and I know he liked being with me. And that felt good.

"Did you know there are over nine hundred missing-persons reports filed in Clark County each year?" he asked as he shuffled between files.

"Your point being?"

He was staring at a group of photographs. The cheerleaders. "They seem like nice girls, don't you think? I hope the Bad Man doesn't do anything mean to them."

Poor sweet Darcy. "I could be wrong. But how else do you explain their disappearance?"

"Spontaneous combustion?"

"Seems unlikely."

"White slavery ring? Did you know that

white slavery rings are still active in Kuwait and many Middle Eastern nations? But I don't know about Las Vegas."

"Let's hope that isn't it." What kind of books did O'Bannon have in that library? "I can't be certain, Darcy. But my instincts tell me Edgar grabbed these girls. And I've learned to trust my instincts."

"Me too," Darcy said, surprising the hell out of me. "You're usually right."

"Well, I don't know if I'd go that far."

"Ninety-three point six six percent of the time so far."

"Thanks, Spock." I wasn't going to ask how he'd calculated that. Or what he considered to be my mistakes.

His head tilted to one side. "You smell good today."

"I do? Oh—you mean no coffee breath."

"Uh-uh. Something else."

And I guess I knew what that was, too. I'd made it through the night again without taking a drink. And I could do it again. I knew I could. I had the strength now. And the really strange thing was that I knew I was getting that strength—at least in part—from Darcy.

"I didn't like that funny smell. I like Susan smell better."

Good thing I knew he was autistic. Otherwise I might have him arrested.

We didn't know that Tiffany was dead. But I still found my voice choking, my eyes tingling, throughout the interview. Was this the first time I'd done something like this since David? Or perhaps, was this the first time I'd done something like this sober since David?

"It seemed such an innocent, harmless activity," Mrs. Glancy said. "Cheerleading camp. What could happen?"

It's not your fault, I wanted to tell the woman. But it wasn't my place. "The team sponsor says she and the others disappeared after dinner. Around nine."

"And that is so unlike Tiffany." She dabbed her eyes. She was medium-sized and of medium weight, with a pleasant face that had probably aged twenty years in the last twenty hours. She did all the talking. Her husband was a physician, and like most doctors I had encountered, words were not his best thing. He sat beside her, not speaking, barely moving. Stunned.

Tiffany was their only child.

"She's never run off before?"

"Of course not," the mother said. "Tiffany is a good girl. Responsible. She's on the honor roll, you know."

"I, um, didn't."

"She's not just some dumb blond cheerleader," her father said, speaking for the first time. Apparently this was a point he felt compelled to make. "She had a real head on her shoulders."

"And so kind," the woman continued. "So considerate of others." Her face flattened for a moment. "I'll bet it was that JJ's idea. I never cared much for her."

"That was one of her friends, right?" I checked my files. "One of the other cheerleaders who disappeared."

"I often told Tiffany she should be more careful. People judge you by your friends. But you know girls that age. They don't listen. Do you have a girl that age?"

"Niece," I offered.

"Oh, well then, you know. They don't listen. Not a bit. Even the smart ones."

Darcy sat in an overstuffed chair, picking at the armrest. I knew he was uncomfortable. All this misery—he absorbed it like a sponge. He might not understand emotion, but in a way, that could increase the discomfort of being around it. I just hoped he wouldn't have another breakdown. I couldn't deal with that now.

"Does she have any friends in Las Vegas?"

"Not that I know of."

"Does she have an interest in gambling?"

"Of course not."

"Rock and roll? There are several rock stars playing the Strip this week."

"She's more interested in Broadway. Show tunes, you know."

"Does she like to . . . dress up?" Had to tread carefully here. But I hadn't forgotten that Helen had a secret life her mother knew nothing about. It was possible this one did, too. Possible they both made the same mistake that put them in Edgar's clutches.

"Dress up? How?"

"Oh . . . provocatively. Sexy."

"My Tiffany would never do that."

I had to push. "Those cheerleading skirts are usually pretty short."

"That's entirely different. That's a sign of school spirit."

Mmmm. "You think she'd have any interest in sex clubs?"

Mrs. Glancy clutched her bosom. "I—I— never—!" She looked at her husband, who was no use at all. "Are you planning to help our Tiffany or destroy her reputation?"

"I'm planning to find her, ma'am. And that means I need to know as much about her as possible."

Dad cleared his throat. "I think maybe I should call Dick Conners."

The family lawyer, no doubt. That would

gum up the works. And frankly, I didn't have the time. Not with the clock on these girls already ticking. "Does she have any hobbies? Interests?"

The woman was still glaring at me, but she eventually answered. "She likes to collect Dumbo figurines. You know, the flying elephant. She must have a hundred of them. And she wants to be a policewoman."

That's one you didn't hear every day. "Tiffany wants to be a cop?"

"Yes. Especially after nine-eleven. She always has been very respectful, even worshipful, around our public servants. Heroes, she calls them. Police, firefighters. All that."

A cheerleading policewoman. Couldn't hurt. "Is she friendly? Outgoing? Would she talk to strangers?"

"Very friendly. But I would hope she has the sense not to talk to someone she doesn't know. Especially in Las Vegas."

I folded up my notepad. This was getting nowhere. Time to search the girls' room. They would protest—I might even have to sit through a phone call to Dick Conners—but eventually they would relent. Because whatever their faults or foibles, they wanted their little girl back. And they knew the longer she was gone, the less likely that became. As did I.

It was nice being with Susan again. She's almost like she used to be before the Bad Man took her but sometimes her hands shake and I can tell her stomach hurts and she looks like she's going to cry but her smell is better and she's back and she let me read to her while she drove the car. I wish I could drive the car but they wouldn't let me get a license and I know I could do it but not unless they let me try and maybe Susan would let me after we catch the Bad Man and her hands don't shake so much anymore. I know she likes me. I know she likes me.

Next time I'm going to ask her about babies.

Tiffany was the strongest, as it turned out. Who would have guessed that the spoiled rich girl would be the most resilient of the threesome? Hidden depths, he supposed. Dark secrets such as the prophet often saw lurking just beneath the surface. But those depths held dangers. They had to be eliminated.

He'd taken her through the entire "Pit and the Pendulum" scenario, just as he had the other two. But whereas Judy and JJ had disintegrated into hysteria, Tiffany had kept hold of her senses, even after the blade gave her a few rather significant slices. She had remained defiant, even through her pain.

Additional measures were required.

When Tiffany awoke, she found herself strapped to the table, still naked. It was amazing, he noted, how nakedness and physical discomfort increased their vulnerability. He had made the room positively frigorific, so much so that her body was covered with goose pimples.

"Good morning, Tiffany."

"You can't hurt me," she said through dry and cracked lips.

"I'm glad to hear that, my dear. It will make what I have to do next so much less trying. Are my hands cold?"

He pressed the palms of both hands down on her abdomen. She flinched.

"I feared they might be. Hard to keep warm this time of year. The temperature is having a rather remarkable effect on your body."

"I don't know why you're doing this, you sick fuck, but it isn't going to work! I'll never do what you want. If you're going to rape me, then go ahead and do it. Get your filthy rocks off so I can get out of here!"

"My dear Tiffany, you mistake my intentions altogether. And you have a mouth like a sewer."

"You're a disgusting little creep. I bet your thing is just as short as you are. That's probably why you have to get your thrills hurting teenage girls."

"My darling—"

"Where're Judy and JJ? What have you done to them?"

"They're in another room."

"Are you torturing them, too?"

"Not at all. They're being quite compliant. Only you are—"

"Then let me see them!"

"I'm afraid that isn't possible yet. But in time—"

She twisted and strained against the straps, trying with all her might to get free.

He laid a hand on her shoulder, gently pushing her back to the table. "You've cut yourself." He pointed to an abrasion across her left breast, just above the nipple.

"It was your damned pendulum, you—"

"Looks nasty. Could be infected. Needs attention."

"Leave me alone!"

"Fear not, I know just the thing." He lifted a bucket and placed it on the edge of the table where she could just see it. "Heavy. Needs to be stirred." He took a large wooden ladle and swirled it through what appeared to be a thick gray muck. "There. That's better."

"What is that? What are you going to do with it? Are you going to put that on me?"

"Of course not. This is not the salve. This is but the living environment." He dipped the ladle into the bucket, this time just skimming the surface.

It came back with something.

He brought the ladle around so that she could see it, letting a splotch of gray goo splash down on her neck. It was small, thin, and writhing, greenish black in color. As he held it close to her face, the putrid smell made her turn away.

"What the hell is that?"

"Don't you know, Tiffany? It's the best thing for an infection. In the prophet's time, all the best physicians used them, a practice that has sadly fallen out of favor." He leaned in closer, pressing the lip of the ladle against her cheek. "It's a leech."

"Get it away from me!"

"No, no, you don't understand. It's a good little creature. It'll clean your wounds. Suck out the poison."

"I said, get it away!"

"Don't be silly. You'll hurt his feelings. Now where was that wound? Oh, yes." He tilted the ladle until the leech slowly oozed out and plopped onto her left breast.

"Get it off me! Get it off!"

"Don't fuss so. Let it do its work."

"Get it off!" Her voice screeched, panic rising. She squirmed as the slimy creature oozed its way across her. "Get—it—off!"

"Many hardy souls such as yourself are quite resilient when it comes to physical torment or fear, yet still have a weakness. Spiders, perhaps. Loud noises. But I suspected that you might have a touch of tactile defensiveness. We all do, of course, to varying degrees. But your case might be more extreme." He smiled. "Oh, look. The little beastie has found the wound. Engaging suckers."

"Please make it stop." She was sobbing, her voice bubbling, tears streaking. "Please make it stop."

"Just leave it to him. He knows what's best for what ails you. Oh—look! Another wound." With his fingertip, he traced a line up the inside of her upper thigh. "Fortunately, I have more of these salutary animalcules."

"No! Not there!"

He plopped another leech onto her leg. Tiffany writhed and shivered, thrusting herself forward and backward, right and left, trying to shake it off, to no avail.

"Is that a pimple on your face? Oh, I hate those."

"Please don't. Please don't."

"Here comes another helper."

"Not on my face! Please! Not on my—"

He dropped it just above her upper lip. It immediately began to slither toward her mouth.

Her eyes widened with fear and helplessness. She didn't dare speak, but she bucked against the table, thrusting her hips, squirming, trying to relieve herself of the slimy creatures.

"Honestly, Tiffany, you will carry on, won't you? About three puny leeches? The way you're behaving, I might as well—you know what? I think I will."

He tilted the bucket and dumped it, gray ooze and leeches alike, on top of her. Tiffany was deluged with the muck, in her eyes, in her mouth, every crevice and orifice.

She sputtered and spit, trying to keep it out of her mouth, but it was useless. She spat out a leech, gagging. She shuddered, unable to hold still. Her eyes were wide as balloons, her breathing a rapid-fire succession of jagged intakes, her chest heaving. She couldn't speak, but was reduced to making incoherent guttural noises, vacant and horrifying.

"How does it feel?" he asked, truly curious. "Having that sucking sensation all over your body, on your hands, your face, even your most private parts? Is it too awful? Or is it, as you young girls say, a turn-on?"

"Please make it stop, please make it stop, please make it stop . . ."

"Oh, Tiffany, my dear, you don't need me to do that. It will stop, sooner than you might imagine. You see, those leeches are more than just disgusting. They are poisonous. Instead of ridding your body of toxins, they are actually infecting you, tainting your bloodstream with a potent cyanide derivative." He looked at her levelly. "You will be dead soon, Tiffany. And then you won't be able to feel the little creatures at all."

"Pleeeeeeeeeeeease!" At least, that's what he thought she was saying, but her shrieks were so piercing at this point he couldn't make it out with any degree of fidelity.

"Goodbye, Tiffany. I'll let you spend your final moments in peace." Even as she cried and pleaded with him, he laid down the bucket, wiped his hands on a towel, and left the room.

She screamed for more than an hour before it was over.

"Who the hell is the leak?" Patrick bellowed, slamming the front door behind him.

I looked up, as did virtually everyone in the building. Outside, I could see reporters' faces jammed up against the glass like trick-or-treaters with their own perverse way of celebrating the forthcoming holiday. We were under siege. Had been all day.

Patrick stomped through the aisles, pushing aside locals and feds alike. I had never seen him in such a state. "It's one thing to leak our theories. New developments. But we don't even know for sure that Edgar took these girls!" He pounded his fists against the staircase banister. "For all we really know, they could be holed up at the Flamingo with their quarterback boyfriends!"

I knew what he was talking about. The morning papers had leaked the names of the three potential abductees—Tiffany and Judy and JJ. While cautiously reporting that the LVPD was investigating the possibility, they strongly suggested that it was a fact—that the girls were now dead and that it was all our fault.

"Is this tirade supposed to accomplish something?" I asked when he made it to my desk.

"Excuse me very much," he spat back. "You may be used to this kind of amateurism, but at the Bureau, we don't countenance leaks. They compromise the investigation!" He headed down the stairs. "I'm going to talk to our criminalists."

Because those FBI guys are so much smarter than I am? Even though they don't have the sense to take off their sunglasses when they come inside? Even though they dress like extras from **Men in Black**?

I gave the desk a shove, kicked back in my chair. I shouldn't let it get to me. He was just frustrated, like everyone else connected to this case. But he doesn't have to take it out on me. Especially after all I've been through. After all that we've . . . shared.

Damn. Amazing how much less sexy guys are when they're acting like assholes.

Tiffany did not die. The leeches were infected with a mild paralytic, enough that she might well think she was dying (and did). But not nearly enough to kill her. He had planned it that way.

She had screamed and begged for mercy till her voice was shredded and her tears were dry and there was nothing she could do but wait to die. But she did not.

"Tiffany! Still with us? Lovely." She was shivering, making quiet sobbing noises, her naked body covered with dried slime, leeches, and the remnants of leeches. They had sucked all over her body; her flesh was variegated with bruises and discoloration. Her eyes were cloudy and her expression was vacant, but he could see she was still there. Part of her, anyway.

"I'm sure you must be thinking horrible thoughts about me right now, thinking I've been terrible to you. If only you could understand that it is not so. Per contra, this has all been for your benefit."

She shuddered, trembled, but did not attempt to answer.

"I know you're probably not able to speak, so I won't expect you to hold up your end of the conversation. I'll do it for you. Look what I brought."

He loosened the straps just enough that she could peer up and see what he had brought with him.

Two bizarre hairy orange costumes. Orangutans.

"I knew you were anxious to see your two friends, so I brought them with me. They're quite agreeable these days. They put on their costumes without any hesitation. I hope you will, too." He leaned closer. "I'm afraid I exaggerated a bit beforehand, my sweet. The leeches drugged you, but they didn't poison you. This time."

She stared at him, shivering, her eyes wide and lost, like a broken doll.

"No need to feel left out, my dear. I've got a costume for you, too."

It was like the others, except that a huge section was cut out at the bosom, with a similar cutaway at the groin.

She trembled as she spoke. "If—if—if—if if

if if if I put it on, will you get this . . . slime off of me?"

"My dear, you'll be able to do it yourself. I'll provide the soap and water. You can pass the day away in indulgent lavation."

He unstrapped her. She took the suit like an automaton, barely thinking. He handed her a towel and she wiped herself off, wiped and wiped and wiped, leaving red abrasions and in some places bleeding. She picked the leeches away, crying as she did it, from her waist, her breasts, her pubis. Some left round sucking circles, others left blood oozing from her skin. But she did not scream or misbehave. She just sobbed quietly, desperately.

Then she took the suit. "Seems . . . wet."

"Coated with paraffin wax. I'll tell you why in a moment. Go on now. You must be anxious to get dressed."

She pulled the suit over herself. Her breasts hung out through the opening at the upper torso, while the midriff cutaway exposed her genitalia.

She put it on without complaining.

"What you have to understand," he said gently, almost paternally, "what it took me so long to grasp, is that it isn't enough to simply make an offering. The offerings must be true participants. Willing."

He took a book of matches from his pocket,

struck one, then lit a small torch—a club with oily rags wrapped and secured at the top.

"Hard to imagine, isn't it? That all this might have some wondrous purpose? But I can assure you that it does. One day, all humanity will give you its thanks. Your suffering will lead this troubled world to eternal bliss."

He smiled genially, then passed her the torch. "Set your friends on fire, Tiffany."

She looked at him, peering through the eye holes in the orangutan mask.

"Don't worry. They won't resist. They only exist to please me. Set them on fire."

Her arm twitched.

"If you refuse, of course, I'll have no choice but to put you back on the table. Perhaps it will be time to restart the pendulum. Instead of putting it across your chest, we'll let it take off an arm. Or a leg." His eyes narrowed. "Or perhaps I should bring out more leeches. Would you like that, Tiffany? Shall we bring them back?" He paused. "Or perhaps I should give one of your friends the opportunity I now offer you. Remember—you're wearing a suit, too, highly flammable. Perhaps I should ask JJ if she will light **your** fire."

Tiffany hesitated. Her arm moved indecisively.

"What shall it be, Tiffany? Them, or you?"

She took the torch.

"That's a dear. Finish it up now."

She did not cry or wail. It was almost as if sensation had fled from her, as if the idea of resistance was beyond imagining.

"Do it, Tiffany. Do it now."

The wax caught fire immediately. She stepped back from the flame, dropping the torch. One suit caught the other and in only a few seconds both were consumed in a blistering inferno.

"They won't suffer long. The suits will fuse to their skin and the smoke will choke them and they'll die before they experience . . . too much of the burning."

Tiffany crumpled to the floor, the orangutan suit bunched around her, her head buried beneath her hands. Her limbs were limp, as if all strength, indeed the bones themselves, had disappeared. He sensed that she wanted to cry, but no tears would come. There was almost no feeling at all, just a deadness, and a felt horror, not at him, but at herself.

Blessed be the prophet. The time was at hand.

CHAPTER THIRTY-ONE

The phone rang. Lisa.

"Calling to brighten my day with a report on last night's lip-lock?"

"No. You wanna shack up together?"

I drew in my breath. "But Lisa—this is so sudden. We haven't even kissed. And I know how important that is to you."

"I'm serious, Suze. I've found a place. Fabulous. Big. Guy needs a housesitter. He's going to be gone for years. We could have it for next to nothing."

I sat up. Living in hotel rooms and barren apartments was getting way stale. "Sounds too good to be true."

"I haven't even told you the best part yet. It's in L.A."

Everything seemed to go into slow motion. I drew the receiver from my face and stared at it. I noticed I was breathing deeply.

"You mean . . . leave Vegas?"

"Well, it would be a hell of a long commute."

"But—I'd lose my job."

"Technically, you already did that, sweetie. And this consulting thing can't last forever."

"What would I do?"

"I don't know. But you are a trained psychologist, remember? There are a lot of things you could do that don't involve poking around corpses or getting nabbed by serial killers. Personally, I think it would do you good. To get away from all the . . . reminders."

My eyes went into deep focus. There was a certain truth to what she said, of course. She wasn't the first to suggest that I should leave. And if I won the custody hearing, I could take Rachel anywhere I wanted. Maybe I could go back into clinical work. Maybe get a cushy job as a corporate trainer.

I wondered if this house in L.A. had palm trees. I always wanted a house with palm trees.

"I don't know, Lisa. I'll have to think about it."

"Okay. There's no rush. Let's talk tonight, okay, girlfriend?"

After she hung up, I had a hard time getting my head back where it belonged. Police work had been a part of my life for so long. It was the one thing my father and I'd had in common, and then after he was gone, something David and I had always shared. To some extent it had **been** my life, especially after David was gone. But what had it ever done for me? Made my life a misery. Gotten me kidnapped, abused. Reviled by my colleagues. Driven me to drink.

And there would always be room for another shrink in La-La Land, right?

I might still be thinking about it if Granger hadn't burst into what I laughingly called my office. "Are you as sick and tired of these goddamn Feebs as I am?"

"Probably not," I said honestly. "Why?"

"They've taken over the whole damn investigation!"

"And this surprises you? Granger—it's what they **do**."

"Hey, wouldn't it be great if you or I could crack this case? Show up those Junior J. Edgars?"

"Yeah. Especially if it were me."

Darcy shuffled in behind him. He'd been acting like the department errand boy all day, couriering things from one department to the other, delivering messages, even going for coffee. Anyone else his age might've found it demeaning, but Darcy wanted to be on the premises, even when he and I weren't doing anything. And not an hour passed that he didn't find some reason to come by my desk.

"Have you been thinking about that cheerleader one, Tiffany? 'Cause I've been thinking about that one."

"Really? Why?"

"Did you know that when most children run away from home, they have some kind of place in mind where they're going?"

I slowly rose out of my chair. "Are you saying you think Tiffany was running away from home?"

More shrugging. Staring at the carpet. "Not exactly." His hands began to pump the air. "But I don't think she'd leave unless she had someplace she wanted to go."

He was giving me all the bread crumbs, but I wasn't following the trail. "We've quizzed everyone. They say she had no friends or family around here."

"She was interested in police work. She wanted to be a policeman." His chin rose. "Lots of people wish they could be a policeman."

"So what are you saying? Maybe she decided to visit headquarters?"

"Did you watch the news last night? 'Cause I watched the news last night. It was all about Edgar."

"Yeah, it has been for—" Wait a minute. Praise God, I was starting to see the glue. "Tiffany would've known about the Edgar murders. And she was interested in police work."

Granger jumped in. "So she might've decided to do a little investigating?"

"Come on, Granger, we see it all the time. Whenever a case gets a lot of attention. The rubberneckers turn out at the scene of the crime, at the courthouse, whatever. Some people thrive on this kind of stuff."

"But where would she go? That shack out by the dam? That strip joint?"

I knew the answer before he'd finished speaking, knew it with a clarity that startled even myself. "Where the first body was found. Where Fara Spencer was killed. The Whitechapel of this whole case." I paused. "The Transylvania. That's where he grabbed them. Because that's where he is."

The girls were in their respective stalls, performing their nine-thirty poses.

They sat on the cold, bare floor in a confined area with nothing to do, nothing to look at, cold, dirty, naked. Every waking hour he would bring them a picture, usually something torn out of a porn magazine, always a woman in some demeaning pose. He would give them whatever they needed to re-create the scene. And then he would wait.

Not a word need be spoken. They knew what he wanted. And he rarely had to wait long to get it, certainly not after the first day. They knew what disobedience would bring. No food, for starters. No water. Not even a clean pan for their excrement. And quite possibly a return visit to the pendulum. Or the leeches. Or whatever else was required.

There had been no disobedience for a long time.

After they assumed the pose, whatever it was, he snapped their picture with his Polaroid, then posted it on the wall next to them. A little something to remind them who and what they were now. What they had become.

His. They belonged to the Raven, heart and mind and soul.

Judy and JJ had not been in those orangutan suits, of course, although it would've been magnificent, their ashes rising in an incandescent blaze, a magnificent incarnation of the prophet's tale of little Hop-frog's revenge. But the shock of thinking she had killed them—willingly—had been more than enough to break Tiffany. She had ended up even more deeply subservient than the two who had crumbled first. She was a sock puppet with his hand inside her.

Now the three of them were so compliant,

so eager to please him, that a picture was not even necessary. As soon as he entered the room, Tiffany began to assume a variety of poses, running through her repertoire, reenacting the photos on the wall. Anything to please him.

Perfect.

Everything at the hotel was proceeding apace. The Poe room was gone, The Hunchback of Notre Dame tableau was all but complete. It was not one of the prophet's works, but it would serve his purposes just the same.

All he lacked was the Vessel. Susan. Perhaps he had given her too much time, hoping that the time bomb he'd left ticking in her head would bring her to him of her own accord. One way or the other, once he had secured the Vessel, all his preparations would be complete.

Tiffany slithered up to him and wrapped herself around his feet. She pointed to her mouth, begging for food. Pathetic thing. He shook his head; he had not even brought a cube of sugar. Didn't matter.

She pulled up his pant leg and began to lick his ankle, purring.

CHAPTER THIRTY-TWO

I ripped the information out of the printer just as quickly as it emerged. For once, even my inner Luddite was glad we lived in the computer age. Once I convinced the management of the Transylvania that we should be permitted access to their records—by giving them no choice whatsoever about it—getting what we wanted was a relative snap. Compiling a list of all the guests who had stayed at the Transylvania since the body of Helen Collier was found was a cinch. Then we winnowed it down to a shorter list of all male guests who fit the current profile. I started with the names of men who had been staying at the hotel for a while and were still on the premises. As soon as I had the names and addresses, I transmitted them by fax to headquarters, where Madeline and Patrick ran Internet and FBI checks on them. She could also tap the DMV records and see if they owned a pickup.

We'd been at it for hours, and so far, we didn't have any suspects who fit all the parameters. But I wasn't worried. Names were still flying out of the computer. I knew we were on to something. I felt it in my heart, my bones. We were on the right track, finally.

Most importantly, I felt good. Even though I had no right to, not yet. But I did. I felt strong. I felt sober. I hadn't had a drink for days, and I was dealing with it. The shakiness was fading. I didn't think about it all the time. I had something more important to occupy my brain.

"Still no match?" Granger asked. He pushed away from the computer terminal and stretched. He'd been at it for hours. Turned out he was pretty good with those evil little machines.

I didn't look up. I was scanning names, faxing, periodically talking into my cell, and chatting with Granger, all at once. I don't need a computer to multitask. "Not yet. But he's in there somewhere. Give me some more names."

"That's going to take a while. We've covered Tower One, but they keep Tower Two in a separate database. It'll take a while to load."

"All right. No point in me standing around while you work." I grabbed my coat. "I'm going to slip out for a minute. I'll be back soon."

"You're leaving the hotel?"

"Right."

"There are about a zillion bars out there."

My buoyancy submerged, but only for a moment. "I'm going to visit my niece. I am not sneaking out to get a drink, Granger."

"I know," he said.

That caught me by surprise. He did?

"But—why make life difficult for yourself?"

"You want me to wear a chastity muzzle?"

He smirked. "You're still a potential target. Take one of the uniforms with you. Take Berman."

"I outweigh Berman by fifty pounds. How's he going to stop me from doing anything?"

"He's Church of Christ. He sees you order a drink, you'll get a lecture so harsh it might save even **your** soul."

Against my will, I found myself smiling. Why did Granger have to display these occasional flashes of human-beingness? It made it so much harder to hate him.

He'd been more than a bit worried when he saw Susan at the hotel. He had followed her discreetly, just to make sure she wasn't getting too close. Happily, she never came near the ballroom. But after she left the hotel—

He had no idea what an astounding discovery he would make.

How had she managed to keep this from him so long? He had researched everything he could find about her. He'd hacked into her police file, searched the newspaper morgue, performed repeated Internet sweeps, quizzed her when she was barely conscious and unable to resist. But somehow, through it all, she had managed to withhold one detail.

There was another Pulaski. A little girl.

Just the age he liked them.

He'd run a computer search through the city database and come up with a name: Rachel Pulaski. A daughter? No. If she and her deceased husband had procreated, it would have appeared in the public records. Same for any adoption. A cousin?

A niece, as it turned out.

Her brother, the one who died in the traffic accident. That must be the answer.

But why was the girl living with strangers? Why wasn't she with Susan? She must've lost custody, or been unable to obtain it. So she was reduced to occasional visitation.

A rapid-fire synaptic flurry crackled in his

head. New ideas flooded to the surface. Was this why he'd been unable to break Susan, why she had not become his willing partner like Tiffany and her friends? His quest for Susan was always marred by the fact that she was not suited to be an offering, much less the Vessel.

But Rachel was. She so perfectly, delicately, wonderfully was.

His premonition had been right. The name Pulaski would be writ in the roll call of Dream-Land. But not Susan Pulaski. **Rachel.**

He must have her.

Originally, he'd been trying to reincarnate Virginia as she once was. Of course that was impossible; her flesh was dust. But like the prophet's Ligeia, her spirit could be recaptured, brought back to the earthly plane. If only he had the proper Vessel.

He would have to remove her, to condition her, and he had little time. But he was sure it could be done. And then Virginia would return to him. And together, they would leave this horrid world behind. And create a far better one.

The only thing worse than Granger acting like a human being was Granger trying to be consoling.

"It's not your fault, Susan. It was a good theory. I thought we were on to something, too. But even the best theories don't pan out sometimes."

"He's here. I know he's here."

He actually laid a hand on my shoulder. And the worst of it was, I let him. "We went through all the records, Susan. Twice. And we didn't come up with anything."

I pressed my palms against my forehead, running every scrap of Edgar-data through my brain for the millionth time or so. "We must have something wrong. In the profile. The description. Something."

"Susan, you've looked at everyone who has stayed here in the last month who even remotely fits your profile. You came up with zip."

Truth hurts. He was right. I'd played my best hand and come up short. The review of the Transylvania's guests had yielded nothing.

Where was all my buoyancy now? All that blinding self-confidence? The girl who was going to catch the bad guy and never drink again? Where had she gone? Now when I looked in the mirror, I just saw a big placard reading LOSER. LOSER—AND DRUNKARD.

My wrist throbbed.

Granger was shuffling papers, obviously making moves to get the hell out of this tiny hotel office. "You look beat. Why don't you let me drive you home?"

So I won't stop somewhere and drown my sorrows in alcohol? "Sure. Thanks. Darce?"

After he'd done everything he could back at headquarters, Darcy had joined us here at the hotel. I don't know why. But I made sure he went over every name, every bio, every scrap of information I had, just in case I missed something. When your PC fails you, put a human computer on the case, right? He'd stared at those lists till his eyes watered.

"Did you know Einstein wrote his Special Paper on Relativity three times before he realized that space was curved? That was what made the whole thing make sense."

I gave him a tired grin. "I'm much too feeble to grasp Einsteinian physics at the moment. Or any other moment, actually."

"Can I go over the lists again?"

"No, Darcy," I said, clapping him on the back. "We're all going home now."

The fax machine pinged.

"Did Madeline have anything else to send us?" I asked.

Granger shook his head. "Madeline has gone home."

That was intriguing enough to keep me by the machine a few seconds longer. And halfway through the cover sheet, I had an even better reason.

"It's from Edgar."

How did he know we were here? I took the sheet and stared at it. Another coded message. But this time it was all ones and zeros.

"He's really taken this multiple-substitution code gimmick to the outer limit."

Darcy snatched it from me. "I think that this must be binary code. Do you think that this is binary code?"

"What, like computer talk?"

"Can I use this please?" He was already scooting in front of the hotel's PC.

"Sure. Ain't mine."

He tapped information into a black screen on the computer, fingers flying faster than I could follow. It all looked like gibberish to me.

"Hey," I said, "this probably won't be important. He wants to brag, impress me, maybe scare us a little. But he won't give us anything we can use to stop him. And I'm not going to stay up all night so I can read a quote from Edgar Allan Poe's grocery list."

"I think that maybe this is a hyperlink," Darcy said, not that it meant anything to me. "The code is much easier than the last one, if you know COBOL."

"Well, that's nice, but it could still take hours and—"

"Got it." Darcy clicked the Enter button a few more times. A Web browser came up, and a few moments later I saw the hourglass symbol that told me it was traveling to a new destination.

"You think Edgar has his own Web site?" Granger asked.

"I wouldn't be surprised. There are plenty of public-access servers that allow anonymous uploads. But what would he post? Poe's Greatest Hits? MP3s for the Golden Age? Photos of his vic—"

My tongue froze in my mouth. The graphic image in the Web browser had begun to resolve.

It was a photograph, presumably taken from a distance with a digital camera. I had no problem recognizing one of the people in the photo. It was me. Didn't have to work much to identify the other person, either. The one I was talking to.

It was Rachel. He knew about Rachel.

"Oh, God," I said as a cold sweat broke out all over my body. "Oh, my God."

"I'm calling for backup," Granger said, already dialing his cell. "What's her address?"

"Oh, God," I repeated uselessly. Rachel. All I had left—

"Susan! Give me her address!"

And I did. Pulling myself together as best I could, I grabbed my car keys and raced for the front door. Please, God, don't let us be too late. Please, don't let us be too late.

But my own words haunted me, even as I

raced out the door and into the stifling desert night air.

He wouldn't give us anything we could use to stop him.

Rachel raised the window and leaned out into the cool night air.

Not a creature was stirring, as the poem went. Excellent.

It was drizzling outside. The white trellis attached to the front of the house was slick. She would have to be careful.

She hoisted herself through the window, flipped her feet around, then slowly descended onto the trellis. The Shepherds were nice folks, but they had to be crazy not to see how easy it was to get out of this room. Just too innocent to consider the possibilities, she supposed. Or perhaps it was some sort of test.

Didn't matter, she thought, as she dropped like Spider-Man down the side of the house. At first, she'd thought the Shepherds were pathetic, hilarious, ridiculous. But over time, she had sort of gotten used to the regularity of life with them. She had found new friends, new interests. It wasn't all bad, really.

But her first loyalty was to Susan. Had to be. She was family. And she knew how much Susan loved her. Knew how much Susan counted on her, needed her if she was to stay sane. When she'd visited earlier today, Rachel could see how edgy she was. Then when she got the call from a co-worker telling her how much Susan had fallen apart, how desperate she was—Rachel knew she had to go to her.

She hadn't packed much, but then, she didn't have much to pack. She'd thrown some clothes in a backpack and scraped together all the money she had—less than twenty dollars. It would be enough. She'd catch a city bus to Susan's neighborhood, then hike the rest of the way to her hotel room. Simple.

She checked carefully in all directions before she emerged from the concealing shadows of the house. No signs of life, not even a car in the distance. She made a break for the sidewalk.

Vegas buses ran all night long. She supposed they had to. Businesses were open all hours and people had to get to work. She crossed the first street, then another, then several more, moving much faster now, making her way toward the bus stop at the corner.

It was lighted; she wasn't crazy about that. A safety precaution, she supposed, but tonight, she preferred to remain in the darkness. She was pretty sure the Shepherds hadn't heard her leave, but you never knew.

She checked the posted schedule. Bus should be along in about five minutes. This time of night, of course, it was impossible to be sure. She decided to move a few feet down the street, out of the light, at least until she heard the chug-chug of the diesel engine or the high-pitched squeal of hydraulic brakes. . . .

"Excuse me, miss. Rather late, isn't it?"

She froze. Where the hell had he come from?

"Mind if I ask where you're going?"

He was wearing a uniform. Wasn't the usual uniform, though. She couldn't read the name on his badge.

"I'm going to visit my aunt. You got a problem with that?"

"No. Do your parents know about this?"

"My parents are dead."

The man gazed at her with an intense focus. She couldn't recall ever being subjected to such severe scrutiny before. What was he looking for?

"I'm sorry to hear that, miss. Is your aunt your legal guardian?"

Rachel hesitated barely a second. "Yes, she is."

"And does she know you're out at this time of night?"

"Ye-es. It was . . . unavoidable. There was a mix-up at school and—"

The man's eyes twinkled. "I think you're lying to me, miss."

"How would you know?"

"Come with me."

She shrugged his hand away. "I'm not going anywhere except on a bus."

"I'm afraid I'll have to insist. Consider yourself under arrest."

"You can't arrest me."

"I can. Suspicion of delinquency."

"Let me see your badge."

"If you know what's good for you—"

"I know not to get in a car with some weirdo just because he claims to be a cop."

The man reached into his wallet and flashed something quickly. "Okay? Now, if you'll just come along . . ."

She grabbed the wallet and reopened it. "This isn't a LVPD badge." She read the small print. "You're just a private security cop. You can't arrest me."

His face seemed to transform, harden. His voice acquired an accent. "Don't be difficult, Rachel, my dear. It's for your own good."

She took a step back. "How do you know my name?" Her eyes widened. "You're him. You're the guy. The one who grabbed Susan."

"It would have been so much easier if you'd simply come when I asked." He seized her arm, his grip so tight it hurt. She twisted back and forth, trying to break free.

"Give up," he said, smiling. "You can't get away."

"Wanna bet, asshole?" She kicked him hard on the kneecap. He buckled. The next kick went into his groin. He released her arm.

Rachel turned to run, but before she could get away he wrapped an arm around her throat, pinching her trachea, yanking her down to the sidewalk. Rachel coughed and sputtered helplessly; she felt the air draining out of her lungs.

Still pinning her to the wet pavement with his left hand, he began fumbling for something in his jacket pocket with his right. Rachel saw her chance—probably her last one—and took it. She brought both fists around and pounded the arm that choked her, knocking it away. Before he could react, she slapped him on both sides of the head, right over his ears.

He screamed. His face contorted with pain and, even more, astonishment.

"You hurt me," he murmured.

"About time someone did." Rachel fled. Without looking back, she tore across the street and dove between two houses. Now she wouldn't mind so much bumping into a cop, but what were the chances? She raced down the slick pavement, slipping and sliding, gliding down alleyways, creating shortcuts between houses and crisscrossing through residential streets. At least she knew the neighborhood. She had that advantage. Her sneakers slipped on a wet patch and she went flying feetfirst into a chain-link fence. She was dazed and her face was scratched, but she knew she couldn't indulge herself in rest.

She checked over her shoulder, down the alleyway. Was he still there? She didn't see him, but somewhere in the darkness, she thought she heard the footfalls of someone, someone running. She couldn't keep this up. She'd never make it back to the Shepherds' house on foot. She needed help.

She raced out into the street. Surely someone would come, even this time of night, anyone, it didn't matter, just so she could get out of here before that guy caught up to her. Please!

In the distance, she saw the gleam of a pair of headlights. She shouted and waved, but it did not slow. What had Susan taught her? If you're not sure someone will cooperate, don't give them an alternative. She ran out in the center of the road, waving her arms wildly, forcing the oncoming vehicle to stop.

When it did, she ran to the passenger side. "I need a lift. Please! Someone's chasing me. I think it's that guy, the Poe freak."

The young girl poised behind the wheel was about Rachel's age. She seemed confused initially, but after a moment she said, "Get in."

Rachel did. The second she closed the door, the truck peeled out. Rachel whipped around, peering out the back window, searching for a trace of the man who had been chasing her. Nice try, you sick pervert, she thought to herself. But you can't have me.

"Where do you want to go?" the driver asked.

"Back to my—no, just take me to a gas station or something. Anything public that has a phone."

"I think there's one on the corner of Maple."

"Great." Rachel tried to relax. "I really appreciate this. You've saved my life, and I'm not exaggerating."

"Glad I could help."

"You and me both." Rachel crumbled against the back of the cab. She was still breathing hard; her pulse was racing. But she was safe. "By the way, my name is Rachel."

"I'm Tiffany." All at once, the truck ground to a halt.

"Wait a minute. What are you doing?"

The girl did not respond. Her face was like a mask, expressionless. Her eyes were wide and hazy.

The passenger side door opened. Rachel screamed.

"We meet again." It was him, the security guard. The killer. He was leaning into the cab. He held a hypodermic needle in his left hand.

"Help!' Rachel tried to crawl out the other way, but the woman driving would not budge.

"You've done a good job, Tiffany," the man

said as he crawled after his prey. "You will be re-warded."

"Leave me alone!" Rachel tried desperately to escape, but there was nowhere for her to go. She kicked and clawed at him, without avail. Behind her, the girl called Tiffany grabbed her arms and held her in place.

"So much spirit. Just like your aunt. And my Ginny. You are the perfect Vessel."

Rachel tried to resist, but she was helpless, powerless, and even as she thought about somehow trying to get away, the needle jabbed her in the throat.

"Your devotion to your aunt is admirable. I was quite certain that phone call would bring you out."

The instant the needle left her neck, Rachel felt her strength fading, the lights dimming.

"S-Susan . . ." she said as her eyelids fluttered closed.

"Susan can't help you now, my sweet. You will not see her again." He put the syringe back in his pocket, zipped it up, and gently slid his arms under her still, limp body. "But the happy thing is, after you've been with me for a while, you won't want to."

Two squad cars were already parked out front by the time Granger and I made the scene. Two uniforms were at the front door. I whipped the car around, tires squealing, parked in the middle of the street, and raced across the lawn.

They didn't answer the doorbell, just as they hadn't been answering the phone. I looked up and saw a window open. The window in what I knew was Rachel's room.

I kicked the damn door open.

We raced inside, guns raised. Circling in formation, we flooded the downstairs, the living room, the kitchen. No signs of life, good or bad.

We found the Shepherds huddled upstairs in their bed. They'd thought it best not to open the door this time of night. They'd tried calling the police but couldn't get a dial tone.

"Damn," Granger said under his breath. "He must've cut the phone line."

I bolted into Rachel's room.

The breeze coming through the open window put a chill in the air. The lace drapes fluttered up and down. The room was silent.

She was gone. He had her.

CHAPTER THIRTY-THREE

Rachel woke screaming.

She was naked and strapped to a wooden chair in the middle of what looked like a basement. She couldn't get free; she couldn't move. She was barely able to squirm.

Only a few seconds later, he entered the room carrying a large oaken bucket.

"Where am I now?" she shouted. He'd repeated this pattern over and over again, ever since he abducted her, taking her to some new location, bringing her around for a few minutes, then drugging her again. She'd lost all sense of time and place.

"A little change of scenery while I finish my preparations. There's so much to do. Did you like what I showed you earlier? Did it not seem a wondrous staging ground to ring in the Ascension? You'll be returning later, after we've had a little fun."

"Where are my clothes, you pervert?" Her voice was hoarse and strained. "Why did you take them?"

He smiled pleasantly. "I didn't wish to get them wet." And then he dumped the bucket on her.

It was filled with water, ice cold. It hit her like an arctic tidal wave. She thought she was going into shock; for a moment, it felt as if her heart actually stopped beating. She shivered uncontrollably, convulsing. She had never felt so bitterly frozen in her entire life.

"C-C-C-Could I please have a blanket? Or s-s-s-something. I-I-I—"

"I'm sorry. That isn't an option."

"B-B-B-But I'm s-s-s-so c-c-cold."

"Yes. But fear not—later you'll be hot. So terribly hot. Then cold again, then hot. Cold, hot, cold, hot. All the livelong day."

She peered up at him, her eyes cloudy, her flesh a mottled pink covered with chill bumps, her arms clutched as tightly as possible to her exposed chest. "Why?"

"I should think that was obvious. To eliminate that trademark Pulaski stubbornness. Happily, I don't require your total subservience. There simply isn't enough time remaining. I already have my three offerings. You're the Vessel. But fear not—it's a most important role."

She drank in air in deep, convulsive gasps. "Why . . . are . . . you . . . like this?"

He looked at her for a long moment. "A curious question. Why are any of us the way we are? There's no satisfactory explanation, is there? Would you like me to tell you a sad story? Blame it all on my tragic childhood? Mommy didn't love me. Daddy hit me with a hairbrush. Simplistic balderdash. We are what we are." He adjusted the lay of his vest. "I am the Raven. Everything else was mere prologue."

People were talking to me, shouting in my ear, demanding answers to their endless questions. I couldn't process it all, couldn't deal with it. Why had he targeted Rachel? How had I known he was coming here? Why hadn't I done something about it sooner? Each time I started to give a coherent answer something else interrupted, a new demand, a false hope, a neural spasm in my brain. This could not be happening. This could not be happening.

Rachel!

"Everybody out of the house!" Patrick

shouted. And when had he shown up? At least someone had the sense to preserve what was now a crime scene. God knows I hadn't.

"Call the techs. Get Crenshaw. Get O'Bannon!"

Patrick barked out orders with impressive efficiency and organization. It should be me, I heard the voice inside my head say. It should be me.

Rachel!

All at once, every single living memory, every photograph, every reminder of what that man had done to me flashed through my head.

And now he had my niece.

Patrick pulled the questioners off me. I knew the respite would be a brief one, but I was determined to make the most of it. I found a sofa and sat, steadying myself. My hands were shaking again. My stomach was sick, tossing, craving. I knew what I wanted, what I needed. I felt it with an urgency I had not experienced before, not since I woke up by the dam, not even when I saw the pictures.

He had won, he and the bottle. I knew I would get drunk tonight. I knew I would get drunk and stay drunk and be a drunk for the rest of my life. I had tried so hard. But I wasn't strong enough.

I felt a sharp aching in my left wrist. God, I'd

almost forgotten that was there. If only I'd done it right. I might be gone, but Rachel would be safe.

This was my fault. This was all my fault.

Next thing I remembered was Patrick sitting beside me, Darcy hovering behind him. Patrick was careful to keep his face sympathetic but calm, strong. And Darcy was expressionless. Was that because he wasn't picking up on the nonverbal clues, didn't comprehend my fear and sadness? No, I think he got it, perhaps more than anyone. He just didn't know what to do about it. Who could?

"We have to ask you some more questions, Susan. Not just about what happened tonight, but about Rachel in general. Anything you can tell us about her that might be helpful."

I felt so useless. I couldn't speak. Couldn't even raise my eyes to his.

"But I don't know why it has to be done here," Patrick continued. "Best if we take it back to headquarters."

So I won't be around if the crime techs start making discoveries? Like Rachel's blood? Evidence of her death or torture?

"Why don't you ride back with me? I'll get a sergeant to bring your car—"

"No, I'll drive," I said, snapping out of it with a suddenness that startled both of us.

"I don't think that's wise."

"I can do it. I'll meet you back—"

He grabbed my wrist and held it tight. "We need you on this, Susan. We need you one hundred percent."

I knew what he was saying. He knew why I wanted to drive myself. But it was all so far beyond my control.

O'Bannon crouched down beside me. "Susan, I'm sorry to have to do this to you, but you're off the case."

"What?"

"Your niece is a victim now. You're too close. I could overlook your own involvement, but not hers. Effective now, your consulting contract is canceled. You can keep the desk. I'll try to assign you something else when an appropriate case comes along. But as for now—"

That was when the phone rang, cutting him mercifully short. I don't know what I thought I was doing. But I was sitting right next to it. So I picked it up.

No. I have to be honest. I knew who it was. And I knew it was for me.

"Yeah."

"I have her."

"Son of a bitch." I clenched the receiver so tightly my fingers turned white. "Why Rachel?"

"I needed her. She's the Vessel."

"You said you cared about me, you bastard!" I shouted, feigning a toughness I did not feel. "If you do anything to her, anything like what you did to me—"

"Please calm yourself, dear. This is pointless."

"I'll make your god Poe look like an unimaginative grandma when you see what I can do. Have you hurt her?"

"Of course not."

"What is it you want?" I cried. "What is it you want from me?"

"Now? Nothing. Nothing at all."

"Then why—"

"I just called to tell you that you needn't worry. I have Rachel, and I will take good care of her, after my fashion. There's no chance that you'll catch me or recover her. So relax and enjoy what little time is left."

My head felt thick and unresponsive. There must be something I should do, something I should say. But what was it? "What do you mean, what little time is left?"

"I've told you before, Susan. The end times are upon us. I have everything I need now. Everything."

"Let me talk to her. If you really haven't hurt her, let me talk to her."

A long sigh. Followed by: "Five seconds."

The phone passed. "Oh, my God, Susan, it's

him. It's really him. I haven't been this scared since that day when we rented a video just after my parents—"

"Time's up."

"Bastard!" I wailed, my voice hoarse. "You could at least let her finish the sentence."

"I'm afraid we must go, just in case you're tracing."

"Can I talk to her again tomorrow?"

"I . . . doubt she'll be . . . able to communicate clearly." I heard him sigh. "I wanted so much to save you, Susan. But I couldn't do it. And who else is going to try?"

"What are you talking about?"

"I think you know. Good night, Susan. Try not to make a mess of it this time."

The line disconnected.

While they were all babbling about the trace and the recording and what it meant, I stumbled to my car and drove away, fast, before Patrick got up the strength or numbers to stop me. My heart was pounding and my brain was racing. A thousand thoughts cruised through my head at once. It was like being drunk without being drunk. Was this what they called a dry drunk? I couldn't focus. Couldn't get a grip on myself, on anything.

Except one thing. I knew where I was going. Gordy's. Back where this all began. It was appropriate, no? Symmetrical.

Had I ever really thought for a minute I could give up drinking? Who was delusional now? The bartender would still serve me, I thought, and if he didn't, there was a liquor store next door. Hell, that might be quicker. What did it matter? No shortage of places to get drunk in Vegas.

Soon as I got there, I parked, popped open the car door, put one leg out—and froze.

Not voluntarily. I wanted to move. I kept telling myself to move. It was as if I'd lost all control, as if some alien being had taken over my body.

I closed my eyes and saw Darcy—Darcy, of all people—in my mind's eye. The autistic savant, the boy who didn't comprehend emotion, but who nonetheless had given me so much emotional support. He was just staring at me. He liked me, I'd have to be blind not to see that, but he wasn't happy to see me. He was sad. So sad.

Rachel wasn't sad. Worried, not sad. I saw almost everyone I knew, Lisa, Patrick, Granger, the chief, my parents, my suspects, all of them, all of them, all of them.

David.

They were so sad.

That's what he wants you to do.

I somehow managed to get my leg back inside the car and close the door, but that was such a strain that I decided to forget about trying to move again for a while.

Try not to make a mess of it this time.

My wrist throbbed. Throbbed, like an aching in the hollow of my heart.

"Don't let him win, sugar bear."

"It's so . . . hard," I said, even though I knew I wasn't speaking.

"Naturally," David replied, with his understanding smile. "It's meant to be."

"I wish you hadn't done it, David. I wish you hadn't." I folded over on the seat, hands tucked into my lap, cradling like a fetus. "I just wished you'd loved me enough to stay."

David looked at me with heavy eyes. "I'm sorry, Susan. It's hard to admit, but—there are times when love has nothing to do with it."

I lay on the seat like a pathetic baby, which is exactly what I was. "I don't forgive you, David. Not now, not ever. I will not forgive you."

His eyes only deepened. "This is my last visit, Susan."

"What? Why?"

"Because you need to get on with it. And you won't, as long as I'm around."

And then he was gone. And I lay across the front seat of my beat-up car, crying into the vinyl, hurting, hurting so much.

But I was still inside the car.

CHAPTER THIRTY-FOUR

When I woke up, I didn't know how much time had passed. Somehow, all the smoke and cobwebs that once had fogged my brain had cleared, like someone had gone in with a mini-vac and sucked it clean. The aching, the craving, was still there. But it was manageable. I could make it. I knew that I could make it.

Rachel needs you, the voice in my head insisted. You have no more time to waste.

And yet I didn't immediately start the car. I sat up straight and stared into the mirror. All I could see were my eyes, but somehow, that was enough.

I could catch this man, I told myself, looking right into those red, tired, mismatched eyes. I had the means, the gift. If only I could put it all together . . .

I tried to let my mind drift, free-associate. I thought if I opened things up enough, I might spark a connection, discover whatever it was I knew but my conscious mind had not yet seen.

Relax, I told myself. Breathe in, hold it, release. Breathe in, hold it, release.

I had been so sure I had him, back at the Transylvania. I could almost feel him in my grasp. But I'd come up short.

Pull back, Susan. Let your mind wander. . . .

Had the three cheerleaders come to the Transylvania? Had the others?

Helen is a good girl. She would never do something like that. . . .

Annabel was brilliant, an honor student even at MIT. I made sure she knew how to apply herself, how to turn heads. . . .

The most important facet of the narcissistic personality is the absolute certainty of his own superiority, that he's right and everyone else is wrong. . . .

He's smart, phenomenally smart. Deranged, but smart. . . .

She made scrapbooks, just like I did as a girl. She even posted some of her art on her personal Web page. . . .

My eyes opened.

Uniforms.

That was the key, damn it. Uniforms.

What did Helen have on the walls in her bed-room? What did she have pasted into her scrap-book, on her Web page? Not rock stars. Not TV hunks. Cops, firemen, doctors, pilots . . .

And what did they have in common? Uni-forms. Where did she sneak out to in her black leather bad-girl getup? A biker bar? The teen stud club? No. The Army grunt hangout. Be-cause that's where she would find men in uni-forms.

Helen had a thing for uniforms. She liked them.

She trusted them.

Tiffany admired policemen, firemen. She dreamed of one day being a cop herself, because she admired them so.

She trusted them.

There's more, I heard a voice within me say-ing. Keep working it, keep digging. . . .

Darcy had shown me the burn mark where the door had been forced, the door to the ball-room where Helen Collier was found. But why was that significant?

Because it pointed **away** from the room, not toward it. Because the chain had been torched from the inside.

Edgar had already been inside when he brought out his acetylene torch. He'd had access to the room. Breaking the chains and forcing the lock had been just another clever trick to throw us off his trail.

My respiration spiked. I was breathing hard and heavy, my heartbeat racing. I was getting there. I knew I was getting there.

I stormed into headquarters, taking them all by surprise. The feds appeared to be reorganizing our offices into an FBI hostage crisis center. Which wasn't a bad idea, in theory. But I knew that by the time they were finished, it would be too late for Rachel.

Patrick was in the chief's office, conferencing. Darcy sat silently behind O'Bannon's desk.

"Susan!" O'Bannon bellowed. "Where the hell have you been?" He looked at me suspiciously.

"Go ahead, sniff my breath. I haven't been drinking."

"Then what? Damn it—this is your own niece."

"I know that," I said firmly. "I also know he won't kill her. Not yet. He might . . . do things to her. But she's strong. She'll survive. I did."

"Susan, our investigators have a thousand questions—"

"And I'll answer them. But in exchange, I want five plainclothes answering to me and complete freedom."

They stared at me, all of them, speechless.

"And I'd like Patrick, if the Feebs can spare

him. And Darcy," I added. "Most importantly, Darcy."

O'Bannon stared at me uncomprehendingly. "Have you taken complete leave of your senses?"

"Just the opposite. Regained them, finally."

He looked as if he were about to burst a blood vessel. "Even given the bizarre assumption that I said yes, what do you think you'd do?"

"Go back to the Transylvania."

"You already played that hunch! It was a good theory. But it didn't pan out. None of the guests—"

"He isn't a guest. He works there."

Patrick stepped forward. "Susan, I looked at the employee rolls. I didn't see anyone who—"

"Then we need to line them up and let me look. I'll recognize the rat bastard."

"Are you sure?"

"Positive. I don't know why I didn't see it before. It's obvious, once you know."

"Know what? What do you think he does?"

"I'm not sure. But I know he wears a uniform." I paused. "I think there's a good chance he's a cop."

He frowned. "A cop?"

"Or something like a cop. Don't they have security at the Transylvania? I thought I remembered seeing some."

"Of course they do. But they might contract

the security out, like most of the big houses."
He snapped his fingers. "Which would explain
why he didn't turn up on the employee rolls."

"I need to get over there immediately." I
turned to O'Bannon and looked him square in
the eyes. "With your permission."

He barely hesitated a second. "Consider
yourself back on the case."

"Good. I'll stay in touch."

"You won't have to. I'm coming with you."
He pulled out his desk drawer and tossed something onto his desk. A gun. My gun. "I think
you may need this."

"I don't know. If you're not—"

He pressed it into my hand. "I insist."

"We need to blanket the hotel," Patrick said.
"Make sure he doesn't slip out before we iden-
tify him. How much time do we have till this
Day of Ascension?"

I checked my watch. "Only a few hours."

"**Hours?** Then the Day of Ascension—"

"When else?" I led the way to the door.
"Today. Halloween. At the witching hour."

CHAPTER THIRTY-FIVE

"You think this place will be ready in time, Ernie?" Martin asked.

He was calm and confident. "I don't see why not. The grand opening isn't until midnight."

"But there's so much still to do." Both pairs of eyes scanned the ballroom. The façade of the Notre Dame cathedral was largely in place, but some of the surrounding decorations were in pieces on the floor, waiting to be assembled. Exposed scaffolding occupied a corner of the room. "I hear the hunchback is still experimenting with his makeup. And what's with these bells?" He gestured toward the huge six-foot bells that were being hoisted into place at the front of the cathedral. "Those mothers are huge.

And heavy. Why would the hotel lay out so much for bells?"

"You can't do **The Hunchback of Notre Dame** without bells."

"Hey, I been meaning to ask—what were you doing in the ventilation shafts last night?"

He stiffened. "Last night?"

"Yeah. I saw you crawling out of that shaft over at the north end of the casino. I didn't even know that was big enough to get into. What were you up to?"

"One of the patrons reported smelling smoke. I didn't detect it myself, but I thought it best to be certain."

"Huh. Well, they never covered that when I came on. Maybe you can show me how to get in there later tonight."

He touched the syringe in his pocket. He could take this man out if necessary. Quickly and quietly. "Tonight would not be a good day, what with all the work going on. Perhaps after the Halloween celebration."

"Good point. Okay."

His hand relaxed. Just as well. Another dead security officer would draw more attention to the hotel—and he had directed too much attention here already. "If you'll excuse me, I, uh, need to check on something in the storeroom."

"You've been spending a lot of time in there

lately." Martin chuckled. "You got a naked girl up there?"

He smiled. "Yeah. Four of them."

He left the ballroom and headed for the elevator bank. There was still much to be done, so many arrangements to finalize. Everything had to be right, just perfect. But soon he would be able to cordon off the ballroom so he could finish his preparations. Rachel would not participate willingly, but the other three would, and they would help him with her. He had put so much time and effort into this, not just with the offerings, but everything. Obtaining the C4 on the Vegas black market. His unbroken brown study of radio signals and electronics and incendiary agents. Everything that was required.

The hotel had spent thousands advertising this event, generating publicity for the grand reopening of this ballroom. But they would be celebrating ever so much more than those dullards imagined.

This celebration would be a cataclysmic event. An apocalypse for some, an ascension for others. The end of days.

"No, it can't wait until tomorrow!"

I pounded my fists together for emphasis. I wasn't trying to threaten the man—well, actually, I was, wasn't I? If I couldn't convince him of the urgency of the situation one way, I was prepared to try another.

"But today is a very special day," Bloomfeld insisted.

"You don't know the half of it."

"All our resources are taxed to the limit." This guy had annoyed me when I was investigating the first crime scene and he hadn't grown on me any in the interim. He was probably perfect for micromanaging the organizational details of a hotel but he was useless to me. "Our hotel is booked to capacity. Our Halloween celebration is generally considered the best anywhere. Thousands of people come to the Transylvania from all over the world."

Patrick stepped between us. "I don't give a damn about your tourists getting their ghost and ghoul fix. Four girls have been kidnapped."

"My staff is already being pulled six ways at once," Bloomfeld continued.

I shot him the harshest look I could muster. "I'm chasing a serial killer here, a killer who— unless he's stopped—is going to try something very bad tonight, probably at midnight, which is less than three hours away. I think that's a little—"

This was where Bloomfeld did his best to pretend he had a backbone. "I have a responsibility to my guests. They expect a party that—"

"I'll cancel the damn party if you don't cooperate with me! I'll shut the whole hotel down."

He froze, his face more horrific than any of their gargoyles. "You can't do that."

"I can and I will. I won't let another girl die because you were too busy entertaining to help. Now you can deal with me, and we can go through your security contractor's employment records, or I can shut the whole joint down. What's it going to be?"

As if he had a choice. I held all the cards. And I had to admit—it felt good to be effective again, to be back on top of my game. Or getting that way.

Bloomfeld started gathering the records.

"Great technique," Patrick said quietly. "Where'd you study, Nazi Germany?"

I suppose I should've been more respectful to Bloomfeld, since we were in his office in his hotel. Well, next week, I'd send him a Hallmark. Right now, I had a job to do. And some lives to save.

By eleven P.M., I had winnowed it down to five names. Five possibles who fit most of the criteria. The women were eliminated, of course. All the men of the wrong age group. Everyone who was physically too large to be Edgar. I classified them by economic group, by educational background, by family relationships. Anyone who listed a parent as a Person To Contact in an Emergency was eliminated. And in the end, I had five names.

One of them was Edgar. I was certain of it. But which one?

I peered at the pictures, the files, everything that was known about them. Darcy hunched over my shoulder. I had seen this man, damn it. I had talked to him. I should be able to pick him out of a photo lineup. Shouldn't I?

Three of them were private security, where we had focused this search, but I was also considering a part-time tennis instructor and an actor who worked in the evening Spookapalooza show playing Edgar Allan Poe. I phoned Madeline and told her to run Net checks on all of them—to learn as much as she could as quickly as possible. I instructed Bloomfeld to round up all the suspects. And I let my mind do what it did best. From here on out, I knew finding Edgar would not be a matter of logic or analysis. Intuition had to take over. My instincts had to tell me which of these men kidnapped Rachel. And how to get her back.

The more I dwelt on it, the more I gravitated toward the three security officers. The tennis dude wore a uniform of sorts, but was it a uniform that instilled trust? Would Annabel, the MIT student, have given him the time of day? Judging from his photograph, he was a cute guy, not much older than she was. But somehow, I just didn't believe it.

The actor who played Poe was an obvious choice—too obvious. If his Poe connection were that apparent, would he have given us the Poe-derived clues, the quotations, the literary death methods? I had seen this guy on television once or twice since the Poe connection was leaked, being interviewed as a local expert on "the Dark Bard of Baltimore." No, he was way too high-profile. I didn't buy it.

And then there were three. Damon William Cantrell. Jeffrey Henry DeMouy. Ernest Lee Abbott.

"What do you think, Darcy?"

Darcy stared at the pictures. His brain was in motion, I could tell that. But this wasn't what he did best, was it? When he met them, he might notice the telltale smell of perfume or the stain of a certain kind of ash found only in Sumatra or whatever. But what could he do with a photo?

"I don't think I like this one," Darcy said. He pointed to the file photo of Cantrell, but I noticed he wasn't actually looking at it. "His hair is like John Wayne Gacy's hair."

"Anything else?"

"Did you know that John Wayne Gacy is considered the most successful American serial killer? He made even more deaths than Ted Bundy."

"Anything else?"

He tapped another picture, the one of Abbott. "I think that maybe I have seen him before."

"Really? Where? In the hotel?"

His face twisted up. "I don't remember," he said—words I never expected to hear coming out of that mouth. But such was the irony of being autistic. He could remember chapter and verse about anything he read. But he was useless with faces. Some researchers thought autistic people didn't really even see faces, their expressions and distinctions. Just a pink blur. Which would explain why they were so poor at picking up on visual clues, facial expressions, and body language.

Darcy was not going to pick the lucky winner.

"Where is Patrick, anyway?" I said. I wanted to get his opinion on this, before Bloomfeld arrived with the suspects. "He should be back by now."

"I'll go look," Darcy said. He probably realized he wasn't much help here. So he would be of use another way.

And I continued to stare at the pictures. Will the real Edgar please stand up?

I have to find Patrick Susan wants me to find Patrick and she's so worried and scared about her niece Rachel who seems nice but I hope she doesn't like Rachel more than me or she can like us both and is Rachel like her baby because I want her to have real babies and maybe she won't maybe she won't if something happens to Rachel like Mommy never had any more babies after me and Dad tells people that they couldn't but they could I know they could Mommy told me they could but they weren't going to because I was a difficult boy and they didn't want any more difficult boys. We have to stop the Bad Man because he hurt those girls and he hurt Susan and he might try to hurt more people and it's not right to hurt people. I would never hurt anyone. Hurting is bad.

I can't find Patrick there are so many people in this gambling room and so much smoke I hate smoke I don't know why people smoke it's bad for you and it's disgusting and it should be illegal it makes my eyes hurt so I went into the ballroom with all the weird decorations. I couldn't see Patrick but I saw this guard guy and he was in a big hurry and I don't know why I even looked at him except he was carrying an axe and that seemed weird and then I looked at him some more and I wasn't sure if I knew him I never know if I know people but he smelled like someone I knew his smell was familiar and then he said something and I heard his voice and I remembered the guy on the street and all that talk about how tall he wasn't except then he had a mustache and a different color hair and glasses and he looked different but he said something again and I knew it was him.

He must be the Bad Man.

He recognized me too and I made a joke about did he have any more good puzzles I could solve and he didn't and I could see he was going to hit me just like the kids at school used to hit me and I should've done something about it. I should've stopped him but then I would have to hit him and it isn't right to hit people it isn't right and I don't want to hurt anyone and I didn't do anything and then he took the other end of the axe and he hit me and I fell down and then there was nothing.

"Please," Rachel gasped. "I can't stand it anymore. It hurts."

"Only for a little while, my dear. Soon it will all be over."

She'd been hanging upside down for far too long. Blood rushed to her head, making it throb so intensely she could barely think. "Where's Tiffany? And the others. Where did they go?"

"They're such dear girls, so eager to please. Nothing I ask is too much."

"Because you've tortured and brainwashed them."

"Rachel!" He tightened the ropes around her wrists and ankles, making sure she was secure.

"Don't speak like that. I've told you what is at stake. I've explained to you about the Ascension, about Dream-Land. About my sweet Virginia. The whole majestic plan."

"I don't want any part of your plan!"

He took her chin—upside down before him—and held it in his palm. "Would you prefer to be like the other heathens, those who remain on this plane and melt into nothingness? Or would you be translated into a Golden Age?"

"I would rather be at home in clean clothes."

"Don't be petty. Why can't you see what I can see?"

"Because I'm not insane."

He clamped the chloroform-soaked cloth over her nose and mouth, his hands shaking with rage. She was unworthy, but that spirit would soon be gone, replaced with that of his lost Virginia, and once he and she were reunited, nothing else would matter.

I was practically out of my mind when I finally heard the doorknob click. It was barely half an hour before midnight. Did they not understand? Midnight was the dreamtime, according to Poe. Later would be too late. Especially for Rachel.

Bloomfeld had two men trailing behind him whom I immediately recognized from their file photos. Two suspects. Two Edgar possibles.

But only two.

"Apologies," Bloomfeld said. He could be quite polite, once you put the fear of death into him. "Couldn't find the third officer."

"We need him," I said.

"We'll find him in time, I'm sure. He's supposed to be working in the ballroom, but no one could locate him. It's already packed in there— hundreds of Halloween revelers. Ran into your partner, though, that FBI man. Sent him into the crowd to find the guy while I brought you these two."

I stared at the photo of the missing security guard, Ernest Lee Abbott. I mentally added a mustache, changed the hair, put dark glasses on him.

"He's normally very reliable. That's why we asked him to help with the crowd control. Everyone is doing the work of three."

I could imagine the man's lips moving, his face. His eyes taking that somewhat menacing, somewhat sorrowful expression that told so much about him.

"If you want, I'll go back to the ballroom and look some more. He's probably behind the cathedral, helping with some last-minute crisis. Whose idea was it to do the Hunchback, anyway? I always thought it was too literary. Kids today, they don't know anything about French literature. They probably think—"

"Hunchback?" I closed my eyes and let my mind wander again, but this time, it went straight to the source. The key clue. The one that hadn't fallen into place before.

I haven't been this scared since the day we rented a video just after my parents— That was what Rachel had said, during that brief phone call. Everyone thought she was terrified, babbling, me included. But we were wrong. Rachel is a tough girl, a smart one.

She was trying to give me a clue.

What was the movie? What was the damn movie?

Of course.

We'd rented **The Hunchback of Notre Dame.** The Disney version. The first day I brought her home. After her parents were killed.

"Take me to this ballroom," I said, rising out of my chair. "Now."

Bloomfeld stuttered, "B-B-But I rounded up your suspects—don't you want to interrogate them?"

I shook my head. "It's the other one. Abbott. He's Edgar."

By the time I made it to the ballroom, I still hadn't found Patrick, Darcy hadn't returned, and it was barely ten minutes until midnight. Ten minutes.

Rachel! I wanted to scream out her name, but I knew that wouldn't help, not in this earsplitting chaos. Please, God, don't let me be too late. Don't let me be too late.

Even though the Halloween party had not officially started, the ballroom was packed. I could see where Bloomfeld might've had difficulty finding one security cop in this swarm. I might have trouble finding myself in here. At least half the partygoers were in costume, many of them masked. If Edgar was one of them, how would I ever find him?

Think, Susan. **Think!**

He wouldn't be out here mingling, would he? He has some tremendous master plan in the works, something wonderful, something terrible. Something involving Rachel. He couldn't have her out here, whether she was costumed, dead or alive. Could he?

While I was trying to crawl into Edgar's brain, I saw Chief O'Bannon enter the ballroom. I showed him the photo of Abbott.

"You're sure it's him?"

"Damn straight."

He smiled a little. "Good girl. Knew you could do it."

He took the left side of the room and I surged into the right. I saw the great façade of the cathedral of Notre Dame at the far end of the ballroom, a focal point for all the festivities. I moved toward it. I've never been to Paris, but it looked pretty damn real to me, except that it wasn't quite finished. There was still some scaffolding, several raised platforms on wheels, off to the side. The ballroom was festooned with confetti and orange and black ribbons and banners. And where was the hunchback? He would emerge later, I guessed, probably from the top of the cathedral, ringing those four huge bells, two on each side of the central spire.

I moved toward the cathedral. It seemed like the place Edgar—Abbott—was most likely to be. And I knew Rachel had seen it before, right? That was the whole point of the clue.

Someone dressed in a jester costume fell into me, tumbling backward. I went for my gun. Jesus, was I on edge. I shoved him out of the way and tried to plow a trail through the dense horde. They were getting increasingly crazed, ebullient, nutty, which I suppose was to be expected as the clock approached midnight. I could smell alcohol breath every which way I turned. It made me sick.

Which was certainly a good sign.

Eventually I forced my way to the back of the room. It was a high-quality cathedral, made of some kind of molded fiberglass, stained to the proper shade of gray. Someone had spent some real money on this. After trying several false apertures, I found a door on the far side that worked.

I stepped into the cathedral, such as it was. It was dark back here, darker than I liked. The cathedral touched the ceiling and, despite the openings for the bells, little light crept through.

This was his place. I knew it, as sure as I'd ever known anything in my life. I could feel it.

I drew my weapon. I'd let IA argue later about whether I had cause or not. Right now, I wanted a gun between me and him.

I stepped into the darkness, marking a path I thought was parallel to the front of the cathedral. The entire area was small, close, silent. And dark. Did I mention that it was dark?

I took baby steps, inching forward, fighting the desire to rush ahead. I wanted to find Rachel. I had to find her before it was too late. But Edgar had proven how dangerous he could be, how smart. I had to be careful. I couldn't save her if I were dead.

I kept moving forward, one dark step at a time.

Till I saw someone.

At first, I couldn't make out who it was. His face was masked by shadows. He was sitting on the floor, looking up at me.

"Patrick!"

He was staring with a strange, vacant expression on his face. I holstered my gun and ran toward him. "Patrick!" I said, grabbing his arm. "Patrick! What are you—"

I gasped.

His head fell forward into my lap. Just his head.

I screamed like a siren, like a child at a horror movie, like the weakest sister who ever lived. Blood spilled all over my turtleneck, my pants. The head fell to the floor but didn't roll. It just impacted with a sickening splat and lay there, staring up at me. It had been sliced clean—by a pendulum? I wondered—at the base of the neck.

My God, my God, Abbott killed Patrick, he **killed** him, and if he killed Patrick—

An even deeper horror clutched at the base of my spine.

It was so unlike him to be gone so long. . . .

"Darcy!" I turned and ran back the way I came, feeling stupid, feeling powerless, terrified. He'd gotten to Patrick, he'd gotten to Patrick but please not Darcy please please **please** not Darcy . . .

That was when the bells began to ring. Did that mean it was midnight? Even with all the noise out front, the ringing of the huge bells was deafening. I was just beneath them, and the unrelenting clanging seemed to crush my skull. It was oppressive and mind-numbing. Why would the hotel want to—

I looked up.

My heart stopped. I couldn't breathe. My fingers were cold, as if all the life had been sucked out of me.

Rachel!

Because the apertures were recessed, it wouldn't be visible from out front, but back here I had a clear view of four young girls strung up one to a bell, tied to the clappers, dangling head-down. Swinging back and forth. Their heads smashing against the sides of the bells.

"Rachel!" I shouted, even though I knew she couldn't possibly hear me. Even if she were alive. If the sound was killing me down here, what must it be doing to them?

"Rachel!"

I forced my brain to calm, slow down—**think**! There must be something I could do. The bells had to be activated by some sort of mechanism. I needed to find the controls. Maybe I could ask someone. If not, I could climb up on that scaffolding out front. . . .

I raced toward the door. And I had almost made it when a hand burst out of the darkness. It grabbed me by the throat and slammed me against the wall. Before I could react, his other hand took my gun.

"Hello, Susan," Edgar said, smiling. "Good to see you again."

CHAPTER THIRTY-SIX

"Aren't they magnificent?" His eyes rolled up in his head, even as his hand remained tight around my throat. " 'The throbbing of the bells! Of the bells, bells, bells, bells, bells!' "

I tried to speak but couldn't. His grip was too tight.

"I hope you've enjoyed my little tableau. Your friend Patrick tried to spoil it, you know. But I couldn't allow that. Not when I'm so close."

He loosened his viselike fingers just enough that I could speak. "Why did you have to kill him?"

"I'm afraid I lacked the time for a more subtle response."

"Those bells are killing Rachel. And the other girls."

"Not killing. Translating."

"Have you hurt her?"

"I haven't put a mark on her."

"I said, have you hurt her?"

"Not as much as you have."

I thought I was going to explode. "What the fuck are you talking about?"

"Nothing you don't already know. You've damaged that poor girl with your drinking, your temper, your self-indulgent weltschmerz, your flights of martyrdom. She's felt alone in the world, unwanted. Forgotten by the only family she has."

"Let me take her down." The anger had left my voice. I was begging. "Let me save her before it's too late."

"You won't be able to get to her."

"And why the hell not?"

He removed a small radio transmitter from his jacket pocket and pushed the first button on the keypad. "Because the hotel is on fire."

The building exploded. That's what it seemed like. The sound was deafening, utterly drowning those bells, which had been unbearable only moments before. I couldn't see them, but I could hear the crowd screaming, running, crying. I could imagine the pandemonium that must have descended. And even though I couldn't hear it anymore, I knew Rachel was still getting her brains splintered by that damn bell.

"This is just the start," Edgar said, almost giggly with excitement. "I've got ten C4 charges set all over the hotel, conveniently close to the gas mains. Disconnected the sprinkler system, too." His eyes were wide and manic. I could barely stand to look at him. "This whole place is crumbling! Isn't it wonderful?" He was totally consumed by his delusion, far worse than when I had seen him last. All vestiges of sanity, of humanity, were gone. "It's 'The Fall of the House of Usher,' the greatest of the prophet's stories, coupled with the greatest of his poems. 'By the mystical magical tolling of the bells, bells, bells, bells, bells!'"

It was getting hot back here. The fire outside was superheating the ballroom. Smoke inundated this dark, narrow passage behind the cathedral as well, making it difficult to speak or breathe.

He pushed a button and I heard another explosion. This one was farther away, but I was certain it was still inside the hotel. Maybe the casino. Maybe the spa. No telling how many people would be hurt or killed.

"It's not too late for you," he said breathlessly. "You could be Madeline to my Roderick. You could join us, Susan, join Rachel and Ginny and me. We'll unite as comrades in the Golden Age."

I thought fast. "I'd like that."

"This can be the Day of Ascension for all of us, a passage from this virulent world to one of—" In the midst of his rapture, he loosened his grip on my neck and body. And that was all the invitation I needed. Mustering my strength, I bodychecked him against the cathedral. His head slammed back against a wooden beam. While he was momentarily stunned, I knocked the detonator out of his hand.

"No!" he screamed, but he was much too late to stop me. I scooped the detonator off the floor and shoved it into my pocket, then raised my fist to deliver a knockout blow to his solar plexus.

And he raised a gun. My gun.

"You don't deserve to ascend," he said bitterly, blinking from the pain, blood dripping down the side of his head. "You will die right here in this miserable world where you belong."

He fired.

O'Bannon swore, but it wasn't productive, because no one could possibly hear him. What the hell had happened? There'd been an explosion, and seconds later the whole ballroom was on fire. Within moments the front doors were congested and blocked. Bedlam ensued. Rabid partygoers were punching, screaming, crying, reeling, desperate to get away from the flames. Smoke billowed through the enclosed area, making it difficult to see or breathe. The air was thinning. Without an alternative exit, they'd all suffocate, maybe even before they burned.

Fighting his way through the mass hysteria, O'Bannon got to a side door—led to the kitchen, if he wasn't mistaken. There was a crowd around, trying unsuccessfully to open it. Seemed to be locked from the other side. Well, he had the cure for that.

"Stand back," he bellowed. He pulled out his weapon and fired three times at the lock mechanism.

Good thing it wasn't chained, or even that might not have worked. As it was, the bullets weakened it enough that he could kick the door open. As soon as he did, the crowd surged through it, coughing, crying, gasping for air. But they had a way out. At least until that one was blocked.

A second explosion rocked the room. My God, he wondered, where did that one go off? How the hell did he stop this?

And what happened to Susan?

Last he'd seen of her, she'd headed behind that fake cathedral. She hadn't emerged, at least not that he'd seen.

He scanned the still-packed room. No sign of

her, and he couldn't believe she'd just leave, not in the midst of all this chaos.

There was only one reason she would be back there while this turmoil was raging.

Cautiously, gun still in hand, he made his way toward the cathedral.

The bullet missed, at least in the sense that it didn't kill me on the spot. It seared my right arm, creating a fierce burning pain that brought sudden tears to my eyes and gave me a bad case of the shakes.

"I hate this," he said, and to my astonishment I saw that he had tears in his eyes as well. "The brutality of it. Firearms. This is not the way it should be. Why are you making me do this, Susan? Why?"

He lifted his arm and I could see that he was going to shoot again, going to shoot to kill this time, from a distance so short he couldn't possibly miss.

I'm sorry, Rachel, I thought. I failed you. Just as I've always failed you.

"Susan! Duck!"

I recognized O'Bannon's voice, but even if I hadn't I would've obeyed. A bullet whizzed over my head and struck near Edgar—but not near enough. Edgar gritted his teeth, shifted his aim

DARK EYE   665

and fired, not once but three times. I heard a grunt that told me one of the slugs had made contact, followed by the sickening thud of a body hitting the floor.

"Nooo!" I screamed. I rushed forward while Edgar's attention was focused on his new victim, tackling him under his gun arm. He fell back against the façade. The gun went flying. In this darkness, there was no way of knowing where it had gone. I punched Edgar again and again and again and he didn't resist. I didn't give him a chance. I wanted to hurt him. I wanted to beat him senseless.

When I was sure he wasn't going to get up again, I ran to the chief.

The bullet had caught him in the lower stomach, below his vest. It didn't look as if it would be fatal if he got help in time. But I knew that stomach wounds were the most painful an officer could suffer.

He was shaking, too stricken to speak. I told him not to try, then called for immediate medical assistance. I assumed the ambulances were already converging, given the conflagration outside. I gave them O'Bannon's location.

"You're going to be okay," I told him, and hoped he believed it. "Just stay put. Don't try to move."

I wanted to remain with him, but I couldn't.

Rachel was still up there, and the other girls. Every additional second they spent upside down in those things could be fatal.

I realized Edgar must've used the scaffolding to get the bodies up into those bells. So I would do the same to get them down.

By the time I ran through the cathedral door again, the ballroom was perhaps half empty, which was a damn good thing, because the flames were spreading fast. At least a third of the room was already ablaze. The air was thick with dense black smoke. Everyone was coughing and choking, black stains under their noses and mouths. I was finding it hard to breathe myself. But I put that out of my head. I had to get to Rachel.

The scaffolding levels were maybe seven feet apart. Edgar had no doubt used a ladder, but he hadn't left that behind for me, so I just vaulted it. Up on the first level, I found round steel pylons, buckets of mortar, tools, signs of a barely completed construction process. I leaped up, grabbing the edge of the next level, my bullet-creased arm aching, and swung myself around. On the next riser, I was level with the bells.

Up close, I saw that Rachel was tied tightly across her entire body, ensuring that she couldn't move or escape. But the other three girls were only bound at the feet, just enough to keep them on the clappers. Why hadn't they escaped?

Was it possible they'd let Abbott put them up there?

Rachel's eyes were open, but I couldn't gauge how conscious she was, hanging upside down for so long, her head thumping against the bell, that incredible noise shattering her eardrums. The side of her head closest to me was bleeding—not a good sign.

"Rachel!" I shouted. No reaction of any kind.

There was a narrow catwalk on the front of the cathedral, probably to give the workmen access to the bell chambers. With a cautious, tentative step, I edged off the riser onto the catwalk. From there, I was able to reach out and grab the edge of the bell.

It fought me. Nearly knocked me off the cathedral. I wobbled and teetered, noticing for the first time just how damn high up I was. But I held on to that damn bell.

It stopped. No more swinging. Rachel hung motionless in the center.

"Rachel!" Still no response.

I didn't know whether I should untie Rachel first or stop the swinging of the other girls' bells. And while I was deciding, the cathedral suddenly shot out from under my feet and I tumbled down into the smoky abyss.

Correction: my feet were knocked off the platform. By Edgar.

CHAPTER THIRTY-SEVEN

Somehow I managed to grab the edge of one of the risers and swing myself onto the second level. Edgar jumped down on the other side.

His face was bruised, bloodied. He was wheezing with each breath, coughing. And he had my gun.

"You've ruined everything." His voice was harsh and gravelly from the smoke, and perhaps my beating. "My ascension. Virginia's return. Dream-Land."

"You need help," I managed. "I told you that before."

He held out his hand. "Give me the detonator."

"So you can set off the other eight bombs? And kill even more people?"

"It's for the greater good."

While we talked I mentally measured the distance to the next riser, the chances of me making it before he could shoot. Where were the cops, the firemen? They were bound to appear soon. If I could just stall, just keep him talking. . . .

"You're starting to sound like me," I said.

"I'm nothing like you, Susan."

"You are. You're rationalizing. Trying to justify the horrible things you do."

"I'm trying to give us a new world. A better world! One that isn't so . . . hard. You of all people should appreciate the value of that."

"You have a good heart," I said, and I truly believed it. "Maybe we all do. But it went wrong somehow. You haven't done anything wonderful. You've killed innocent people."

"No!" He fired. It missed me, but not by so much that I didn't feel my heart skip several beats. "I've studied the prophet's words. I was given the secret."

Down below, the flames were everywhere. I knew it would not be long before the entire room, infrastructure and all, came crashing down. Where was my backup?

"Give it up, Abbott. Let me get you some help."

He inched forward. "I want the detonator! Now!"

"Not gonna happen. Not now. Not ever. No matter what you do."

He rushed me. I was caught off guard by the sudden change, not to mention the fact that I was on the edge of a riser some fourteen feet off the floor. I wrapped myself around his body and wrestled him down. He couldn't get me in his sights, so he clubbed me over the head with the gun butt. That hurt. I fought to block out the pain, keep myself conscious.

He seemed possessed, as if one of Poe's worst monsters had taken over his body. He kicked me repeatedly. I pushed up to my hands and knees and he kicked me again, flattening me. I felt something in my chest snap.

"You don't have to do this," I said, spitting blood. He kicked me in the mouth, loosening a tooth. "Like Poe said in **Eureka,** we're free spirits. We can chart our own destiny."

"In Dream-Land."

"No. That's where you got it wrong. He was talking about finding your own Dream-Land. He was talking about making **this** world a Dream-Land."

"Liar. False prophet."

I hauled myself up, hoping to make one final run at him, but he saw me coming. With both hands, he grabbed me by the neck and flung me backward. Off the riser. Into the flames.

I woke up and there were noises everywhere there were noises everywhere and they were so loud and it was just like the inside of my head except it was outside and the room was on fire everything was on fire and I don't like fire I'm afraid of fire. Everyone was running and fighting to get out and I was going to get out too except I heard my dad calling and he sounded just like he did that time when he told me my mommy was dead and I wouldn't get to see my mommy anymore. I ran to him and I saw him and he was hurt and he had red all over him. He was crawling and barely pulling himself along and his gun was in his hand and I don't like guns I don't like them at all but he was too weak to lift it up. I shouted for someone to help but no one was listening until someone told me he'd talked to the hospital and ambulances were coming and I tried to get my dad out of there before the entire room burned down and there was a scream! There was a scream I knew it was a scream and I knew who it was even before I saw her it was Susan and she was falling falling and she fell so far please God don't let her be dead please don't please don't please don't please don't let the Bad Man take away our babies. Susan is my friend doesn't he know Susan is my friend just like Brian in the fifth grade was my friend until they took him away to another school but Susan is still my friend and I want her to stay to be my friend. Please don't hurt her. People should not hurt each other! People should not hurt each other!

I hit the floor back first, head tucked, then rolled, like they teach us at the academy, but I was certain I'd broken my right arm. Maybe a leg. It sure hurt enough. Possibly had a concussion. I didn't have time to do a personal inventory. As soon as I opened my eyes, he was standing there, hovering over me, his foot between my legs.

"You know I loved you. You know that." He looked like Satan, with belching smoke and billowing flames in the background.

Blood trickled out of my mouth when I tried to speak. I knew I couldn't escape. He could pump three rounds into my skull before I could blink. "You had a damn funny way of showing it."

"I let you live."

A silence fell, blocking out the fiery chaos surrounding us.

"I did that for no other," he continued. "It was not the will of the Raven, but I did it, because I so desperately wanted you to see the path." His lips trembled. "You must hate me."

"No." And as I spoke, staring up at his twisted, pathetic face, I realized it was true. Whatever anger I'd had, whatever enmity I'd borne, was gone now. "I don't hate you. I did. But not anymore. I told you already. We're a lot alike."

"We are?"

I nodded. "Both haunted. Both screwed to the max." I wiped the blood from my mouth. "I used to think you were evil. Like if I demonized your psychosis, that somehow made it easier to deal with." I laughed. "Hell, you're not evil."

"I'm . . . not?"

"No. You're just a poor schmuck who misses his sister. Like I miss my husband."

He hovered over me, gun still pointed, listening.

"I couldn't forgive my husband for what he did. And I channeled all that anger against you. But that's no way to live. I'm not going to spend my whole life angry, tearing myself apart. I forgive you."

"You—what?"

"You heard me. I forgive you."

He hesitated, gun wavering, sweat and blood trickling down the sides of his face. "You know I can't let you live."

I spat more blood out of my mouth. Something inside me was broken. I couldn't remain conscious much longer. "So if you're going to kill me, do it already. What do I get, the axe? I don't think you have time for dental surgery."

His face knotted up. "You are so . . . **hard** on me." He pressed the gun against the side of my head. "I'm sorry, Susan. Goodbye."

The gun fired. I winced. And waited, expecting to feel the intense pain—and release—that did not come. Always I think I've made it, but it never, never comes.

I opened my eyes. Abbott had crumpled to the floor. And behind him stood Darcy, shaking from head to foot, his normally inexpressive face contorted with pain, his eyes streaming tears.

He was holding his father's gun.

CHAPTER THIRTY-EIGHT

After that, everything got kind of fuzzy. I know police and fire teams invaded the ballroom, and I know they got me out of there. Darcy hovered by my side the whole time. He was horribly torn up about what he had done. I knew it would haunt him for a long time, maybe forever. But at that moment, all he seemed to care about was me.

Next couple of days were pretty much a haze, too, but I eventually got the lowdown on what had happened in the aftermath. There were surprisingly few casualties from the fire. Many injuries, lots of smoke-inhalation-related respiratory problems, but only a few fatalities, mostly because O'Bannon had blasted open an exit to speed up the evacuation. That ballroom and the one adjoining it were wrecked, but most of the rest of the hotel was still sound. I'd prevented Abbott from detonating the remaining incendiary bombs, which were found and removed.

O'Bannon was seriously wounded and would be in the hospital for months. He'd already had his phone rerouted to his room in the recovery ward and had all his open files sent over. He might be laid up, but he was definitely not out of commission.

Patrick had been killed with an axe, which Abbott had apparently brought along to cut the rope he used to string up the girls. We assumed he'd come upon Abbott at work and Abbott killed him. Hid the body where he thought no one would find it, at least not before the explosions started. What a waste. He was a good man, a kind man. A rarity, in our field. I miss him.

Abbott died, almost instantly. Darcy's gunshot got him in the brain. Although I could empathize with the pain his life had brought him, I had no regrets about his execution. He had crossed the threshold into utter psychosis. No drug therapy ever would have brought him back. It was better this way.

Rachel was alive. The bells hadn't been as hard as they looked—not real iron. She still had a concussion and had suffered some hearing loss, at least temporarily. But she was alive. And the docs told me that if I hadn't gotten to her when I did and stopped that bell, she might not have made it.

That was something, anyway.

The other three girls, Tiffany and Judy and JJ, were also alive, but seriously messed up, far worse than Rachel. They hadn't been in their bells as long—apparently they had helped him secure Rachel—but they were suffering severe psychological trauma from their time in captivity. It would be a long while before they were normal again, if indeed they ever were. But they were alive, and where there's life, there's hope. Right?

This time, I let the docs keep me in the hospital just as long as they wanted. I was in no hurry, and it gave me time to do some thinking. Which for me, was long overdue.

After six days, I was released. My arm was in a cast, my leg bore a brace, and I had a cracked rib, but I was out of there. Lisa picked me up at the hospital.

"You're sure you want to do this?"

"Positive." I wondered if I needed a friend who was a better driver, because each little bump of her Porsche radiated through my tethered arm and leg. "Thanks for being my chauffeur."

"Hell, honey, you're unsafe at any speed

when you're well. No way I'm letting you drive." She paused. "But this could wait."

"No, I want to do it now." I reached out and lightly ran my fingers across her cheek. "I love you."

She kept her eyes fixed on the road. "Tell me the trauma of your near-death experience hasn't made you realize that you are at heart a lesbian."

I smiled. "No."

"Not that there's anything wrong with that. God knows you couldn't be a worse kisser than some of the male lovers I've had."

"No. Just wanted to tell you. I know you've been taking care of me. Not just the big stuff, like driving and finding places for me to live, moving me and taking care of my life while I drank myself into oblivion. I know you're the one who put Sugar Babies in my empty holster. Who quietly replaced my ratty old black turtleneck with a much nicer new one. Who kept taping Dr. Phil and leaving it on my VCR."

Lisa's eyes crinkled. "That's what friends are for."

I laid my head on her shoulder. "Alcoholics don't usually have friends. They don't deserve them. But you stuck with me through it all. I won't forget it."

She blushed, actually blushed. "Have you given any more thought to L.A.? It's a great house in a great town. Swimming pools, movie stars. It would be good for you."

"I know it would. You're right, as always."

"You flatterer. So . . . chick night tonight? TNT is running a **MacGyver** retrospective."

"You're on, girl."

My esteemed lawyer, Quentin Delacourt, stared uncomprehendingly across his desk. I knew I should be taking his mystification more seriously. But he was wearing a red bow tie, and how can you take anyone seriously when they're wearing a red bow tie?

"I don't understand," he said. "You want to give it up?"

"Right. Throw in the towel. Call it quits."

"But—"

The Shepherds were also in his office, at my invitation. "I just wanted you all to know. The battle is over."

"But Susan—" The lawyer leaned forward. "Do you understand what will be the consequences of this action?"

"Yeah. I get that." There was a sudden thickness in my chest that I tried to ignore. At any rate, I wasn't going to let it show. "Just get me some visitation rights, okay? So I can see her every now and again."

"That won't be any problem," Mr. Shepherd said. "Whatever you want."

I turned toward him, shutting the lawyer out. "You've been pretty hostile to me in the past."

He cleared his throat. "It's possible that . . . my opinion has changed."

His wife cut in. "I don't want to intrude, but . . . may I ask why you're doing this?"

I sucked in my breath. "Because you're better for her than I am. I know that now. I guess I always did, really, but I didn't want to admit it. I'm not saying this is forever—I'm going to try like hell to pull myself together, and if I do, I'll want to talk about custody again. But for now—this is best for Rachel."

Mr. Shepherd held out his hand. "You're doing the right thing, Lieutenant."

I took the hand with my good arm and shook it firmly. "I know I am. But that doesn't make it hurt any less. Take good care of my girl, okay?"

"We will. And Lieutenant?"

"Yeah?"

"You take good care of yourself."

One last stop before the hearing. I could tell Lisa didn't think this was a good idea, but she took me anyway. Let me stop by the florist, then onward.

Not many people at the cemetery this time of day. A groundskeeper, a few scattered mourners. Found David's grave in no time at all. It looked pretty scruffy, barren, unkempt. 'Course, I hadn't been here since the day he was interred.

I stood there just staring at the grave for the longest time before I finally spoke. "Look, it's not like it was a gigantic surprise or anything. I knew that you were . . . confused. I knew your interest in me . . . sexually . . . was declining. I'd seen the way you turned away whenever a hot-looking guy passed us in the mall. How unconvincing you were, laughing much too loudly whenever Granger made crude remarks about a Super Bowl cheerleader's anatomy. And I know, intellectually, as a psychologist, that it was no reflection on me. Not that that's stopped me from engaging in humiliating, degrading affairs, desperately trying to prove to myself that I might actually be desirable to someone."

I drew in my breath, then slowly released it. "My point is, I had my suspicions for a long time. I just didn't expect to have them confirmed the way I did. To come home and find you . . . you . . ."

I pressed the heel of my hand against my forehead, trying to stop the mental movie from replaying. "I'm sorry I threw that huge fit in the office. I had no right to do that, not in front of your friends, co-workers, even if they didn't know what the hell I was talking about. They still don't know. I never told anyone and I never will. But what you did, David—" I felt myself tearing up, something I promised myself I would not do. I steeled myself, then started again.

"I mean, bottom line, I didn't care about any of that. You were what you were. But whatever you were . . . I needed you. Rachel needed you. And to just . . . leave us like that, leave me feeling guilty and betrayed and . . . alone. That was what hurt, David. That was what screwed me up the most. That was what I couldn't forget— or forgive. We didn't get a chance to work it out. I didn't even get a chance to say goodbye."

The wind whistled through the barren oaks that dotted the yellow field. A few crows circled overhead, singing their sad songs. "But you were right. It's time to move on, sugar bear."

I crouched down and laid a single red rose across his resting place. "Consider yourself forgiven."

The Bad Man still comes for me, but he comes in my dreams. Daddy says that it isn't real but it is real I know it is just like I dreamed that Mommy would leave and she did and she never came back and now the Bad Man is dead but he keeps coming for me and I don't know when he will ever stop.

I saw Susan in the hospital and she looked broken but better and I asked one of the doctors who looked at me like I was a weirdo but he told me she could still have babies and that made me happy.

I don't miss the Bad Man but I miss being a policeman. I'm glad Susan is getting out of the hospital so I can be a policeman again. Susan is my friend. Everything has been better since she came to see my dad that night and I don't know if she knows that she makes me happy but she makes me get tingly when she winks at me and has sort of a happiness beam that she shoots out and I feel like I could do more things when she's around I feel like I could do anything I could focus like my dad tells me to focus focus and I could be of use to people. If Susan wanted me to.

It's lonely here without my dad. I used to dream about being alone and not having my dad scowling and being disappointed in me all the time but now that he is gone it isn't nearly as nice as I thought it was going to be.

I was feeling fairly buoyant when I hobbled into the hearing. And devastated when I left.

Like what little I had left had been ripped away from me. As if I had nothing, nothing at all.

Never being one to display much decorum, much less sense, I confronted him in his hospital room.

"You did this to me, didn't you?"

O'Bannon sat up. "What are you talking about?"

"I had my hearing today. With IA. For reinstatement."

"How did it go?"

"I thought it went brilliantly. They complimented me on my work on the Edgar case. Talked about the pleasure they got from the fact that all those FBI dudes went home empty-handed while one of theirs made the collar. Talked about my impressive courage and resilience. How I seemed to be conquering my personal demons. I thought I had it made in the shade."

"And?"

I punched his pillow. "And then they pulled out the report you filed. You blackballed me, you son of a bitch."

"Hardly that. I just said—"

"You knew they wouldn't reinstate me against your wishes. Your recommendation was critical!"

"Susan, listen to me."

"Why should I, you bastard? I did your dirty

work for you! I caught your killer. I even—I even—what he did to me—" I broke down. Just lost it.

O'Bannon intervened. "Susan, stop."

"Why should I?" I screamed. "I wanted my job back! Don't you understand—it's all I have left!"

He looked at me with tired, cheerless eyes. "You're not ready, Susan."

"Who the hell are you to judge?"

"You know it as well as I do. If I reinstate you, that means you carry a gun. That means maybe a partner depends on you for their life. Are you ready for that kind of responsibility?"

"I caught Edgar!"

"You're an alcoholic, Susan. We both know it. I think you're trying to pull yourself out of that gutter, but how can I know whether you'll make it? You're a brilliant behaviorist, but until I'm certain you're one hundred percent, I will not put another officer's life in your hands."

I fell back in my chair, feeling all the pain, the hurt, the futility wash over me. "What can I do?"

"You can go back to those IOP meetings, for starters. Join AA. Get a sponsor. Read the Big Book. Work the steps."

"I'm not the talky-feely type."

"You'll force yourself. You'll get better. And when your doctor tells me you're solid, I'll put you back on the team. In the meantime, your consultation contract continues. Believe me, I can find plenty for you to do. You won't be bored."

He fiddled with the controls on his hospital bed, raising himself. "And now that we've got that out of the way, would you mind dropping by the house to check on Darcy? He called the front desk—he's having some kind of problem. He's been all by himself since I went into the hospital. He's a good kid, but—you know how he is. He needs someone looking out for him. And God knows there's no one he likes better than you."

"Oh, that's not—"

"Don't kid a kidder, Susan. He adores you. I'm his old man, sure, but I know the score. I love him, but he's wary of me. Too much discipline—or attempted discipline, anyway. Too many mistakes. Too many unresolved issues. And I'm laid up. So would you run by and see what's going on? He probably just needs someone to hold his hand for a minute. Would you do that?"

"If I say yes, will you reinstate me?"

"Hell, no. But I'd consider it a personal favor. I think your daddy would, too."

Bastard would play any card in his deck, wouldn't he? "Fine, I'll go. But you can stuff your damn consulting contract."

"Are you sure? Why?"

"After I see Darcy, I'm blowing town."

I rang the bell and Darcy came to the door almost immediately. His eyes were like balloons. His hands were flapping. He ran around in circles, screaming, barely coherent, even worse than when I'd taken him to that sex club. "Fire! Fire!"

I raced inside. The kitchen was indeed on fire, flames shooting out from the microwave oven. Looked like he'd been reheating some Pizza Hut chicken wings, but he'd left the food in the box with the foil wrapping. Darcy ran circles around the kitchen table, screaming, running his fingers through his hair. He collided into the wall. He fell backward against the table and hit his head.

I grabbed him and held him in place. "Darcy, where is the fire extinguisher?"

He was so messed up he couldn't talk, could only point. I opened the pantry door and grabbed the extinguisher. A minute or so later, the fire was out. But the kitchen was a mess. As was Darcy.

He crumpled on the floor, hunched over the linoleum, rocking back and forth, babbling incoherently, hitting himself in the face.

"I called and asked Dad about dinner but

Dad couldn't fix dinner so I thought that's fine I'll fix my own dinner and I did but the oven was mad at me and it started a fire and I didn't know what to do and . . ."

On and on and on. He hit himself so hard he made bruises.

I had to do something. I reached around him with my good arm and grabbed both hands, restraining him. Becoming his human straitjacket.

"All I wanted was something to eat but there was no one here and there's never anyone here anymore and I was all alone and I didn't know what to do and did you know that sixty-seven percent of all domestic fires begin in the kitchen but I opened the microwave and the flames just leaped out they just leaped out like they were trying to get me they wanted to punish me because I did a bad thing a really really bad thing . . ."

I hugged him tighter and tried to speak in a soft, soothing voice. I figured it didn't really matter what I said. He just needed to hear someone. It was hard, because I had one arm in a cast and the other ached at the wrist, but I held on to him.

"It hurt so much and I was all alone and I didn't know why the Bad Man came why the Bad Man always comes when I'm asleep I didn't want to hurt him I didn't want to hurt anyone I didn't hurt Mommy I really didn't but he was going to hurt Susan because I wanted to ask you about babies and I couldn't let him hurt Susan . . ."

God, my heart ached for him. He couldn't be left on his own like this.

I whispered into his ear. "It's all right, Darcy. Susan is here. Susan is right here."

"And sometimes it's dark and I hear these noises and I don't know what the noises are and I don't like it when people touch me why do people always want to touch me I want to be touched but when they touch me it makes me want to run away and I don't want to be here by myself anymore I don't I don't I don't . . ."

I felt myself choking, feeling his pain, wondering what it must have been like for Chief O'Bannon, raising this boy by himself all those years, dealing with this kind of panic attack not just once when you happen to drop by but every day, every day of your life.

The words tumbled out of me. I didn't even think before I spoke. This boy had done so much for me, had supported me throughout this whole horrific case. Maybe it was time I returned the favor. "It's all right, Darcy. I'm here. And I'm not going anywhere."

I held him like that for more than an hour before he calmed down. I didn't mind. Even though it hurt, I didn't mind. Once he was calm again, I fixed a proper dinner, then cleaned up the kitchen mess and made myself a place to sleep on the couch.

I took a shower, and when I stepped out of the bathroom with—thank God—a towel wrapped around myself, I found Darcy standing outside the door.

He was gasping for air and dripping with perspiration. And he was holding a frozen custard in each hand.

"I hope that you are in the mood for custard. I thought that you might be in the mood but I wasn't sure so I ran all the way to Third Street. And back."

"Just because you wanted me to have a bedtime snack?"

His face was like a shimmering sheet of tinfoil. "Because any day you have a custard is a Very Excellent Day. And I thought that maybe you could use a Very Excellent Day."

That night, before I fell asleep, I cried. Streams of tears, endless flows of salt water, cascading down my face. But it was a good cry. One I'd been saving up for a long time.

Guess I won't be going to L.A. after all.

ACKNOWLEDGMENTS

No writer can ever tackle anything so large and daunting as a novel without getting a lot of help, and I'm certainly no exception. I want to thank everyone who helped me during the time I spent creating Susan and Darcy's world and who assisted with the enormous research required to bring the characters to life.

The United States is currently in the midst of an autism epidemic—and no one knows why. Autism Spectrum Disorders have increased over 500 percent in the last decade; the Department of Education reported an 18 percent increase in those seeking special services for autism from 2003 to 2004. In 2004, the Department of Health and Human Services issued an Autism Alert to the nation's pediatricians in an effort to improve data collection to try to determine the cause of this epidemic and to aid in earlier diagnosis. I want to give special thanks to perhaps the leading pioneers in autism research, Ivar Lovaas and Bernard Rimland. Lovaas pioneered the use of behavioral intervention, which has been incredibly useful to many parents trying to recover a child who seemed lost to this neurological disorder. Rimland pursued biomedical research and, as a result, has produced a therapeutic protocol that many parents believe significantly assisted, or even cured, their children. Both approaches are most effective when instituted in the child's life as early as possible. (In case you're wondering, the only reason Rimland is not mentioned in the book is because his protocol would not have existed when Darcy was a child.) Those wanting to know more about Lovaas and his Institute for Early Intervention should visit www.lovaas.com. Those seeking more information about Rimland and the Autism Research Institute should visit www.AutismResearchInstitute.com or consider attending one of his periodic DAN (Defeat Autism Now) conferences (www.DANconference.com). Parents reeling from the shock of this diagnosis and wondering where to begin would do well to read **Let Me Hear Your Voice** by Catherine Maurice, the inspiring story of one parent's successful battle against this strange and terrifying disorder.

It would be impossible to write a book about a criminal behaviorist without becoming familiar with the work of the two best-known names in the field: John Douglas and Roy Hazelwood. Douglas developed criminal profiling techniques during his twenty-five years with the FBI and subsequently wrote fascinating books based on his experiences, such as **Mindhunter** and **The Anatomy of Motive.** Hazelwood built on and expanded his work; his psychological insights are perhaps the best recorded in his book **Dark Dreams.** I also must thank my friend Dave Johnson for his insight and information about the inner life of a police station and those who work there. If the characters in this book do not always behave as model police officers, however, it's not Dave's fault; it's because these characters, like most people I know, are not perfect.

And those who want to know more about card counting and other blackjack techniques developed at MIT and elsewhere may wish to read **Bringing Down the House** by Ben Mezrich, and the classic **Beat the Dealer** by Edward Thorp. If you're thinking card counting will allow you to go to Vegas and get rich quick, though, please think again.

I also want to thank the many fellow writers who agreed to read an early draft of this book, indulging my friendship, not to mention my insecurity about a book I knew was a departure from my previous work. Many thanks to Jodie Nida, John Wooley, K. D. Wentworth, James Vance, and my wife, Kirsten. The worst of it is, the only compensation they received was having characters in the book named after them. But at least none of their namesakes were tortured by poisonous leeches.

Very special thanks to my agent, Dan Strone, who believed in this book from the start, and my long-standing friend and editor, Joe Blades, who supported this effort just as he has everything else I've tried for the past fifteen years. No writer could possibly be more fortunate than I've been.

I invite readers to send me their thoughts via email at WB@williambernhardt.com. You can also visit my website at www.williambernhardt.com.

As the academician in the book says, Edgar Allen Poe's contributions to American literature are enormous, and if you haven't read any of his work, this might be a good time to start. Just don't take it too seriously, okay?

—WILLIAM BERNHARDT

PHOTO: RICK STILLER

WILLIAM BERNHARDT is the author of many novels, including **Primary Justice, Murder One, Criminal Intent, Death Row,** and **Hate Crime.** He has twice won the Oklahoma Book Award for Best Fiction, and in 2000 he was presented with the H. Louise Cobb Distinguised Author Award "in recognition of an outstanding body of work in which we understand ourselves and American society at large." A former trial attorney, Bernhardt has received several awards for public service. He lives in Tulsa with his wife, Kirsten, and their children, Harry, Alice, and Ralph. Readers can e-mail him at WB@williambernhardt.com or visit his website at www.WilliamBernhardt.com.